ROAD OF DECEPTION

A Wartime Story

Of

Treachery And Betrayal

Douglas W. Jacobson

*For our dear friends, Antoine and Jet, who lived
through the German occupation of Belgium.*

Acknowledgments

For my friend and editor, Jackie Swift, whose skill and patience kept me going through the writing of three books.

"Thus, when all the trumpets sounded, every class and rank had something to give... but none gave more, or gave more readily, than the common man or woman."

Winston Churchill

PART ONE

BELGIUM
SEPTEMBER, 1943

Chapter One

Near Grote Brogel—Seventy Kilometers East of Antwerp

1st Lieutenant Jack Richards hit the ground hard, stumbled forward and rolled over on his back. He lay there for a moment, trying to catch his breath, then slowly pushed himself into a sitting position and stared at the massive white parachute tethered to his shoulder harness, fluttering a few feet off the ground.

He tried to stand, but a sharp pain shot through his right ankle and dropped him to his knees. He quickly unsnapped the harness and pulled in the chute, gathering it in both arms, furiously bunching the unruly mass of cloth into a ball and securing it with the harness straps.

He looked around, trying to get his bearings. He knelt on firm, lumpy soil in what appeared to be a plowed field that smelled of manure and freshly cut hay. But it was broad daylight, and he was completely exposed. He spotted a stone wall about fifty yards away.

He crawled slowly toward the wall, his ankle throbbing in pain, dragging the sloppily secured parachute. Sweat poured down his forehead and into his eyes, as he clawed his way forward, expecting a shout or gunshot at any second. He kept crawling and crawling and finally reached the wall.

He dug a shallow hole in the soil with his fingers. He stuffed the parachute into the hole along with his flight helmet and covered everything as best he could with dirt and a few loose rocks. Then he sat down and leaned back against the wall, trembling from the exertion and fright.

He closed his eyes, and immediately, the horrific images of those last moments inside the bomber flashed through his mind—the huge plane pitching wildly to the right with the starboard engines in flames, oil pressure and fuel gauges bottoming out, and the reading on the altimeter diving fast below 3000 feet. Icy wind roared through the smashed windshield, then the final, bone-jarring explosion... the fire... and the screams.

His stomach heaved, and he scrambled to his knees, vomiting against the rough stone wall. Heaving violently a second and third time, he braced himself with his right hand to keep from falling forward. Slowly, the nausea passed. He waited another minute until his stomach settled, took several long, slow breaths, and then looked over the wall, searching for his co-pilot and friend, Alex.

He crawled further down the wall, slumped against it, and grasped his aching right ankle with both hands. He thought about trying to remove his boot to examine the injury, but the ankle hurt too damn much.

He unzipped his canvas bailout bag and took a few sips from the canister of water. He rummaged through the other items in the bag. Besides the water and a tin of hard biscuits, there was a pocket knife, a first aid kit, a compass concealed in a tunic button, and two silk maps, one of Belgium and one of the Netherlands.

He glanced at the map of Belgium, wondering if it would do any good. In all their survival briefings, the main rule the experts from the British Intelligence unit, MI9, drummed into his head was *'Escape and Evade.'* Avoid capture at all costs. Stay off the main roads and away from towns, try to seek shelter as soon as possible, and find friendly locals.

He zipped up the bag, reached for the holster sewn into the left side of his flight vest and felt the grip of the Colt 45, relieved he at least had a weapon. He took another sip of water.

Think! Think!

The explosion had destroyed the entire aft section of the plane, and the only other crew member who had made it out was his co-pilot, Alex.

Where is he?

Where am I?

Jack scanned the field in front of him but didn't see anything except neat rows of cultivated soil. The stone wall he leaned against was about three feet high and extended several hundred yards before intersecting tree lines in either direction.

He took another sip of water and then froze at the sound of an engine and tires crunching on gravel. The noises got louder, coming closer. He set the canteen on the ground and, ignoring the pain in his ankle, got up on one knee and peeked over the wall.

Shit!

A gray truck with a canvas-covered back approached the road less than ten yards from the wall.

Germans!

He dropped back down and leaned against the wall. He flicked the snap off his holster, removed the 45 and clutched it tight to his chest with both hands.

The truck stopped.

He heard a door slam, then a voice speaking. He couldn't understand German, but the tone of voice was clear, tense, and worried.

With his thumb, Jack flicked off the safety, struggling to control his breathing.

He heard other voices, two, maybe more.

He caught snatches of the incomprehensible conversation. They were looking for something... or someone.

Probably me!

One of the voices came closer.

Hunkering down as low as possible, Jack gripped the pistol with both hands, his eyes glued to the top of the wall. Then he heard the sounds of another vehicle roaring to a stop, tires skidding on the dirt and gravel.

A new voice, loud and angry, shouted to the others. Then, the second vehicle sped away.

A flurry of boots crunched across the gravel. Truck doors slammed, the engine gunned, and the truck pulled away, tires spitting dirt and stones.

What the hell?

Jack counted to five, then, very slowly, got to his knees and peered over the wall. The truck rumbled down the road, throwing up a cloud of dust, following a long black auto. After less than a hundred meters, the auto stopped, and the truck pulled up behind it. Two soldiers in black uniforms got out of the auto and pointed into a field on the other side of the road.

Jack looked in the direction they were pointing. A white parachute lay on the ground, partially buried and barely visible, a small section fluttering in the breeze. Beside it lay a figure. Alex!

Three soldiers in grayish-green uniforms jumped from the back of the truck and sprinted into the field toward the white parachute.

Alex jumped up and sprinted away in the opposite direction.

One of the soldiers fired a shot in the air.

Alex paused, then took off running again.

The soldier dropped to one knee and fired again.

Alex stumbled forward and then fell, face-first, into the field.

Jack crouched at the stone wall, unable to breathe, his fingernails scratching against the rocks, his eyes clouding up as he watched the soldiers approach Alex lying on the ground.

Jack shuddered, and his mind went blank as he watched the soldiers grab Alex's arms and drag him back toward the road.

Was he still alive?

Jack wiped tears and sweat from his eyes and glanced back to where the auto and truck were parked. The two black uniforms stood at the edge of the field, paying little attention to the action. One of them lit a cigarette, casually chatting with his partner as though they were discussing the weather.

Slowly, Jack extended his right arm, aiming the Colt 45 at the smug, black-uniformed bastard. He clamped his left hand over his right wrist to keep from shaking and zeroed in. Sweat trickled down his forehead as his finger slowly wrapped around the trigger.

Then he slumped to the ground and slammed his fist into the dirt. What the hell was he thinking? At this distance, he'd be lucky to hit the damn truck, let alone a person.

A minute later, truck doors slammed shut, engines revved up, and the two vehicles drove away.

Chapter Two

Jack sat on the ground behind the stone wall, his mind racing. The sun had descended in the western sky, and it would be dark soon. What then?

He couldn't sit here all night. Someone would surely spot him in the morning and report him. But he had no idea where he was if there was a town nearby, and even if there was, would he dare to go there? And *how* would he go there? He could barely stand, let alone walk.

His thoughts drifted to his crewmates; the nose gunner was killed instantly when the fighters attacked, and six others screamed and died in the fire. And Alex... shot down like a dog in a farm field.

The nausea returned, and he closed his eyes, clamping a hand over his mouth.

Goddamn it! How could it happen?

He hadn't spotted the enemy fighters until they had burst from the clouds above and to his right. It was over in minutes. The hammering sound of shells tearing through the fuselage, icy wind and gasoline fumes whipping through the cockpit. Then, the final, jarring explosion in the aft section... the fire... and the screams.

The screams... the agonizing, paralyzing sounds of the screams!

He took a long, deep breath, counted to ten, slowly and deliberately, then opened his eyes and looked out into the field again.

He spotted something moving toward him. He stiffened and gripped the pistol, rising slowly to his knees.

The object moved closer, a black silhouette against the setting sun, growing larger. Then he heard a sound, a slow chugging and sputtering.

He got to his feet and clambered over the stone wall, landing squarely on his right foot. A searing pain shot through his ankle, and he struggled to concentrate as he listened to the sound of the engine, getting louder by the second.

A tractor?

Jack took a deep breath and squinted into the sunlight.

That's exactly what it was... a tractor... an old farm tractor moving slowly across the field, heading right toward him.

Jack shifted his weight to his left foot and pointed the Colt 45 at the tractor as it moved closer.

When the ancient vehicle was so close that Jack could smell its exhaust, it finally stopped. A man climbed down and stood perfectly still, hands at his sides, staring at him. After a moment, the man took a few steps closer. He looked to be older, perhaps in his sixties, his face clean-shaven but weathered. He had dark eyes and a shock of gray hair under a brown knit cap. He wore a tattered gray jacket over a plaid shirt. Slowly, the man raised his right hand and pointed at Jack's gun. He shook his head. "No shoot," he said in English. "No shoot. Friend."

His accent was strange, a bit like German but different. It wasn't French. Flemish? Didn't they speak Flemish in the northern part of Belgium? He seemed to remember something like that from the MI9 briefings.

The man stared at Jack, eyeing his flight suit. "*Amerikaans?*" he asked.

Jack stood unsteadily, bracing himself against the short wall with his left hand. Finally, he lowered the pistol and nodded. "Yes, American. American aviator, pilot, my airplane was shot down."

The man squinted at him, then nodded, "*Ja, vliegtuig...* airplane. He made a gesture with his right hand, a parachute falling from the sky.

"Yes, we bailed out, parachuted. Did you see?"

"*Ja, see.*" Then, the man motioned with his head toward the tractor. There was a small cart hooked up to it. He held out his hand and said, "*Komm.*" He tapped his finger on his chest. "Friend. Help. *Komm.*"

Jack hesitated, remembering the MI9 briefing instructions to find friendly locals who help Allied aviators.

Could he be one of them?

Jack holstered the gun and tried to crawl back over the wall but faltered, wincing in pain. The old man quickly stepped forward, gripped him under the arm and, with amazing strength, eased him over the wall and into the cart.

Chapter Three

SS-Hauptsturmfuhrer Konrad Becker lit another cigarette and leaned against the fender of the black German-built Horch parked on the main street of the small farming village of Grote Brogel. He was a tall man, broad-shouldered, with short-cropped blond hair and ice-blue eyes. Except for a slightly deformed left ear—a result of his years in boxing—he was the perfect caricature of the Aryan Nazi.

He nonchalantly glanced around at the simple row houses that lined the narrow, cobblestone street, the red tile roofs, and the ubiquitous brown bricks he'd seen throughout Belgium. The street was quiet, the shutters on all the windows were closed, and the people inside were obviously afraid to venture out, fearing they might be next.

The Wehrmacht soldiers lifted the badly wounded American aviator out of the truck and carried him across the road to a shabby, two-story building that served as the headquarters of the local *gendarmerie* and what passed as a medical clinic. Becker thought it seemed a bit grotesque to do it so casually, in broad daylight, but it was standard SS procedure. If the locals witnessed this sort of thing, it kept them in line.

Becker hated this job—tracking down Allied aviators and escaped POWs. He had no sympathy for them; of course, they were the enemy, and they got what they deserved. But it all seemed beneath him, undignified for an SS officer with his training and skill. Fortunately, this was only part of his assignment, and other matters were far more important.

The local *gendarme* walked briskly across the road and handed Becker the form he'd signed, verifying the delivery of the wounded aviator. Another of the pointless clerical tasks required by SS procedure. Becker took the form, glanced at it for a second, then tossed the cigarette butt into the street. This one probably wouldn't make it through the night, so at least he'd be spared the fruitless task of interrogating him. "What about the other aviator that made it out of the plane?" Becker asked in English because he didn't speak Flemish and didn't care to learn.

The *gendarme* shrugged. He was a short, serious-looking man with dark eyes and a pencil-thin mustache, his blue uniform tunic freshly pressed, the brass buttons highly polished. The uniform of someone who never got his hands dirty, Becker thought with disdain.

"Are you looking for him?" Becker asked, stepping closer, towering over the shorter man and growing impatient. He knew the *gendarme* spoke a bit of English and had understood him the first time. It was just another reason Becker didn't trust the *gendarmerie.* Even though they were forced to take orders from the SS, they were seldom helpful and, many times, deceitful.

This time, the *gendarme* responded, nodding vigorously as if to demonstrate his willingness to help. "Of course, we search, will find."

Becker grunted and dismissed the *gendarme* with a wave of his hand. Most likely, the other aviator had already been rescued by operatives of the local escape organization and was hidden away in someone's attic, cellar or barn. Becker knew all about that secretive and elusive group, and he knew it was discreetly financed by MI9, the British Intelligence unit. He had even arranged for a collaborator to infiltrate the organization last year, and some key arrests were made, but they had failed to completely shut it down. Obviously, the disappearance of the other aviator was proof they were still operating. For all Becker knew, this worthless *gendarme* might even be one of them.

Chapter Four

Jack sat in the wooden cart and gripped the sides to keep from falling out as the elderly farmer drove the tractor through the lumpy field. They stopped briefly at a two-story brick house nestled between several large trees, where the man dismounted and disappeared inside. Jack tensed but relaxed a moment later when the man returned and handed him a wooden cane.

The farmer climbed back on the tractor, and they sputtered away, past a barn and into what appeared to be a large apple orchard. The cart rocked back and forth, bumping over rocks as the man steered the tractor along a narrow path through the orchard and finally came to a stop next to a large brick building. It looked to be abandoned, with several boarded-up windows and a sagging roof.

The sun had set, and it was getting dark as Jack slowly slid out of the cart and steadied himself with the cane. He followed the man along the side of the building to a large wooden door that creaked on rusty hinges when he pulled it open. Hobbling slowly with the cane, Jack stepped inside the dark building. It was damp and cool with a strange smell that Jack thought was familiar but couldn't quite place. The man followed him in, pulled the door closed and lit a lantern.

Jack glanced around at what he could see of the expansive building. It had a high, beamed ceiling, sagging noticeably in certain spots, and seemed mostly empty except for several large, wooden vats. That's when he recognized the smell. It was gin.

Jack followed the man across the earthen floor to the far side of the building, where a crude ladder descended from a loft. The man said something and motioned for Jack to climb the ladder. Jack glanced at the old man, then slowly climbed the ladder and crawled into the straw-covered loft.

The man walked away without another word.

Jack sat in the darkness for several long minutes, listening to the silence. Gradually, sounds of the night filtered in: crickets chirping, an owl hooting, something scampering along the roof. His neck tingled, wondering what else was out there and what he'd gotten himself into. Would the black-uniformed SS officers show up and bust down the door? Would the old man's friends show up with pitchforks and shotguns?

He thought back over the last few minutes of the flight. They had crossed the border from Germany into Belgium just a few minutes before they were shot down, so he had a vague idea of where he was. He had a map and a compass if he had to make a run for it, wondering if it would come down to that. The thought scared the hell out of him.

Eventually, thirst and fatigue won out over fear. He unzipped the bailout bag and took a long drink from

the canteen. Then he felt around in the dark,
discovered a coarse woolen blanket, laid back and
closed his eyes.

Chapter Five

Jack woke with a start when the door creaked open with a burst of sunlight that forced him to shield his eyes. A figure stepped through the doorway, and for a terrified moment, Jack fumbled around for his gun.

The figure took a few steps toward the loft, and Jack realized it was a woman. "You may come down now. It's safe for the moment." She said, in very good though slightly accented English,

Jack was so startled to hear her speak English that he didn't respond.

"I said you may come down," she repeated. "Are you able to?"

"Yes, yes... sorry," Jack mumbled, then slowly climbed down the ladder.

She stepped closer and held out her hand, "Welcome to Belgium."

Gripping his cane in his left hand, Jack extended his right and tentatively shook her hand, surprised by the strength of her grip and not sure what to say.

She smiled at him, "You may call me Claire."

"First Lieutenant Jack Richards, US Army Air Corps," he responded.

She was petite and slender but not thin, with dark, penetrating eyes and short black hair tucked under a knit cap. She was dressed in a black turtle-neck sweater, black trousers, and muddy boots and carried a wicker basket in her left hand. "I brought some food for you," she said, tilting her head toward the basket. "There's an old workbench over there and a couple of stools. It's the best we can do right now. So, hobble over there if you can, and I'll have a look at that ankle.

As though she'd done this many times before, Claire carefully removed his boot and then wrapped her hands around his ankle, slowly but firmly twisting it back and forth and up and down. His eyes watered, but he clenched his teeth, refusing to utter a sound.

She looked up at him. "So, you're a tough guy, is that it?"

"Not really," Jack grunted.

"Well, it's not broken. But it's quite a bad sprain." She reached into the basket, produced a long strip of cloth and, quite expertly, wrapped his ankle. "Keep the weight off it for a few days, but I think you will live. Now, have something to eat."

While Jack devoured the first of two ham sandwiches, Claire poured what appeared to be a thin, watery beer into two metal cups. She took a sip and sat quietly, watching him.

When he'd finished the sandwich, Jack took a large gulp of the beer and then looked at her, suddenly feeling guilty. "Sorry, I was starved." He paused, then asked, "Do you know anything about my other..." He shook his head to clear away the vision of the soldiers dragging Alex from the field.

She nodded slowly. "Yes, the one they shot in the field—"

"I know, I saw it!" Jack snapped, interrupting her. He paused and took a breath. "I'm sorry, I didn't mean..."

"I know that he was badly wounded and was taken to the *gendarmerie.* There is a small clinic there, but..."

"His name is Alex."

She nodded but didn't say anything.

"What will happen to him?" he asked.

Claire had a look in her eyes that reminded Jack of a high school teacher or a coach who was about to deliver disappointing news to a student. "I'll be honest with you, Lieutenant—"

"Jack," he said, interrupting her again. "Please, call me Jack."

"Okay... Jack. Your friend is in the custody of the Germans. If he recovers from his wounds, he'll be interrogated. I was told that his wounds are very serious so, as terrible as it sounds, it may be better for him if he—"

"If he what... if he *dies?* What the hell, wait a minute, you don't understand. Alex is my friend, my co-pilot. We went through flight school together. We've been through twelve missions together!"

Claire stood up. She walked to the door and pulled it open just enough to stick her head out. She looked left and right, then pulled the door closed again and stepped back to the workbench. "Listen to me carefully, Jack. I am very sorry for your friend, but this will not work out well for him. The Germans consider him an escapee—an enemy soldier who did not surrender—and if he lives, he will be interrogated and probably tortured by the SS or the Gestapo. They are very brutal. So, as I said—"

Jack's stomach started to roll again, and he held up his hand. "Yeah, okay, I get it. My God... Alex... and the rest of them... gone! All except *me!*"

She waited for a moment, then said, "You were very lucky that Gaston found you, Jack."

"Gaston, that's his name? He must have seen me come down in the field."

She nodded. "Gaston is a spotter. There are several like him in the area. They watch for Allied planes, and if they see one go down, they follow the parachutes and try to get there before the Germans. Sometimes they succeed... as in your case."

He was quiet for a moment, then shook his head, trying to purge the gruesome thought about what might happen to Alex. "So, who are you... and Gaston... who are, I mean... what is it that you do?"

"We are a very secret organization, Jack, so secret that most of us only know one or two others in the organization, and then only by code names. We try to help Allied aviators who have been shot down over

Belgium. We've helped many before you, and if we're careful and follow protocol, we'll be able to help many more after you."

"So, Claire is not your real name?"

"I said you may call me Claire."

"How can you help? Can you get me out of here?"

"Perhaps, if we're lucky, and if you cooperate and do everything you're told. But this is a dangerous business. The SS and the Gestapo are very tenacious. And they have spies everywhere, especially in this part of the country."

The words of the *Escape & Evade* experts flashed through his mind. "Spies? You mean... other civilians?"

"Yes, Belgian civilians, collaborators, Nazi sympathizers. As I said, it's a dangerous business, a dangerous time. We must be extremely careful."

Jack was quiet for a moment, suddenly feeling very alone. "So, what happens now?"

"You will remain here until your ankle heals, and we can find a more suitable place for you to stay. Most likely in the home of someone who can be trusted. Hopefully, it won't be long, a few days perhaps. In the meantime, Gaston will bring you food and some different clothing. The sooner we get rid of that flight suit and boots, the better."

"And Alex? Will I ever find out what happens to him.?"

She hesitated, looking him in the eye. "We have contacts in Grote Brogel, and we may find out what happens, but we might not."

"And I'm supposed to just go on ahead, following instructions from people I don't know, and leave him behind without ever knowing? No, that's not right, I can't do that!"

She didn't respond right away but kept her eyes locked on his. "You may not think it's *right*," she said slowly and quietly, as though forcing herself to be patient. "But that's the way it must be. And these people you don't know? They're risking their lives for you."

She turned and started for the door.

Jack stood up, leaning on the bench. "Claire, wait! I'm sorry... I didn't think."

She stopped and turned back to him. "It's okay, Jack, I understand. You've suffered a terrible loss. You're in a strange and dangerous place, and you don't know who to trust."

"I trust you... I think."

"Well, that's a start. The best thing you can do now is to stay where you are and be patient. These things take time."

Jack held up a hand and glanced around the vacant building. "By the way, what is this place, and where are we?"

"It's an old gin distillery, been abandoned for years. We are in Limburg Province, seventy kilometers east of

Antwerp. The village of Grote Brogel is just a kilometer
away."

"Is that where you live?"

"I can't say."

"Will I see you again?"

"Perhaps." Then she pulled the door open and was
gone.

Chapter Six

The next day passed in frustrating slowness. Claire brought him some aspirin along with bread, jam and cheese for breakfast, then checked his ankle and re-wrapped the bandage. As she started to leave, Jack asked if she could stay for a while and talk, but she said she had chores to do.

After she left, he tried walking around a bit to test the ankle. But even using the cane and taking it slowly, he could only make it halfway around the interior of the distillery before the pain forced him to stop. After one complete lap, he crawled back into the loft and massaged the throbbing ankle. Then he lay back and listened to the silence.

Shortly after noon, Claire returned and brought more bread, a thick slice of sausage and an apple, along with a container of the watery beer. It made him yearn for a cold bottle of Pabst. She had brought enough food for the two of them and sat down at the bench to join him.

"So, do you live here on the farm?" he asked.

She nodded. "Yes, for now at least. Gaston is an old friend, and his wife died from tuberculosis two years ago. Help is very hard to find with the war going on, so in exchange for a place to live, I help with all the chores.

"Are you from this area originally?"

She shrugged. "I can't say it's not safe." She took a sip of the watery beer and looked directly at him. "I don't mean to be rude, Jack, but the less we know about each other, the safer it will be for all of us. If you are discovered by the Germans, you can't tell them what you don't know."

He paused, wondering why two perfect strangers would risk their lives for him. "Your English is quite good. Did you learn it in school?"

"My father was a teacher, and he spoke some English. He always thought I should learn it, so I spent two years at university in London before the war."

"I went to college back home but didn't do very well with languages," he said. "I tried French, not sure why, but it never sunk in. Guess I'm more of a technical guy."

They were both quiet for a moment before Claire reached into the wicker basket and produced a book. "I brought something for you to help pass the time," she said, handing him a leather-bound copy of *Treasure Island* by Robert Louis Stevenson. "It's the English language version, perhaps you've read it before, but I thought—"

Jack's eyes lit up with a jolt of excitement. "Yes, I have," he cut in, "but it was a long time ago, in high school, so I'll gladly read it again, anything to keep from staring at these walls. Thank you."

"I have a few other English language books if you finish that, though I hope you won't have to stay here that long—" She stopped short and shook her head, "No, I'm sorry. What I meant is that—"

Jack held up a hand, interrupting again. "I know what you meant. I'm such a nice, charming guy. You'll hate to see me go."

She almost laughed, then seemed to catch herself and looked away. She stood up and grabbed the basket. "Enjoy the book. Gaston will bring your supper."

Chapter Seven

The plane jolted and pitched violently downward. Metal screeched. Shells hammered the fuselage. Then, a thunderous, bone-jarring explosion; gasoline fumes and smoke filled the cockpit. His crewmen screamed again and again. Icy wind whipped up the fire and smoke, blinding, choking. "Bail out!" He yelled, "Bailout... Bail... out... Bail..."

"Jack, wake up!"

Someone gripped his shoulder, shaking him.

Jack blinked. He opened his eyes... a light... a face.

Claire?

"Jack, wake up," she repeated, quieter this time. Her hand was on his shoulder. "You were dreaming."

He blinked again and sat up. "Dreaming?"

She nodded. "I heard you from outside. You were shouting something, quite loudly, over and over. It must have been a nightmare." She sat next to him in the loft, her legs crossed, her hand still resting on his shoulder. The lantern hung from a wooden beam. "Would you like some water?" she asked, handing him the metal canteen.

He took a long drink and handed it back.

"What were you dreaming about?" she asked quietly.

He took a deep breath, blinking again as the vision slowly dissipated in his mind. "It was the plane, the fire... just before we..." He shook his head. "The screaming... I'll never forget the screaming."

She looked at him in silence for a moment before responding. "I have some news for you about your friend, Alex."

"Did he die?"

She nodded. "Yes, earlier today. Gaston found out just a few hours ago."

"Did they, the SS, did they—

She shook her head quickly. "No, Gaston was told that Alex never regained consciousness. He died peacefully."

A tear formed in the corner of his eye, and he wiped it away. "He was like a brother... we went through so much together... and they just shot him down like a dog. I'll never forget that. And I knelt there behind that wall and watched, helpless, like a child... I'll never forget that either."

"There wasn't anything you could have done, Jack. I know that doesn't ease the pain. Perhaps, in time, it won't hurt as much, but you're right, you won't forget these things. They're terrible tragedies. You couldn't, no one could."

He looked at her curiously. He hadn't seen her since she left abruptly after lunch, and he realized that he missed her. "So, you know psychology as well as a first aide... a woman of many talents." He glanced at his watch. It was after midnight. "You're up late. Were you out for a walk, or did you come out here to tell me?"

She shrugged. "I couldn't sleep. It happens sometimes, and walking through the orchard at night is relaxing... then I heard you shouting."

"Good thing I didn't wake up the neighbors. Are there any, by the way, neighbors?"

"No, none close by, but you never know who might be sneaking around."

"Hmm, a high-crime neighborhood, is it?"

"Yes, it's a real problem. Just last week, a fox broke into a henhouse and stole a chicken. And then—"

"Yeah, okay, I get it. Nothing to worry about out here except a few Nazis with machine guns."

They sat quietly for a little while, and then Claire patted his hand and said, "Well, I should let you get some sleep."

"I doubt I'll get back to sleep anytime soon. Do you want to stay a while and talk? You said you couldn't sleep either."

She looked at him with a doubtful expression, then smiled. "Okay, for a while." She glanced down at the book lying on the hay. "Did you start to read it?"

"Yeah, I spent most of the afternoon with it—not much else to do—and it all came back to me, Long John Silver and his secret pirate buddies sneaking around. Seems a lot like what's going on around here, not knowing who to trust, and all that. Is that why you gave it to me?"

She looked at him with a wry smile and raised eyebrows. "My, my, that's pretty deep thinking... and you've only just arrived. Actually, I just grabbed it off the shelf, though I have to admit it's always been one of my favorites: young Jim Hawkins coming of age, far from home and surrounded by dangerous enemies, secrets revealed, all the elements of a good adventure story. It was on the reading list when I got to university, along with all the other classics by British and Scottish authors."

"Were you studying literature? No, wait, that's wrong, let me guess... psychology?"

"What, psychology? Why, because of my comment about your dream? No, I was much more practical than that. I did have to take an English literature course, but I was in nursing school, even thought about medicine."

"Of course, nursing, expertly bandaging my ankle, I should have guessed. Shall I call you 'Doctor Claire'?"

She laughed and lifted the lantern off the beam. "Now, you're getting delirious. You really do need some sleep."

Chapter Eight

A day passed, then another. It was late in the evening, and Jack crawled back into the loft after walking slowly around the inside of the distillery three times. He even made it halfway around the third time without using the cane, though his ankle now ached.

He desperately needed the exercise and the diversion, anything to occupy his mind when Claire wasn't there. Talking to her—and re-reading *Treasure Island* when there was enough light—was the only thing that kept him from reliving the loss of his plane and crewmates... and going stir-crazy. He always wished she would stay longer.

In the four days he'd been confined to this gin-soaked hideaway, Claire usually started each of her visits with the same blunt, matter-of-fact demeanor, though she'd softened a bit since the night she woke him from the nightmare. She would even laugh a bit at his futile attempts to learn a few words of Flemish, but he still knew very little about her. She'd told him that she was originally from Antwerp, and he guessed that she was close to his age, early twenties. She was quite attractive, in a self-assured, casual way, someone who didn't concern herself with disheveled hair or dirt under her fingernails. But, other than that, she was a closed book.

He pulled off the boots Gaston had given him and started massaging his ankle when he heard the creaking sound of the door opening. He sat bolt upright, instinctively reaching for his gun. It was dark outside, but a light showed in through the open door.

"Jack, it's me. Don't shoot."

Despite the tension, he felt every time the door opened, he had to smile. It was exactly something he'd expect her to say.

Carrying a lantern, Claire stepped into the building and quickly closed the door. "Come down," she said with an urgency in her voice, "we have to go. I've brought you a hat and a sweater."

Her abruptness snapped him back to the moment. "Go now?" he asked, tossing the boots down from the loft and then climbing down the ladder.

"Yes, now. Hurry!"

He sat on the dirt floor as she knelt in front of him and helped slip his right boot over the still-swollen ankle. He grimaced a few times as she tightened the laces, then took her out-stretched hand as she helped him up.

"Take a few steps," she said, still holding his hand.

He held the cane with his other hand and, not using it, walked slowly toward the door. "Yeah, it'll be fine... but you can still hold my hand if you want."

She abruptly dropped his hand. "You better use the cane." Then she handed him a turtle-neck sweater and a black beret. As he put them on, she took a step back and looked him up and down. "Not bad," she said. "The trousers Gaston gave you are a bit short, but if you don't speak to anyone, we may be able to pass you off as a Belgian."

"Where are we going?"

"Somewhere safer. It's not far."

When they stepped outside, Jack was surprised to see Gaston standing next to the building. "He's here to clean-up," Claire said, "so there will be no trace you were ever here. Now, give him your pistol."

Jack flinched. "What? Give up my gun... in enemy territory? You can't be serious."

"I am completely serious. You cannot carry a weapon. If we get stopped by the SS or the Gestapo, and they find a weapon, it's a death sentence... for both of us. Give Gaston the gun. We must leave right now. Someone tipped off the local *gendarmerie,* and they've been asking questions. They could be here any minute. You can't stay here any longer."

Jack hesitated for a moment, then pulled the Colt 45 from the waistband of his trousers and handed it to Gaston.

Claire quickly grabbed his arm at the sound of automobile tires crunching on the gravel driveway.

"We must go. *Now!*"

They walked quickly without speaking. Stepping gingerly with the support of the cane, Jack just barely kept up with Claire's pace. His ankle ached, and his back and legs were stiff after several days of little activity.

It was a clear, starry night with a crescent moon, and though Claire had left the lantern with Gaston, it wasn't difficult to see where they were going. At first, she led them down a narrow dirt path away from the distillery for about a quarter mile. Then she turned onto a smaller path that led through a thicket of pine trees.

As they skirted past another field, Jack spotted the outline of a distant farmhouse, barely discernable in the darkness. Suddenly, the quiet night erupted into the jarring sound of barking dogs. Claire stopped abruptly, held her hand up, and they stood in silence.

Jack stared into the dark open field as the barking got louder, and they both stepped off the path into the shadow of the trees. "Stand perfectly still," he whispered.

A moment later, he spotted them: three dogs charging across the field, menacing black shapes in the moonlight, racing directly toward them. When they reached the path, the dogs stopped abruptly, less than a meter away, barking and snarling.

Jack stood ramrod stiff. Out of the corner of his eye, he saw Claire standing still as a statue, their shadows blending in with the trees. He was used to dogs and knew the best defense was to do exactly what they were doing. What worried him was the loud commotion alerting the people in the house at the far end of the field.

Gradually, the dogs stopped barking, giving way to growling, snarling, and pawing the dirt.

Then a man's voice shouted something. It sounded like a command, calling the dogs. Jack glanced at Claire, but she shook her head, obviously signaling it was someone she didn't want to meet.

The man shouted again, louder, and clapped his hands. The dog in the middle—the biggest of the three—turned his head toward the man, then abruptly turned back, growling at them again, pawing the ground, circling closer.

Another shout, this one even closer and, in the moonlight, Jack spotted the silhouette of a figure walking into the field, carrying what looked like a rifle. He glanced at Claire again, who stood perfectly still, staring into the field. He doubted the man could see them but couldn't be sure.

The man moved closer and shouted again, "*Wie is darr?*" This time, it was loud enough for Jack to make out the words, and even though it was in Flemish, he knew what it meant. "Who is out there?"

Finally, the lead dog started to back away slowly, still staring at them and snarling. Then, after one last hesitation, the big, husky animal abruptly turned and bolted back into the field, followed by the other two.

Sweat poured down the side of Jack's face, the salty taste seeping into the corner of his mouth. After what seemed like a very long time, the man finally bent down and patted the big dog's head. Then he turned and walked slowly back in the other direction, glancing back over his shoulder every few seconds, the dogs following at his heel.

They stood perfectly still until the man disappeared from their sight. Then Claire reached over and tapped his shoulder, pointing down the path. "Stay in the shadow of the trees," she whispered.

They walked slowly, keeping silent for another quarter of an hour until they crossed a bridge over a small stream and stopped at a clearing overlooking yet another farm field. Beyond the field, Jack saw a house with lights in the window.

"That's where we're going," Claire said. "We'll wait here until the light goes out in the ground floor window on the left and the one on the right comes on. That's the signal." There was a fallen tree lying nearby, and she sat down, motioning for him to sit next to her.

"Who was the guy with the dogs?" he asked. "Apparently not someone you wanted to meet."

"No, he's not someone I wanted to meet, certainly not with you along, that's for sure."

"You think he suspected anything?"

"I hope not. Perhaps he thought the dogs spotted a deer or a fox. I'm glad you were with me, or I might have tried to run. I'm not fond of dogs."

"Was he the one who called the *gendarmes?*"

Claire shrugged. "It's possible. Gaston has never trusted him, and I wouldn't have come this way if we weren't in such a hurry. I thought he kept those damn dogs in the barn at night, but I guess I was wrong. I'm sorry, that was a very close call." She pointed to the house with the lights on. "You'll spend a night or two in that house, perhaps longer, depending on when we can arrange the next move."

"Who lives there?"

"An elderly couple connected with our organization. They have helped others before you and can be trusted. But do not introduce yourself, and do not ask their names.

"Where are *you* going?"

She glanced at him with that same schoolteacher look, then softened a bit. "To make some arrangements. I'll come back to you in two or three days. In the meantime, the woman will try to teach you a few simple phrases in Flemish. Hopefully, she'll have more success than I did. She will also help you learn to keep your fork in your left hand when eating. It may sound trivial, but it could save your life someday... and mine."

Jack thought about that. The dogs and the man carrying a rifle, at least, that was something he might be able to handle. But being discovered because of eating with your fork in the wrong hand? That scared him... and embarrassed him. And being alone in a foreign country where he couldn't even speak the language. He wondered what he would do if Claire didn't return.

Then, she suddenly stood up and took his hand. "There's the signal. Let's go."

Chapter Nine

SS-Hauptsturmfuhrer Becker was furious. He stood in Gaston's kitchen and ran a hand through his short, blond hair, glancing around, knowing he was being lied to. The dogs barking in the distance confirmed he was just minutes too late. He carefully replaced his hat and glared at the *gendarme,* then at the old farmer who had met them in the driveway and shown them into the house. "You *know* what will happen if you are lying to me," Becker snapped, speaking English again, knowing that at least the *gendarme* understood. "I will have both of you shot in the street, in front of your families and neighbors!"

The *gendarme* nervously translated to the old farmer and then nodded at Becker. "He understands, *Hauptsturmfuhrer.* I understand as well. He is telling the truth. Has not seen an aviator. Was not here."

"Then why the hell did his neighbor call us and report it? Those dogs have obviously spotted something."

The *gendarme* shrugged. "As you see, no one here."

Becker turned away and stormed out the door, thinking he could easily shoot both of the lying bastards right now, and no one would do a damn thing about it. He stood in the driveway and lit a cigarette, taking a deep drag, letting the nicotine settle his frustration.

There were those among his fellow SS officers who would have done exactly that: shoot them right then and there and not think twice about it. He'd seen it happen a hundred times when he was on the eastern front in Russia, civilians—women, old men, even children—shot down in cold blood. He'd come close to doing it himself, several times, after seeing his men get ambushed in some crappy Russian village, knowing that the locals had tipped off the Red Army.

Becker ground out the cigarette in the dirt and walked back to his car. He'd been lied to; he knew that. But shooting a couple of civilians wasn't the answer. Hell, if he were in their shoes, he'd probably have lied as well. Besides, he had more important things to tend to.

Despite his distaste for tracking down aviators, he had learned something about the civilian population in the occupied countries, which had proven useful in carrying out his real assignment. While there were partisans willing to help the Allies, there were also collaborators willing to help the Germans... you just had to know where to find them.

And Becker did.

But the pressure was mounting. In the months following the disaster at Stalingrad, the prospects of victory were slipping away, and certain people in Berlin—important people who depended on him—were getting nervous. They could *not* get caught in Germany if the war was lost. Becker could not let that happen. He had to capture these damn allied aviators, get that escape line shut down for good, and press on with his real mission.

Chapter Ten

Claire returned early on the morning of the third day, and Jack had never been so glad to see anyone in his life. It wasn't that the elderly couple had been rude or didn't treat him well. On the contrary, they had been very kind and went out of their way to make sure he was comfortable, though he hadn't slept very well. The isolation had set his mind racing again, conjuring up a dozen crazy schemes of how he would escape on his own if Claire didn't return.

This morning, it was the brusque, schoolteacher version of Claire who returned, but he was still glad to see her. She exchanged a few words with the woman of the house and then led Jack out into the yard. There was a small wrought iron table and two chairs under an apple tree where they sat facing each other.

"Did you learn any Flemish?" Claire asked.

Jack hesitated then said, *"Ja, ja. Godemorgen, goedenacht, dank u wel."*

She stared at him for a moment, then shook her head. Okay, I can see that's going to need some work."

"Well, her English isn't very good, so it was a little tough. But I can also say, *Hallo, gag, ik begrip het nacht…"*

Claire smiled, reached across the table, and put her hand on his arm. "It's *niet... ik begrip het niet.* And it's *dag, not gag.*"

"Yeah, well, it's only been a few days."

She sat back, and the serious look returned. "While we're still in Belgium, you will *not* speak Flemish to anyone unless you absolutely have no choice. Your accent will be a dead giveaway. I will try and make sure you don't have to."

"Then why am I trying to learn it? Maybe I should try French. I had two years in high school. Don't you also speak French here?"

Claire sighed. "Belgium is a very complicated country, Jack, and it would take years to explain it all. Yes, French is spoken, primarily in the south, the Ardennes area, and in Brussels. But here in the north, in Flanders, we speak Flemish. German is also spoken, but only down in the far southeastern area of the country, also in the Ardennes but very near the German border." She paused for a moment, obviously noticing his bewildered look. "The important thing for you to remember is that there are divided loyalties in Belgium, and many people, in all regions of the country, are sympathetic to the Germans and actively collaborate with them. This is a very dangerous place right now, and it is hard to know who to trust. Learning a few Flemish phrases will be useful once we cross the border into France, especially on the trains or at checkpoints. Very few French or German officials understand Flemish. If you are asked a question, those few phrases, especially *ik begrip het niet*—I don't understand—will usually prevent further questions."

Jack thought about it for a moment, wondering how he could ever pull that off.

Claire continued. "There are some things you need to know about what happens from this point forward. They are extremely important, and while they may seem trivial, remember it's the little things, the details, that make the difference between life and death."

"Sounds like flying an airplane," Jack replied.

She paused for a moment as though considering that. "It's a good way to look at it, I suppose. There is one big difference, however. For you, flying an airplane is by now rather second nature, I suspect, whereas this—

Is it completely unnatural?"

"Yes, I'm certain it is. And what will be *most* unnatural for you is that this will be the last time we can speak English unless we are completely alone, and even then, only if I initiate the conversation. Understood?"

"Ja, ja natuurlijk."

"Heel goed. The accent is still a problem, but you're getting there. Now, some other things: when we are walking together, especially in a city, I may occasionally take your hand. Two young people walking hand in hand can look more natural and less suspicious. Don't make anything of it; it's just for effect."

Jack nodded. He thought he'd enjoy that.

"There are other times, however, when I may walk twenty paces ahead or not sit next to you on a tram. It will depend on the circumstances. You'll just have to follow my lead and not question it."

"How many others have you escorted before me?"

"Several."

"Other Americans?

She shrugged. "I can't say."

"Ah, the secrets, again."

She stood up. "We should go back to the house. Gaston will arrive soon with a truck. He'll drive us to Antwerp, where we have a safe house and a connection with someone who can provide you with a new identity card."

Jack stood up slowly, placing his hands in his pockets. Safe houses, trains, checkpoints, it seemed like something from a very bad movie, one that probably didn't have a happy ending.

She seemed to have guessed his thoughts and said, "You will have to trust us, Jack. We've done this before, many times."

"Successfully?"

She looked directly at him. There was a sadness in her dark, penetrating eyes. "No, not always. We *have* successfully helped several hundred aviators get to Spain and then back to Britain in the last few years.

But there have also been some who did not make it and were captured."

"Like Alex."

"Yes, like Alex." She paused, then added, "In *all* cases, however, when Allied aviators are captured, their escorts—the people in our organization, people like me—are usually executed on the spot."

Jack's mouth was suddenly very dry, and he tried unsuccessfully to swallow. "Why do you do it? Why do any of you do this... risk your lives for people you don't know?"

She hesitated for a moment. "The only thing that has kept me going for the last few years is the belief that this war will not last forever," she said quietly, "and that one day, we will be able to live our lives, to trust our neighbors, to have hope again. We do it for freedom, Jack. You would do the same thing."

As they started back to the house, he wondered if that were true. Would he do the same thing? Would he risk his life for someone he didn't know?

Claire glanced at him and said, "You're walking better. How's the ankle?"

"Much better. See, no cane."

"Yes, I see. But don't put your hands in your pockets. It's very American."

Chapter Eleven

Antwerp

Claire's nerves tensed the moment they arrived in Antwerp. It happened every time she escorted an escapee through a big city. The crowded sidewalks, noisy trams, and hundreds of people created a thousand risk factors where something could go wrong. Not to mention the German soldiers.

She knew, of course, there would be German soldiers in Antwerp, just like Brussels and Paris and every other city they would travel through. And she had instructed Jack to ignore them and not make eye contact. But it was always a risk; you never knew when one of them would get curious and ask a question or say something.

That's when everything could change in an instant.

Gaston had dropped them off on the outskirts of the city center, where they boarded a tram. The car was crowded, and suddenly, she and Jack stood face-to-face with two Wehrmacht soldiers. They were young, barely more than teenagers, and they bantered back and forth in German, laughing about some unknown joke as though they were on their way to a soccer game. Claire realized Jack was staring at them, probably remembering the soldiers who shot his crewmate in the field and wishing he had his gun. She stepped on his foot to get his attention, and he turned away but with a smoldering look in his eyes.

When they got off the tram in the city center, Claire immediately took hold of Jack's hand. Blending into the crowd, she led the way down *De Keyser Lei,* a broad, bustling avenue lined with shops, cafés, and diamond merchants that she had walked a hundred times in the years before the war. The difference now was that few of the shops had anything to sell... and all the Jewish diamond merchants had vanished. They still passed German soldiers on the street, but now Jack looked away.

At the end of *De Keyser Lei* stood Antwerp's central railway station, a colossal, five-story stone structure topped with an enormous arched dome flanked by smaller gothic towers on either side. Claire turned right and headed down a narrow, cobblestone street that ran parallel to the train tracks. The street eventually curved under the railway tracks, where it intersected a quieter street lined with three-story, brick row houses.

Claire stopped in front of a house practically identical to every other house on the block. She'd been here several times before, and a bit of her tension melted away as she glanced up at the familiar number *14* embossed in a stone lintel above the wrought-iron door of the safe house. Getting off the streets was her first priority.

She pulled the door open and motioned for Jack to follow, touching her lips with a finger and signaling for him to stay quiet. They stepped into a small, dimly lit alcove with a marble floor and a row of three mailboxes along one wall. To the left of the mailboxes were buttons corresponding to the names of the tenants. Claire pushed the button next to the name *Vandenberg*.

There was no reply.

She tried again.

After a moment, a soft female voice she recognized came over the intercom. *"Hallo?"*

"We zijn gekomen om de piano te zien." Claire replied, asking about a piano, the same phrase she had spoken many times before.

There was a moment of silence on the other end before the voice spoke again. But it was even softer now, halting, nervous. *"Het is verkocht."*

Claire blinked and was silent for a moment, wondering if she had heard correctly.

The piano was sold?

Her heart pounded, and she swallowed hard as the message sunk in.

The safe house was compromised!

Perhaps it was being watched; perhaps *they* were being watched.

Her mind was racing, but she finally took a deep breath and said, quite loudly, *"Ja, ja, sorry. Dag."*

She took Jack by the arm and pushed the door open. Outside, she kept her arm in his, ignoring his look of surprise, and walked quickly back the way they came. The hairs on the back of her neck bristled, and it took every ounce of her discipline not to look back over her shoulder.

How could this happen?

When they crossed back under the railway tracks, Claire finally stopped and looked back down the street. A train rumbled slowly overhead, and she glanced left and right, making sure they were alone and out of sight for the moment. She leaned close to Jack and said, in English, "We can't stay there. It's no longer safe."

"What happened?"

"The house has been compromised."

"When just recently?" Jack's eyes were wide, a stunned expression on his face.

"Yes, *very* recently. I checked the day before yesterday, and we were cleared to stay there, but that's changed."

He stood quietly for a moment, staring at her. "So, now what?"

Claire rubbed her forehead, trying to think. She knew there was a backup plan. They could stay with Lukas. He would know what to do. He might let them stay at his safehouse, but they couldn't just show up. There was a protocol to follow in any situation where the original plan was compromised. They would go to the Café Brig in the area of Antwerp's old port. She knew the code words. She'd memorized them long ago... if only they hadn't changed. "There is an alternate plan," she said, trying to sound a lot more confident than she felt. "But I've never used it before, so let's get going,"

"You've never used it before? Isn't this your home? I thought you said you were—"

Claire cut him off. "Yes, this *was* my home. I was raised here. But that was before. Everything's changed now. I can't tell you any more than that. We have to go."

She took Jack's arm again, trying desperately to look and act like a casual young couple. But a hundred thoughts raced through her mind, wondering what the hell had happened; was someone in the safehouse with the proprietor? Did someone else know she and Jack were going there? Were they being followed right now?

As they walked past the central station, she briefly thought about just getting on the train for France but dismissed it. The safehouse in Paris needed to be cleared, and Jack still needed an ID.

They crossed the street where they had exited the tram and continued toward the old city where streets were busier, and she felt less conspicuous. She tried to set a casual pace, occasionally glancing at half-empty shop windows as though they were out for a stroll... but it suddenly seemed like there were many more German soldiers around.

They entered the old city and strolled through the medieval square dominated by Antwerp's thirteenth-century cathedral. Claire nudged Jack in the ribs to stop him from gawking like a tourist and stepped up the pace, leading the way through a narrow, winding street that eventually opened onto the Grote Markt, a large market square lined with outdoor cafes, small shops, and gabled-roof buildings.

Occupying the entire west side of the square was the *Stadhuis,* Antwerp's colossal, five-story, renaissance-style city hall. She glanced at Jack, who stared at the huge red flag with the white circle and black swastika hanging from the top of the building's richly ornamented central tower. Her stomach knotted whenever she saw it, and she wondered how he would feel if that flag were flying over the city hall in his hometown in America.

They continued walking arm-in-arm and eventually arrived at a broad avenue fronting the River Schelde. Trying to recall the directions she had memorized months ago, Claire turned toward Antwerp's immense seaport and continued along the avenue, also busy with pedestrians. One or two buses passed by, but other than the occasional long, black Citroen or Mercedes Benz favored by the SS and Gestapo, there were almost no private autos.

As they continued north along the river, the pedestrian traffic eventually tailed off, and just a few trucks rumbled past. A few minutes later, they came to a quiet, seemingly deserted street. She'd never been here before. Her mouth was dry as she read the street name on the side of a building: *Amsterdamstraat.* This was it, and they turned onto the narrow cobblestone street.

To their left was an ancient dock, one of the oldest in the port of Antwerp. Two barges filled with coal lay alongside the quay, a dank, fishy odor emanating from the stagnant water. To their right was a line of drab commercial buildings, and, in the middle of the long block, she spotted a shabby, red brick building with large, dirty windows on either side of an open door. Just as it had been described to her. Above the door was a wooden sign with faded, red letters that read *Café Brig.*

Claire stopped well back from the door and glanced up and down the street. They were alone. She turned to Jack, noticing the skeptical look on his face. She felt bad for him, knowing he must be terribly confused and must have a hundred questions but had been sworn to silence. "This is the place," she whispered in English, hoping she was right. "Do you have the Belgian francs that were in your kit?"

He nodded. "But I have no idea—"

"Ten francs will be enough. I will order, but it will look better if you pay. And do *not* say anything in English."

It was a long, narrow, dimly lit tavern that smelled of beer, grease, and human sweat. Surprisingly, given the deserted street, all the stools at the bar were occupied by rugged, middle-aged men who looked like dockworkers or truck drivers. Claire suddenly felt very conspicuous. A few glanced at her, realized Jack was with her and returned to their glasses of beer and conversation.

Claire took a seat at one of the booths lining the wall opposite the bar. Jack followed her lead and sat across from her. It was obvious from the creaky wooden floor, cracked leather seats, and maritime artwork yellowed with age that the *Café Brig* had been here a long time. A backwater. Most of the men at the bar had also been here a long time by the looks of them. But at least there were no German soldiers.

Before long, the bartender stepped over to their booth, carrying two menus. *"Goedemiddag,"* he said casually, as though young couples stopped in here all the time. He appeared to be in his mid-forties, thin and wiry with a shock of curly brown hair, roughly matching the description she recalled from the instructions. Now, if only she remembered the code correctly.

"Goedemiddag," she responded. *"Twee Trappist Ales. Uit Liege."*

She held her breath, her heart pounding as the man blinked and stood silently for a moment, staring at her.

Finally, he shook his head and said, *"Dat hebben we niet."*

It was the expected reply, and Claire took a breath. *"Leffe?"* she ordered instead.

"Ja, ja," he replied and stepped back to the bar. He did not leave the menus.

The bartender disappeared into the back room for several minutes, and Claire tapped her fingers on the table, purposely not looking at Jack for fear she'd give away the anxiety that was lingering in her gut.

What if I got it wrong, and he's calling the police?

What if someone—

Finally, the bartender emerged from the back room, poured two glasses of beer from a tap, set them on a tray and returned to the booth. He placed two coasters on the table and set the glasses on the coasters. Then, with a glance at Claire, he placed a small metal plate on the table with a neatly folded slip of paper that was presumably the bill. Without another word, he returned to the bar.

As they sipped the beer, Claire withdrew a small map from the vest pocket of her jacket and spread it on the table between them. It was a city map of Antwerp, and she had previously explained to Jack that she might use it if they needed to pretend to be doing something except sitting in awkward silence. She pointed to the map and, speaking softly in Flemish, asked Jack, "Should we continue on and check out some of the other docks and then head back toward the Grote Markt?"

Jack again followed her lead, looked down at the map and grunted a response, *"Ja, Okay."*

Given everything that had gone wrong so far, she thought he seemed to be holding up quite well. He was probably feeling more than a little self-conscious, certain that everyone at the bar was listening. He would occasionally run a hand through his dark brown hair, which had grown out a bit since he arrived, but didn't appear outwardly nervous, wasn't looking around like he expected the police to show up, wasn't sweating or showing any outward signs of stress.

So far, so good.

We just need to get out of here.

They finished their beers and stood up to leave. Claire glanced down at the bill, and Jack picked it up, looked at it and dropped a ten franc note on the table. Claire picked up the bill and slipped it into her pocket.

They crossed the street and walked alongside the old dock, heading away from the river. There was nothing on this side of the street except two parked trucks. Claire pulled the bill out of her pocket and glanced at the hand-written note. She crumpled the bill and tossed it into the muck-covered water. "We're to meet someone at the Steen Castle at 17:30," she said.

"Who are we meeting?"

Claire shrugged, "I don't know." She had an idea who it might be, but Jack didn't need to know. If it turned out she was right, everything could work out. If she was wrong and it was a set-up... her stomach churned.

The late afternoon sky had clouded over, and a stiff breeze blew across the River Schelde. Claire shivered and turned up her coat collar, not sure if she was cold or just anxious. The compromised safehouse had unnerved her, though she was trying hard not to let it show. She was also worried about who would show up to meet them. She had no reason not to trust the bartender, though the protocol she had followed to go to the *Café Brig* was at least a year old. The escape line had been infiltrated since then by an unknown collaborator, and anything could have happened.

She took a breath to clear her mind and glanced at Jack, who was examining the nooks and arches of the ancient castle that over-looked the river as though he were a tourist. "It's the oldest structure in Antwerp, built by the Romans in the thirteenth century," she said quietly in English. They were early, and there was no one else around.

"Was it a fort to protect the city from attack by the river?"

Claire nodded and motioned toward a small alcove where they could get out of the wind and stay out of sight. Whoever was coming to meet them, she would rather see them first. "It's quite common in Europe," she replied. "We keep fighting the same wars over and over."

Jack was quiet for a moment, studying the view of the old city from their vantage point. Then he turned to her and said, "You told me this is where you're from, and you studied in London for a couple of years, then moved to Grote Brogel to help Gaston."

Claire nodded but didn't respond.

"So, is there anyone else in your life, a boyfriend or—"

Claire held up her hand, cutting him off.

Jack quickly backed off. "I'm sorry, you don't have to answer. I know it's dangerous."

She hesitated for a moment, glancing around again. She had escorted six others before Jack: three Brits, a Pole and two other Americans. They all asked questions, some more than others, about where she was from, if she was married if she had a boyfriend, the usual things to make conversation. She understood their need to have some level of human connection, something to take away the fear and loneliness. But her training was precise. You deflect the questions; you don't answer. Finally, she looked Jack in the eye. "Any information we give an Allied soldier evading the enemy could lead to capture, torture, and execution if that soldier is caught. There are spies and collaborators everywhere. And no one can stand up under interrogation by the Gestapo."

He nodded. "Yeah, I understand…, but since I don't even know your real name or anything about you, I just thought—"

She hesitated again, then reached out and put her hand on his arm, squeezing it gently. "No, I don't have a boyfriend, and I've never been married. So, no more questions."

"Oh… okay then, good to know, thanks."

Claire held his gaze for a moment, wishing she could answer his questions, wishing they could just sit quietly, holding hands, and talk. She wanted to know more about him, wanted to—

She spotted someone out of the corner of her eye, a tall, silver-haired man, walking swiftly up the castle's cobblestone carriage ramp. A wave of relief washed over her as she recognized Bart Peeters. She blinked back tears.

Jack turned and looked over his shoulder. "What's wrong? Who is that?"

"It's fine. His name is Bart, an old friend of my family. I've known him my whole life. Wait here and stay out of sight. I'll be right back." She stepped out of the alcove and waved to Bart.

Bart smiled as he waved back and hurried over. He embraced Claire and kissed her lightly on both cheeks. "It's all clear, and Lukas is expecting you," he said. "You and your friend had better get going. I'll join you there later."

Chapter Twelve

Jack noticed a change in Claire's demeanor the moment they arrived at Lukas' apartment. She suddenly relaxed, and it was obvious from their warm embrace and easy banter in Flemish—which lasted for several minutes—that she and Lukas were very close friends. He was a slender, serious-looking man, a few inches shorter than Jack and appeared to be in his late twenties or early thirties. Jack noticed that he walked with a slight limp, though it didn't seem to bother him.

After a laugh over some private joke, Claire abruptly turned and said, "Jack, come and shake hands with my dear friend, Lukas. He owns the shop downstairs."

Lukas smiled and extended his hand. "My English is not good, but I am pleased you are here. You like some coffee?"

Jack nodded, "Yes, thank you."

Lukas turned and walked down a short hallway that apparently led to a kitchen. Claire followed him, saying something in Flemish.

Jack stood idle for a moment, glancing around the neat but sparsely furnished room, which appeared to be a combination parlor and dining area. There was a sofa at one end with a floor lamp and a low coffee table. On the other end of the room was the only window and a square, wooden dining table with four straight-backed chairs. In a corner near the window stood a much smaller, small round table with a lamp and single framed picture. Jack stepped closer and picked up the picture. It was a grainy photo of two young children standing with their bicycles. One appeared to be Lukas, and the other one was very definitely Claire. It was the only picture in the room.

Jack set the picture down and glanced out the window, which overlooked the street below. The building was situated in the center of the old city with a partial view of the cathedral. Directly across the street was a grassy, tree-lined plot, like a small park. He recalled that when they arrived at the building, he had noticed a rather cluttered-looking shop on the ground floor. Claire had led him past the shop's entrance to a separate door and staircase that led up to the apartment. Through the shop windows, Jack had noticed an assortment of hand tools, gloves, ladders, and machine parts that reminded him of a rural hardware store back home. He wondered if Lukas was some type of handyman.

A moment later, Claire and Lukas emerged from the kitchen, still casually chatting in Flemish. Claire blushed slightly and glanced back at some comment Lukas made, then set a tray of cups and a plate of biscuits on the coffee table. Lukas followed her and poured coffee.

"It not good coffee," Lukas said, glancing at Jack, "but Claire say you don't mind."

"No, not at all... thanks."

Claire sat down on the sofa and motioned for Jack to sit next to her. Lukas pulled up a chair from the dining table and sat, balancing the coffee cup on his knee. Almost immediately, he initiated another conversation in Flemish with Claire that continued for some time while Jack sipped his coffee. Lukas appeared to be a friendly sort, though he seemed a bit awkward or ill at ease. Perhaps seeing Claire escorting an allied aviator unnerved him, though he'd likely seen her in this situation before since he operated a safe house. Perhaps he feared for her safety, which would be understandable.

This was the first time Jack had been with Claire when it wasn't just the two of them, and it suddenly felt very strange—and isolating—since he had no idea what they were talking about. He had felt isolated and lonely before when he was confined in the loft in the old gin distillery, but Claire would always come by and brighten his day. Then, it was just the two of them, and even though it was a bizarre and dangerous environment, he somehow felt... connected. But now, sitting here in the presence of her long-time friend, speaking their own language, he felt more isolated than he did in the loft.

Eventually, the conversation ended, and Claire and Lukas both set their cups on the coffee table and stood up. Claire smiled and motioned for Jack to follow them. "Lukas will show us where you'll be staying."

Chapter Thirteen

Jack stood in the middle of the tiny room, wondering if he would ever see anything that would surprise him more than this. It was located under the eaves of the building and accessible only through a cleverly concealed trapdoor in the ceiling above a hallway. Lukas was obviously very proud of his handiwork as he showed Jack how to access the trapdoor and integral ladder.

The room was clearly used as a hideout, sparsely furnished, with a single bed, a small round table with one chair, a chest of drawers and a small, braided rug in the center of the rough, plank floor. There was a skylight in the ceiling, which, thankfully, could be propped open a few inches to let in some air, but no electricity, the only light coming from a candle on the table.

Wondering how many other Allied aviators had stayed in this room, Jack sat on the floor, pulled off his boots and rubbed his feet.

Claire sat on the bed watching him. "They don't fit that well, do they."

He looked up at her and shrugged. "A little tight, but I'm not complaining."

"How's your ankle?"

"It feels better, just a bit stiff from all the walking. The tight boots actually help."

"I'm sorry about all that," she said, "but there was no other choice. I thought you held up rather well considering the circumstances."

Jack shrugged. "Obviously, the thing at that safehouse was something you weren't expecting. Has that happened before?"

"Yes, things like that do happen. But this was a shock because just two days ago, Lukas said the house was clear."

"Is that what your conversation with him was about, the safehouse?"

"Yes. He didn't know what happened. Perhaps the woman who runs the house got spooked by something, or one of her neighbors asked too many questions. Some new arrangements will be made going forward. Lukas and Bart will work it out."

"So, tell me about Lukas, another old friend of the family, like Bart?"

Claire smiled and nodded. "Yes, that's not a secret. I've known Lukas practically all of my life. He's three years older than me and lived in the neighborhood when we were growing up. I'm an only child, and he was like a big brother to me, always my 'protector' when I got in trouble with older kids."

The image made Jack smile, and he asked, "Did that happen often? Were you a troublemaker?"

She shrugged. "Often enough, I guess. I was never the type to play with dolls. I preferred to play football, but at times, I got too competitive and that led to some problems. But Lukas would always be there to make sure things didn't get out of hand. He's also an only child, so we had a sort of bond if you know what I mean."

"Yes, I could see that right away when we got here. Obviously, you two are very close."

She looked at him for a moment before answering. "I guess you could say that. We are close... close *friends*, I mean... not anything more. I love him dearly, as I would a brother, and I know he would do anything for me, but... well, that's it, we're friends."

"Why does he limp?"

"It was a bicycle accident when he was thirteen, and it never healed properly, but it doesn't prevent him from doing anything."

"Has he always owned the shop? I mean, was it in his family or something like that?"

"No, not at all. He had a difficult time as a kid. His father was some type of engineer or inventor. I never really knew much about it, but he could never hold a steady job. The family never had any money, and when Lukas was a teenager, his father became very reclusive, drank a lot and could be very mean. Lukas would spend most of his free time at our house."

"So, do you see him often?"

She shook her head. "Not all that often, it's hard with... what we do."

Jack sensed there was more she wanted to say about that but probably couldn't, and he let it go. "And what about Bart," he asked instead, "your other 'old friend of the family'? I assume Bart and Lukas are not real names either, are they?"

"My, so many questions. You may call them 'Bart' and 'Lukas.' And Bart is exactly that, an old friend of the family. He has been sort of a mentor for me, a rock, so to speak, ever since I lost my parents."

Jack flinched at the mention of her parents, not sure what to say or how much to ask, but he could tell that something had just struck her.

Claire closed her eyes for a moment and rocked back and forth. A moment later, she looked at him, shaking her head. "I don't know why I'm going on like this, telling you all these things, boring you with my—"

"No, please," Jack broke in, "it's certainly not boring. I would like to know, but I don't want to pry."

She cocked her head and smiled. "You're very sweet, Jack, and it's really the first time I've felt comfortable talking with someone outside of our little circle. The constant vigilance and secrecy of our world, always looking over your shoulder, always on alert, never knowing who to trust, it takes a toll after a while."

He suddenly felt like getting up and taking her into his arms. For the first time since they met, she seemed to have let down her guard; she seemed vulnerable, but he didn't want to break the spell. He wanted her to share her stories with him. "Tell me about your parents," he said quietly.

She sat very still, staring at the wall as if the memories were flooding back. "My parents were arrested... almost three years ago, not long after the occupation began." She turned to look at him. "The Gestapo showed up one day and just... took them away. They had a warrant accusing them of being 'traitors and subversives, enemies of the state.'"

Jack could scarcely believe what he was hearing, thinking about his own parents, but he sat quietly, wanting her to go on.

"I was in Brussels that day, interviewing for a job. When I returned home, my neighbor told me what had happened. I stayed with her that night and contacted Bart the next day. He found a safe place for me to stay for the next few weeks while he tried to intercede with some of his contacts but was unsuccessful. Then he took me to Grote Brogel, to Gaston's farm, and I never went home again."

"And your parents, do you know where they are?"

She shook her head. "Eventually, Bart learned that they were sent to *The East*. That's what they say when people are sent to concentration camps in Germany or Poland."

Jack got up and sat next to her on the bed. He reached over and took her hand. Her eyes were moist, and a tear trickled down her cheek. "Claire, I'm so sorry." He paused and looked down at their hands. "You said it's been a long time since you could talk with anyone... so I'm glad it's me."

Suddenly, he heard a sound.

Tap, Tap,

Tap, Tap, Tap

He stiffened and glanced at Claire, but she just patted his hand and stood up. She went to the trap door and tapped twice in return. "It's just Lukas signaling us that supper will be ready soon."

Jack took a deep breath, his heart racing.

She sat down again. "Thank you for listening to me... and for caring." But before he could respond, she abruptly returned to schoolteacher mode. "Before we go down, there is something you really *do* need to know. Bart will arrive; he may be there now, and he will ask you some questions."

"What, an interrogation, you mean?"

"Well, you could call it that. It is standard procedure with downed aviators trying to evade capture. You won't have any problem with it."

"How do you know?"

She smiled again. "I think I know."

Chapter Fourteen

Bart was indeed waiting for them when Jack and Claire descended through the trapdoor. They joined him at the square dining table, passing by the tiny, blue-tiled kitchen where Lukas stood at the stove, stirring a pot. Lukas glanced at them, then turned back to the stove.

On the table was a plate with four slices of heavy, dark bread and a block of cheese next to an unlabeled bottle of red wine. Lukas emerged from the kitchen a few minutes later, carrying a pot of vegetable soup.

As Jack sipped the soup, trying to guess the origin of the unusual taste, he joined in a casual conversation about Belgium's ever-changing weather and how it compared with his home in America. For Jack's benefit, they spoke in English, though Claire would occasionally touch Lukas' hand, lean close and whisper a few words in Flemish to clarify what had been said. It was a simple act of kindness between two close friends, which Jack found somewhat gratifying, making him feel a bit less of an outsider than he really was.

Bart, on the other hand, was completely fluent in English, a sophisticated, urbane sort of man with an easy smile and a direct, no-nonsense manner of speaking. Jack guessed he was in his mid-sixties and was the type of person who could easily take charge of a conversation without appearing to dominate it, like a seasoned, well-connected politician.

"Where is your home?" Bart asked as the simple supper proceeded.

"A small town in Wisconsin called Sturgeon Bay."

"Wisconsin... that's somewhere in the center?" Claire asked.

Jack nodded with a sudden flash of homesickness. "Yes, we call it the 'Midwest.' Wisconsin is about ninety miles north of Chicago."

They all nodded—even Lukas—with recognition at the mention of Chicago.

So, did you play sports in high school?" Bart asked casually.

"Yes, I played basketball. I was the point guard and... do you know basketball?"

Bart nodded, "A bit, it's not a popular sport here."

"I know you have to throw a ball through a hoop," Claire said, drawing a round of laughter.

"Yeah, well, the 'point guard' sort of directs the play and tries to get the ball to the taller guys who can 'throw it through the hoop.'"

"So, is that like the captain of the team?" Claire asked.

"Not necessarily, but in my case, I was also the team captain."

"What else do you like to do besides play basketball?" Bart asked.

"I like to go fishing. There is a small lake near our house, and I like to row the boat out just before dark and cast into the lily pads. I find it very relaxing. Sometimes my younger sister, Mary, goes with me, but she usually gets impatient if we don't catch fish right away."

They were all quiet for a moment, but Jack caught Claire's eye as he took another sip of wine. She cocked her head and smiled, then looked away and also took a sip of wine.

Bart very artfully steered the discussion toward questions about Jack's military service, and it soon became obvious that the 'interrogation' was underway. Bart turned out to be quite well-versed in American politics, sports, and entertainment, as well as military matters, and Jack quickly realized that an enemy infiltrator pretending to be an American would be in a great deal of trouble if he didn't know who won the last World Series.

An hour later, Bart, apparently satisfied that Jack was indeed an American, stood up and extended his hand. "Good luck to you, Jack. Lukas will take care of you until Claire returns. Then you can be on your way back to Britain and help us win this war."

Jack stood and shook the tall, silver-haired man's hand. He glanced at Claire, not realizing until that moment that she was also leaving.

She smiled and said, "I'll be back in a day or two... as soon as we work out a few details. You're in good hands."

Claire waited about fifteen minutes before leaving, indicating that she and Bart should not be seen together, and then she was gone.

A half-hour later, Jack was alone again, sitting in the cubbyhole of the room under the eaves. Lukas had taken his photo and left the house, apparently to visit another unidentified person who would prepare a new identity card.

During the next two days, Jack had to restrain himself at least a dozen times from crawling through the skylight and escaping over the rooftops. He knew how stupid that thought was, but the tiny room was closing in on him, and it was against his nature to sit and wait. He'd been programmed his whole life to take initiative, to be proactive and to take charge. He'd been the captain of his high school basketball team and president of his college fraternity. When he enlisted in the army, he had qualified easily for officer candidate school and had excelled in the Air Corps flight school. He loved flying because he was in charge, in control of his own destiny.

Then he lost his plane and all of his crew, and suddenly, there was *nothing* he could control. There wasn't one damn thing he could do except sit in this tiny room and wait, listening to noises on the street below, half-expecting the black-uniformed SS troopers to burst through the trap door at any moment.

Three times each day, Lukas signaled for him to come down to the apartment for a meager meal of bread, soup, an occasional potato, and bitter ersatz coffee. Though Lukas' English was very basic, Jack found that each time they were together, it improved. He seemed a humble sort of man, a bit standoffish perhaps, but they were able to carry on simple conversations.

At lunchtime, the day after Bart and Claire left, he asked Lukas about the shop downstairs and how he learned the hardware business just to put off the isolation of the tiny room for a bit longer.

"After high school, I go to France," Lukas explained, "to find work. Things very bad in Belgium then. There was no work. I had a friend who worked in the same type of shop near Lyon, so I went there and learned the business, learned how to *reparative...* you know, how to...

"Oh, to repair, to fix things?" Jack asked.

Ja, ja, repair, fix things, motors, tools, you understand?"

Jack nodded, "Yes, I understand. So, then you came back to Belgium and started this business?"

"*Ja,* I come back here and... a friend... help find this shop. Good business... very busy."

"So, does your friend help you in the shop, like a partner?"

Lukas quickly shook his head. "No, no partner... work alone." He was silent for a moment, then got up from the table and said, "I go now to get your *identiteitskaart.* Then must work in the shop. You go up to the room. We have supper later, maybe some *groenten...* ah, how you say... vegetables?"

"Yes, vegetables, that would be very nice. I'll see you then."

It was another long afternoon, and Jack regretted that he'd finished reading *Treasure Island* before they had quickly left Gaston's farm. He doubted that Lukas had any English language books. At supper that evening, he initiated another conversation with Lukas to pass the time and, giving in to his curiosity, asked about Claire. "I understand that you and Claire have been friends since you were children. Has she always been so self-confident?"

Lukas looked at him as though he didn't quite understand. "Self con... fid...?"

"Uh, self-confident it means strong, determined, willing to take charge."

"Ah, *sterk, zelfverzekerd, ja, ja,* strong," he said with a laugh. "Always strong, take charge, yes, always. Even when very young. No *broers of zussen,* had to be strong. Me as well, always very *goede vrienden,* you know, like this." He emphasized their close relationship by clasping his hands together.

Even with Lukas jumping back and forth between languages, Jack understood what he meant. Lukas leaned across the table and said quietly, "Our work is... *gevaarlijk...* how you say... ah, danger?"

Jack nodded, "Yes, dangerous, I know."

"But I look after Claire. Try to keep her safe. After the war is over, perhaps Claire and I *Ga trouwen.* How you say in English... get married?"

Jack looked at the thin, serious man and nodded slowly, "Yes, that's how we say it."

Chapter Fifteen

Nightfall came, and the darkness in the tiny room under the eaves was almost absolute. Jack lay on the bed, looking out the skylight. He could see a few stars, and there was a faint glow from the streetlamps down below. Noises drifted in, clopping horse's hooves and creaking wagon wheels, voices, and bursts of laughter from the area of the park across the street.

Time passed, and voices from the park became louder and more boisterous, reminding Jack of the fraternity parties in college and the pubs in England packed with servicemen, when the noise level always increased with the amount of alcohol consumed.

Gradually, the tone of the voices seemed to change. They became even louder, shrill, and harsh, and the laughter turned into shouting.

Jack couldn't understand the words, of course, but the voices now sounded angry and gruff, like men cursing each other. Then, the voices drew closer as though they had crossed the street, heading toward the apartment building and Lukas's shop. Did he hear Lukas' voice? He thought so but couldn't be sure.

Suddenly, glass shattered in the shop below, and Jack sat up abruptly.

More shouting, louder than ever.

Then, from off in the distance, the distinctive two-tone wail of police sirens.

Jack stared into the blackness of the room, straining to listen. The shouting and cursing escalated as though everyone was trying to get their last licks in before the cops arrived.

Was Lukas involved? Was he injured?

A thought raced through Jack's mind that he should get down there and help Lukas, but the foolish notion vanished when the commotion suddenly stopped with the sound of screeching tires and slamming car doors.

Then it was quiet. Minutes passed, and different sounds drifted through the open skylight: official-sounding voices barking commands, men complaining and grumbling, and feet shuffling across cobblestones.

Car doors slammed again, and vehicles sped away.

Time passed, it was hard to know how long, but perhaps five or ten minutes before another vehicle arrived, a car door slammed, and he heard a different voice, a sharp, direct voice... speaking German.

Then he heard Lukas' voice, this time he was sure of it... but also speaking German, though slowly and deliberately.

A moment passed, and he heard the authoritative German voice again, but this time, it wasn't coming from outside. It came from below, inside the building, in the shop perhaps, or the stairway to the apartment.

Lukas' voice, then the German's, both louder now and very clear.

Are they in the apartment?

Jack knelt on the bed, barely breathing, listening to the sound of the two voices. The sharp, authoritative German voice sounded familiar as if he'd heard it before. He thought back to the farm field, recalling the long, black auto driven by black-uniformed SS officers.

How could that be possible?

We're in Antwerp, that was in Grote Brogel.

Both voices, Lukas' and the other one, still speaking German, sounded now as though they were in the hallway, right below the trapdoor.

Jack's leg suddenly cramped, and he shifted his weight, causing the bed to move scraping the floor. He tensed, holding his breath, waiting. He thought about the trapdoor in the ceiling.

Did I close it all the way?

If I didn't, there is a small crack that—

The authoritative voice once again, and the sound of boots shuffling in the hallway.

Jack tried to visualize his tiny room in the darkness, thinking of anything he could use as a weapon.

Why the hell did I give up my gun?

He thought about his boots.

Christ, did I leave them in the hallway?

No, he was sure he didn't. He couldn't see anything in the darkness, but he was sure his boots were in the room, tucked neatly under the table. Did he dare to try and get to them and risk making a noise? And what good would they be against an armed SS officer?

He sat, waiting, listening, trying to control his breathing. His leg began to cramp again, but he dared not move for fear of making another sound. More than frightened, he felt pathetic and helpless. Just a few days ago, he'd been the captain of a US Army Air Corps B-24 Liberator, a lethal warplane, in command of his crew as they wreaked havoc on the enemy from the skies. Now, he hid like a rodent, quivering in a cave.

I really wish I had my gun.

Then he heard Lukas's voice again, quieter now, and the sound of footsteps moving down the hallway. The footsteps descended the staircase.

Then it was quiet.

Chapter Sixteen

Lukas stood on the landing at the bottom of the stairs, waiting patiently while *SS Hauptsturmfuhrer* Konrad Becker went out to his automobile to get something. When he returned, he handed Lukas a cardboard box containing a dozen eggs.

"*Danke, Hauptsturmfuhrer,* that is very kind. I haven't had fresh eggs for some time."

"*Bitte,* I am glad to help. Fortunately, we in the SS have some privileges." Becker then took a step closer and spoke slowly and quietly. "One last question before I go, 'Lukas.' Have you heard anything about the American who escaped from Grote Brogel? Is he one of yours?"

Lukas' stomach tightened, but he kept his eyes fixed on Becker. "*Nein,* I have not heard anything. He is not one of mine and has not been here."

"You will tell me if you hear anything, *verstehen?*"

"*Ja, verstehen.*"

"You don't mind if I use your code name, do you, 'Lukas?' I find it an amusing little game among those in the escape line."

The back of Lukas' neck tingled as he shook his head. "*Nein,* I don't mind."

Becker smiled, though his ice-blue eyes retained their intense glare. "You have done good work for us since you infiltrated that traitorous organization. Many of the conspirators you identified have been arrested and dealt with appropriately. Along with some of the Allied aviators who have stayed right here in your little attic. Very good work, indeed. You will be rewarded when we achieve our final victory."

"I want no reward, *Hauptsturmfuhrer,* you know that. The triumph of the Reich, the New Order, will be reward enough."

Becker nodded, "*Sehr Gut,* Lukas. I know I can trust you. We have been friends and partners, have we not?"

Lukas nodded but remained silent, having learned to say no more than necessary when conversing with Becker.

"But there is more to do," Becker said, "this escape organization must be shut down completely. And, after that, I have an even more important task for you."

"*Ja, Hauptsturmfuhrer,* you can count on me."

After Becker left, Lukas leaned against the wall for a moment, trying to relax. He knew exactly why Becker chose to show up tonight, and it wasn't because of some simple act of vandalism. Just like he knew the so-called fight in the park and the broken window were staged by Becker's thugs to send him a message—the same message he always wanted Lukas to remember— that he was being watched. And then Becker would abruptly step out of character and show a small act of kindness, like bringing a dozen eggs.

Lukas knew that everything Becker did was part of a plan to keep him off balance and always on guard. It was all part of their mission. If the New Order was to be achieved, absolute discipline and complete loyalty were demanded. Becker had drilled that into him from the first time they met.

Lukas closed his eyes, thinking back to that fateful night in 1941. He had just returned to Belgium from France but found himself alone and adrift in an occupied country. Everyone was gone: his family, Claire and her family, Bart, everyone he knew. Homeless, out of money, and desperate for work, he had answered a small, obscure ad in the newspaper for a job as a laborer on an estate near Namur.

Provided with simple meals and a small cot in one of the outbuildings, Lukas worked hard, starting early and finishing late, always taking on extra chores. Eventually, the estate's owner, known to Lukas only as the *Viscount,* took a liking to him and, after a time, introduced him to other young men in his employ.

They were eager, energetic young men who strutted proudly through the streets of Namur in brown shirts and black boots. One night, the *Viscount* encouraged Lukas to join the other young men at a special meeting. There were many others there, all young men about his age, some even younger, all of them dressed in the same brown shirts and black boots. For the first time in a long while, Lukas began to feel like he belonged.

After dinner, a tall blond man wearing the striking, black uniform of the SS delivered a passionate message about the coming of a New Order and the promise of a bright new future for Belgium and all of Europe. Lukas had listened intently, hanging on every word.

The man was *SS-Hauptsturmfuhrer* Konrad Becker.

That was the beginning.

Chapter Seventeen

After what seemed like an eternity, Jack heard a car door slam and an engine roar to life.

The auto drove away, and it was quiet again.

Jack waited.

What the hell just happened?

If the SS, or the Gestapo, or whoever the hell it was, had arrested Lukas, Jack knew he was finished.

I should get the hell out of here while I still can.

Climb out the skylight and escape over the rooftops.

He decided to wait. Alone, on the streets, he wouldn't last a day. He couldn't speak the language, couldn't buy a train ticket, or couldn't even order a cup of the rotten coffee they served.

Time passed. It seemed like hours, but he was certain it wasn't. He wondered about Claire. What if something happened to her? The Gestapo had arrested her parents right here in Antwerp. What if they knew she'd returned? What if someone had recognized her and called the police? That German voice... was it the same one he'd heard in the farm field? His mind was running wild when suddenly—

Tap, tap.

Jack stiffened and stared into the blackness, waiting for the rest of the signal, his heart beating so hard that he was worried he wouldn't hear it.

Tap, tap, tap.

Two taps followed by three. The signal meant it was safe to come down.

He tapped twice in response, as he recalled Claire doing when they were here together. Then he slowly lifted the trap door, still wishing he had his gun.

It was Claire... looking up at him.

"They're gone," she said quietly.

Jack lowered himself through the trapdoor and followed Claire down the hallway. His legs felt like rubber as he sat down across from her at the square table.

"Lukas is cleaning up his shop," Claire said after a moment, "The front window is smashed."

"Is he okay? I thought I heard him yelling."

"He's fine; he's just pretty upset about the mess. Apparently, some local guys were drinking in the park, and a fight broke out. It got rather ugly, and one of them threw something through Lukas's shop window. He started yelling at them, and then the police showed up, followed a few minutes later by the SS."

"I know. An SS guy came up here with Lukas. They were both speaking German, so I have no idea what they said."

Claire nodded. "Lukas said the SS officer interrogated him for a while, wanting to know who those hoodlums were. We both speak a bit of German, not as well as French or Flemish, of course, but it comes in handy sometimes. "

"Where were you? Did you see it?"

"I was on my way back and about to cross the street when it started. I ducked into the alcove of a building on the other side of the park and waited until it was over." She paused for a moment as if there was more, then said, "Let me see your new identity card."

"What?"

"Your new identity card, Lukas had one made, didn't he?"

"Yeah… sure. But I should go and help Lukas clean up the shop."

Claire looked at him like he was crazy. "Jack! Don't even think about it. If anyone saw you or heard you utter so much as a word, that would be the end of all of us. You can't ever—"

"Okay, okay, I get it. Sorry, I wasn't thinking." He pulled the card from his pocket and handed it to her.

She looked at it for a long time, glanced at him, then back to the card. Finally, she handed it back to him. "Well, you're certainly more handsome in person than in that picture, but the card looks genuine. As you can see, we've changed your first name to *Jacques,* which is pronounced very much like 'Jack.' It will make it easier for you if someone tries to call you by your first name. But we had to alter the surname to something that sounds more Flemish. So, you'll have to remember to respond if someone says, *"Monsieur De Ridder, or Herr De Ridder."*

Jack looked at the card for a moment. *"Jacques* looks like a French name, but isn't this supposed to be in Flemish?"

Claire smiled. "Remember what I said about Belgium being a very complicated little country, Flemish in the north and French in the south. Culturally, the two regions are quite different from each other, but it's not uncommon to have some crossover with first names."

"Jacques De Ridder, Jack mumbled as he slipped the card back into his pocket. "I guess I should repeat it over in my head a few thousand times."

"And where are you from, *Monsieur De Ridder?"*

Jack abruptly pushed back from the table and held up his hand. "Wait, wait, hold on a minute! Let's back up. This thing tonight was a pretty close call, wasn't it? Or does it happen all the time? The SS, or whoever the hell they were, arrest a bunch of people right outside the door, then came barging into the house while I'm sitting up here like some cornered rat. I thought they had arrested Lukas. For Christ's sake, Claire... I thought they may have arrested *you!"* He paused, suddenly feeling foolish like a kid complaining to his coach about sitting on the bench instead of being in the game. "And why the hell did you make me give up my gun!?"

She didn't react right away but sat very still, looking him in the eye. Finally, she reached over and put her hand on his arm. "And I was terrified that they would find *you*. Yes, this sort of thing does happen, Jack, not all the time, but it happens. You're a soldier; you're trained for action, so I know this is hard for you to deal with. But in a situation like this, the only thing you or I can do is exactly what we just did... stay out of the way, be patient, and let it play out. And by the way, I'm damned glad you *didn't* have your gun, or we probably wouldn't be sitting here right now."

Her eyes had that dark, penetrating look, boring right through him. He noticed that she wasn't wearing the knit cap, and her short, dark hair was disheveled and frizzy. He thought she was beautiful. "Have you always been this tough?"

She continued to stare at him for a moment, then smiled. "I'm really not that tough. I've just seen some things you probably haven't—"

"I saw my best friend murdered in a field!" Instantly, he felt like an ass. At least his parents hadn't been sent to a concentration camp.

They were both quiet for a while. Then Claire squeezed his wrist and said, "I know how difficult that must be for you. And I'm truly very sorry."

"Certainly, nothing like you losing your parents. I guess I'm a bit like Jim Hawkins, seeing things he could never imagine."

She smiled, "Well, you're certainly not *anything* like young Jim Hawkins. Perhaps I should have chosen a different book. Let's see, maybe something about Sir Lancelot and the Knights of the Round Table?"

Jack laughed, "Sure, that's it. If I can't have a gun, how about a nice big sword?"

Chapter Eighteen

When Lukas returned to the apartment, Claire and Jack were sitting at the table, laughing about something.

Jack looked up at him. "I'm sorry about what happened," he said. "Is there anything I can do?"

Lukas walked past them without stopping. "No, it is all cleaned up."

"Would you like some tea?" Claire asked. "I was just going to make some for us."

"No, I don't—" Then he stopped and glanced back. She had gotten up from the table. "Yes, tea would be fine. I'll just clean up a bit."

He went into his bedroom, stripped off his shirt, and then went to the toilet to wash his face. He had seen Claire with other Allied aviators, some of whom stayed right here in the room under the eaves. But she had never gone up there with any of them before. What was different with Jack? Was she attracted to him? How could that be? She barely knew him? But he'd noticed a certain look in her eyes when she and Jack were together.

When he returned to the table, they were still talking about something and laughing again. Claire looked up at him. "I gave Jack a copy of *Treasure*

Island, and we were wondering if he was anything like the character, Jim Hawkins."

"Have you read it?" Jack asked.

"No, don't read English very well." He sat down and picked up his cup of tea. He noticed Claire glance at Jack. Then she looked at him. "Can the window be replaced?"

He shrugged. It bothered him that they had to speak in English. "Yes. But will take time. Boarded up for now."

"Who were those guys?" Jack asked.

Lukas looked at him, wondering why he would care. What did he know about any of this? Didn't he just want to get back to America? "Just some hoodlums. Is of no concern."

"Is there anything I can do to help?" Jack asked again.

Lukas wanted to say that he could help by leaving but remained silent and shook his head. He finished his tea and set the cup down. "I am tired. Going to bed now." Then he got up and walked back to the bedroom.

As he got undressed, he heard the two of them talking. It was very late, but it went on for some time. Wasn't Claire leaving to go back to stay with Bart, which she usually did when she had to stay in Antwerp? But as time passed, he still heard them quietly talking as he lay in bed, staring at the ceiling.

When Lukas woke up the next morning, he was surprised to hear Claire's voice in the kitchen. He quickly pulled on some trousers and a shirt, ran a hand through his hair, and left the bedroom. He noticed Jack sitting at the dining table.

He stepped into the tiny kitchen where Claire was making coffee. She turned toward him with a smile. "Good morning, Lukas. I'll have some coffee ready in a moment. I see you also have some eggs. What a surprise. Wherever did you find them? Would you like one?"

Lukas stared at her for a moment as he realized that she must have stayed all night.

She smiled again and shrugged as though she knew what he was thinking. "It was pretty late, so I just spent the night sleeping on your sofa." She looked past him at Jack, who had gotten up from the table and joined them. "I'm going to make some eggs. Would you like one?" she asked.

"Sure, an egg would be great," he said. "I'm starved."

Lukas stood silently for a moment, suddenly feeling out of place in his own home. Had Jack spent the night up in the room under the eaves or with Claire on the sofa? He turned away, trying to put the thought out of his mind. "Just coffee for me," he said. "I have work to do in the shop. Your train leaves at 1400. I'll be back before that."

Chapter Nineteen

Later that morning, Lukas sat at the desk in the back of his shop, trying to handle some paperwork but not getting much done because he spent most of his time brooding about Claire. She had never stayed overnight in his apartment before, not even on those few occasions when it was just the two of them having a simple dinner. He had certainly hoped she would, many times, but he'd never dared to ask, and she never did.

He had always assumed that one day, they would become more than just close friends. It was only logical. They had known each other their whole lives; he knew she cared about him, and he'd been in love with her for so long that it seemed only natural that she would love him one day, too. But would she? Would Claire ever think of him like that, or would he always just be her closest friend, someone she cared about but could never be in love with?

And then Jack showed up. It certainly seemed like she was attracted to him. He saw how she acted with him, the look in her eyes that he had never seen before when she was escorting other aviators.

A look in her eyes I've never seen when she looks at me!

He stood up and paced around the dusty, cluttered shop to clear his head, reflecting on his conversation with Becker last night, another dimension in his complicated world. There were times when doubts would creep into his mind about his commitment to Becker, to the *Viscount,* and to the cause, the New Order. And it always happened whenever he was with Claire. Her courage and devotion to the Resistance, to the escape line, and her hatred of the Nazis was so intense that it sometimes frightened him. If she ever found out that he was a collaborator...

But he shook his head and remembered it was the *Viscount* who had saved him and led him to Becker, who explained how the world would be changed for the better under the New Order. With encouragement from the *Viscount,* it was Becker who set him up in this very shop, who provided the apartment upstairs, asking in return only Lukas' complete loyalty to their mission. It was a new lease on life, and Lukas had committed himself to the cause. There was no turning back.

But he needed to do something about Jack.

And very soon.

Chapter Twenty

The local train left Antwerp Central station at 1500—an hour late—headed for Gent and then to France. It was crowded, but Jack and Claire eventually found a compartment with two open seats. Jack placed the small suitcase Lukas had given them on the overhead rack and took a seat by the window. Claire slid in next to him. The other four passengers were all men, dressed in well-worn but neatly pressed suits, seemingly content to read their newspapers. Fortunately, none of them seemed interested in conversation.

Jack stared out the window and silently reviewed the scenario Claire had explained to him back in Lukas' apartment. They were on their way to Paris and then to Toulouse and somewhere beyond that. He, *Jacques De Ridder,* is an electrical technician whose company is sending him to France to inspect some machinery they wish to purchase. Since he doesn't speak French, Claire is being sent by the same company to serve as his interpreter. Apparently, she is carrying some documents that verify this charade.

He thought it all seemed a bit sketchy, but Claire had assured him they had used similar schemes many times before. He was going to ask how often they succeeded, but what good would it do? He had to admit, however, that of the two of them, the one he trusted the most to keep their cool was Claire.

It was mid-morning the next day when they finally arrived at the *Gare du Nord* in Paris after so many stops and delays that Jack had lost count. He felt groggy from lack of sleep, but when they stepped off the train, he was instantly awestruck by the cavernous railway station. Twelve tracks wide, under a towering roof of steel and glass, the terminal throbbed like a giant living creature, bursting with throngs of human bodies moving in every direction amidst a mind-numbing clamor of steam-belching locomotives, shouted conversations in unknown languages, and announcements bellowing from above like commandments from heaven.

Claire took his arm and led the way, briskly pushing through the crowds until they finally burst through one of the double doors onto a wide avenue lined with glass storefronts and teeming with pedestrians. It reminded Jack of pictures of Paris he had seen in travel posters... except that the somber, poorly dressed people he passed on the street bore little resemblance to the carefree, elegant Parisians in the posters.

A half-hour later, they stopped in front of a drab, three-story building on a quiet, tree-lined street named *Rue Lobineau.* Claire quickly glanced up and down the street, then pulled open the door. The narrow, cramped vestibule reminded Jack of the one in Antwerp. He hoped they had better luck this time. Claire pressed the button next to the name *Du Bois.*

"Madame Du Bois is one of ours," she whispered as they waited, "We call her Martine. She has operated this safehouse since the beginning. I've been here twice before."

When the buzzer sounded, they stepped through a second door and climbed the stairs to the third floor. A thin, pale-looking woman with gray hair pulled tightly into a bun stood at an open door and ushered them into the apartment. She closed the door and smiled at Claire. They exchanged a few words in French, and then Claire introduced *Jacques De Ridder.*

The woman extended her hand and said in English, "Welcome, it is a pleasure to be of service." She glanced at her watch and then said to Claire, "I must leave now for an appointment. But first, let me show you how to prepare some coffee, such as it is."

Jack sat on one of two upholstered chairs in the parlor and glanced around the room as Claire followed Martine into the kitchen. It was small and tidy, furnished with bright colors. Two chairs were positioned on either side of the single window, and a sofa was centered on the opposite wall. There was a floor lamp and a small round table with a couple of books and a picture of two elderly people. Perhaps her parents?

Jack could hear Claire and Martine speaking French in the kitchen. He picked up a few words he remembered from his high school French class, but not enough to follow what they were talking about. A minute or two later, he became curious when the conversation continued beyond what it would take to explain how to make coffee. Claire raised her voice once, sounding concerned about something, then quickly lowered it and seemed to be asking questions. Martine's voice, on the other hand, was calm and deliberate, as though passing along information or instructions.

When Martine emerged from the kitchen, she slipped on a coat and hat and said, "Please relax a bit, have some coffee and something to eat. I will return in a few hours." With that, she picked up a purse and was gone.

Jack waited for a moment, and when Claire didn't return, he got up and stepped into the kitchen. It was a bright, high-ceiled room with two curtained windows, white painted walls, and a gray, tiled floor. Claire turned around and smiled. "Would you like some coffee?"

"Sure, that'd be great." She seemed a bit preoccupied, which made him wonder about her conversation with Martine. There was a small round table with a red and white checkered tablecloth under the windows, so he pulled out one of the two chairs and sat down.

Claire set two cups of coffee and a plate of biscuits on the table and sat down in the other chair. "The coffee isn't any better here than it is in Belgium, but I guess it's better than nothing."

Jack took a sip and grimaced. It seemed like a lifetime since he'd had real coffee. He picked up one of the hard, crisp biscuits and took a bite. "You and

Martine seemed to be discussing something. Is anything wrong?"

She shook her head. "No, not really, just a change in plans."

"What kind of a change?"

She sipped her coffee, looking at him as though she were trying to decide what to say. Finally, she set the cup down and folded her hands with both elbows on the table. "Our organization was decimated several months ago," she said quietly. "The SS arrested our founder and more than a dozen senior operatives. It was the result of an unknown collaborator who had infiltrated the organization. Since that time, we've been forced to make changes to routes, procedures, safehouses, that sort of thing. It's still going on. This is just one more thing."

"Sounds like the military," Jack said, "battle plans are great until you meet the enemy."

She smiled. "Well, I'm hoping the Allied armies have a lot more resources and backup plans than we do. But we *are* a lot like a military organization. It may not appear that way, but we have strict chains of command, protocols, and operational procedures."

"That's why you weren't supposed to tell me anything about yourself, nothing personal, right?"

"I've certainly told you more than I should have already."

"Well, only about your parents—and I am very sorry about that—and being forced to leave Antwerp. A bit about Bart and Lukas, but nothing else, like what you do when you're not doing this."

She shook her head slowly, looking into his eyes. "Perhaps, in some other time, some other life... it could be different." He started to respond, but she quickly switched back to her school-teacher mode and pressed on. "So, here's what's going to happen. We won't be staying the night, as I had planned. When Martine returns, she will go with us to the *Gare d'Austerlitz,* the station that handles all trains heading south. Along the way, she will stop and pick up our tickets from another contact. Then we will board a train for Bordeaux. That's the change in plans. We were originally going to Toulouse."

"Why the change?" Jack asked.

Claire shrugged. "I don't know. Lukas called Martine last night and said there was an issue in Toulouse. He made new arrangements for us to travel through Bordeaux, then on to Dax, Bayonne, and Saint-Jean-de-Luz. It will take longer with an extra overnight stay in Bayonne, but it is apparently safer. Eventually, we will be led by a Basque guide over the Pyrenees Mountains into Spain."

Jack sat quietly, thinking about this. They'd never discussed the entire trip.

Basque guides? Crossing mountains?

Claire smiled, then reached over and squeezed his hand. "So, do you think Jim Hawkins would mind being stuck with me for a bit longer?"

He placed his other hand over hers and smiled, "I don't know about Jim Hawkins, but Sir Lancelot certainly won't mind."

Chapter Twenty-One

Walking arm-in-arm with Jack, Claire glanced around the quiet neighborhood two blocks from the *Gare d' Austerlitz* and spotted the *boucherie,* a small, glass-fronted shop with green awnings. Martine had left the apartment ten minutes ahead of them and was just now emerging from the shop carrying a small, brown paper bag, which Claire knew contained two croissants and two train tickets. They followed Martine to the corner where Claire took the bag, stuck it in her purse, and she and Jack set off toward the station. With nothing more than a slight nod of her head, Martine walked away in the opposite direction.

The trip was uneventful, though slow and tedious, taking most of the night. They got off in Bordeaux and, two hours later, switched to an even slower, older train to Dax that was filled to near capacity with men who appeared to be laborers headed off to their jobs. Claire scrunched next to Jack on the stiff, leather seat. They shared a compartment with four middle-aged, weathered-looking workers. The stale air was ripe with body odor, onions, cigarettes, and a variety of other smells Claire couldn't identify.

Just before the train pulled out, Claire spotted another man as he made his way down the aisle past their compartment. He was a heavy-set man wearing bib overalls with a red and white checkered scarf around his neck. She took a breath and relaxed a bit. He was the man Martine had told her to look out for.

The sun was up when they arrived in Dax, discernable as a railway station only by a single sign tacked to a post. When the train wheezed to a halt, Claire nudged Jack awake, and they got off the train, following the working men carrying lunchboxes and newspapers.

Mingling in with the group, they walked along a gravel path leading to the city center. As they crossed a bridge at the first intersection, the stocky man with the checkered scarf peeled off to the left. Claire took Jack's arm and turned to follow him.

The man led them to a dilapidated brick building located in an industrial area that had seen better days. Inside the building, it was damp and musty and reminded Claire of the abandoned distillery on Gaston's farm, minus the smell of gin. There was an old tractor up on blocks, a pile of worn-out tires, and a jumble of what appeared to be old machinery parts. There were also at least a dozen bicycles.

The man lit a kerosene lantern, pulled the door closed, and then looked at Claire. "*Bonjour,* you may call me Karl," he said in French. "You must be Marie?"

Claire smiled and shook her head. It was what exactly Martine had told her to expect. "No, Marie is my sister," she said. "My name is Claire."

Karl nodded, then pointed to the bicycles, speaking to Claire in French, which she translated for Jack. "We'll be traveling by bicycle from here down to the coast at Saint-Jean-de-Luz. It's about forty kilometers, so we'll spend the night near Bayonne and enter Saint-Jean early in the morning to blend in with workers arriving in the city. We will ride single-file, and Karl will take the lead. You will follow him but at a good distance, at least fifty meters back, so it appears as if he is not traveling with us. You and I are traveling together, and I will follow you. Just try to keep Karl in sight."

Jack nodded, casually looking over the bicycles.

Claire nudged him and looked him in the eye. "And this is the most important part," she said. "You and I may be traveling together, but if either of us is stopped by the authorities, do *not* say anything. If you are asked a direct question, you know how to respond."

He nodded. "*Ik begrip het niet,* I don't understand."

"Okay, very good. Now, if either you or I are stopped by the authorities, Karl will ride on and wait a kilometer or two down the road. If Karl is stopped, you and I must do the same thing. It must appear as if we are *not* traveling with him, so you do *not* stop. Act as if we are strangers and *ride on.*"

Karl stepped up and spoke to Claire in French, gesturing toward Jack. When he was finished, Claire nodded and smiled, then translated for Jack. "Karl said that he wants you to know he is proud to help American soldiers. He thanks you for being here."

Jack didn't respond right away, looking surprised. Then he reached out and extended his hand to Karl.

"Please tell him I am very grateful for his help, and I will not forget it."

Chapter Twenty-Two

It was just a short walk from Lukas' shop to Bart's apartment on the Schelde Kaai, south of the city center, but Lukas didn't waste any time. It wasn't often that Bart called and asked to see him.

Bart was waiting for him after Lukas rang the buzzer and walked up the stairs to the second floor. He'd been to Bart's home several times, a bright, spacious apartment with three large windows overlooking the river. This time, however, someone else had arrived before him, a stocky, bald man wearing gold-rimmed glasses and the uniform of a police officer.

Bart closed the door and followed Lukas into the room, placing a hand on his shoulder. "Lukas, I'd like you to meet a good friend of mine. This is Captain Niels DeVos with the Antwerp Police Department." DeVos stepped forward and nodded. "Pleased to meet you, 'Lukas.'"

Lukas glanced at Bart, surprised to hear someone outside the organization use his code name.

Bart smiled and motioned to a grouping of chairs around a coffee table. 'Let's have a seat, and I'll pour the coffee.

When they were seated, and Bart had poured coffee, he said to Lukas, "Captain DeVos is a long-time friend... and a supporter of our work. He has been helping our organization quietly for some time, and I wanted you to meet him. I think he can be of some help to you."

Lukas took a moment before responding, wary of a police officer getting involved in his operation. "Help me in what way?" he asked.

Captain DeVos set his coffee cup on the table. "I understand you had some trouble at your shop the other night," he said.

Lukas shrugged. "Just some guys with too much to drink. A fight broke out, and it got out of hand. Your officers took care of it, so thank them for me."

"No thanks are necessary," DeVos said, "that's their job. But I also understand the SS got involved. That's a different matter."

"Yes, an SS officer showed up and asked some questions. He wanted to know if I knew any of those men and if I'd ever had trouble with them before. I told him the truth. I had no idea who they were. That was it; he wasn't there very long."

"A bit unusual for an SS officer to involve himself in something like that. Did he give his name?"

Lukas shook his head. "No, and I certainly didn't ask."

DeVos turned to Bart. "Well, it would be wise to be cautious about this, wouldn't you agree?"

Bart nodded. "I agree. We want to be very careful with the SS snooping around."

"I'll have some of my men watch your building for the next few weeks," DeVos said, "very discreetly, of course, no uniforms or anything. They'll just keep an eye on things."

Lukas had no idea where this was going, but there was only one possible answer. "Yes, that would be fine. I'd appreciate it."

DeVos glanced at Bart, then stood and picked up his hat. "Very pleased to meet you, Lukas," he said. "I will stop by and see you from time to time, and we can discuss how I may be able to help."

After DeVos left, Bart refilled their coffee cups and then sat back in his chair. Lukas took a sip of coffee and waited, as he usually did in conversations with Bart.

"I'm sure you're a bit surprised by this, Bart said, "so let me give you some background. I first met DeVos back in 1938, shortly after I joined the Department of the Interior. In that position, along with being a city councilman, I was able to help arrange additional financing for his family's business, a company called *Produits Agricoles Echange,* a manufacturer of fertilizers. Because of his job on the Antwerp police force, Niels was not directly involved with the day-to-day operation of the company, but we've kept in touch over the years and become friends.

"He is a patriot—a bit zealous about Flemish rights, perhaps—but a Belgian patriot, nevertheless. And since the occupation began, he has been a strong supporter of our efforts in the Resistance. His family had some resources, and with his position on the police force, he had many contacts. He has been quietly helping us in our work," he paused and took a sip of coffee. "But, earlier this year, everything changed. The Germans very abruptly commandeered the company and forced the family out. Shortly after that, his father died of a heart attack. Niels is very bitter about it, and not long ago, he came to me and said he wanted to do more to help us."

"Help how?" Lukas asked.

"He was aware of our escape organization and offered to help. DeVos knows people all over Belgium and, most importantly, people who can be trusted. He can help us with new escape routes and safe houses. You know how difficult it's been since the infiltration and sabotage of the line—and we still don't know who the goddamn collaborator is—so I think we could use someone I know and trust."

Lukas' skin tingled as it always did when he and Bart talked about the infiltration and sabotage of the escape line—*his* infiltration and *his* sabotage. It was the one part of his connection with Becker and the New Order that greatly conflicted him. Bart was a friend, a mentor of sorts, and had always looked out for him. He would never do anything that could hurt him... or Claire. But he was treading a thin and dangerous line, and he would have to be very cautious. He was certain Bart did not suspect him... or he would be dead already.

Bart continued, "The exposure of the safe house near the Central Station here in Antwerp a few days ago is a perfect example. The sabotage is still going on... and that's the place Claire was going with Jack!"

Lukas nodded, his skin crawling again at the thought, "Yes, that was a close call. Fortunately, she had the discipline to use the backup plan."

Bart smiled, "We both know that Claire is as tough and resourceful as anyone in the organization. But we could use help, don't you agree?"

Lukas nodded, "Yes, absolutely."

Bart smiled, "Very good. Now, I have not told Claire about DeVos wanting to help the escape line. She knows of him vaguely; she knows he's with the police and is a friend of mine, but I don't believe they've ever met. At any rate, she has no real need to know about this. It's safer that way."

Lukas nodded, "Yes, understood." He finished his coffee and stood up to leave. "I will look forward to talking with Captain DeVos when he comes to see me."

Lukas walked home slowly, trying to sort everything out in his mind. It was stressful enough keeping secrets from Claire and Bart without having a police officer involved who was a close friend of Bart's. He knew he would have to tell Becker about this, and there was no telling how he would react.

The whole conversation with Bart about the escape line being infiltrated had unnerved him, as it always did when he allowed himself to think about it. Good people had been hurt—some even killed—because of him, and that disturbed him, sometimes to the point that he wanted to get out. But he couldn't. He knew that. He was in too deep and had no choice but to see it through to the end. When the Germans prevailed and order was restored, things would be better. He was certain about that.

He put it out of his mind as he always did, and his thoughts returned to that safehouse in Antwerp that Claire almost walked into. That was a complete foul-up, and he shivered just thinking about it. Lukas had set it up with Becker, but it wasn't supposed to happen for another week when he knew that some other Allied aviators would be there. Some of Becker's men must have gotten too eager.

And Claire almost got caught!

Goddamn it! If anything had happened to her...

He took a deep breath and tried to relax. Bart was right; Claire was smart and resourceful, and she obviously had the good sense to get away as soon as she realized what had happened.

Then, another thought struck him. If that safehouse had *not* been compromised, Claire wouldn't have come to his house that night, and he might never have found out about her and Jack. So, perhaps some good came out of it. But he knew he'd have to be very careful with the plan he was putting in motion—a plan to take care of Jack—and protect Claire at the same time.

Chapter Twenty-Three

The road was hilly as open meadows and farm fields gradually changed to thick, wooded forestland. It became cooler and darker in the shade of the trees, giving Claire the feeling that the three of them were alone in the world.

She had never taken this route before, having usually been directed further south through Toulouse and then onto the Spanish border. And she'd never felt quite the same at this point in the journey as she did now. Every other time, she had been focused solely on getting to the border and sending the aviators safely on their way back to England, relieved of the tension and danger. But this time, it was very different. Now she dreaded the end of the trip when she would have to say goodbye to Jack, knowing she would probably never see him again.

She took a deep breath and glanced up ahead as they started a long uphill climb. Karl had disappeared over the crest of the hill, and for the moment, she and Jack were alone on this beautifully isolated stretch of road.

If only it could stay this way forever.

When they finally crested the top of the hill, Claire looked up again, past Jack, and spotted Karl. The stocky Frenchman had gained some distance and was already at the bottom of the hill, approaching a crossroad.

Suddenly, a truck burst into her view at the bottom of the hill. The grayish-green vehicle barreled into the intersection from the right at high speed, then skidded sideways and slammed into Karl's bicycle, throwing the Frenchman into the ditch like a rag doll.

Instinctively, she braked to a stop, staring in disbelief at the horrific scene. Ahead of her, Jack did the same thing, but an instant later, he started riding again, pedaling hard down the hill toward the crossroad.

She shouted at him in Flemish not to stop. But as soon as he arrived at the crossroad, Jack jumped off his bike and ran to the ditch where Karl lay on his side, not moving.

Claire immediately set off down the hill as two German soldiers scrambled out of the truck, waving their arms and shouting at Jack, one of them pointing a rifle at him.

Claire arrived at the bottom of the hill and skidded to a halt next to the truck. She cautiously approached the two soldiers, forcing herself to stay calm as she glanced into the ditch where Jack knelt next to Karl. Blood streamed from a gash in the unconscious Frenchman's forehead, and his right leg was twisted at a ghastly angle, with bone protruding through his torn trousers. Jack removed the checkered scarf from Karl's neck and pressed it against the profusely bleeding wound.

One of the German soldiers, the taller of the two, shouted, *"Steh jetz auf!"* motioning for Jack to get up and come to the road. The other soldier, shorter and stout, cocked the rifle.

Then, the tall soldier spotted Claire and abruptly turned toward her, an angry look in his eyes.

"Parlez-vous francais?" Claire asked quickly.

The soldier abruptly berated her in French, gesturing angrily toward his truck.

Claire smelled liquor on his breath and knew this could get ugly very quickly.

The soldier turned to Karl and screamed at him in German. *"Du dummkopf!* You almost made us go into the ditch! *Und schau hier!* The fender is dented!"

He spun back to Claire and screamed at her in French. *"Ou allez-vous?"*

"We are on our way to Bayonne," Claire replied, forcing herself to stay calm despite the tingling up and down her back.

"Vos papiers!" he barked, weaving slightly back and forth.

Claire handed her identification card to him, and while he studied it, she quickly glanced at Jack, who had remained in the ditch, kneeling next to Karl. Silently, she mouthed, "Keep quiet."

"You are Belgian? What are… what are you… doing here?" the soldier snapped, slightly slurring his words.

"The three of us were sent here to inspect some machinery at the foundry in Bayonne," Claire responded, thinking quickly. "We have the day off and decided to visit Dax. We are on our way back." She knew the story was weak, but it was all she could come up with.

The soldier glared at her, shifting his weight unsteadily from one leg to the other, then turned to Jack and asked for his papers.

"I'm afraid he doesn't understand French or German," Claire said quickly. "He's an engineer brought in to inspect the machines and only speaks Flemish. I am the interpreter."

The tall soldier continued to stare at her.

The short one kept his rifle trained on Jack and shouted to his partner in German, "*Schnell, schnell,* we are late for the meeting!"

The tall one yelled back, "*Ja,* I know!"

Claire concentrated on following their conversation in German as the short one gestured with his rifle toward Karl. " *Was ist mit ihm?* He's badly hurt."

The tall soldier glanced at his watch again, appearing uncertain what to do. "Verdammt! We have no radio in the truck!" He was silent for a moment, then looked at the short soldier and flicked his head toward Karl.

The gunshot was so jarring that Claire stumbled backward, grabbing her bicycle to keep from falling.

She looked up as Jack suddenly bolted from the ditch and ripped the rifle from the short soldier's arms. He swung the weapon from the barrel and smashed the soldier in the head.

The short soldier slumped to the ground, and Jack shot him in the chest.

Her head pounding and her ears ringing from the gunshots, Claire turned toward the tall soldier who fumbled to unsnap the holster of his pistol. She charged forward and rammed her bicycle into him, knocking him into the ditch.

The momentum sent Claire sprawling into the ditch over the top of the soldier. As she scrambled away, the blast of another gunshot hammered her eardrums.

She rolled over and looked up to see Jack holding the rifle.

Slowly, she got to her feet and looked at the three dead bodies in the ditch. Then she turned to Jack. "What the hell did you think you were doing?" she snapped. "We talked about this... *You don't stop! You keep going!*"

Jack lowered the rifle and raised a hand, palm up. "I know, I didn't think. When I saw the truck hit him, I just... reacted."

"That could have been the end! They could have shot *you*! That could have been it, right there!"

"They *would* have shot me, and they would have shot you too if—"

"Yes, I know. Damn it!" Claire closed her eyes and pressed her fingers to her temples, trying to think. She heard Jack say something and looked at him. "What?"

"We should drag these bodies into the woods," he said.

"Yes... yes, of course." She looked up at the road, turning in both directions. No one was around.

Jack grabbed the body of the tall soldier under one arm, and Claire grabbed the other arm. They trudged up the slope of the ditch and into the trees on the other side. "Should we cover him up... some leaves, branches?" she mumbled, her mind racing, the hairs on the back of her neck on fire.

Jack shook his head. "No, let's grab the other two and drag them up here before someone comes along."

They dragged the short one up the hill and dropped the body next to his partner. When they got back into the ditch, Claire dropped to her knees and put a hand on Karl's forehead. Her stomach turned at the thought of leaving Karl's body lying in the woods with the two German soldiers who murdered him. But there was no other choice.

Jack put his hand on her shoulder.

She nodded, stood up, and grabbed Karl's body under the arm.

They lay Karl's body several meters into the woods beyond the two Germans and stood in silence for a moment. "I don't even know his real name," she said.

When they got back to the road, Claire pointed at the truck. "Drive their truck a few hundred meters up the road and run back. Then we've got to get the hell out of here."

They rode for the next hour in silence, the blast of the gunshots reverberating in Claire's head. Her stomach was in a knot, and her hands were smeared with blood. She wiped them on her trousers, but it did no good.

They had just killed two German soldiers, a crime for which there would be only one punishment. But what else could they have done? If Jack hadn't reacted as quickly as he did, the soldiers would almost certainly have shot them as well. They had obviously been drinking and certainly wouldn't have left any witnesses.

But at least there are no witnesses to *their* crime. They hadn't encountered anyone else along the isolated road, so it was unlikely anyone would know what happened or who did it. The thought was of little solace to her. When the truck and bodies were discovered, she knew the Germans would terrorize the citizens of Bayonne and Dax and everywhere in between until they discovered the perpetrators. Hopefully, she and Jack would be over the mountains and at the Spanish border by that time.

She spotted a small path that led off the road into the trees and stopped. Jack pulled up behind her. She glanced up and down the deserted road, making sure they were alone. "Let's stop and rest for a few minutes," she said, then walked her bike along the narrow path until they came to a small clearing next to a stream.

She laid her bike down, walked over to the stream, knelt down, and washed the blood off her hands.

Jack knelt next to her and did the same. She looked over at his dirty, blood-spattered face, then scooped some water with her hands and gently wiped away the blood, dabbing it dry with her shirt sleeve.

He knelt silently, looking into her eyes. Then he slowly shook his head. "I've never shot anyone before... I didn't even think about it. I just... did it. It all happened so fast that I—"

She reached up and put her hand on his cheek, noticing there was still a speck of blood on his forehead. "If you hadn't, we'd both be dead. You know that, don't you?"

He nodded, then took her hand as they both stood.

He slid his arm around her.

She wrapped her arms around his waist and held him close. She felt the warmth of his body and closed her eyes.

If only...

The planned overnight stay in Bayonne changed abruptly upon their arrival. The matronly woman who owned the safe house paced nervously around the tiny parlor, shaking her head after Claire told her what had happened. "*Non! Non!* You cannot stay," she snapped. "*C'est dangerex!* They will find the bodies and come here! *Non!* You must go!"

Claire took a deep breath and held out her hands, palms up. The woman's eyes were wild, flitting around. Terrified. *"Oui, oui,* I understand," Claire said, her voice low and steady. "We do not want to put you in any danger. We will leave, but we need help. Can you help us?"

The woman stopped pacing and stared at Claire. "They will come… the Germans." She shook her head. *"Non!* You go."

Claire bit her lower lip, forcing herself to stay calm. "We could leave and go on to Saint-Jean-de-Luz. But I don't know the way. Do you know someone who could show us the way?"

The woman's eyes darted around again between Claire and Jack as though she was trying to make up her mind. Then she stomped out of the room.

Claire turned to Jack and shrugged. She'd never been in this situation before and had no idea what to do if they couldn't get help.

A few minutes later, the woman stepped back into the kitchen. She looked at Claire and nodded, *"Oui,* perhaps I know someone. I will go and see. You wait here." Then she put on a hat and coat and left the house.

"Where the hell is she going?" Jack asked, his eyes wide.

"To get someone who can show us the way to Saint-Jean. At least that's what she said."

"Do you trust her?"

“I don’t know.”

Chapter Twenty-Four

Saint-Jean-de-Luz

Jack opened his eyes and glanced around. The room was dark, and for a fleeting moment, he imagined he was back in the loft at the gin distillery. He sat up slowly, wondering how long he'd been sleeping. A thin shaft of moonlight showed through the window, illuminating the silhouette of a person sitting on the edge of the narrow bed.

"Claire?"

"I'm sorry, I didn't want to wake you... but I..."

Jack reached out and took her hand, gently pulling her closer.

She slid over and put her head on his shoulder. He could tell she'd been crying.

As the fog of sleep lifted, he remembered that when they arrived at the safehouse in Saint-Jean-de-Luz, Claire insisted he take the single bed in the small upper room. The owner had let them in and then left them alone with instructions to stay inside and keep the shutters closed and the door locked. Claire said she would nap on the sofa in case anyone came to the door.

"It's about Karl, isn't it?" he whispered.

She nodded. "I didn't even know him... and now he's..."

Her voice trailed off, and she wiped away the tears, shaking her head. "I feel terrible about him, but... it could have... it could have been *you!*"

Jack was silent for a moment, then said quietly, "When I heard the gunshot, in that instant, the only thing I remember thinking was... I can't let it end like this."

She turned her head and looked up at him, tears streaming down her cheek. "I don't know what I would have done if it had been you. I don't think I could—"

He wrapped both arms around her and kissed the back of her neck. "But it wasn't. We're both still here, together."

"I don't want to lose you, Jack."

He gently wiped away her tears and kissed her forehead, then her lips. "And I don't want to lose you. I want to be with you more than anything I've ever wanted."

The first time they made love, it was fast and breathless, still partially clothed, as though it was the only moment they were ever going to have together. Later, it was slower and softer, their bodies and minds coming together, making Jack feel certain he would be utterly content if this one night could last forever.

When he awoke again, she was gone. He sat up quickly and blinked, looking around the small, dark room. Then he heard voices, soft and muted, coming from below. He pulled on his trousers, sweater, and boots and slowly descended the staircase.

Claire sat at a table in the middle of the main gathering room of the modest cottage. The shutters were still closed, but the room was bathed in a warm glow from two kerosene sconces on the rough plaster wall. Sitting across from her was a sturdy-looking, olive-skinned man with thick, dark hair and a black beard.

They both stood when Jack appeared, and Claire quickly came over and took him by the arm. "Jack, let me introduce you to Andoni. He will be leading us across the mountains into Spain."

Jack shook the stocky man's outstretched hand, wincing slightly at his iron grip. He was about Jack's height but broader in the shoulders with a thick neck and hands the size of small dinner plates. His face was creased and weathered as though he'd spent his entire life outdoors, which Jack guessed he probably had.

Andoni smiled at Jack, nodded, and then turned back to Claire. He said something in a language that sounded like French but, judging by how intently Claire listened, was probably a combination of various local dialects. After a few exchanges back and forth, Andoni nodded again to Jack and turned to leave. As he opened and closed the heavy, wooden door, Jack saw that it was light outside but overcast and drizzling.

"I've made some coffee," Claire said, "would you like some."

"I think I need it," Jack replied, rubbing his eyes and rotating his head to get the kink out of his neck. He glanced at his watch. It was 11:30 in the morning, "My God, I've slept over six hours. Did you get any sleep?"

"Yes, I did… finally," she smiled and kissed him on the cheek. "I just woke up about a half-hour ago when Andoni knocked on the door."

"Maybe we should just stay here and tell Andoni we've changed our minds."

She handed him a mug of coffee. "That would be wonderful, wouldn't it… until the SS kicked in the door."

"Oh yeah, I forgot about them." He sighed and sat down at the table. "When do we have to leave?"

"Just after dark."

"Have you worked with Andoni before?"

Claire poured coffee for herself and sat down at the table. "No, this is the first time we've met."

Jack sipped the coffee. The room was damp and chilly, but the coffee, though still bitter, was hot and felt good, "Do you trust him?"

She shrugged. "As much as I trust anyone these days. The woman back in Bayonne came through for us, so I guess I do. You can never be completely certain, but the Basques are the indigenous people in this region. They are fiercely independent and were terribly brutalized by Franco and the German Nazis who propped him up during the Spanish civil war.

Besides, they're the only ones who know the ancient smuggler's routes over the mountains into Spain."

"You're coming with us into Spain?"

Claire took a sip of coffee, then set the cup down and shook her head. "No, my orders are to go only as far as the Bidasoa River."

They sat in silence for a while, Jack staring into his cup. Then he looked up at her. "So, our last two days together will be spent trekking over a mountain in the rain."

Claire reached over and took his hand, "This wasn't supposed to happen, you know."

He nodded. "I know."

"No, I mean it. It's against the rules."

He was silent for a moment, then burst out laughing. "Rules? There are rules about this?"

She glared at him, then stood up and turned away.

Jack got up and put his hands on her shoulders. "You know, I didn't like you very much that first day."

She was silent, then turned around and stared at him, her deep, penetrating eyes boring into his soul. "Well, Lieutenant Richards, I had a job to do. And you were a bit annoying."

He could see she was trying to look angry, but it wasn't working. She stared at him for a moment longer, then slipped her hand around the back of his head, pulled him close, and kissed him.

"So, we have the rest of the day here, right?" he asked.

She nodded, then slipped her arm through his as they climbed back up the stairs.

Chapter Twenty-Five

SS Hauptsturmfuhrer Becker arrived at Lukas' shop just after dark, wearing plain clothes to avoid any suspicion from nosy neighbors. When Lukas told him about meeting DeVos, he smiled and lit a cigarette. "I know. I arranged it... with DeVos, of course, not the esteemed Councilman Peeters."

Lukas stared at him for a moment, then took a seat at the desk. "I don't understand... you knew?"

"Yes, of course. Niels DeVos and I have a long history. He's a passionate Flemish separatist and a very loyal fascist. He's a member of the VNV and one of the earliest collaborators with the Third Reich. We first met in 1938 when he came to Berlin seeking funding for the VNV. I helped him with that, and we've been very close ever since. He's one of our most trusted collaborators... as are you, of course."

"But he's a police officer, a captain, no less."

Becker smiled once again and exhaled a precise ring of smoke. "Yes, and that turns out to be very convenient."

"But what about 'Bart,' Councilman Peeters—?"

Becker interrupted, leaning forward. "Councilman Peeters is completely unaware of anything. He believes DeVos is his friend. It has taken years to cultivate that little deception, and that is how it will remain. DeVos approached him recently with an offer to help with the escape line, and that's the reason your friend Peeters brought him to meet you. I have plans that will eventually require the councilman's, shall we say, 'cooperation.' But, for now, it is important that you continue your normal relationship with him."

"He told me that DeVos' company was taken over, and—"

Becker interrupted him again, getting a bit impatient with the questions. But Lukas was loyal and competent and, unlike DeVos, could be trusted. And he would need Lukas for the most important part of his mission when it started. "It is all part of a larger plan, Lukas. Not something you need to worry about now. It will become clear eventually when you learn the full extent of our mission. For now, your job is to bring down this escape line. And DeVos may be able to help you with that." Then Becker crushed out his cigarette and stood up to leave. He looked down at Lukas. *"Verstehen?"*

Lukas stood as well and nodded, *"Ja, verstehen."*

Becker got in his stretched, black auto and drove through the old city, heading toward the river. Ten minutes later, he pulled over and parked behind another auto. DeVos, also dressed in plain clothes, got out of the car, approached Becker's auto, and slid into the front passenger seat.

"How did it go?" DeVos asked. "Do I need to do anything about him?"

Becker sighed. It was just the type of thing he expected a treacherous, money-grubber like DeVos to say. The only reason he was still on the police force, much less a captain, is because Becker had made it happen. *"Nein,"* Becker snapped. "There is nothing you need to do except exactly what we planned. Lukas understands the situation. Your job is just to keep an eye on him. Help him out by recommending some 'safehouses' where your goons can arrest some of these damn aviators and the traitors who are helping them. Lukas will cooperate, so stay in the background and let him make the calls. We will need him later." He paused and looked directly at DeVos. "Your job is to take care of the money. More is coming, much more, to the usual rendezvous point in St. Vith. Take good care of it, hide it well, and you will be rewarded... and the rest of your family will remain safe. *Verstehen?*"

"Ja, verstehen."

Chapter Twenty-Six

The Pyrenees Mountains

The Basques called it *xirimiri,* a cold, dampness, somewhere between drizzle and fog that drifts up from the sea. To Claire, it was a clammy, bone-chilling annoyance that was slowly siphoning off the last of her energy. The rocks were slippery, the pathways sticky with mud, and the low-hanging branches dripped wet, salty water across her face.

They had left the intimate confines of the safehouse in Saint-Jean-de-Luz just after dark, and most of the first night had been an easy trek along winding country paths that led past orchards and farm fields dotted with cone-shaped haystacks and grazing sheep. In the light of the rising moon, she could just make out the white-washed, chalet-style farmhouses with heavy wooden shutters and tile roofs.

After skirting past the village of Urrugne, the going got tougher. Andoni led the way, Jack followed him, and she stayed behind Jack in single file. The slopes became steeper, the pathways narrower and rock-strewn. Soon, the overcast sky blanked out the moonlight, and the *xirimiri* set in.

When he returned to the safehouse to collect them, Andoni brought walking sticks for both of them. He had also brought along soft, rope-bound shoes called *alpargatas* that he insisted they wear in place of their rugged, leather boots. Claire had not taken this route over the mountains before, and as they trudged up the steep, slippery inclines, stepping over rocks and tree roots, she was glad to have both.

Throughout most of the next day, they climbed higher, trudging along step by step in the cold dampness. Her face was wet, her hair plastered to her forehead, and her woolen sweater soaked through to the bone. Finally, they stopped for a brief rest on a plateau and took refuge under a stand of trees. Andoni opened his pack and produced chunks of cheese, hard bread, and a flask of cognac. Claire was exceedingly grateful for the warmth of the cognac.

She had a short conversation with Andoni and then translated for Jack. "Andoni says it will be about three or four hours to the summit and then all day tomorrow down to the river."

"Is there a bridge?" Jack asked.

"There is a bridge, but it's always guarded by German soldiers. You will have to wade across the river about a half-mile upstream."

He shrugged. "Well, at least getting wet is no longer a problem… and the cognac definitely helps."

A few minutes later, while Andoni busied himself with re-packing the cheese and cognac, Claire took Jack's hand and led him back down the path a bit. "Tell me again about fishing," she said.

"What?"

"Fishing at your home in Wisconsin."

He smiled and wiped the rain off his forehead, then ran a hand through his shaggy hair and put his arm around her. "Yes, well, there is a certain lake we go to. It's not very big, but it's quiet, surrounded by thick pine forests. We row the boat out, just past the lily pads, and cast our lines back toward the shore."

"And you like to go in the evening, just before dark," Claire said, picking up the story he'd told while having dinner at Lukas' apartment, "And you go with your younger sister, but she sometimes gets impatient."

He laughed, "Yeah, that's right."

She rested her head against his shoulder and whispered, "Well, 'Sir Lancelot,' I would never get impatient."

Just after dark the next day, Claire stood on a flat rock formation and looked down at the Bidasoa River. It was cold and misty, but the rising moon had broken through the clouds, and she could see the lights on the bridge a half-mile downstream. On the other side of the river was Spain and, for Jack, freedom.

She knew that there were still risks ahead for him. He might be spotted wading across the river or run into spies on the other side. And even if he made it safely back to England, he'd soon be back in the war, and anything could happen.

She also knew she might never see him again. Just like that, it would be over. They'd only known each other for a few weeks, but she was in love with him. She was certain about it. How was it possible? She had no idea. They really had nothing in common. They were from different worlds and had lived entirely different lives, but...

He came up and took her hand. They stood in silence for a time, staring at the river. "Promise me you'll be careful on the way back," he said, finally. "You'll avoid Bayonne and Dax?"

Claire nodded, swallowing hard. "And you know what to do after you cross the river?"

He squeezed her hand. "Yes, Lukas' instructions were thorough." He was silent for a moment, then said, "You're going back to Grote Brogel and continuing on with the escape line?"

"Yes, of course, until it's over."

"So, you can rescue other lost souls again and again until someone turns you in, and you wind up in a Gestapo torture room?"

She turned abruptly and glared at him. In the faint moonlight, she could see his face and the furl in his brow. "Damn it, Jack, don't make it harder than it is."

"I'm sorry, I—"

"Yes, I know. I'm sorry, too. This wasn't supposed to happen. I've done this before, and I've always stuck to the rules. Do your job, be cautious, and, above all, do *not* get personally involved. Then *you* come along... you 'point guard' person from Sturgeon Way and mess everything up."

Jack smiled at her. "Bay," he said, "It's Sturgeon *Bay.*"

"What?"

"The name of my hometown, it's... never mind, it's not important." He took her other hand, "The war won't last forever, and—"

"No! Don't say another word. You're going back to England. You're going to climb into another airplane and risk your life all over again."

"And you're going to risk your life on another rescue mission."

They looked at each other silently, standing on the flat rock above the river. Andoni had already started down the embankment to make sure it was safe.

Very quietly, she said, "The chances that we both survive this are—"

He put a finger to her lips, "Now it's my turn. Don't. Neither of us can predict the future, so we have to let it happen." He paused, still looking into her eyes. "What now?"

She put her hand on the back of his neck and kissed him. "Now you have to go."

He pulled her close and returned the kiss, long, sensual, and loving. Then he turned away and started down the embankment.

PART TWO

BELGIUM
NOVEMBER 1944

Chapter Twenty-Seven

Antwerp

Claire stood in the middle of a crowd of distraught citizens, staring in disbelief at the pile of smoking rubble. A company of firemen, sweat running down their blackened faces, sifted through the remains of Antwerp's largest movie theatre, searching for bodies. A few hours earlier, a V-2 rocket launched in Germany had dropped in ghostly silence from an altitude of thirty kilometers and scored a direct hit.

Claire shook her head, brushed away a tear, and glanced at Bart Peeters. "My God," she whispered, "four hundred people, half of them children, just watching a film." Shivering against the damp air, thick with the acrid odors of smoke and charred wood, she wrapped her arms over her chest, "Will they ever quit?"

"You know what they're like," Bart said. "It doesn't matter that France and Belgium have been liberated. The war isn't over, and Hitler will never allow the German army to surrender. They won't quit until Allied tanks are rumbling through the center of Berlin."

Claire shook her head and sighed. Just a week earlier, she and Lukas had joined a jubilant crowd that had spontaneously gathered in the Grote Markt, celebrating the second entire month since the liberation, the second whole month of freedom since the Nazis were driven out. And now this. "Yes, I know what they're like," she said. "But isn't there one drop of honor anywhere in Germany? Can't just one of their officers summon up the courage to kill that bastard and finally end this?"

Bart gently took her arm, "We should be going."

It was a short walk to the small cafe, tucked away on a quiet street between a bakery and a boarded-up shop that had previously housed a Jewish diamond merchant. They were the only patrons, and the proprietor, a friend of Peeters, led them to a table. He uncorked a bottle of white wine, filled two glasses, and departed with a smile and a brief whisper that the filet of sole would be ready soon.

Claire took a sip of the wine, trying to forget the gruesome scene at the theater. "White wine and filet of sole, how is it possible? I haven't tasted sole in five years."

Bart beamed. "A small shipment arrived at the port. Soon, we will have regained full access to the sea, and some things may return to normal."

Claire looked at the silver-haired man with a wry smile. In all the years she had known him, she never ceased to be amazed at the full extent of his contacts. As 'Councilman Peeters' he was widely connected with business leaders and government officials throughout Belgium and Great Britain. As 'Bart,' he had used those connections as one of the very early organizers of the Resistance movement in Belgium. "Return to normal?" she asked, "like real coffee, perhaps? Or coal for heating?" Claire had unbuttoned her coat but left it on.

"Don't get your hopes up. But I do have some news for you, good news, a reason for our little celebration."

"What is it?"

Bart took a sip of wine and leaned forward. "There is a position for you at the Interior Department if you're still interested."

"Interested? I'm thrilled. When can I start? What would I be doing?"

"You can start on Monday. It's in the Relocation Section, helping displaced persons find shelter, ration coupons, that sort of thing. The office is in the Antwerp city hall. The pay isn't much, but—"

"Whatever they pay will be fine, Bart. I need something to do. I'm delighted."

The sole was prepared the way Claire remembered, lightly floured, and sautéed in butter, another rare treat. Her mood had brightened considerably by the time the proprietor brought out two cups of coffee. "This was a real treat, Bart, though I feel absolutely decadent about the sole." She took a sip of the coffee, still bitter and watery, but it didn't matter. "Did I tell you that I wrote a letter to Jack?"

"No, when?" he asked, a note of surprise in his voice.

"Two weeks ago.

"You had his address?"

"Well, not exactly. But he had told me he was based at Hardwick Airfield in Great Britain, so I sent it there."

Peeters gave her a hard look but softened a bit when she reached over and patted his arm. "I know what you're thinking about not letting things get personal, but I think you know it *is* personal with Jack and me. Ever since last year, when Lukas assured me that Jack made it back to England, I've been waiting for the chance to write him and make sure he's still safe. And now, since we're starting to get mail, I've got to try."

"No harm in trying, I suppose. But I wouldn't get your hopes up. The war's still going on, you know."

That night, in the tiny room under the eaves of Lukas' apartment, Claire had trouble falling asleep. It was too dark to see the brass alarm clock on the nightstand, but she guessed it was after midnight. Following Belgium's liberation in September, the escape line was disbanded, and Claire left Gaston's farm in Grote Brogel. She moved back to Antwerp and needed a place to stay, but the memories of her parents were still very raw, and she couldn't bear the thought of returning to her home. So, Lukas quickly offered her the room, even modifying the trapdoor and staircase to make it easier to access.

Now, every waking moment she spent in the space under the eaves reminded her of Jack, which she found comforting, though she missed him terribly. She knew how irrational it was. They had known each other for only a few weeks, and it had been almost a year since they parted. But she was completely in love with him, and deep in her soul, she knew he was in love with her.

She knew it was possible they'd never see each other again. Bart was right; Belgium may have been liberated, but the war was still going on, and Jack had probably been thrust back in harm's way. But then she rolled over on her side, immediately pushing the dark thoughts out of her mind, preferring to remember the night they made love in the safehouse in Saint-Jean-de-Luz.

Chapter Twenty-Eight

The work was tedious and stressful, at times overwhelming, but for Claire, it was a Godsend, keeping her busy and her mind occupied. Processing requisitions from the citizens of Antwerp for housing, ration stamps, and reconstruction permits could have seemed dull after the intense experience of being an operative for a covert escape organization. But the hundreds of people who queued up in the corridors of City Hall every morning was a grim reminder of the difficulties people faced in newly liberated Belgium, especially with the war still ranging just over the border in Holland and Germany.

For three hours each morning, Claire took up her post on the second floor, interviewing the weary and confused souls struggling to emerge from four years of deprivation under Nazi occupation. They were searching for housing and jobs, extra ration cards, and medical assistance. They were searching for news of friends, relatives, and loved ones lost in the chaos and wreckage of the war.

The questions were endless, and the answers were few. Every person and every family had a story. They were all different, all unique and distressing in the way their lives had been shattered. And Claire listened to them all, her heart aching when no solutions could be found and soaring whenever she could provide even the smallest dose of help.

In contrast, the afternoon hours of mindless paperwork offered a respite from the stress and exhaustion of the morning interviews, and Claire eventually found she welcomed the mundane task of reviewing and filing a never-ending stream of documents.

Early one afternoon, midway through her second week on the job, the section manager, Dora van Houtte, walked up and dropped a stack of papers on Claire's desk with a thump that startled her. She was a prim, serious woman who had apparently been with the department longer than anyone could remember, and rumor had it she knew everything about everyone. Apparently noticing Claire's look of surprise, van Houtte shrugged and said the Financial Section needed help with filing. Then she moved on, dropping other stacks of papers on other desks.

Claire leaned back in her chair, stretched for a moment, then sighed and began thumbing through the new stack of documents. After a few minutes, she stopped and went back, looking over the documents more carefully, her interest piqued. Rather than the usual requisitions for housing, jobs, and ration cards, these were different. They were financial documents and notifications of transfers of foreign funds into Belgian bank accounts.

Interested in doing something different, she looked through them slowly, studying the notations. A few of the transfers had been made by individuals, but most appeared to be on behalf of businesses, corporations of one type or another, many of them German or Austrian.

Halfway through the stack, one document caught her eye. It was a notification of the transfer of five hundred thousand Swiss francs from the bank account of a German company named *I.G. Farben* to an account in Antwerp. It had caught her attention because the amount of the funds was significantly higher than any of the others. The bank account in Antwerp was in the name of a Belgian company named *Produits Agricoles Echange,* located not far from Antwerp.

Curious now, she pulled the document from the stack and thumbed through the pages. They were filled mostly with dense legal and financial data until she came to the last page, where signatures appeared. One signature was that of someone named Gerhard Wagner, Chairman of the Board of

I. G. Farben. The other was that of a person by the name of Niels DeVos, listed as the Principal Owner of *Produits Agricoles Echange*, acknowledging receipt of the funds.

The second name triggered something in her mind.

Niels DeVos

She thought about it, trying to remember.

Niels DeVos

Bart's friend? A captain with the Antwerp police department?

It couldn't be the same person.

Or could it?

An hour later, Claire sat in Bart Peeter's office on the fourth-floor of the Department of the Interior, waiting as he flipped through the document a second time. He frowned, studied the last page for a long time, then glanced up at Claire. "It's remarkable this happened to pass over your desk since you're not working in the Financial Section. This is just a routine notification, like a thousand others. Normally, a financial clerk would have just filed it."

"I would have as well," Claire said, "except that the amount of the transfer was so large compared to all the rest it caught my attention, probably because I've never seen these documents before. Apparently, the financial group needed help, and Dora van Houtte asked me to file these."

Bart nodded but didn't respond.

"Is this the same Niels DeVos as your friend who is a captain with the police force?"

"Yes, it is. *Produits Agricole Echange* is DeVos' family company, a manufacturer of fertilizers started by his father. Niels is the principal owner of the company, but being on the police force, he was never very involved in running the family business. He's a true Belgian patriot and, for some time, had been quietly helping me with some of my activities in the resistance. Then, last year, the company was abruptly taken over by the Germans, and the family was forced out. It was tragic. Niels' father died of a heart attack a few months later. He was very bitter about it and came to me saying he wanted to do more; he wanted to strike back at them. He had resources and connections, so I introduced him to Lukas to help out with the escape line."

Claire flinched at the comment. She hadn't heard anything about that before.

Bart apparently noticed and said, "I assume Lukas never said anything about it."

"No, he didn't. You probably told him not to." Before he could respond, Claire waved her hand dismissively and continued, "If the family was forced out of the business last year, why is DeVos' signature on the funds transfer?"

Bart was silent for a moment before responding, "To be honest, I don't know."

"And this document was signed here in Antwerp three weeks ago, shortly after the liberation." She added.

Peeters stood and paced around the room for a moment, then stopped and looked at her. "There must be an explanation for this. I'll look into it, discreetly of course, and let you know what I find out."

Chapter Twenty-Nine

Frankfurt, Germany

SS Hauptsturmfuhrer Konrad Becker stood in front of the expansive façade of the *I. G Farben* headquarters. He was conflicted with mixed emotions. He felt the same awe and pride he always felt whenever he visited the enormous, modernistic structure, the largest office building in Europe. It was a fitting tribute not only to Germany but to the company itself, the largest chemical company in the world. But on this day, he also felt the pressure of what he knew was coming next.

He'd been back in Germany since last September when the Allied armies liberated France and Belgium and drove the Wehrmacht back across the border. The war appeared to be lost... and now his real mission was about to begin.

Twenty minutes later, Becker entered the seventh-floor executive office suite and was ushered into a mammoth conference room of glass and oak-paneled walls. The sole occupant of the room was a slender, gray-haired man who stood at the far end of a long conference table, facing away from the door, looking out one of the floor-to-ceiling windows. The man's name was Gerhard Wagner, who was Chairman of the Board of Directors of *I.G. Farben*. He was also Becker's father-in-law.

Becker stood silently as Wagner slowly turned away from the window and looked at him. Becker flinched at the sight of his father-in-law's face. It was pale and heavily lined; his normally intense blue eyes were blank and distant as though he hadn't slept well, which he probably hadn't in some time.

After a long moment of silence, Wagner spoke, his voice surprisingly steady and clear despite his outward appearance. "The time draws near, Konrad. I fear the war will be lost. Is everything in place?"

Becker nodded and placed his uniform hat on the table, though he kept standing. His relationship with his father-in-law was formal and dignified. He would never take a seat in the man's presence unless it had been offered. "Yes, sir. Everything is in place. And the individuals who will be leaving, they are the same ones you identified earlier?"

"Yes. The same ones, twelve in all. There are others who will take a different route, but they are not your concern. These twelve are the most important, which is why I entrusted the mission to you."

Becker stiffened, "I understand, sir. I will not let you down. I trust you will be the first?"

"Yes. The Viscount is prepared, I assume?"

"Yes, sir. He is awaiting your arrival and the others that will follow. His estate, as you know, is ideal for our purposes, and complete secrecy has been established."

Wagner was quiet for another moment, glancing out the window as though he was taking a last look at the Fatherland. Then he sat at the head of the long table and motioned for Becker to take a seat next to him. He folded his hands on the table and said, "They would never understand. The Americans and the British would never understand that we were doing what had to be done. Europe was a disaster. The Communists were taking over, and the Jews were helping them. It had to be done, and our Fuhrer was the only man strong enough to do it. But he went too far; Russia was a mistake." He paused for a moment, his gaze fixed on Becker. "You understand, Konrad, the importance of our mission. We have come too far to stop now just because this war is lost. You know we are on the cutting edge of something unique in all the world, the development of a new weapon so powerful that it's mere existence will propel us back into power. You know this, and you know that the people critical to the success of our mission must get out of Germany, along with the money necessary to complete our work. The Reich cannot—will not—die. We cannot fail." He paused for a moment before continuing. "So, we will be entering Belgium through St. Vith, as we had planned?"

Becker nodded. "Yes. It is the safest place to cross the border. The American troops in the area are either new recruits or veterans taking a rest from the war. And the population, as you know, is largely German and sympathetic to our cause."

"Who will be leading us to Namur? Not this police officer who is handling the money, I hope. What is his name?"

"DeVos," Becker said, "Captain DeVos. And no, he will not be involved with you or any of the others. His role is confined to transporting and safeguarding the money. You will be met in St. Vith by a young man I have been training for two years. He successfully infiltrated the largest escape line in Belgium and helped to bring it down. His name is Lukas, and I trust him completely. He is also arranging all the details for your eventual exit from Belgium and Europe. The Viscount also knows him well and trusts him. You and your colleagues will be in good hands."

"Very well, I expected nothing less. There is, however, one thing that concerns me."

"What is it, sir?"

"I have been informed that the British Intelligence unit, MI9, has been investigating certain transfers of money from Germany to Belgium."

Becker was silent for a moment. He hadn't heard about this, and it disturbed him that his father-in-law knew it before he did. It didn't surprise him, though, because the old man always seemed to have people whispering things in his ear.

Wagner continued before he could respond. "Do you know who in Belgium has a connection with MI9?"

Becker nodded. "Yes, his name is Peeters; he was a city councilman in Antwerp before the war. We have been watching him. But I don't know the identity of his contact at MI9."

"Well, you had better find out and take care of it. We cannot take any chances at this late date. Everything depends on the success of this mission."

Wagner stood, and Becker did the same.

"I will look into it immediately, sir. And I will telephone you when the day of your departure is certain," Becker said.

When he left the conference room, Becker by-passed the lift and walked down the seven flights of stairs to the ground floor, preferring to be alone with his thoughts. The time had finally arrived. This war may be lost, but Wagner had made it abundantly clear, as he always did, that the Third Reich would continue on, provided that the most important people, those with the best minds and the most power, could be safely transported out of Germany and Europe.

Becker knew what was at stake. He knew about the work being done on the new weapon and its capabilities even more than Wagner did. He'd made it his business to know. And he certainly knew more than any of the other 'important people,' each of whom only knew about isolated portions of the whole project.

The Reich will continue on... but with a new leader.

Wagner?

Or perhaps someone else?

And now it was up to him. It would have to be done in absolute secrecy. If the Fuhrer ever got wind of it, they would all be summarily executed. Becker would send a message to Lukas that it had begun. He knew Lukas was prepared and had been making the necessary travel arrangements for months. He would be ready.

But how did MI9 find out about the money? Was it DeVos? Did he get careless and say something to the wrong person? Or was it Peeters? Becker knew the former councilman had an important position at the Interior Department, where he could have seen money transfer documents. That seemed more likely. Either way, he would find out and take care of it.

He exited the building and walked to his car, thinking about his wife, Ursula, Wagner's only child. He wouldn't tell her about his conversation with Wagner today. She had barely spoken to her father in the last five years since her mother died, blaming him for neglecting her mother's long-time illness.

As he reached the car, Becker thought that perhaps, when this was all over, he and Ursula would live in South America or Australia. Perhaps they would have children and one day even return to Germany.

As the leader of the new Reich?

Perhaps.

Chapter Thirty

Antwerp

Niels DeVos hated this kind of place: a small, dirty café tucked into one of Antwerp's back alleys, a place respectable people didn't know existed. That's why, undoubtedly, they were alone. For someone in his position, he also hated sneaking around dressed in grubby street clothes, like some criminal, and, most of all, he hated associating with people like the beady-eyed mongrel sitting across from him. DeVos knew him only by his code name, *Socrates,* which was enough of a joke. But what he was hearing was no laughing matter.

"Tell me again where you got this information," DeVos said.

Socrates lit up another cigarette, his third in the twenty minutes they had been sitting there. "Can't give you her name, you know that. She's a section manager at the Interior Department. Always been reliable, committed to the cause."

The cause.

DeVos almost laughed in his face. It seemed incredible to him that people like this actually believed all the Nazi, Third Reich bullshit. He knew the name of *Socrates'* contact at the Interior Department; it was his job to know, but he always liked to test these people, these *believers* in the cause. At least I'm only in it for the money, DeVos thought smugly. That kept him apart from these nut cases.

But now there was a problem, and he had to deal with it. He stared at the shifty little man through the haze of cigarette smoke. "And this 'section manager' was sure she knew who she was talking about. You're sure she got the right name."

Socrates nodded impatiently, "I told you, she's one of our best inside contacts. And she was quite specific; it was that Councilman, Peeters, he's been there for years, one of the big bosses or whatever."

"And Peeters asked her to go through their records to find any documents about my family's company. Do you have any idea why?"

"No, that's all she said." Socrates took a sip from his glass of beer. "So now It's *your* problem... and you have to fix it."

DeVos smoldered inside. He'd thought he was finished dealing with people like this. But he had only one final mission to complete for Becker, and then he would be gone for good. It wouldn't bring his father back, but if Becker kept his word, the rest of his family would be safe, living in comfort in Switzerland with all that money.

DeVos waited until Socrates had left and was out of sight. Then he left the grimy café and walked quickly toward Groenplaats, mixing in with the late afternoon crowd. He descended the stairs to the tram station and stood at the back of the platform, seething with anger. He'd have liked nothing better than dragging that little son-of-a-bitch out into the street and kicking his balls in. But Socrates was very well connected with a band of collaborators who were still out there and very committed to the cause... and very dangerous, even to a high-ranking police officer.

Socrates may be well connected, but he didn't know everything, DeVos thought. He didn't know anything about the money and never would... he would see to that. As much as he loathed the man, DeVos knew that Socrates had just done him a great service.

Chapter Thirty-One

Claire left Lukas' apartment and walked briskly across the Grote Markt on her way to work. It was a damp, cool morning, and there was a misty fog settling over the ancient market square, almost obliterating the giant bronze statue of Brabo, the symbol of Antwerp. She remembered with a smile how Jack had stopped and stared at it that day they were walking through the city to the Café Brig. The shops still had little to sell, but at least the German soldiers were gone, as well as the disgusting Swastika flag.

When she arrived at her desk, there was a note from Bart asking her to stop by. It had been three days since their meeting, and she wondered if he'd learned anything. She walked up the flight of steps to the fourth floor, down the hall to his office, and stuck her head in the open door.

He motioned for her to come in and close the door. "There have been some developments," he said quietly.

Claire sat at the small table in the corner of the office while Peeters poured two cups of coffee from a silver pitcher. He sat in the chair across from her. "The money is gone," he said. "I contacted someone I know at the bank, and the day after he signed that document, DeVos apparently arranged for four hundred thousand Swiss francs to be wired to a numbered bank account in Switzerland."

"What about the rest of it, another hundred thousand?"

"DeVos took it in the form of a cashier's check."

"A cashier's check for a hundred thousand, whatever for?"

Peeters shrugged and took a sip of coffee. "I have no idea. But there is something else that is strange. I asked Dora van Houtte to gather up any documents the department has on file regarding *Produits Agricoles Echange.* She reported back that there are no files on record for that company."

"Really, no records at all?"

"Apparently not. Aside from the document about the money transfer, which you gave to me, and I still have, there is nothing else in the files. Not even the original incorporation documents, which would normally be there." Peters paused for a moment, then continued. "So, I checked with my contact at British Intelligence, MI9, to see if he knew anything about the *Produits Agricole* business. Well, it turns out that two weeks ago, a special unit of the British army visited the *Produits Agricole* factory. The building was locked and boarded up, but they forced their way in. The facility was vacant, no machinery, no barrels, crates, storage tanks, nothing. Everything had been dismantled and hauled away. But one of their investigators discovered a small metal canister that had apparently been over-looked when the building was cleaned out.”

“A canister? What was in it?”

“A pesticide called Zyklon-B.”

Claire shook her head, confused. “So, the plant also produced pesticides; I don’t understand why the British army would be interested—”

Peeters interrupted. “Zyklon-B is a deadly compound that releases poisonous gas. It’s the same chemical the Russians discovered when they liberated one of the Nazi extermination camps in Poland this past July.”

Claire stared at Bart. Her stomach suddenly turned sour, and she pushed the coffee cup aside. She’d heard rumors about these camps, where hundreds of thousands of Jews and other ‘undesirables’ were reported to have been exterminated, gassed to death, and their bodies then burned in ovens. Her *parents* may have been sent to one of those camps. And now, this same deadly poison was found in the DeVos family’s factory?

“My MI9 contact also told me the name of the German company that developed

Zyklon-B.”

Claire swallowed, trying to push aside the notion of her parents and poison gas. She held up her hand. “Let me guess, *I.G. Farben,* the same German company that transferred five hundred thousand Swiss francs to the account of *Produits Agricole.*”

"Precisely."

"But how did the British know about DeVos' company? What made them investigate?"

"For some time, MI9 has suspected that the Germans are smuggling large sums of money out of the country. They have established secret conduits for bringing the money into other countries, Belgium possibly being one of them. Sometimes the money is paid to companies they have taken over—"

"Like *Produits Agricole,* for example?"

Bart nodded. "Yes, but they also suspect large sums of cash, probably Swiss francs, are also being transported out of the country."

"Getting it out before they lose the war?"

"Yes."

Claire suddenly felt uneasy, as though she had stumbled onto something that was a lot bigger and more dangerous than she could imagine. "Do they know where it comes in, or who else is involved?"

Bart shrugged. "My contact didn't say. He only mentioned DeVos' company but wasn't sure how involved DeVos himself was in the rest of the operation."

"And since DeVos is your friend and a high-ranking police officer, I suppose it would be awkward for you to question him about this," Claire said, trying not to sound sarcastic.

Peeters shrugged, "Yes, I imagine it would. But I'm still looking into it."

As Claire started to leave, she glanced down at the newspaper lying on Bart's desk and pointed to an article she had read earlier. "Another one of these murders of a former collaborator," she said. "This one took place just a few blocks from here and seems particularly brutal. Broke right into his apartment and stabbed him."

Bart picked up the paper. "Yes, I saw it. Some character who went by the name of *Socrates*, of all things. You're right; it was brutal. The murderers could have been some Belgian patriots settling an old score, or it could have been other collaborators wanting to shut him up so *they* don't get caught. You know how dangerous this has become. Former collaborators will do *anything* to keep their secrets. It's a difficult time right now, so you must be very careful, Claire. We both need to be careful, Lukas as well; I've told him that. With everything we were involved in, it's very hard to know who to trust."

Chapter Thirty-Two

Stalag Luft POW Camp, Sagan, Germany

The 'cooler' was a solitary concrete cell that measured 10 feet long and five feet wide, with a tiny, barred window eight feet off the floor. In one corner of the concrete floor was a wooden pallet with an inch-thick straw-filled mattress, and in another corner, a chamber pot that was rarely emptied on time. The average length of stay in the cooler for incorrigible Allied POWs was seven days.

Jack was on his sixty-first day.

Except for an hour of interrogations every morning, he had been completely alone for two months, enveloped by darkness and silence, which had been slowly grinding him down. He knew it and struggled every hour of every long day to keep his mind occupied on something... anything at all, no matter how trivial, or he knew he'd eventually go mad.

He spent at least an hour each day—or was it more? He had no way of really knowing—picking the lice from his hair... and counting them, keeping track to determine if the problem was getting better or worse. He spent another hour each morning and again in the afternoon doing push-ups, sit-ups, and jogging in place, the time of day determined only when the tray of bread and watery soup was pushed through the slot in the bottom of the door.

He was determined to maintain his mental and physical condition, though the meager meals and constant darkness were taking their toll. As the days wore on, he spent more and more time lying on the thin, straw mattress just because he was tired. But he rarely slept.

In spite of his growing fatigue, the one single task he had absolutely forced himself to do was to keep track of the number of days since he'd said goodbye to Claire. It had been easier in the months before he was confined to the cooler. At least then, he could mark on a wall or even ask a guard or another prisoner what day it was. But in the constant darkness of this damp, hellish cell, the only thing he could count on was the predictable, routine nature of his German captors. The guards brought him two meals every day, without exception, and by forcing himself to mentally keep track of the number of meals he received—and the number of interrogations—he had managed to keep track of the days since he had held Claire in his arms, kissed her passionately, then said goodbye and walked down the embankment to the Bidasoa River.

Jack sighed and shoved the empty metal tray across the damp, concrete floor, sending a rat scurrying after it. He slumped down on the mattress and wrapped his arms around his knees, alone in the dark with his worst fear... that Claire had also been captured. He knew what that would mean; she had told him what the Germans did to escape line operatives, and the thought was more than he could bear.

Once again, he recalled the details of that fateful day... the day he was betrayed.

When he waded across the river into Spain that night, the landmarks on the other side were precisely as Lukas had described them: railroad tracks that ran parallel to the river, a single-lane dirt road that led into a wooded area, and a farmhouse situated on the left side of the road just beyond a narrow, wooden bridge. Everything had gone according to the plan... except for the officers of the Spanish *Guardia Civil* who were waiting for him in the house.

For the next six months, he sat in a filthy jail cell in San Sebastian, surviving on soup and chunks of stale bread. Spain was technically a 'neutral' country in the war, and the jailer assured him it probably wouldn't be long before American or British diplomats would negotiate his release. It usually worked that way, the greedy-looking man had said, provided that Jack wasn't wanted by the German SS or Gestapo... and that certain 'gratuities' were paid. But for six months, it never happened as he languished in the grubby, rat-infested cell, his isolation and boredom broken only by fights with the drunks and thieves the jailer would throw in next to him.

Then, early one morning, it *did* happen. Two German Luftwaffe officers showed up and, following a long discussion with the *Guardia Civil* jailer, led Jack out of the jail. A week later, he was in Germany, sitting in an interrogation room at Stalag Luft, a POW camp for Allied airmen.

Every day, for the next sixty-one days, a series of Luftwaffe interrogators asked the same questions over and over...

Who is your contact at MI9?

How did you send reports to England?

Why were you in Belgium?

How did you get there?

They kept repeating that he was a *besonder fall,* which he eventually realized meant that he was a 'special case' though he had no idea what that meant.

Occasionally, the word *Gestapo* would be mentioned and then dismissed with a shake of the head or a wave of the hand by the interrogators. Jack came to realize that, though they were tasked with interrogating him, they were Luftwaffe officers, airmen like himself. And the unwritten code of conduct of airmen taking care of other airmen thankfully took precedence. Solitary confinement was better than Gestapo torture, they explained every time they led him to the cooler and slammed the door shut.

Chapter Thirty-Three

Antwerp

Niels DeVos sat at a table in a small windowless room on the second floor of an abandoned warehouse building near the port and decoded a wireless transmission from *SS-Hauptsturmfuhrer* Konrad Becker. It read,

MI9 is aware of the money transfer

Need the identity of Peeters' contact person

Must create diversion

Urgent!

DeVos re-read it, then propped his elbows on the table and rubbed his temples. Now, he had to deal with Peeters sooner rather than later. Peeters must have learned about the recent money transfer from *I.G. Farben*—why else would he be asking about documents on the company—which was bad enough. But now MI9 is involved. That was a major problem. DeVos knew Peeters was the primary connection with MI9 in Belgium and had been since before the war. But he had no idea who Peeters' contact person was. It was a secret Peeters would never give up. But that would not satisfy Becker.

He sat at the table for a while longer, considering his options. He read the decoded transmission one last time. Then he set a match to it, ground out the ashes on the concrete floor, and left the room.

The next evening, DeVos returned to the second-floor room above the warehouse and telephoned Peeters at his home.

"To what do I owe the pleasure?" Peeters said when DeVos identified himself.

"You may have read in the newspaper about a German collaborator who was murdered in his apartment a couple of days ago."

"Yes, I read the article," Peeters said, "the one who went by the name *Socrates.*"

"That's the one. Nasty chap. At any rate, we searched his apartment, which led us to another location he had been using. We've found some documents here that I would like you to examine. They concern the escape line." He was certain this would pique Peeters' interest.

"What kind of documents?" Peeters asked.

"Well, there are quite a few lists of names, locations, that sort of thing. It would be helpful if you reviewed them before we log them into evidence so we don't waste our time tracking down things that don't mean anything. Probably wouldn't take very long. I can have my men pick you up in twenty minutes. Would that be possible?"

DeVos knew that nothing like that would ever have been written down, at least not by an operative of the escape line. But the line *had been* infiltrated, and even though Belgium had been liberated, operatives of the line were still at risk from collaborators. There were scores to settle, and he knew Peeters couldn't ignore information like this.

"Of course, that would be fine," Peeters replied. "I'll meet them in front of my building."

"Very good. They won't be in uniform, of course, since this is an undercover operation.

DeVos hung up the phone and paced around the small room. The warehouse building itself was a large, dimly lit space with high ceilings and a cobblestone floor. It was damp and cold and mostly empty. The building, of course, had not been used by *Socrates* or anyone else for a long time. But since DeVos obviously couldn't conduct this particular meeting at the police station, this was a perfect spot. No one would ever know they were here.

While he waited for Peeters, DeVos reflected on their relationship, which dated back to 1938, shortly after he returned from his visit to Germany. It had been Becker, of course, who suggested—or, to be more precise, insisted—that he seek out Councilman Peeters for help in arranging financing for his family's business. Becker had told him that Peeters could be useful for his purposes, and that was all he needed to know. It had been easier than he expected. Belgium was in dire economic straits in those days, and all levels of government were eager to help businesses create jobs. His own job as a police officer had given him some credibility with Peeters, and everything evolved from there.

It was a masterful idea, part of Becker's plan of establishing a conduit for transferring money out of Germany in the event the outcome of the war went the wrong way. DeVos knew few of the details in those early days, but he had quickly realized that Becker was well connected at the highest levels in the Third Reich. Again, that was all he needed to know.

A part of him was disappointed that his association with Peeters would end this way. They weren't exactly friends—DeVos didn't cultivate friendships—though he knew Peeters thought of him as a friend. He respected Peeters for his courage and organizational skills in the Resistance movement and the escape line, though he always thought of it as a futile gesture. Peeters was passionate in his patriotism, and unlike himself, the outcome of the war mattered to him. That aside, their relationship had indeed been useful. It had established *Produits Agricole* as an important part of the money conduit. And it had led DeVos to the escape line, both of which enhanced his standing with Becker.

But now Peeters apparently knew about the money transfer, and that changed everything. How could he have found out? Transfer documents like that are ubiquitous, obscure forms that are normally buried in the mountains of paperwork generated by governments, even in wartime. Someone in Peeters' position would never see documents like that. Someone else must have discovered it and shown it to him. But who? And why? And what else does Peeters know?

These were all problems, of course, but at this moment, they were not as important as Becker's urgent need to know the name of Peeters' MI9 contact and create some type of diversion, something to send MI9 off in a different direction. DeVos had laid awake half the night thinking about that. And now he had a plan.

When Peeters arrived and entered the small, dingy room, the councilman glanced around, frowning, a look of concern in his eyes. He turned to DeVos. "What's going on, Niels?"

DeVos pointed to the other chair, satisfied that he'd caught Peeters off guard. "I understand you've been searching for information about my company. So, have a seat and tell me what you want to know."

Peeters stared at him for a moment, then sat down and said, "I was wondering why your company just received five hundred thousand Swiss francs from a German company called *I.G. Farben.*"

"Why is that any concern of yours?"

"Oh, no particular reason, except for the fact that your family was supposedly driven out of business last year, and you were so angry about it that you offered to help me with the escape line... to strike back at them, I believe were your words. At least that's what you told me at the time."

"And now, I have been paid what they owed me for the business."

"Really? Paid by the Germans for a company they forcibly took over? That would be a first. And paid quite handsomely, I would say... unless it was payment for manufacturing Zyklon-B."

That caught *DeVos* off guard, and he took a moment before he responded. "It's very unfortunate that you happen to know about that," he said.

"So, it's true. You're a traitor." Peeters retorted.

DeVos abruptly leaned forward and pointed a finger at him. "Don't even think about preaching to me about collaborating with the enemy. You're just as guilty as I am."

Peeters flinched. "What? *Am I* guilty? What the hell are you talking about?"

DeVos picked up a briefcase, opened it, and removed a single file folder. He'd prepared the contents of this and other folders right after the meeting with the late *Socrates*. "I asked you to come here and look at some documents," he said calmly, holding out the folder. "Here they are. I suggest you look through them carefully."

DeVos watched Peeters closely as he opened the folder and removed the three sets of documents inside. The first was a copy of the loan application DeVos had filled out in 1938 when he was arranging financing for *Produits Agricole*. It included a letter Peeters had written to the bank on behalf of the Department of the Interior in support of DeVos' company, encouraging them to grant the loan. The second document was a copy of an annual report, including a list of the Board of Directors of *Produits Agricole,* filed with the Department of the Interior at the end of that same year. Peeters' name was on the list of directors, each of whom was to be paid fifty thousand Belgian Francs every year for their services.

Peeters tossed both documents on the table. "This is all a complete distortion of the facts, and you know it. Yes, I encouraged the bank to finance what I believed to be a legitimate company, and I agreed, at your request, to serve on the Board of Directors. None of that was illegal. And, as you know very well, I resigned from the board when you told me about the Germans commandeering the company. And I certainly had no idea the company produced Zyklon-B!"

"Then why would *Produits Agricole* have paid you a hundred thousand Swiss francs for your 'consulting services' just two days ago?"

Peeters blinked. "What the hell are you—"

DeVos cut him off. "Look at the last document inside that folder, and we can stop wasting time."

Peeters frowned, then picked up the third document.

DeVos smiled as he watched Peeters stare at it in silence. It was a carbon copy of a cashier's check from the account of *Produits Agricole* for one hundred thousand Swiss francs made out to him. The notation on the check read, 'For consulting services through

October 1944.' There was also a deposit slip verifying that the check had been credited to Peeters' personal account. "You obviously haven't checked your bank account recently," DeVos said. "Not only were you a member of the Board of Directors, you also provided consulting services to the company right up to—"

Peeters abruptly pushed his chair back, stood up, and shouted, "Is this what you've become, Niels... a traitor, a criminal?'

DeVos looked up at him and shrugged. "I think you should sit down and relax for a moment. There are some additional things I must share with you."

"I wouldn't take a single franc from you. I will instruct the bank to immediately return that check."

DeVos smiled thinly, then opened his briefcase again and removed another file folder. This, he knew, would be the clincher.

Peeters sat down and snapped. "How many other policemen on the force are also Nazi collaborators?"

DeVos ignored the question, opened the folder, and removed another document. "I believe this will be of interest to you," he said, handing it to Peeters.

It was a bulletin from the Antwerp Police Department, along with Peeters' photo.

COUNCILMAN PEETERS

WANTED FOR TREASON

The Antwerp Police Department has issued a warrant for the arrest of Councilman Peeters, also

Peeters stared at the bulletin for a long time, then dropped it on the table. "What do you want, Niels? Why am I here?"

DeVos took back the document and put it in the folder. "That's more like it. I really don't want to send this bulletin out if I don't have to. But I need your help. More precisely, your cooperation."

"My cooperation? With what? Helping the enemy? Why are you doing this, Niels? *Why?* How could you possibly collaborate with those people? How could you even *think* of helping them after what they've done to millions of innocent people—"

DeVos slapped a hand on the table, cutting him off. "That's enough! Save all the righteous indignation crap for someone else! It doesn't matter who wins the goddamn war! It only matters whether you're on the winning side! That's where the money is!"

Peeters' face flushed, and he shouted, "The money? The fucking *money*? That's it? That's why you're doing this... ?" His voice trailed off, and he slumped in the chair, shaking his head.

DeVos stood up, collected the documents from the table, and put them back in his briefcase. "I'm leaving now," he said tersely. "But we will meet again tomorrow. After that, you will have a decision to make. You can join us and help with our mission...or you can refuse. If you choose to join us, you could live a very prosperous life when this is all over."

Peeters stood as well and looked him in the eye, "And if I refuse?"

"I think you know the answer to that question." DeVos said. Then he left the room, closed the door behind him, and walked down the stairs. He nodded to the two men who had picked up Peeters. "I'll drive my own car home. You know where to take him."

Chapter-Thirty-Four

Claire walked quickly across the Grote Markt and glanced at her watch as she entered the city hall building. She weaved her way past the dozens of tired-looking, dejected citizens already lined up in the ground-floor hallway. They were of all ages: men carrying battered suitcases, women holding babies in their arms, elderly couples clinging to each other for support. The air in the cramped hallway was stuffy and smelled of body odors, and the line of people stretched all the way up the main stairway to the second floor. It was eight-fifteen, and she didn't want to be late for her morning shift, but she wanted to see if Bart was in his office. She hadn't seen him for the last two days.

Claire made her way through the crowd in the second-floor hallway, pushed through the double doors into the open work area, and hurried to her desk, situated in a corner at the far end. Typewriters clacked away, telephones rang, and cigarette smoke already filled the air of the noisy, over-crowded space. Claire shoved her purse in the bottom drawer of her desk and made her way down the hall and up the stairs to the fourth floor. But when she arrived at Bart's office, the door was closed, and through the frosted glass, she could tell it was dark inside, the same as it had been the last two days. She sighed and walked back down the stairs.

The morning shift seemed to take forever. Claire struggled to focus on the endless problems presented by the long line of displaced people, but her mind wandered, wondering where Bart had gone.

When the shift finally ended, she hurried back up to Bart's office, but it was still dark. She stood and stared into the darkened office as if hoping the light would suddenly snap on and he would be at his desk. She heard footsteps coming down the hallway and turned to see Dora van Houtte. "Have you seen Councilman Peeters today?" Claire asked.

Van Houtte stopped and looked at her curiously as though surprised to see her up on this floor. The woman glanced at the darkened office and shrugged. "No, I have not."

"Do you know if he had a meeting out of the office today?"

Van Houtte frowned, "Well, you know the councilman is quite a busy man. He has meetings quite frequently all over the city. I suspect he'll be in later. Is there anything I can help with?"

Claire instantly felt a bit foolish, knowing it was an odd question to ask about someone in Peeters' position. But it had been two days. "No… thank you, it's not important. I'll talk with him later."

"Very well," van Houtte said, "I'm sure you have quite a bit to do."

When Claire arrived for work the next morning, she went immediately up to the fourth floor to check Peeters' office. She felt a rush of elation as she walked down the hallway, seeing his door open and the lights on. It instantly evaporated when she stepped into the office. Dora van Houtte stood behind Peeters' desk, leafing through a stack of papers.

"May I help you?" van Houtte asked, peering over the top of her glasses.

"I'm still looking for Councilman Peeters, and I'm worried about him," Claire replied. "Have you heard from him?"

"I expected to meet with him this morning," van Houtte replied," but he hasn't come in. Perhaps he's ill."

Claire took a step further into the office. "It's been three days. I called his home, and he was not there. Perhaps we should check the hospitals."

Van Houtte glanced at her watch. "I'm already late for a meeting with the director, and I need some files from the councilman. That's why I stopped by."

"Shall *I* call the hospitals?" Claire asked.

"If you like, but I really must hurry along."

Claire stared at her for a moment, then left the office, frustrated by the woman's indifference. A tingling sensation crawled up her spine.

What the hell is going on?

Chapter Thirty-Five

DeVos drove along a narrow, overgrown dirt road in the countryside several kilometers south of Antwerp and stopped next to an old, abandoned chapel, partially hidden in a grove of threes. A policeman—one of those who had picked up Peeters two days ago—stood outside the chapel. DeVos got out of his car and glanced at the chapel. It was a stout, stone building with a thick wooden door and no windows. The policeman stood near the door, smoking a cigarette.

"Has he caused any trouble?" DeVos asked.

The burly man shook his head. "Nothing serious. Keeps demanding to see you, curses at me when I don't answer, but that's about it." The policeman dropped his cigarette butt in the dirt and ground it out with his boot. "Have you heard from Becker?" he asked.

DeVos nodded. "Yes. More shipments are on the way, coming to St. Vith, same as before. But there is—" He stopped and glanced at the heavy wooden door, then stepped back toward his car and motioned for the policeman to follow. He continued, keeping his voice down. "There is a potential problem with MI9 that we'll have to deal with. And we'll have to get rid of Peeters sooner than we thought."

The policeman shrugged. "Just let me know, and we'll take care of it."

"Well, go get him out here."

The policeman stepped over to the chapel door, pulled a brass key from his pocket, and opened the door. "Stand up!" he snapped. "Stand up and get out here!"

Peeters slowly emerged from the darkness of the chapel, blinking and shielding his eyes from the sunlight. He was hunched over, a stubble of beard on his thin, pale face, his silver hair disheveled. He stood unsteadily for a moment, blinked again, then slowly straightened up. He pointed at DeVos and croaked, "About goddamn time, you traitor!"

DeVos looked at Peeters and shook his head. He was still acting like the proud 'defender of freedom' that he'd always been. Except the esteemed councilman didn't look quite so proud now. "Let's take a walk," DeVos said.

DeVos started down a path overlooking the river with Peeters and the policeman following him. The area was isolated and heavily wooded, the only structure within sight being the old stone chapel. Despite the partly sunny sky, there was a chill in the air and a brisk, damp wind coming off the river.

After a few minutes, they arrived at a clearing, and DeVos stopped. He thrust his hands into the pocket of his overcoat and looked at Peeters, who glared daggers at him. "So, now that you have had some time to think, can we expect your cooperation?" he asked.

"Cooperation, with what?" Peeters snapped. "I'm not a traitor... and I'm not going to betray my country!

So, if you want to send out that ridiculous bulletin, go right ahead!"

DeVos removed his gold-rimmed eyeglasses and slowly cleaned the lenses with a handkerchief. He put them back on and said, "I don't want you to betray your country. I merely want you to set up a meeting with your contact at British MI9."

Peeters blinked, then stared at DeVos for a moment before answering. "A meeting with MI9? For what purpose?"

DeVos shrugged, "Oh, just some intelligence we've picked up. I'll give you the specifics when the time is right."

"Are you asking me to commit treason?"

"Of course not. You only need to set up a meeting, nothing more. I'll take care of the rest."

"That's not possible. Contacts with MI9 are classified; you should know that. I'm the only one he would meet with."

DeVos expected this. "Well, your MI9 contact doesn't need to know that anyone else will be present. Just set up the meeting in your usual manner. After that, you'll be free to go and live well. The hundred thousand Swiss francs in your bank account should help you do that."

"What kind of 'intelligence' are you planning on giving him?"

"That is not your concern. But it will be information he will find useful."

"These people aren't fools. What makes you think they would take any 'intelligence' you give him seriously? They'd want to know where the information came from and how you happened to learn something they didn't already know."

"That will all be taken care of, and it's not your concern." DeVos watched Peeters closely as his defiant demeanor seemed to slowly fade away, as though he now realized he was trapped.

Finally, Peeters nodded, "Very well. May I return home now?"

DeVos smiled. "Not just yet. But be assured we will make you comfortable until our work is finished."

Chapter Thirty-Six

Kransberg Castle—Germany

SS-Hauptsturmfuhrer Konrad Becker sat alone in one of the countless rooms of the medieval Kransberg Castle, now serving as the headquarters of Field Marshal Gerd von Rundstedt. He sipped a cup of coffee and looked out the window at the magnificence of the Taunus Mountains, reflecting on the first time he'd traveled to this area.

It had been a camping trip with the scouts in the summer of 1934 when Becker and his friends in the Hitler Youth felt like they were invincible. They strutted through the mountain villages in their brown uniforms, heads held high, singing songs of the glories of the Fatherland. They learned to build fires and pitch tents, how to use a compass, and find their way through the forests. And they learned to shoot, straight and true, like the good soldiers they knew they would become. Becker especially enjoyed boxing, a sport he excelled in despite suffering a battered left ear, which he regarded as a badge of courage.

Now, as the sun was setting over the mountains, Becker finished his coffee, thinking about how long ago it all seemed. He thought about the heady days of 1940 when he and his fellow soldiers lounged in the sidewalk cafes of Paris, celebrating their first easy victories through the Netherlands, Belgium, and France. But those celebrations had dissipated rapidly two years later during the gruesome battles on the icy, barren steppes of Russia.

Russia!

Becker's memories of that grim wasteland were never far from the surface, and a chill came over him now as the visions returned: the thousands of mangled and frozen corpses, his comrades-in-arms lying forgotten in the snow and ice, the never-ending onslaught of poorly clad, poorly armed Russian soldiers slogging ever forward like so much cannon fodder. And the burning villages reeking with the stench of charred bodies, men, women, and children, young and old.

Fortunately, Becker had been wounded rather than killed during the Battle of Karkov and was transferred back to the western front in 1942 and posted to Belgium. His service in Russia, dangerous as it was, had been necessary to establish himself among the SS officer corps. A vital step in concealing the real mission he'd been trained to conduct.

He stood up and walked to the windows, thinking about the complex and highly secret mission, going over the details once again in his mind, as he had several times since his last meeting with Wagner. It was now very likely that the war may be lost. But Wagner and his colleagues could *not* get trapped in a defeated Germany. It was his responsibility to make certain that did not happen. Everything depended on it.

Becker turned toward the door, jolted from his thoughts by the sound of voices and boots clicking on hard marble floors. He stood at attention as the door opened and *Sturmbannfuhrer* Wilhelm Steiner entered the room.

Steiner closed the door behind him, stepped briefly across the room, and tossed his hat on the table. "Is there anything stronger than coffee?" he asked, motioning for Becker to be at ease.

"*Ja, naturich,*" Becker replied as he opened his briefcase and produced a flask of cognac.

"*Sehr gut,* that's the first sensible thing that's happened all day."

Becker poured a healthy dose of cognac into a coffee cup and handed it to his superior officer. He silently waited for Steiner to inform him of the purpose of his meeting with the Field Marshal and other high-level officers. The meeting had been called on very short notice by the *Fuhrer,* which was never a good thing.

Steiner took a long swig from the cup and ran a hand through his gray hair. Then he drained the cup and motioned for a re-fill. "Our illustrious *Fuhrer* apparently believes the war can still be won." He took another long drink and set the cup on the table. "He is ordering a new offensive. One that he is certain will strike a fatal blow at the Allies and win the war."

Becker flinched, not sure he'd heard correctly. "A new offensive? Now? With the Americans, British, and Russians at our doorstep?"

Steiner nodded glumly. "Von Rundstedt thinks it's foolhardy, of course, and Model agrees with him. But the *Fuhrer* cannot be dissuaded. He is convinced it will be the final decisive battle that will ensure our victory."

Becker stared at him. This was insane. "When would it happen?"

"Soon. Very soon. He is ordering twenty divisions to launch a strike through the Belgian Ardennes within a month."

"A strike through the Ardennes next month, in the middle of winter?"

"*Ja*. And it is to be organized and carried out in complete secrecy. It has no chance of success, of course, but there is nothing to be done."

Becker suddenly felt a cold chill. He wondered if Wagner knew anything about this. Possibly not if the offensive was being organized in such secrecy. And the heart of the Belgian Ardennes was St. Vith, the same location he'd chosen for the money and people to cross into Belgium. He had laid meticulous plans for this operation months ago, and they couldn't be changed now. This could ruin everything. He'd have to contact Lukas and—

Steiner interrupted his thoughts by tapping his empty cup on the table. His superior was clearly as shaken by this turn of events as he was. Becker refilled the cup, and Steiner drained it in one swig, then looked him in the eye. "You have done good work in Belgium, *Hauptsturmfuhrer.*"

"Danke, Herr Sturmbannfuhrer," Becker replied, worried about what was coming next.

"So, as a reward for your efforts, I have arranged for you to get back into the action."

Becker hesitated, then abruptly straightened up and stood at attention again. "That is... good news, *Herr Sturmbannfuhrer.* Where will I be going?"

"You have been assigned to the 1st Panzer Division, the very unit that will spear-head the offensive.

Chapter Thirty-Seven

Antwerp

When Claire returned to Lukas's apartment that evening, there was a letter in the mail slot addressed to her real name, Mariette Janssens. When she saw the return address—USAAF, RAF Hardwick, Suffolk, England—she ran up the stairs to the kitchen and tore open the envelope.

Dear Ms. Janssens,

We have received your letter addressed to Lieutenant Jack Richards. I regret to inform you that Lieutenant Richards is listed as Missing in Action following his last mission in September of 1943. I can assure you that all efforts have been and will continue to be made to account for all military personnel. But with the continuation of hostilities in Europe, I'm sure you can understand that the task will be difficult.

With sincere condolences,

Colonel Edward Marks

USAAF, 20th Combat Wing

RAF Hardwick

Suffolk, England

The letter slipped from Claire's hand as she stumbled backward and slumped into a chair.

No! It's a mistake... it can't be.

She reached down and tried to pick up the letter, but she was dizzy, her eyes blurry. Her stomach suddenly heaved, and she covered her mouth with her hands.

It can't be true... it can't—

Lukas suddenly appeared. "Claire, I heard you run up the stairs. Is anything wrong?"

His voice sounded like it was far away. She turned and looked at him, tried to focus, and then pointed to the letter lying on the floor, her hand trembling.

Lukas picked it off the floor and read it. When he finished, he sat down across from her. "Claire, I'm so—"

She abruptly pushed away from the table and rushed to the toilet at the end of the hallway. She hunched over the sink, her stomach heaving, tears streaming down her face. She dropped to her knees on the cold tile floor and buried her face in her hands.

After some time, she managed to stand, gripping the sink for support. She took a sip of water then wiped her eyes, turning away from the small mirror on the wall, unable to look at herself.

How could this happen?

He was safe... he was crossing the river, he...

Oh God, Jack... I am so sorry... I can't...

When she returned to the kitchen, Lukas was sitting at the table. He had made a cup of tea for her.

Still dizzy and nauseous, she sat down, then reached out and took her trusted friend's hand. "I don't understand... you told me he made it back!"

"Yes, that's what I heard. He made it back to England, so I don't—"

Claire waved him off, then stood up and stared out the kitchen window at the growing darkness. She wrapped her arms around her chest as all the memories flooded back in a torrent: the time she woke him from his nightmare, the laughter over Jim Hawkins and Sir Lancelot, the night they faced down the dogs, and the horrible day with the two drunken German soldiers they had to kill. And then... the night they finally made love in the safehouse before starting the long trek over the Pyrenees Mountains. Tears streamed down her face as she remembered their last embrace and the long, sensual kiss, over-looking the Bidasoa River. She let the tears flow and didn't bother to wipe them away.

Jack, I'm so sorry.

Finally, she took a deep breath to clear her mind and turned back to Lukas. "Tell me about Niels DeVos."

Lukas blinked, looking surprised. "What... Niels DeVos?"

"Yes, Niels DeVos, Bart's friend, the police captain. I know Bart introduced you to him last year."

Lucas cleared his throat. "Captain DeVos, yes, of course. Bart introduced us a few days after that fight in the park when my shop window was broken. He thought DeVos may be of some help to us. DeVos's family company was taken over by the Germans, and he was very bitter about it and wanted to help get back at them. That's what Bart said."

"And did he help?" Claire asked, "With the escape line, was he able to help?"

Lukas shrugged, "Yes, he did help a bit. He had some contacts and names of people who could provide safehouses. I know he arranged some of those, but I never knew all the details. Why do you ask? Bart instructed me not to tell you about DeVos, so I never did."

Claire sat down again and propped her elbows on the table, rubbing her forehead, not sure she had the energy to tell the whole story after the news about Jack. But she finally did; the document she discovered, the money from *I.G. Farben*. And every word darkened her mood, deepening her despair.

"And you haven't seen Bart since you discovered all this last week?" Lukas asked.

Claire shook her head. "No, and I think DeVos has something to do with that."

"DeVos? Why would you think—"

Getting impatient, she cut him off. "Something is *wrong*, Lukas. I know it; I can feel it. A man like Bart disappears for almost a week, and no one seems to give a damn!"

Lukas stared at her for a moment, then finally reached over and put his hand over hers. "Well, *I* give a damn. Now, where do we start?"

Chapter Thirty-Eight

Just after six o'clock the next evening, Claire met Lukas at Bart's apartment on the Schelde Kaai. Lukas rang the bell next to the nameplate, and when no one answered, he produced a key and opened the door to the vestibule. Earlier in the day, he had managed to track down Peeters' lady friend, who had a key to his apartment.

They climbed the stairs to the second floor, and Lukas opened the door. As they stepped inside, Claire held her breath, praying they wouldn't find him lying on the floor.

She wasn't feeling well, having barely slept all night, and when she did, she was tortured by an ominous dream of Jack walking into a forest and slowly disappearing into the darkness.

The apartment was clean and neat, furnished in the elegantly masculine style of a sophisticated man who lived alone. There was no sign of Bart. They checked through the papers stacked on his desk, found the key to his mailbox, and looked through his mail. They checked his closets and found them full of clothes, an empty suitcase stored on an upper shelf.

They returned to the parlor and sat in the chairs on either side of the coffee table. Claire leaned forward, elbows on her knees, and shook her head. "I just don't understand what could have happened to him?"

"Let's go over it one more time," Lukas said. "Bart told you that he asked some section manager in your department to gather up files on DeVos' company."

"Yes, Dora van Houtte," Claire replied. "She reported back to Bart that there was nothing in the files."

"And Bart thought that was strange?"

"Yes, very strange... something is wrong."

Lukas was silent for a moment as though thinking about something. "Have you considered that Bart's disappearance might not be related to DeVos at all? That it could be something entirely different, you know, with all the retributions going on, collaborators trying to shut people up, that sort of thing. Have you gone to the police and reported Bart's disappearance?"

Claire flinched. "The police? No, of course not. I think Captain DeVos might be involved in this, and I certainly don't want him to know *my* name."

Lukas nodded, "Well, how about this? DeVos knows me and my connection with Bart. And, as I said, he did help us with the escape line. I could go to him and tell him I've been looking for Bart and that I'm concerned. I could just ask if he's heard anything and see how he responds."

Claire rubbed her temples, thinking. The coincidence of Bart's disappearance right after her discovery of the transfer of funds to DeVos' company seemed very suspicious. But perhaps Lukas was right. Maybe it *is* something different. "Would you know if he was telling the truth?" she asked.

"Yes, I think I would."

Chapter Thirty-Nine

Stalag Luft POW Camp

On the morning of Jack's sixty-second day in the cooler, he was let out. With no explanation, a guard suddenly appeared, motioned for him to get up, and led him across the camp to the barracks area. The guard was tall and thick-chested, with short hair cropped in a crew cut. The name tag on his uniform identified him as Bucher.

Groggy from lack of sleep and walking unsteadily, Jack plodded along, following Bucher, vaguely aware of dozens of inmates staring at him. Bucher turned to him and smiled, gesturing to the inmates with his thumb. He said in heavily accented English, "They all ask about you. Now they see you, a famous person who survives sixty days in the cooler."

Jack glanced at him and grunted hoarsely, "Don't need famous, just a real bed."

They arrived at one of the barracks, and Bucher pulled the door open, motioning for Jack to enter. "Sleep good," he said, "hope days in cooler over."

Jack nodded. "Thanks, I hope so too."

Several inmates were present inside the wooden barracks building, a few sitting at a round table, others lounging on the bunks. One by one, they came over and introduced themselves, all fellow American or British airmen. Since Jack had seen nothing since his arrival except the interrogation room and the cooler, he asked a lot of questions and was astounded to learn of the size of the camp.

Stalag Luft was a massive, sixty-acre facility consisting of dozens of single-story barracks, each with triple-tier sleeping bunks. The camp—run by the Luftwaffe for captured allied airmen—included a substantial library, a theater where prisoners put on weekly shows, and a well-organized recreational program for the inmates, including a basketball league between the fifteen different barracks. It was certainly a far cry from the squalid POW camps run by the SS, and none of the men were complaining except about the food and that they wanted to get home.

It took Jack some time to regain his strength and mental clarity after all the long months in the Spanish jail and the cooler. But eventually, he felt fit again and was able to join in the basketball games. He had apparently earned some notoriety with his extended stay in the cooler. And, as his ball-handling and leadership skills on the court returned, he caught the attention of his barracks captain, a brash, broad-shouldered New Yorker named Ned Barrows, a P-51 fighter pilot and former basketball player himself.

Late one afternoon, after the basketball game ended, Jack picked up the ball and started back to the barracks. Ned Barrows shouted at him in his grating, New York accent. "Hey, Boxcar driver, come on over here; I want you to meet some guys."

It was typical of Barrows' style, the flashy P-51 Ace joking about bomber pilots, especially those who flew B-24s, which resembled flying boxcars. He turned around, walked up to Barrows, and abruptly flicked the ball to him from three feet away.

"Asshole," Barrows grumbled as the ball bounced off his chest.

"If you could hang on to those passes, we'd win more games," Jack retorted.

The two other aviators whom Jack had seen around but never met stood on either side of Barrows and burst out laughing.

"Yeah, I know, he's a smart ass," Barrows said.

"So, you're the guy they kept in the cooler for two months," one of the aviators said, extending his hand. "I'm Arnie Thompson. What the hell did you do to deserve that?"

Jack shook the slim, blond-haired man's hand and replied, "Jack Richards, and I have no fucking idea."

They all laughed again, and Barrows introduced the third aviator, Bill Simmons, a short, stocky guy with an iron handshake. "Ok, let's take a walk," Barrows said.

They walked slowly around one of the barracks, identified with a large letter 'C,' that faced the basketball court until they reached the back side of the building, which was situated about fifty meters from the fence line. Beyond the fence was another ten or fifteen meters of open space fronting a thick stand of pine trees.

Barrows stopped and lit a cigarette. Looking directly at Jack, he said, "Do you understand what's expected of officers detained in an enemy POW camp."

Jack nodded. "Escape and Evade."

"Well, what I'm about to tell you is the escape part, and this is the spot. We're going to dig a tunnel from inside this barracks building and extend it all the way under the fence line. A couple of teams have already loosened the floorboards under one of the bunks and started the excavation."

It was obvious to Jack by the way Thompson and Simmons didn't react that they were already part of the escape plan and had probably concurred with Barrow's decision to bring him in. He also knew that while the Luftwaffe guards often looked the other way over minor infractions, the one concrete, unbreakable rule was that escape was absolutely forbidden and never tolerated. "Has this been tried before?" he asked.

Barrows flicked his head. "We should keep moving, but the answer is yes, it's been tried before, and no, it didn't succeed... either time."

Jack wondered who had tried and what happened to them but decided he didn't really want to know. "What do you want me to do?" he asked instead.

Barrows glanced at Thompson and nodded.

"We want you to do two things," Thompson said. "One is to join Simmons and me on our excavation team. We'll work at night, a three-hour shift three times a week. I'm the team leader."

Jack thought about that for a moment, wondering about digging a tunnel that far. "How do you do it?" he asked Barrows. "I mean, don't you need supplies like shovels, lights, stuff like that? And how do you get all the dirt out of the tunnel?"

Barrows clapped him on the shoulder, "Ha, a technical guy. I thought so." He glanced around quickly, then lowered his voice. "Some of the stuff we steal, some we jerry-rig together from what we find around the camp, but a lot of it arrives from the Brits, the MI9 guys. They pack it in boxes supposedly from the Red Cross with clothes, snacks, and stuff. They're quite ingenious, but don't tell any of the Brits here I said that."

Jack wasn't surprised that MI9 was involved, remembering all his briefings. He felt certain they had helped the Resistance and the escape lines as well, though Claire had never mentioned it. He glanced at both men and nodded. "Okay, you said there were two things. What's the other one?"

Barrows responded. "Play basketball, of course. We selected C barracks because it overlooks the court. We'll have excavation crews working during the day, coinciding with every basketball game. Each game will have one designated spotter standing on the sidelines as a sub. It's his job to keep an eye out for the guards. If the spotter notices anything strange, he goes into C barracks and stops the dig. As of right now, it's your job to designate the spotter in every game."

Jack nodded again. "Ok, got it. When do I start?"

"The new basketball schedule goes out tonight," Barrows said. "Games are scheduled every day at 0900, 1100 and 1300. Cheering and arguing are important; it cover up any noise from inside the barracks. Thompson will give you the schedule for your evening digs."

They walked on in silence for another few minutes before Simmons finally spoke up. "Hey, we all got our asses shot out of the sky and survived, so this should be a piece of cake."

None of the others responded.

Chapter Forty

Antwerp

It was just a little past four-thirty in the afternoon, but it was already dark outside as Lukas sat at the desk in his dusty, cluttered shop, wondering what he would say to Claire. He'd told her he would question DeVos about Bart's disappearance, but the truth was he didn't trust DeVos.

Lukas had always felt uneasy about DeVos, though he was never completely sure why. DeVos *had* arranged some phony safehouses and set traps for Allied aviators, but it was nothing more than Lukas had done before on his own. Perhaps it was the duplicity of DeVos' role as a Belgian police officer, but then again, Lukas knew that wasn't any worse than the duplicity of his *own* life. In the end, he decided just to tell Claire that DeVos didn't know anything about Bart's whereabouts and try to protect her as best he could.

Lukas pushed his chair away from the desk and was about to close up for the day when the door opened, and a man stepped into the shop. He was short and thin, wearing a dark woolen coat and a felt hat. Lukas didn't recognize him but stood up and said, "*Goedemiddag,* can I help you?"

The man approached the desk, glanced around the shop, and said in German-accented Flemish, "I have a message from Becker." When Lukas didn't respond, the man said, "He wanted to know if you enjoyed the eggs."

Lukas remained silent a moment, then slowly nodded. He had, of course, never told anyone about Becker giving him some eggs, and he'd almost forgotten about it himself. Becker had retreated to Germany with the rest of the German army when Belgium was liberated last September. The comment about the eggs was obviously a code so Lukas would know that whatever message the man delivered actually came from Becker. "What is the message?" he asked.

"Becker will meet you at the Hotel Zur Post in St. Vith at Midnight tomorrow."

Chapter Forty-One

Frankfurt, Germany

It was just past eight o'clock in the evening as Becker sat behind the wheel of the SS staff car and glanced up at the stone turrets that stood like sentries at either end of Gerhard Wagner's palatial estate. He wondered if he'd ever set foot in the mansion again. He rather doubted it.

A light still showed from the highest window in the western turret where his father-in-law kept his office. Becker knew Wagner was probably still on the telephone making whatever last-minute calls to whichever of his most trusted confidants within the Reich might be able to tell him this foolish notion of a last-ditch offensive had been called off.

The light went off, and the turret turned dark, a stark silhouette against the moonless night. Several moments later, Wagner emerged from a side entrance of the mansion wearing a black overcoat and carrying a briefcase. He slid into the passenger seat and silently flicked his hand forward. Becker put the car in gear and drove down the long, winding driveway.

They drove in silence for almost a quarter of an hour through the suburbs of Frankfurt. Just after they turned onto the autobahn heading west toward the Belgian border, Wagner finally spoke. *"Du hattest*

Recht, you were correct," he said, "the *Fuhrer,* in his ultimate stupidity, has sealed our fate, and any chance of a negotiated peace is over."

Becker glanced at him. "Was there ever a real chance of that?

Wagner grunted. "Short of assassination, probably not." He was quiet for a moment, then asked, "How has this affected your plans? Can you still get everyone out?"

Becker's jaw tightened, but he controlled his annoyance at being asked the same questions he'd already answered several times since advising Wagner of the planned offensive. "It has affected everything, but it will be worked out once we meet Lukas in St Vith tonight."

"He doesn't know about this yet?"

Becker glanced at his father-in-law. "*Nein,* he doesn't know anything yet. All I could do was get a message to him to meet me in St. Vith at midnight tonight. To communicate anything further would be too much of a risk."

"Has the *Viscount* been advised of—"

"Yes, of course." Becker cut him off, something he rarely did with Wagner, but his father-in-law's obsession with the importance of his long-time, aristocratic friend was more than annoying and could eventually become a liability. He'd always believed the *Viscount's* loyalty to the German Reich was no stronger than a thin reed blowing in the wind. He had been useful during the occupation of Belgium and in preparing for this mission. But beyond that? It was one more thing he would have to deal with.

They continued on mostly in silence, driving through the dark German countryside, Becker's mind churning through these latest complications. Not only did the coming offensive force him to accelerate the escape plans for Wagner and the others, but now, thanks to the orders he received from Steiner, he would be thrust directly into the battle himself.

He hadn't mentioned that last complication to Wagner, knowing it would do little good at this point. His father-in-law had many connections within the Reich, but when it came to interfering with the hierarchy of the SS in wartime, that was strictly off-limits. Not even Wagner could touch that without the top brass of the SS wanting to know why. He had managed to keep the entire operation secret, including everyone from the *Fuhrer* on down, and that's the way it would stay.

Becker stared at the dark road ahead and reflected on the enormity of the secret they had been keeping, especially considering the status of the individuals involved. They included other executives of *I.G.* as well as top executives and scientists from some of Germany's most powerful corporations. It came as no surprise to Becker that Wagner's list did not include his own daughter, Becker's wife, Ursula. It would, of course, add to the risk and complicate things, but he also knew Wagner well enough to know where his priorities were. Fortunately, he had anticipated this many months ago and made separate arrangements for Ursula. She also understood her father's priorities.

Becker took a breath to clear his head and focus on the route out of Germany. Checkpoints had already been set up at the intersections of all the major highways in anticipation of the stream of armor and infantry that would be moving into position over the next few weeks. But the SS flags on his staff car should get them through.

A little over three hours later, they descended from the snow-covered hills of the Eifel region in Germany and approached Belgium's densely forested Ardennes region. Becker had chosen this area carefully, knowing that it was the least guarded by the Allies of anywhere along the German border, perhaps the only part of the *Fuhrer's* insane notion that made any sense.

A little less than a kilometer before the Belgian border, Becker pulled off the main road onto a narrow country lane he had discovered two years ago while Germany still occupied Belgium. It was narrow and rutted, isolated from any of the towns, winding through stands of forest, farm fields, and meadows. Further on, Becker pulled into a farmyard and stopped in front of a dilapidated barn that stood just behind an equally dilapidated brick farmhouse.

Wagner looked at him skeptically as Becker turned off the headlights.

"It's deserted," Becker said confidently. "No one has lived here in over a decade, and my contact in St. Vith purchased the property shortly after I discovered it."

Wagner grunted but didn't comment.

Becker got out of the car, walked up to the barn, unlocked the padlock of the stout wooden door, and slid it open. Inside the barn stood a ten-year-old French-built Renault equipped with Belgian license plates. He fired up the engine and backed the Renault out of the barn. Wagner got out of the SS staff car, and Becker drove it into the barn. He removed Wagner's two suitcases, which he'd packed into the trunk earlier in the day, and re-locked the barn door.

When he returned to the Renault, Wagner was already sitting in the passenger seat. Becker put the suitcases in the trunk and got behind the wheel.

Wagner turned to him and nodded. "Seems as though you thought of everything," he said. "I hope your man got the message."

Becker shrugged. It was as much of a compliment as he would ever get from Wagner, but he'd gotten used to that. "He'll be there," he said as he backed the Renault out of the driveway and turned toward St. Vith.

The streets of St. Vith were dark and deserted as they entered the city from the southeast a few minutes before midnight. Becker stopped the Renault in front of the Hotel Zur Post, a solid, non-descript three-story building on Hauptstrasse. Becker retrieved Wagner's bags from the trunk, and they stepped quickly into the hotel.

As they approached the front desk, Becker was relieved to see Frau Brunkhorst waiting for them. She was a sturdy, serious-looking woman in her mid-thirties, who had been his contact in St. Vith since he first arrived in Belgium. He set the suitcases on the floor and extended his hand. "Frau Brunkhorst, I'm pleased to see you again. Thank you for accommodating us at this late hour."

She smiled thinly. "It is my pleasure, *Hauptsturmfuhrer*, as always." She shook his hand with only the slightest glance at Wagner. "If you will follow me, your associate is expecting you."

Becker and Wagner followed Frau Brunkhorst into the dining room, where Lukas sat at a table sipping a cup of coffee. He stood up the moment they entered and nodded at Becker. "*Guten Abend, Hauptsturmfuhrer.* I hope you had a pleasant journey."

Becker glanced at Frau Brunkhorst, who immediately left the room and then turned back to Lukas. "There are certain events taking place that require our plans to be executed more quickly than we had planned, starting tonight. Will that present any problems?"

Lukas shook his head. "*Nein, Hauptsturmfuhrer,* I will have to change some things, but it can be done."

"*Sehr gut,* I knew I could count on you." He gestured toward Wagner but did not introduce him. "You will escort this gentleman to the *Viscount's* estate immediately and explain the change in our plans to our mutual friend. I'm sure he will understand that I cannot contact him directly under the circumstances."

Lukas nodded but remained silent.

Becker continued, "There will be four additional arrivals every other day beginning the day after tomorrow. Eleven men in all, traveling two or three at a time. Each rendezvous will take place at this same time at this same location. Is that understood?"

"*Ja,* I understand."

"Then I must go. I trust you will execute this assignment with the same efficiency you have shown in the past. Tell the *Viscount* I look forward to seeing him soon."

Becker turned abruptly to Wagner, detecting a slight look of concern in his father-in-law's face, which actually pleased him. He extended his hand and said, "Have a safe journey. I will see you soon." Wagner's hand felt cold, which also pleased him.

Chapter Forty-Two

Antwerp

Niels DeVos was in his office at the Antwerp central police station when his secretary buzzed him and said that he had a telephone call.

"Who is it?" DeVos asked.

"She said her name is Dora van Houtte, from the Department of the Interior."

DeVos hesitated for a moment. It was very unusual for van Houtte to call him at the office, and he wondered if it might have something to do with Peeters missing from work. Van Houtte was a valuable contact within the department, but he hadn't confided in her about Peeters' disappearance. "Yes, please put her through," he said finally.

Thirty minutes later, DeVos, wearing a plain dark trench coat over his uniform, met van Houtte in front of the cathedral. They walked slowly along one of the narrow, cobblestone streets leading toward the river.

"I have some information I thought you should know," van Houtte said as they walked.

DeVos nodded but didn't respond.

"It has to do with a young woman whom Councilman Peeters hired a few weeks ago for the

Relocation Department. She is apparently very concerned about his absence and has come up to his office several times looking for him, even suggesting calling hospitals to see if he'd been injured. It's highly unusual behavior for someone in her position."

"You said she works in the Relocation Department?"

Van Houtte nodded, "Yes, most of the time. But I also had her help with filing for the Financial Department from time to time."

DeVos thought about that for a moment. "What is her name?"

"Her name is Mariette Janssens, but I've heard the councilman call her 'Claire.' I believe she is a family friend of the Councilman's."

"Did you bring her personnel file with you?"

Van Houtte opened her bag and retrieved a thin file folder.

DeVos stepped over to the side of a building and glanced at the file, which included a picture of a petite young woman with short dark hair. His eyes widened when he noticed the home address she had listed. It was the same as Lukas.' He handed the folder back to van Houtte and said, "Thank you for notifying me. I'll take care of it."

Van Houtte put the folder back in her bag and turned to leave when DeVos stopped her. "By the way," he said, "regarding those files I asked you to remove. I assume you gave me everything there was about

Produits Agricole. No other documents would have been filed some other place, like any documents about the transfer of funds?"

The woman shook her head. "No, I checked the files in each department. I gave you everything."

DeVos nodded, "Very well, thank you."

Chapter Forty-Three

Stalag Luft POW Camp

The tunnel was deep and narrow, almost fifteen feet below the surface but only about three feet square. And it was dark, save for the few sections that had been widened where electric lines had been jury-rigged and bare bulbs hung from makeshift supports.

Jack inched his way backward through the tunnel, dragging thin canvas sacks filled with sand. When he reached one of the 'staging areas' where the excavation widened, he was able to conceal each of the bags underneath the pant legs of his baggy trousers, then turn around and crawl forward the rest of the way back to the barracks.

When he arrived at the starting point, he climbed the ladder slowly, weighed down by all the sand, and knocked sharply on the trap door. Simmons pulled open the door and held out his hand, helping him into the barracks. Jack stood up for the first time in an hour and a half and stretched his back and neck to get the kinks out. He blinked a few times, then held the trap door open while Simmons descended into the darkness for his turn hauling sand.

The trap door had been ingeniously concealed in the furthest corner of the barracks, away from the door, and shielded from view by the positioning of the bunks. Several other inmates were lounging in their bunks or sitting at a table near the door playing cards, a neat obstacle for any guard who might happen to poke his head through the door.

As Jack shuffled across the wooden floor toward the door, one of the card players, a hustler from New Orleans everyone called 'Slick,' whistled sharply, a signal to the lookout on the other side. As Jack waited for the lookout's response, he grabbed one of the greatcoats they used to cover up the bulging trousers. While he was putting it on, he glanced at the hand of cards Slick held and laughed. "Hope you're not betting the farm on that mess."

Slick flinched, looked up at him, and then slapped his cards on the table. "Thanks a lot, asshole," he snarled as the rest of the group broke out laughing.

"You're welcome," Jack said, "I just saved you a lot of money."

The lookout rapped twice, indicating it was all clear, and Slick flicked his thumb toward the door. "Hurry back, boxcar driver. Can't wait to deal you in after your shift."

"Sure enough, but save your money; you're going to need it," Jack retorted, then stepped outside, reveling in the cold, clear air after an hour and a half lying on his stomach in the dusty, stifling hot tunnel. He had no intention of getting into a card game with Slick, but he enjoyed needling him.

"Head around to the back of D Barracks," the lookout said, "there's still some cover in the garden area. It'll be good for another two or three loads.

Jack nodded and shuffled off, trying to walk as naturally as possible in case any of the guards happened to come by. It had snowed during the afternoon, and the white ground limited the choices of areas where they could spread the light, brown sand. Hence, the garden area where the weeds, wilted corn stalks, and tomato plants provided some cover.

Jack reached the garden and carefully loosened the strings that sealed the bottom of the bag along his right leg. He moved quickly, allowing the sand to trickle out evenly in a fine, thin spread, a technique that he had learned after many trials and errors.

He switched to the left leg, and when both bags were emptied, he walked back over the same area, grinding the sand into the soil with his boots. Then he headed back to the barracks for a cigarette and some rest before starting his second hour-and-a-half shift.

On the way, he pondered the incredibly massive and complex escape project he was now a part of. More than two hundred of the inmates were secretly involved, divided into work groups for tunneling, carpentry, ventilation, and electrical work. Other specialists worked on forging identification papers, drawing maps, and teaching lessons in rudimentary German for use by those who made it out.

It was a marvel of engineering and ingenuity, many of the plans having been provided by MI9, smuggled in through the Red Cross packages. Jack wondered how many other escape attempts, in other POW camps, in other wars, the agents of MI9 had been involved in... and how many of those had been successful. Using wooden slats from inmates' beds to shore up the tunnels was part of the instructions from MI9, as were the plans for a manual air pump fashioned from specific odds and ends that could be found throughout the camp and ventilation ducts constructed from old milk cans. If he survived the war, Jack thought that one day he might like to meet an MI9 agent and shake his hand.

As Jack approached the barracks, he noticed Ned Barrows standing alone near the door, apparently waiting for him. During his time in the camp, Jack had come to appreciate that Barrows was a lot more than just another cocky fighter pilot. He was the inspiration behind the entire escape project and had the natural leadership skills to keep it all on track in complete secrecy.

"Let's go have a cigarette," Barrows said when Jack walked up. He pulled out a pack of Lucky Strikes, lit it both cigarettes and motioned for Jack to follow him to a picnic table just off the main path. "How's it going? Pretty shitty work, isn't it?" he asked.

Jack shrugged, "No problem. It's gotta get done."

"How's Simmons doing?"

Jack looked at him for a moment, the question catching him off guard. "Uh, he's fine. Works like hell. Why do you ask?"

"That's good to hear. I put you on that team for a reason. Simmons is a good guy, but he can be a bit squirrely at times. I wanted you to be there with him when your team got started, just to make sure everything went smoothly."

"Well, it's really Thompson's team, you know, and—"

"Yeah, yeah, I know, and Thompson said things are fine. But you're a solid guy, and I just wanted your opinion."

They both sat in silence for a moment, and Jack glanced at Barrows out of the corner of his eye, wondering what was really on his mind. "It's a big project," he said to break the silence, "how do you keep it all together?"

Barrows snorted and stifled a laugh. "Christ, that's a hell of a question. The answer is, I have no fucking idea."

"Well, you're doing something right; the guys all seem pretty motivated."

Barrows was quiet for another moment, then said, "All I want to do is get the hell out of here alive and get back to my family."

That was the first time Jack had heard anything from Barrows other than his New York bravado, bragging about the Brooklyn Dodgers and arguing about fouls on the basketball court, "How many kids do you have?" he asked.

Barrows raised two fingers. "Boy and girl, six and four. Haven't seen either of 'em in two fucking years. It stinks. I don't have any idea how my wife holds it together." He took a long drag on the cigarette and glanced at Jack. "How about you, married, kids?"

Jack shook his head. "Nope, neither one."

"There must be a girl back home, though, a good-lookin' guy like you, sports jock and all."

Jack fell silent, his heart aching, thinking about Claire.

"So, is that a yes?" Barrows persisted. "What's her name, let me guess, some nice simple Wisconsin name like 'Betty' or 'Jean?'"

Jack shook his head and sighed, knowing Barrows wouldn't let him off the hook. "Her name is Claire," Jack said, surprising himself at how easily that rolled out... *his 'girl,' Claire.* "And she's not from Wisconsin; she lives in Belgium."

Barrows straightened up. "Really, she's Belgian? How the hell did you meet her? She saved your life when you were shot down?"

Jack nodded. "That's exactly right."

"And then you fell in love? Christ, that's like a fuckin' fairy tale, man."

Jack glared at him, and Barrows quickly raised both hands. "Hey, sorry, I was just kiddin' around. She must really be something special."

Jack nodded, "She is very special."

"So, when we get out of here, that's where you're going, back to Belgium?"

As many times as he'd thought about Claire, as many times as he'd wanted nothing more than to be together with her, he could never bring himself to believe that it could actually happen. Belgium had been occupied when he escaped, and they had killed two German soldiers. He'd been betrayed. Had she also been betrayed? Or is it possible she survived? Would she still be there when he got back?

Barrows broke into his thoughts, "So, was she with one of those escape lines I've heard about?"

Jack nodded. He knew he'd never be able to tell the whole story, so he just said, "Yeah, like I said, she saved my life."

"So, how'd you get caught? How'd you end up here?"

"I was arrested by the *Guardia Civil* in Spain. Someone betrayed me. There were a lot of Nazi collaborators in Belgium; it was a dangerous place."

They both lapsed into silence for several minutes. Finally, Barrows stood, slapped him on the back, and said, "It's good to have someone to talk to, Jack."

Chapter Forty-Four

Antwerp

Two days after he met with Dora van Houtte, Niels DeVos left his office at eleven o'clock, wearing a gray hat that matched his trench coat and carrying a briefcase. He walked to the Grote Markt, hoping to find a table in one of the cafes with a view of the city hall. It was cold and windy, with snow flurries in the air, and when he arrived at the market square, he found the entire area teeming with a raucous, jeering crowd, shaking their fists and shouting obscenities.

DeVos stood off to the side and watched as the crowd slowly parted, allowing a horse-drawn cart to pass through. Six women stood in the cart, their hands bound behind them, their heads shaved, bright red swastikas painted on their foreheads. A group of boys broke through the crowd and pelted the women with rocks, drawing cheers and shouts of *"Filthy Collaborators! Nazi Whores!*

Right then, DeVos was very glad he wasn't in uniform, or he'd feel compelled to do something. He wasn't sure what that would be since most police officers in Belgium were anti-Nazi patriots and would most likely believe those who collaborated with the enemy deserved what they got.

So, he watched in silence as the horses plodded on, pulling the cart slowly across the square, followed by the boisterous, rock-throwing crowd until it entered a narrow side street and disappeared from his view. That street led to the wide avenue fronting the River Schelde, where DeVos guessed another angry crowd probably waited for the condemned women who may or may not survive the trip to prison.

When the mob finally dispersed, DeVos found a table at the *Café Den Engel* and ordered a beer to settle his nerves. He'd seen this before, many times, since Belgium's liberation, and it always rattled him. The retribution inflicted on women accused of collaboration with the Nazis was cruel, even gruesome, but DeVos knew it was far worse for men, many of whom were just tied to a post and shot in the street before they could be arrested. There were deceitful people out there, and he knew it was only a matter of time before someone might point a finger at him. And Bart Peeters was just the one who could do it. Fortunately, he was no longer a problem... but there could be others.

What had continued to trouble DeVos was the question of who had alerted Peeters about the transfer of funds from *I.G. Farben.* The fact that some unknown person was out there who knew about it had kept him on edge, fearing the one thing that could ruin the entire mission.

But now, since his meeting with van Houtte, that problem has also been solved. Van Houtte had removed all the department's files on *Produits Agricole* and given them to him. But one file was missing, the document of the transfer of funds from *I.G. Farben.* The only way Peeters would have known about that was if someone had seen the document and brought it to him directly. And now he knew who it was. He knew her name, and he knew where she lived and worked.

But that raised another question in his mind. According to Van Houtte, the girl is a family friend of Peeters'. And she's living with *Lukas.* What the hell did that mean? Had she been an operative in the escape organization? Was she involved with Lukas? Were they lovers?

His beer arrived, and DeVos took a sip, thinking through the situation. Claire is a family friend of Peeters,' the one who alerted him to the funds transfer, and she's living with Lukas. Is Lukas playing both sides or just trying to protect his girlfriend? Either way, he had to dispense with the girl... but Lukas could also be a problem.

The Grote Markt was quieter now, and no one inside the café seemed to pay any attention to him. He cleaned his gold-rimmed glasses with a napkin, retrieved a newspaper from his briefcase and thought about ordering a bite to eat while he waited. Through the large front window, he had a clear view of the entrance to the City Hall and the offices of the Department of the Interior. And he'd seen Claire's picture, so he knew who to look for.

***

At half-past noon that same day, Claire sat in a café looking out at the fog that hung over the River Schelde, a dreary scene that matched her mood. She took a bite of the cheese sandwich she'd ordered—the only food available at the Riverside Café that day—though she wasn't very hungry. She took another bite and then dropped the half-eaten sandwich back onto the plate, wondering what to do. Bart would not have just left without saying a word; that wasn't possible. Something had happened to him, and she felt helpless.

With no plan in mind, she left the café and hurried along the busy street fronting the river, which, despite the cold, snowy weather, was teeming with pedestrians. She stopped abruptly and stood off to the side, suddenly realizing these weren't just pedestrians. It was an enraged mob tormenting a group of six women with shaved heads being towed through the streets in a horse-drawn wagon.

Claire was shoved back against the side of a building by the incensed crowd as the wagon passed by, and she gasped out loud when she recognized one of the women in the wagon. Her name was Lydia, and she lived in a small village not far from Grote Brogel. She was about ten years older than Claire and was left with two young children after her husband was killed in the early days of the war. With no means to care for their small farm, the woman had taken up with a German soldier who had been kind to her and helped maintain the farm to keep her children from starving.

Claire wrapped her arms around her chest as tears trickled down her cheek, thinking of what might now happen to Lydia's children. She had witnessed this same scene many times since the liberation, and it always sickened her. She detested the collaborators who sided with the Nazis during the war, and none more so than whoever betrayed Jack. But she also knew that many of these women—like Lydia—were guilty of nothing more than what she had done because they were desperate, their husbands dead or missing with children to feed.

The horse cart and the angry mob eventually moved on down the street toward the Steen Castle where she and Jack had waited after contacting the bartender at the Café Brig. She tried not to think about what might happen to these women whose lives had been torn apart by the war and were now being condemned by their former friends and neighbors. More than anything else, Claire just wanted the entire gruesome experience to end and have life return to normal. But she knew that was naïve. It would take years for the wounds to heal.

The Cathedral bells chimed, deep melodic tones resonating off the stone buildings of the Old City, jarring Claire back to the moment, and she glanced at her watch. It was one o'clock. She sighed and took one last glance down the street as the frenzied mob continued to terrorize the imprisoned women. Then she left the river, walked back to the Grote Markt, and entered the City Hall. She had no idea that Niels DeVos was watching her.

Chapter Forty-Five

It was just after six o'clock on Friday evening as Peeters sat on the bed waiting for his evening meal when he heard footsteps outside the door of his small, windowless room. The door opened, and instead of the stocky policeman who had silently delivered food every day for the past week, DeVos stepped into the room. He left the door open, and Peeters could see the policeman standing in the hallway. DeVos glanced around the room then his eyes settled on Peeters. "It's time to go," he said.

Peeters stood up slowly. "Where are..." his throat tightened, and he coughed. It had been a long time since he'd spoken to anyone. "Where are we going?" he asked hoarsely.

DeVos turned and stepped out of the room. "You'll find out soon enough."

It was dark and cold, with a biting, icy snow in the wind. An auto was parked next to the building, and the driver opened the rear door, motioning for Peeters to get in. DeVos got into the passenger seat in the front, and as they drove off, DeVos turned around and said, "It's time to deliver your first message. Just follow my instructions, and everything will be fine."

Peeters turned away and glanced out the window. They drove through narrow, cobblestone streets in an area that he recognized. They were just south of the Groenplaats. Then they turned onto the wide avenue fronting the river, heading north toward the port. A few minutes later, they turned again and stopped in front of the Café Brig.

DeVos turned around again. "Well, Councilman, I'm sure you recognize this place."

Peeters did not respond, wondering how DeVos knew about the place that had been a secret rendezvous location for the Resistance.

DeVos continued, "When you go in, you will see a man sitting at the bar, wearing a tweed coat and a black beret. Take a seat next to him, then give the bartender your usual code. Our people have been watching you for a long time, so don't make any mistakes."

"Go to hell," Peeters said as he turned to open the door.

"There is one more thing you should know," DeVos said.

Peeters stopped and looked back at him. "What is it?" He noticed that the driver had turned just enough so the pistol he was carrying in a shoulder holster was clearly visible.

"I saw your friend, Claire, earlier today," DeVos relied smugly.

Peeters went rigid.

"We know all about her," DeVos continued, "we know that she was the one who alerted you about the transfer of funds from—"

Peeters lunged forward and drove his fist into DeVos' face, knocking his glasses off.

In an instant, the driver drew the gun and pointed it at Peeters' head.

"Don't!" DeVos barked, grabbing the big man's wrist as blood dripped from his nose. He glared at Peeters. "I hope that made you feel better," he said slowly, with an unmistakable tone of menace in his voice. "But if you do not do exactly as I order from this point forward, we will kill her. We are watching her, and we *will* kill her. Now get the hell out of the car!"

There were only a handful of people sitting at the bar when Peeters walked in. He stood in the doorway for a moment and took a deep breath. No one paid any attention to him except the bartender, who made brief eye contact and then looked back down at the glass he was wiping off. The thin, curly-haired man had been a long-time operative of the escape organization, but Peeters knew him only as 'the bartender.'

Peeters spotted the man with the tweed coat and black beret sitting at the far end of the bar and walked toward him slowly, taking time to collect his thoughts before taking the stool next to him. The man was middle-aged, with a thick neck broad shoulders and a broken nose, as though he might have been a boxer in earlier years.

When the bartender stepped over, Peeters spoke up quickly, *"Een Trappist ale, from Liege,"* he said, surprised that he could get it out.

As expected, the bartender replied that he did not have that brand, and Peeters ordered a *Leffe,* which was on tap. The bartender poured a glass and set it in front of him. A moment later, he slipped into the back room.

Peeters sipped the beer slowly, hoping he'd be able to keep it down. He stared straight ahead, clenching his jaw as DeVos' words burned in his mind.

We are watching her, and we will kill her.

The man in the tweed coat made some mundane comment about the weather. Peeters answered with a grunt but did not look at him, fearing if he did, he would be tempted to smash the glass on the bar and cut the man's throat.

He took another sip of beer, thinking about the rest of what DeVos had said or at least started to say. DeVos obviously knew that Claire was the one who found the document about *I. G. Farben.* But how did he know that? Someone in the department must have told him. And that meant there was a traitor in the department, *his* department. But who?

Peeters had let his guard down after the liberation; he could see that now. The Germans were gone, but the country was still in turmoil. Civil law enforcement was in a state of flux and unreliable, and over-zealous patriots were hunting down collaborators and taking revenge into their own hands. It was a dangerous time... and it could cost him his life.

But not Claire!

I will not let that happen!

The man in the tweed coat said something again, and Peeters abruptly blinked and looked around. He had been so buried in his thoughts that he hadn't noticed the bartender standing in front of them.

"Do you want another beer?" the bartender asked.

Peeters glanced at his glass and realized it was almost empty. "Just the check, please." He picked up the glass, drained the last of it and paid by dropping a few coins on the bar, then stood up to leave, taking the check off the bar and slipping it into his pocket.

Outside, he stood for a moment, breathing in the cold night air and stared at the dark water in the harbor across the street. He'd probably be as good as dead if he tried to run, and that was a chance he might have been willing to take. But he couldn't take the same gamble with Claire's life. Even if it meant that he would have to commit treason, he would never risk her life.

He removed the check from his pocket and read the message the bartender had scribbled on the back.

Sunday, 1600.

Then he walked down the street toward the parked car where DeVos was waiting.

Chapter Forty-Six

On Sunday morning Claire sat at the kitchen table sipping a cup of bitter coffee, trying unsuccessfully to pull herself out of the despair she felt closing in. Jack had been betrayed and was probably imprisoned, if not worse. Bart had disappeared, and she had no idea what to do about it or where to go for help. The frustration was building to the point where she was about to scream and throw the coffee cup against the wall when it suddenly hit her.

The Café Brig!

"Of course," she blurted out loud, scarcely able to believe she hadn't thought about it until now.

"Of course, what?" Lukas said.

Claire blinked and looked up at him, not realizing he'd come into the kitchen.

"The Café Brig," she said. "The place Jack and I went before we came to your house that night. It was the bartender who contacted Bart. He might know how to help us now. He might know how to find Bart."

Lukas sat across from her and stared at the table for a moment as though he was collecting his thoughts. He'd been out of town the last several days, apparently helping a friend rebuild some farm machinery, and he looked tired. "Well, that was over a

year ago," he said, stifling a yawn. "Do you still think—
"

"It's worth a try," Claire said, interrupting him. "We don't have any other leads, do we?"

Lukas shrugged, then pushed his chair back and stood. "Okay, let's go to the Café Brig."

"I should go alone," Claire said. "If it's the same bartender, he may remember me, but he could also be spooked if I walk in with someone else. We'll go over there together, and you can wait for me just down the street."

Claire remembered the Café Brig like it was yesterday. The shabby, red brick building with a wooden sign hanging above the door, the narrow, dimly lit bar room smelling faintly of grease and beer. The only thing different was that there were no other patrons in the bar. But it was only a little after ten o'clock on a Sunday morning.

As she hoped, the bartender was the same thin, curly-haired man who was here the last time. He sat on a stool behind the bar with a newspaper spread out in front of him, and looked at her curiously, as though trying to place her, but didn't say anything.

Claire took a seat at the bar and hesitated for a moment, then started to say, *"Een Trappist Ale..."*

Before she could finish, the bartender smiled and nodded, silently confirming the rest of the coded signal.

Claire relaxed a bit and asked for a cup of coffee.

When he brought the coffee, the bartender pulled his stool over and sat down. "I remember now," he said quietly with a quick glance at the front door. "It was about a year ago; you were here with a young man, an American, perhaps?"

Claire blinked. "That's right, but how did you know he was an American?"

The man shrugged. "You did all the talking. I've been a contact for the organization since the beginning. You were not the only one to come here. My name is Jo."

Claire stared at him for a moment, once again struck by the fact that she never knew the full extent of the secretive escape line she'd been a part of for more than two years. "My name is Claire."

"So, Claire, how can I help you?"

Claire took a breath, wondering if she was doing the right thing. But she really didn't have any other options. "Bart is missing," she said.

The bartender flinched, then sat back a bit and placed both hands on the bar. "Missing? He was here two days ago."

Claire was reaching for the coffee cup, but her hand stopped in mid-air. "What? He was here?"

Jo nodded. "Yes, the day before yesterday, Friday evening. He came in and sat next to another man I'd never seen before. It seemed like the man had been expecting Bart, but they never really conversed."

Claire stared at the curly-haired man, trying to process what she'd just heard.

What the hell is going on?

"This other man, what did he look like?"

"Ah, let me think... middle-aged, broad-shouldered, wearing a black beret and a tweed coat. Had a crooked nose, like it had been broken. Bart came in and sat down next to him. Before I could say anything, Bart recited the code, just like you did. After bringing him a beer, I followed the rest of the procedure."

"Followed procedure... what procedure?" Claire asked.

The bartender very deliberately glanced at the front door again as though to make sure they wouldn't be overheard. "I really can't tell you that."

Claire looked him in the eye. "Jo, it's important. Bart has been missing for over a week. I work with him at the Department of the Interior; he hasn't been to work, and he hasn't been home. Something has happened to him. I know it. You can trust me, I was part of the escape line, and—"

Jo held up a hand, stopping her. "Okay, I understand. We've been liberated, but it's still dangerous; a lot of crazy people out there. We must still be careful."

Claire nodded. "Yes, of course, I know that. Bart was my friend, my mentor. You can trust me to be careful."

Jo glanced at the door a third time, then turned back to her, speaking softly. "If Bart ever gave me the code, I was to contact someone called McDonald at British Intelligence, MI9. Ever since the war began, even before that, Bart has been the main contact here in Antwerp with MI9. You must have known this."

Claire nodded. "Yes, I knew, but that was all. Bart never shared anything with me except for what I needed to know about my duties with the escape line. But how could he have just been here? It doesn't make any sense. Something is *very wrong!*"

At that moment, the front door opened, and a man entered the bar. He wore a tweed coat and black beret.

Claire and Jo exchanged a quick glance as the man took a seat a few stools away. He looked exactly as Jo had described him. Jo slowly stepped over, took the man's order, and poured a glass of beer from the tap. But he kept his eyes on Claire and cocked his head slightly toward the door.

Claire gripped her coffee cup with both hands, trying to think. Who is this person, and why was he here yesterday with Bart?

And why is he here again right now?

She slipped off the stool, dropped some coins on the bar and, as casually as she could manage, left the building. Back out on the street, she turned left and spotted Lukas walking toward her. She motioned for him to stay where he was and, when she caught up to him, said, "Let's go quickly."

They proceeded back up the street toward the River Schelde, turned and headed south along the avenue fronting the river. "Did you see the other man who entered the bar?" Claire asked.

"Yes, that's why I was heading your way. I take it he was not just some random customer."

"No, he wasn't. The bartender had just finished telling me that Bart was there on Friday, and—"

Lukas abruptly stopped. "What? Bart was just there... on Friday?"

"Yes, Friday evening. Let's keep walking. I want to get away from here." They turned another corner, and she continued relating what the bartender had told her. "He had just finished telling me how Bart gave him the code to contact MI9—someone named McDonald— when this same man, wearing a tweed coat and black beret, walked in. I didn't know what to do, so I just got up and walked out."

Lukas stopped and gave her a hard look. "That is not a coincidence. Someone has been following you." He looked around and then pointed to a narrow street heading away from the river. "Let's go this way. I know of a place where we can talk."

After a short walk along several narrow, twisting streets, they arrived at a small café not far from the cathedral. The proprietor recognized Lukas and led them to a booth at the rear. He brought coffee and left them alone.

"Do you think DeVos sent someone to follow me?" Claire asked.

Lukas shook his head. "No, I don't. I met with DeVos, like I told you I would. He said he hadn't seen Bart in a couple of months and hadn't heard anything about him being missing."

"And you believe him?"

Lukas hesitated for a moment, then nodded. "Yes, I do. I really don't think he has anything to do with this. But let's get back to MI9. Why would Bart need to contact them, and what did he want to tell them?"

Claire shrugged. "I don't know. Unfortunately, I left before Jo told me anything more. But you know as well as I do that Bart was involved in a lot more than just the escape line."

Lukas was quiet for a moment, then said, "I've got to go back there and find out."

"Did that man in the tweed coat see you when he arrived?"

"Not enough to recognize me again. He walked up from the other direction and headed straight into the café."

Claire thought about it for a moment, then nodded. "The sign on the door said the cafe closes at five o'clock on Sundays. Maybe that would be the best time to talk with the bartender when no one else is there."

Chapter Forty-Seven

The meeting with Peeters' MI9 contact was set for four o'clock Sunday afternoon in a private room on the lower level of the Café Brig. It had been windy and raining all afternoon and had turned to sleet when Peeters and DeVos arrived a few minutes early. Not surprisingly, considering the foul weather and that it was late on a Sunday afternoon, there were only two other patrons sitting at the bar when they entered. One was the man with the tweed coat and black beret. The other man Peeters did not recognize. He was hatless and wore a black leather jacket.

The bartender, who was washing glasses at the sink, glanced at Peeters and said, "The room downstairs is all set for you. I'll direct the rest of your party down there when they arrive." As he said this, he set an empty glass on the bar and slowly turned it so that the *Leffe* trademark was pointed at Peeters.

Peeters nodded and headed for the stairs, his mind working rapidly. The bartender had just given him a well-established danger signal by turning the beer glass to show the label. So, at least the bartender was on alert; that could be helpful, he thought.

Peeters had known, of course, that he would never be allowed to speak to his MI9 contact alone. And what better person to add credibility to whatever deception they were about to deliver than a captain of the Antwerp police department?

As they sat in silence, waiting for his contact to arrive, Peeters considered his options. If he failed to corroborate whatever phony information was about to be delivered, DeVos could easily use the prestige of his position to discredit him, after which he would certainly have him killed... and Claire as well. The two men sitting at the bar upstairs were proof enough of that. If he did as he was instructed and allowed DeVos to deliver the bogus information, he'd be committing treason and aiding the enemy.

Though he and DeVos had arrived together, Peeters knew they would be leaving separately, with DeVos being the only one alive. The two thugs upstairs would make certain of that. He also reasoned that DeVos would leave before the two thugs swung into action so he could not be implicated. But the bartender had given Peeters the danger signal, indicating he knew what was likely to happen. And that may be just the edge they needed to survive.

Peeters was roused from his thoughts by the sound of someone descending the creaking, wooden stairway. A slender, middle-aged man with thinning gray hair and dressed in a dark three-piece suit stepped into the room, closing the door behind him. Peeters had only met the MI9 agent one other time—their other communications had been through coded wireless transmissions during the occupation—and knew him only by the name of McDonald.

Peeters got to his feet, as did DeVos. Seeing the look of concern in McDonald's eyes, Peeters spoke up quickly. "Good afternoon; please allow me to introduce Captain DeVos of the Antwerp police department."

DeVos stepped around the table and handed McDonald his identification card.

McDonald studied the ID and then looked directly at Peeters. "I was not aware that anyone else would be attending this meeting," he said stiffly.

"I apologize, but there was no good way to advise you, considering the urgent nature of the information we have in our possession," Peeters replied, disgusted with himself for the lie.

McDonald handed back DeVos' ID. "And what is your responsibility in the police department, Captain?"

As he listened to DeVos explain his supposed role in a special operations unit tracking down Nazi collaborators, Peeters wondered how many other traitors there were in the Police Department… or in the Department of the Interior, for that matter. If he ever found a way to get out of this, how would he know who to trust?

DeVos explained to McDonald that he had known of Peeters' involvement with the Belgian Resistance and his connection with MI9. "So, when my special operations unit discovered some potentially important information from an informant," DeVos said, "I asked him to set up this meeting."

Peeters was sickened by how smoothly these lies rolled off DeVos' tongue. But McDonald was apparently convinced because he stepped over to the table and pulled out a chair. "Very well, show me what you have," he said.

DeVos opened his briefcase and removed several documents and photographs. He set the documents and photos on the table and said, "The information I'm about to give you was obtained through separate interrogations we conducted of two collaborators whom we had been following for some time and finally arrested last month. When faced with the death penalty for their crimes, they both became very cooperative."

DeVos pointed to one of the photographs. The grainy picture taken at night showed three men unloading a crate from a canvas-covered truck. In the distant background was a bridge that Peeters recognized as the *Passerelle* in Luxembourg City. "This picture was taken three weeks ago in Luxembourg by one of our agents who had been following the collaborators," DeVos said. "The truck was driven from Frankfurt that night, and the contents of the crate included several hundred thousand Swiss Francs." He pointed to a second photo, also taken at night, depicting several men transferring a similar crate from what looked like the same canvas-covered truck to a much larger truck. "This was taken just last week, also in Luxembourg. There are at least one or two deliveries every week from Frankfurt and Stuttgart to Luxembourg City."

Peeters remained silent, wondering where DeVos had gotten this information. Then he recalled the brief snatch of a conversation he had overheard several days ago while he was locked in the abandoned chapel. DeVos was talking to the policeman guarding the chapel, and the policeman asked DeVos about someone named Becker. Could that be the person behind all this?

McDonald studied the photos and then looked up at DeVos. "Are you suggesting that this is an ongoing operation to smuggle large sums of money out of Germany?"

DeVos nodded. "That is precisely what this is." He picked up one of the type-written documents. "Both of these collaborators were involved with the smuggling operation. During our interrogations, they provided names, dates, and details of the conduit. It's all here, in these documents."

McDonald read through the documents, then sat back in his chair and lit a cigarette. DeVos did the same, but Peeters did not. Although the nicotine would be helpful in calming his nerves, he could not bring himself to share a casual moment with someone as despicable as DeVos.

After some time, during which he appeared to be contemplating what he'd just heard, McDonald said, "This is interesting information, gentlemen. We have suspected this type of activity was taking place, so this is very helpful. May I take these documents with me?"

"By all means," DeVos said.

McDonald gathered them up and placed them in his briefcase. He stood, shook hands with DeVos and turned to Peeters. Thank you for arranging this. It is good to work with you again."

As they shook hands, Peeters said, "Give my regards to Colonel White."

After McDonald left the room, DeVos stood abruptly and snapped his briefcase shut. With a thin smile on his face, he glanced at Peeters. "Well done," he said, "Our people will be pleased. We have just one more assignment for you, and then you will be free to go."

Peeters looked him in the eye. "And what might that be?'

"Just a minor task, but important. Wait here, and my colleague upstairs will summon you. If you continue to cooperate, I can assure you that nothing will happen to your friend, Claire." Then he turned abruptly and walked back up the stairs.

Peeters knew it was pure bullshit. The man upstairs in the tweed coat and the other brute in the leather jacket were here for only one reason. But he was banking on the fact that they wouldn't make their move until DeVos was back in his auto and well out of the way. It certainly wouldn't do for a captain on the police force to be involved in a murder in a sleazy bar down on the docks. That would give the bartender a chance to act first, but Peeters knew he had to be ready.

He stepped quietly to the bottom of the staircase and waited, hoping he'd correctly interpreted the silent signal from the bartender. He heard the brief sound of wind and rain from outside as the front door of the cafe opened and closed.

He waited a moment, then two...

Suddenly, he heard the clatter of a barstool tumbling to the floor.

Peeters charged up the staircase as another barstool crashed over. He burst through the doorway and spotted both of the thugs lying on the blood-spattered floor.

The one in the leather jacket lay face down, his head split open like a melon. Tweed Coat was struggling to sit up... pointing a gun.

Peeters lunged at him.

The gun went off.

Peeters felt a hammer blow in his chest and staggered backward. As he slumped to the floor, the bartender flashed through his line of vision, wielding a thick, wooden club and smashed Tweed Coat in the forehead.

Tweed Coat collapsed backward, the gun rattling to the floor.

The bartender kicked it away, whacked Tweed Coat a second time, then knelt beside Peeters.

Peeters looked up at him through glazed eyes, feeling the warm flow of blood oozing through his shirt.

The bartender gripped him under the arm and helped him to his feet. "We have to get out of here, now!" he snapped.

Peeters grimaced and tried to focus as the searing pain in his chest crept into his shoulder and down his back. The bartender wrapped his arm around his waist, and they hobbled together through the cluttered kitchen, knocking over a tray of plates and glasses and out the back door to a cobblestone walkway.

Slipping and sliding in the freezing rain, Peeters desperately tried to remain upright as they made their way down a narrow walkway.

"I know a place we can go, just around the corner," the bartender said. "Can you make it?"

Peeters gritted his teeth against the pain and nodded.

They turned a corner, hobbled down another walkway, and arrived at the back entrance of a three-story building. The bartender pushed the door open and helped Peeters into a dimly lit hallway with a staircase at the far end. He led Peeters to the steps and helped him sit down. "I know someone who lives upstairs," he said. "I'll be right back."

"Who... lives here?" Peeters stammered.

"A friend who owns an automobile. We'll bandage your chest to stop the bleeding, then get the hell out of here."

Chapter Forty-Eight

Sunday evening, Claire paced around the parlor like a nervous cat, trying to make sense out of everything that had happened. Bart was alive and had been to the Café Brig two days ago. But why had he disappeared without a word, and why was he trying to contact MI9?

And where the hell was Lukas? He'd left at four thirty to get to the café before closing, and now it was after seven.

Then she heard footsteps coming up the stairs, and a moment later, Lukas walked in. She could tell by the look on his face that the news was not good as he took off his coat and motioned for her to sit down at the table. He was silent for a moment as though gathering his thoughts, then took a deep breath and said, "When I arrived at the café, the building was cordoned off, and there were two police cars and an ambulance parked on the street. I stood off to the side and waited to see what was happening. A few minutes later, a body was carried out of the café. It was the guy in the tweed coat."

Claire flinched. "What? The man in the tweed coat... is *dead?*"

Lukas nodded. "No one at the scene would say anything, so I walked to the central police station to see if I could get any more information. Fortunately, one of the clerks on duty is a friend of mine. We took a walk outside, and he told me that apparently there was a big fight at the café. The police are not releasing any information yet, but he told me that two men were killed, supposedly both with major head wounds, like they'd been beaten with a club."

"What about Jo… the bartender? Was he…?"

Lukas shrugged. "I don't know. The clerk didn't know anymore. And he advised me not to appear too curious."

"What about Bart, was he there, do you know—?

Lukas stopped her. "I don't know anymore, and the police aren't going to give us any information."

"Well, we sure as hell need to find out," Claire snapped. She thought about it for a moment, then said, "I know someone who is an editor with the newspaper. He's a good friend of Bart's, and I know we can trust him. I'll call him first thing in the morning and ask him to check into it. I will be at work, but I can tell him to call you if he finds anything out, and you could go over there."

Lukas shrugged, "It's worth a try."

Chapter Forty-Nine

Stalag Luft POW Camp

Jack held the trapdoor open as Simmons crawled up the ladder, his trousers bulging from the concealed bags of sand. He helped Simmons into the barracks and was about to lower the trapdoor when he heard a low, muffled *whump* from the interior of the tunnel.

Simmons flinched, "What the hell was that?"

Without answering, Jack scrambled down the ladder. As he peered into the narrow dark hole he was struck in the face by a blast of coarse sandy air and instantly knew what happened. "It's a cave-in!" he screamed. "Get some help down here; I'm going after Thompson!"

Jack heard Simmons shout something but didn't wait and started crawling into the tunnel. He scrambled as fast as he could, crawling on his belly, keeping his face down against the gritty, sand-filled air flowing back through the tunnel to the open trap door.

He reached the first staging area and sat up for a second, blinking and blowing grit from his nose. He covered his face, took a deep breath, and crawled deeper into the tunnel, hoping like hell someone else was following him.

He crawled deeper, keeping his eyes closed and holding his breath as much as he could to keep from choking. The floor of the tunnel became softer as sand fell out of the airstream, and a moment later, he was scraping his way through inches of dirty, gritty sand.

He kept crawling forward, and the sand got deeper. He knew he had to be getting close to where Thompson had been digging, excavating the face of the tunnel. He paused for a second to listen, hoping he'd hear Thompson's voice.

Nothing.

He crawled further. Sweat poured down his forehead, stinging his eyes with dirt and grit. It was deathly quiet, and he was suddenly enveloped in darkness as the last overhead light bulb flickered and went out.

He hesitated, his mind conjuring up fears of being buried alive. He listened for sounds coming from behind him. Nothing.

I should wait for help.

They have to be coming.

He crawled further, the sand now half a foot deep. He clawed a pathway and pulled himself forward, groping in the darkness, straining to hear something, anything, a grunt, a moan, anything to indicate he was close and Thompson was alive.

He reached forward to scrape away the sand and hit something solid.

He reached in with both hands, clawing furiously, feeling around the object.

It was a shoe.

He dug deeper, scraping through the sand.

Two shoes.

He yelled, "Thompson," but choked and started coughing and sneezing. Wet, slimy sand poured from his nose.

He closed his eyes and held his breath, scraping and clawing forward.

A leg.

Two legs.

He grabbed the bottom of Thompson's trousers and pulled.

Nothing, no movement.

He leaned forward, scraping away more sand, digging, reaching further.

He tugged on the pant legs again.

The body moved.

He reached in again, digging deeper.

He tugged, and the body moved again, further this time.

Furiously sweating, his eyes clamped shut, his back staining, he tugged a third time.

Then he felt something from behind, a hand on his shoulder.

"Slide over," a voice said. "Let me get in and help you." It was Simmons.

Jack squirmed to his left, and Simmons scrunched alongside, grabbing the trousers of Thompson's right leg. "Okay, pull," he grunted.

They tugged together, and Thompson's body moved a foot, then two.

"Keep pulling," Jack yelled, then coughed and choked again.

"Come on, keep pulling!" another voice snapped. "We're right behind you."

It was Barrows.

One final tug and Thompson's body was clear, covered in sand, and... motionless.

"Okay, let's move," Barrows shouted. "Drag him out another foot, and we'll flip him over.

Jack was suddenly aware of other voices, other hands, amazed they could all squeeze in. Thompson's body was pulled away, down the tunnel, toward the entrance.

"You ok?" he heard Barrows say, "Simmons, you ok?"

They both grunted, and Barrows said, "Let's get the hell out of here."

An hour later, Jack sat in the far corner of the barracks, carefully rinsing his eyes for the third time. He took another sip of water, choked, and spit out sand. Simmons sat nearby doing the same thing.

A moment later, Barrows appeared. Jack tensed when the guard named Bucher followed him into the barracks and stood near the door. Barrows stepped between two of the bunks and sat down, facing Jack and Simmons. "Thompson's going to live," he said, then glanced over his shoulder at Bucher. "It was pretty damn close, but Bucher ran over to A barracks and grabbed Timmerman, the air corps medic, who gave him CPR.

"I guess Thompson had the presence of mind to keep his mouth closed when it happened and went unconscious without choking to death on sand." He looked Jack in the eye. "It's a damn good thing you got to him right away, a hell of a ballsy thing to do... you dumb shit!"

Jack flicked his thumb toward Simmons. "If he hadn't followed me in, there was no way I'd have gotten him out."

Barrows nodded. "Good work, both of you."

"Now what? What about him?" Jack asked, glancing up at Bucher.

Barrows took his time lighting a cigarette. He offered one to both Jack and Simmons, but Jack declined. "Don't worry about Bucher," Barrow said, "he's with us, hates the fuckin' Nazis. And he's helped keep this contained. If Thompson had died, it would've been impossible to conceal, but for now, we're still good to go. We get the mess cleared away, shore up the tunnel and keep going."

"Yeah, sure, piece of cake," Simmons said quietly.

Jack glanced at him as Simmons took a drag on the cigarette, his hand shaking so badly he had trouble getting it to his mouth. He thought he probably wouldn't see him in the tunnel again.

Chapter Fifty

Antwerp

On Monday, Claire somehow managed to ignore the turmoil in her mind about the murders at the Café Brig and focus on her work, processing requisitions for food coupons, housing assignments, and job placements. The morning passed quickly, and at eleven thirty, she looked up from her stack of papers to see Dora van Houtte standing next to her desk.

Van Houtte smiled and asked, "I wonder if you'd mind running an errand for me?

"An errand, certainly, what is it?"

The woman handed her a thick packet. "These documents need to be delivered to the Museum of Antiquities in the Steen Castle."

Claire nodded. She knew the department kept certain old documents in the museum's files, but she'd never been asked to go there before. "When would you like them delivered?" she asked.

"You should go now. They asked to have them before they break for lunch."

Claire left City Hall, walked across the Grote Markt, past the *Café Den Engel,* and down a narrow street that led to the *Vleeshuis,* an ancient building that had once housed Antwerp's butcher's guild in the 14th century. She turned left and descended a cobblestone pathway along the south wall of *Vleeshuis,* which led to the river and the Steen Castle.

Claire reached the bottom of the hill and passed an arched tunnel, thinking about Bart, wondering what—

Suddenly, a sharp blow to the back of her head.

She staggered and dropped her to her knees.

A thick arm clamped around her throat and dragged her backward.

Dazed and panic-stricken, she thrashed her arms, trying to break free, but the assailant was too strong. She tried to scream, but he squeezed her throat so hard she started choking. One of her shoes fell off as she was dragged into the darkness of the tunnel. Her vision started to blacken.

Then she heard someone shout, "You there! Stop! Stop!"

The assailant dragged her faster, deeper into the tunnel, her feet scraping on the cobblestones.

The other person shouted again, this time louder and closer, "Stop! Let her go!"

The grip on Claire's throat abruptly slackened, and she fell hard to the ground. She rolled to her side and caught a glimpse of a figure disappearing into the depths of the tunnel.

The other person ran up from behind and knelt beside her. She tried to squirm away, but the person put a hand on her shoulder. "Claire, it's me, Lukas! You're safe now! It's Lukas."

She looked at his face, her eyes hazy, her head pounding, not understanding. "Lukas...?"

He gently placed his arm around her and helped her to her feet. He held her by the shoulders, looking into her eyes. "Can you stand?"

She blinked and touched the back of her head, wincing in pain. Slowly, her vision began to clear. "Lukas? I don't... what are you... doing here?"

"I just left your friend's office at the newspaper and was coming to see you. I saw you crossing the Grote Markt and was trying to catch up when I saw that guy grab you. Do you know who it was?"

"No... he came from behind."

"We need to get out of here. Can you walk?"

Claire hesitated as a bolt of pain shot through her head. She swallowed hard. "Yes, I think... I just need a minute." She closed her eyes, breathing slowly.

Carefully, she touched the back of her head again. It was tender, but there was no blood. She took a step forward. "My shoe fell off," she said.

Lukas retrieved her shoe and helped her slip it on. She took a few more steps and then nodded. "Where are we going?"

"I don't know, but away from here."

Chapter Fifty-One

Lukas led Claire to a garage near his shop where he had managed to keep an old Citroen and several cans of petrol hidden during the occupation. He'd used over half of the petrol supply driving back and forth to St. Vith four times, but he couldn't worry about that now.

Claire looked at him with surprise when she saw the auto.

"For emergencies like this," he said. They got in the old car, and Lukas drove along the river, heading south.

A few minutes later, he turned west, skirting the central part of Antwerp and continuing through the adjacent communities of Berchem and Mortsel. He wasn't sure where to go except that he wanted to get Claire out of the area as quickly as possible.

Lukas gripped the steering wheel and stared straight ahead. After what had happened at the Café Brig, Lukas was certain that whoever attacked Claire, it was no random incident. DeVos was behind all of this, and he was furious with himself for underestimating how dangerous he could be. If Lukas hadn't come straight to the City Hall after visiting Claire's friend at the newspaper, she might have been—

"I still can't believe you showed up at exactly that moment," Claire said, breaking into his thoughts as though she was reading his mind. "How could you have known?"

Lukas swallowed hard, a wave of guilt washing over him. "I didn't, of course... how could I? I had just seen your friend... at the newspaper... and I wanted to share the news with you. I saw you leave the building and was trying to catch up." It was true, but saying it out loud made it sound so incredible that he wondered if she'd believe it. He kept looking straight forward, afraid to make eye contact for fear she would detect that he was hiding something. "Where were you going, anyway?" he asked.

It took her a moment to respond. "I was running an errand. Taking some documents to the castle. Dora, the Department Manager... Dora van Houtte... asked me to do it." She was quiet for another moment, then said, "My God, do you think... I mean, could she have known... could it have been...?"

Lukas glanced at her quickly as her voice trailed off. She was leaning against the door, rubbing her temples. The name van Houtte didn't mean anything to him, but the more he knew about DeVos, the more he thought anything was possible. And now the bastard was trying to get Claire.

"So, what did you find out at the newspaper?" Claire asked.

"Your friend was quite helpful. Apparently, the bartender wasn't in the cafe when the police arrived.

But they found a trail of blood and at least two sets of footprints leading through the back room and out into the alleyway. They suspect Jo must have been one of the two who left by the back door."

"Was Bart the other one? Was he there?"

"He didn't know... he said it could have been anyone, it may have nothing—"

Claire cut him off. "No! Something is going on. Something is very wrong. The guy in the tweed coat *can't* be a coincidence; you said it yourself. He was there with Bart, and then he showed up while I was there. And now he's *dead... murdered!*"

Keeping his eyes on the road, Lukas removed a document from the breast pocket of his coat. He handed it to Claire. "You're right about something going on. You had better read this."

He glanced at her as she opened the document and gasped, her eyes widening as she noticed the headline just above Bart's photo.

COUNCILMAN PEETERS

WANTED FOR TREASON

It was a bulletin issued by the Antwerp police department and dated that morning. When Lukas had read it at the newspaper office it turned his stomach. It was the last thing in the world he wanted to share with Claire but knew he had no choice.

"How did you get this?" she asked after she finished reading it.

"Your friend with the newspaper received it early this morning. He was quite disturbed about it and wanted to make sure you saw it right away. That's why I came straight to City Hall. And a damn good thing I did."

Claire looked back at the document, reading aloud some excerpts... *'treason and collaborating with Nazi Germany'*... *'arrest of Allied aviators'*.

"My God, this could be *Jack!* DeVos is behind *all* of this! It says right here, *'Report to Captain DeVos.'*"

"Goddamn it, Lukas, he's the one! He betrayed Jack, and now he's issued an arrest warrant for Bart! What the hell is going on?"

Lukas felt his face flush and prayed she wouldn't notice. He felt like he was caught in a room, and the walls were closing in. "I don't know what's going on," he finally managed to say, thankful he didn't have to look her in the eye. "We've had suspicions that there are collaborators within the police department. Exactly how high up, we didn't know—"

Claire cut in. "Well, we sure as hell know now, don't we? Obviously, Bart learned something important that they don't want to get out." She leaned back, rubbing her temples again, "At least we know he's probably still alive. There would be no reason to release this bulletin if they had already killed him."

"That's right, of course," Lukas said, "but I hope that he's found a good place to hide because every policeman and gendarme in Belgium will be trying to hunt him down."

She nodded. "And I think I know exactly where he went."

Chapter Fifty-Two

Grote Brogel

It was early evening and already dark when Lukas and Claire arrived in Grote Brogel. They drove through the small town and followed the road to Gaston's farm. The light on the porch of the old brick farmhouse snapped on as they drove up the gravel driveway, and Gaston stepped out the front door.

Claire rolled down the window and waved, "Gaston, it's me, Claire.

She could see a look of surprise on the old man's face. Then, he motioned for them to proceed to the back of the house. He met them at the barn and pulled open the door. Lukas drove in and parked behind Gaston's ancient truck. They closed the barn door and hurried into the house.

Claire hadn't seen Gaston in almost a year, but he hadn't changed a bit; he was tall and thin with dark eyes and a shock of gray hair protruding from underneath the ever-present brown felt cap. He gripped her shoulders with his tough, gnarled hands, then took a step back. "It's good to see you, Claire."

She kissed the old man on both cheeks. "Is Bart here?"

Gaston's eyes widened. "So, you know about that already? Yes, he arrived late last night with the bartender from the Café Brig."

Claire started to say something, but she could tell by the look in Gaston's eye that there was more. The old man pointed to the kitchen table. "Please, let's all sit down."

When they were seated, he told them about the fight in the café and Bart getting shot. "The bullet passed right through his shoulder, and he'd lost quite a bit of blood, but he's out of danger and in a safe place. I decided it was too dangerous for him to stay here in the house, so when the doctor came back this afternoon, we moved him."

"I need to see him," Claire said, "Now."

Claire hadn't been back to the abandoned warehouse since she left Gaston's farm with Jack over a year ago, and she had to choke back her tears when they pulled open the heavy, wooden door and stepped inside. She almost expected to see Jack standing there the way he had that very first day, eyes darting around, a bewildered look in his eyes.

God, I miss him!

Gaston put a hand on her shoulder and pointed to the ladder, leaning up against the loft. "He's up there."

She nodded, took a breath, and climbed up, remembering the night she woke Jack from his nightmare.

Bart lay on a mattress under a thick blanket, his head propped up with two pillows. Lukas followed Claire up the ladder carrying a lantern, and they both sat on the floor of the loft on either side of Bart. Claire took her old friend's hand as a tear ran down her cheek. "I have been so worried about you," was all she could manage to say.

He smiled and replied in a soft, hoarse voice. "And I've been worried about you. I'm so relieved... you are safe."

She squeezed his hand, and they sat in silence for a while. Finally, Peeters scrunched up a bit further and said, "There's a lot you need to know."

Slowly, in a weak and halting voice, Peeters related the story of everything that had happened since DeVos picked him up at his home. By the time he had finished, it was obvious he was very tired, and Claire knew they should leave him alone to rest.

"Contact... McDonald," Peeters said, his raspy voice just above a whisper. "Tell him about DeVos and Becker." Then, just before he closed his eyes, he reached out and grabbed Lukas' wrist. "Promise me... you will look after her."

Lukas gripped Peeters' hand. "You know I will."

Claire glanced at Lukas, grateful there was at least one person she knew she could trust.

Chapter Fifty-Three

After leaving the abandoned warehouse, they gathered around the table in Gaston's kitchen. Claire said, "Let's go over what we know. I found out that DeVos' company was receiving money from the Germans and told Bart. Shortly after that, Bart was kidnapped by DeVos and forced to set up a meeting with McDonald at MI9. DeVos gave McDonald information about the Germans smuggling money out of Germany into Luxembourg. But Bart doesn't believe that. He had previously overheard DeVos telling one of his men about shipments coming to St. Vith, and he heard DeVos mention someone named Becker."

"It's just the bits and pieces," Lukas said. "What does it all mean?"

"And why would DeVos go through all the effort of forcing Bart to set up a meeting with MI9?" Gaston asked.

"I think DeVos was acting under instructions from the Germans to plant false information about the smuggling operation," Claire said, "to throw them off track from the real operation in St. Vith."

"Could this person named Becker be the one giving instructions to DeVos?" Gaston asked.

Lukas spoke up again. "Becker is a very common German name. It could be anyone. Maybe Bart is confused about what he thought he heard."

"I don't think Bart is confused," Claire retorted. "And I think something is going on down in St. Vith." She turned to Gaston. "Can you ask Jo to contact McDonald again and tell him what we learned from Bart?" She was silent for a moment, thinking. Then she asked, "Isn't there an American army base in St. Vith?"

Lukas held up his hand, shaking his head. "Wait a minute. You can't just barge into some American army base with a story like this. They'd think you were crazy."

"Well, not just me. I want this MI9 agent, McDonald, to go with me. He's already aware of the smuggling operation, and he needs to know that DeVos is a traitor."

"But you can't go to St Vith," Gaston said.

Claire glared at him. "And why not?"

"Because it's practically on the border with Germany, and half of the population are German speakers who've always resented us, and most of them want the Nazis to win. You know that. You would be in—"

Claire interrupted him. "It's an American army base. I'll be with a British MI9 agent. I'll be fine."

Gaston persisted. "No, it's out of the question. It's not safe and—"

Lukas stopped him. "It's alright," he said. "I'll go with her."

Gaston stared at both of them for a moment, then shrugged. "The two of you need a good night's sleep. First thing in the morning, I'll ask Jo to contact McDonald."

Chapter Fifty-Four

Stalag Luft POW Camp

It was bitterly cold and snowing with a biting wind from the north as Jack descended the ladder, leading the first group of escapees into the tunnel. The cave-in had set back the timetable by two weeks, and Barrows was getting nervous about containing the secret. So, tonight was the escape.

Jack crawled as quickly as he could, followed by nineteen others in the first group. Right behind him was a B-24 navigator from New Jersey named Krueger, whose parents were German immigrants. Speaking decent German, Kruger would be the point person if they encountered any locals on their way to the nearest village and a train station.

Jack passed the first staging area and glanced behind him, making sure they were all following. Krueger flashed a thumbs-up, which almost made Jack laugh. This plan was so full of risks that he figured it wasn't even worth worrying about.

Some of them were wearing shabby peasant clothing under their greatcoats that Bucher had smuggled into the camp during the last month. The rest of the escapees had removed all insignia from their uniforms and soiled them in the dirt and sand as a sort of camouflage. They had directions to the nearest town and train schedules, also provided by Bucher, if they made it that far.

Jack's orders were to lead the first group, find the village and the train station, then double back and make sure the following groups knew what to do. Barrows trusted him, and at this point, there was certainly no turning back.

Jack reached the end of the tunnel and extended both hands upwards to the trap door, which Barrows had calculated would be just inside the tree line. He put both hands on the cold, frost-covered wooden door and pushed upwards.

It didn't move.

He pushed again, harder.

Nothing.

Krueger came up behind him. "Is it stuck?"

Jack nodded. "Frozen, I'll bet. It's been pretty damn cold the last few days."

Krueger crawled in next to him, and they both pushed.

Nothing.

"Lie on your back and kick up with your feet," someone whispered from the group filling in behind them.

Jack thought about it and then nodded. "Worth a try." He squirmed around onto his back and scrunched as low as he could, knees bent. Then he kicked both feet straight up into the trapdoor.

A jolt of pain shot down his legs and into his back as the door creaked but didn't budge. He clenched his jaw, bent his knees, and kicked it again. His legs shot straight up into the night air as the door splintered and flew open with a loud *Crack!*

"Jesus Christ," someone muttered, "I hope they didn't hear that."

"Hell no," Krueger said, "The guard tower is fifty meters away, and they've got the windows closed to stay warm."

Jack squirmed around again until he was back on his knees, hoping what Krueger said was true. It was a hell of a loud noise. He waited for a moment, then put on his gloves and knit cap and slowly stood up until his head cleared the opening.

He blinked and shivered as the ice-cold wind slapped him in the face. The broken trapdoor lay in the snow just to his right. He turned his head toward the camp and was surprised at how close they were to the guard tower. They were inside the tree line but not by much, and the tower was a lot closer than fifty meters.

Jack waited for another moment, watching the tower, his eyes watering from the cold. He stuck his head back into the tunnel and whispered, "We're closer to the tower than we thought, but I don't think they heard anything. I'll crawl out first, then Krueger and the rest of you, one at a time. Stay low, crawl on your stomach, and follow me deeper into the woods."

Jack took a deep breath and then slowly pulled himself out of the tunnel. He lay flat on his stomach and started crawling slowly through the fresh layer of snow, heading into the thicket of trees. After a minute, he raised into a low crouch and, hunching down as low as he could, waddled forward, expecting a bullet in the back at any moment. He heard the sound of men crawling behind him, wheezing, and cursing in low, muted voices.

He forced himself to keep going for another ten seconds, then scurried behind a tree and slowly rose to his feet, his back aching, his fingers numb. He glanced back at the line of men crawling through the snow like lizards and waved them forward, pointing to nearby trees.

When all the men had made it into the trees, Jack pulled out the map they had drawn with the directions to the town. Shielding the map and a flashlight with his coat, he looked around the area, trying to get his bearings. "We know the tunnel exited from the south end of the camp," he said to Krueger, who stood next to him, looking over his shoulder at the crude map.

"And the town is to the west, so we should head in that direction," Krueger said, pointing through the trees toward a rising hillside in the distance. "How far is it?"

"According to what Bucher told us, it's about five kilometers." Jack glanced at his watch. "It's almost midnight, and the next train leaves from that station at 0500. We'd better get moving so I can get back in time to get another group moving out."

"I sure hope Bucher knows what he's talking about," Krueger said, "and isn't setting us up."

Jack looked at him for a moment. "A little late for that, don't you think."

The town turned out to be little more than a collection of a few wood and stucco single-story homes haphazardly situated near an open square, with a feed mill on one side and a whitewashed, wooden church on the other. The train 'station' was nothing more than a wood-planked siding located a couple hundred meters down a dirt road leading out of the completely dark and quiet town.

Jack left Krueger in charge—with the men hiding out in the farm fields and a few clusters of trees near the rail siding to wait for the train—and started back for the camp to assist the next group of escapees. If all went according to Barrows' plan, they could get as many as a hundred men—all selected by lottery—out of the camp tonight. He picked up the pace as much as he could, slogging through the snow-covered forest, knowing he and Barrows would be in the last group.

Jack finally crested the hill that descended to the clump of trees nearest the tunnel exit. He waited for a moment, watching and listening. He waited for another moment, counting slowly to twenty, then started down the hill, keeping low and darting quickly from tree to tree.

He continued until he could see the guard tower, then stopped again.

Nothing, no movement.

He pressed on for another ten meters, then twenty, until he could see the area where they had all gathered, the snow trampled by their footprints. He hunched down and made his way to the same tree where he and Krueger had studied the map, the spot where he had a view of the tunnel exit. He waited and took a few deep breaths, thinking carefully about the signal he was about to give, the owl hoot he had practiced a hundred times.

"Hoot! Hoot!"

Suddenly, he was blinded by a searchlight. He stumbled backward and turned to run in the other direction when a command echoed through the night.

"Halt! Nicht bewegen!"

The guards appeared out of nowhere. Two of them threw Jack to the ground. A heavy boot stomped on his back as his hands were pulled back and clamped in handcuffs. They hoisted him to his feet and shoved him forward in the direction of the camp.

Chapter Fifty-Five

Matthew McDonald lit his first cigarette of the day and sifted through the stack of papers on his desk. Most of it was just the usual junk that piled up whenever he was out of the office—requisition forms for additional staff, outdated intelligence reports, dossiers of suspected enemy agents. Most of it could easily have been dispensed with by his assistant... if he still had one. With France, Belgium and Luxembourg liberated, the end of the war was in sight, and the budget cuts had already started.

He dumped one of the piles in the box for shredding and started on another when one of the few remaining secretaries on his floor stepped into his office. "Colonel Fairbanks has asked to see you."

McDonald nodded and crushed out the cigarette. He'd filed the report of his meeting in Antwerp immediately upon returning. And Fairbanks was just now getting back to him, a pretty good indication that there wasn't much of concern in the report.

Colonel Anthony Fairbanks was in his mid-sixties, a former infantry commander from the Great War who had served as MI9's Deputy Director since its inception. He was a tough nut with an encyclopedic recall of detail and well connected with the top military brass. When McDonald entered his office, Fairbanks motioned for him to take a seat.

"I read your report on the meeting at that café in Antwerp," Fairbanks said. "So, the Nazis are smuggling money out of Germany through Luxembourg. That right?"

"Yes, that is possible, sir," McDonald said. "We've suspected they're smuggling money out through either Luxembourg or Belgium."

"And this chap, Peeters, you've worked with him before, I take it. Always been reliable?"

"Yes, that's right."

Fairbanks paused for a moment, then picked up a document from his desk and handed it to McDonald. "This just came in. Thought you'd better see it."

When McDonald looked at the document, the title slapped him in the face.

COUNCILMAN PEETERS

WANTED FOR TREASON

He glanced up at Fairbanks and then quickly read through the bulletin. Councilman Peeters was wanted for treason and collaboration with the Nazis?

What the hell?

"So, what do you make of that," Fairbanks asked, lighting a cigarette and offering the pack to McDonald.

Relieved to have a few seconds to think while he shook a cigarette out of the pack and lit it, McDonald took a long drag before responding. "I'm stunned. It doesn't make sense. You said this just came in?"

Fairbanks nodded. "According to the date on that bulletin, it appears they issued it the day after your meeting. This Captain DeVos that's mentioned in the bulletin, he was at your meeting if I recall."

McDonald's mind was racing. "Yes, he was. Peeters introduced us when I arrived. I hadn't known ahead of time that he would be there and had never heard of him. But, as you said, I've worked with Peeters before, many times, and even met him on one other occasion. Everything he's ever given us has been checked out. He's been completely reliable."

"Well, it seems he's in one hell of a jam right now. These are serious charges."

McDonald took another drag on the cigarette, exhaling slowly, thinking it through. "What doesn't make sense is that while DeVos and Peeters were both at the meeting, DeVos did all the talking. He said he'd known of Peeters' connection with the Resistance and with MI9 for some time, and that's why he asked him to set up the meeting. And then, the next bloody day, he issues an arrest warrant for him?"

They were both quiet for some time while the question hung in the air. Finally, Fairbanks asked, "Why do you think DeVos wanted that meeting with you?"

"Other than what he told me, I have no idea. His police department had information about this smuggling operation and wanted us to know about it. Seemed straightforward at the time."

"Well, it sure as hell doesn't seem that way now," Fairbanks snapped. "One of these two guys isn't who we think he is. Did the information they gave you check out?"

"I don't know. I gave it all to the analytical boys." McDonald stubbed out his cigarette and stood up. "But I'm going to find out."

Chapter Fifty-Six

McDonald went back to his office, closed the door, and propped his elbows on the desk, rubbing his forehead. Something didn't make sense. In all their past dealings, Peeters had been completely reliable, whether it involved MI9 assisting the escape organization or information Peeters had gathered from Belgian Resistance operatives. But the meeting with this police captain about the Nazis smuggling money out of Germany was something new.

It could be true, McDonald thought. MI9 suspected the Nazis *were* smuggling money out of the country. But more importantly, McDonald also suspected they were smuggling *people* out of the country, high level people, possibly executives of German companies. He couldn't prove it yet, and he wasn't sure of their purpose, but he believed it was happening.

There was a knock on his office door, and one of the secretaries poked her head in.

"Excuse me, sir, but you have a call on the secure line from Belgium."

"Who is the contact?" he asked.

"The usual one, sir, code name 'Brig.'"

"I'll take it in the secure room."

McDonald walked down the hallway, entered the secure, sound-proof room, and closed the door. He sat at the desk and picked up the telephone. "McDonald here. Who is this?"

"Bartender," came the reply. "And we are out of *Trappist Ale.*"

McDonald recognized the voice, and the code checked out. "Continue," he said.

"I have someone with me who has information about the Councilman."

That was unusual. Normally Bartender was the only one on the line.

Information about the Councilman?

Meaning, Peeters, of course.

That piqued his curiosity. He recalled the last thing Peeters said to him at the Café Brig. "Give my regards to Colonel White." McDonald had wondered about that because there was no Colonel White at MI9. It was obviously meant as some type of message or signal. Maybe this was it. "Who is this other person?" he asked.

"Her code name is Claire. She was an operative of the escape line. And she just met with Peeters. She has important information for you."

"Very well, put her on the line."

A young woman's voice came over the line. "Thank you for agreeing to speak with me," she said. "I just left

Councilman Peeters. After you left the meeting on Sunday, he was shot by one of the men at the bar."

McDonald almost dropped the phone. "Did you say… shot? My God, is he—"

Claire cut in. "Yes, he is okay. He was shot in the shoulder, but he will recover, and he's safe for the moment. But he wanted you to know that the meeting with DeVos was a set-up and that DeVos is a traitor."

McDonald listened quietly for several minutes as Claire told him about her discovery of the funds transferred from *I.G. Farben* to DeVos's company, about DeVos kidnapping Peeters and forcing him to arrange the meeting. She explained that the information about Luxembourg was a lie, and Peeters believed some type of smuggling operation might be happening through St. Vith in Belgium. Finally, Claire said, "Peeters also overheard DeVos mention the name 'Becker', who he thinks may be a German officer organizing the operation."

McDonald flinched.

Becker? A German officer?

Could it be the same person?

McDonald's intelligence mind snapped into high gear. "You said Peeters thought Becker was a German officer?"

"Yes, he thinks he was associated with DeVos, who is a Nazi collaborator. Peeters said he heard Becker's name mentioned and then something about more shipments going to St. Vith. Do you know something about Becker?"

McDonald could hardly believe it. Could they really be talking about the same person, *SS-Hauptsturmfuhrer,* Konrad Becker, the son-of-a-bitch he'd been building a file on for over a year? He took a deep breath and said, "I need to see you, Claire. This could be very important."

"I'm on my way to St. Vith. I understand there's an American Army base. Can we meet there?"

McDonald thought about it for a moment. St. Vith was in the German-speaking area of the Belgian Ardennes, very close to the border, and if Peeters' notion about a German smuggling operation was correct, St. Vith might make sense. "Yes, we could meet there," he said. "There hasn't been any enemy activity in that area for months, so there's no real danger. The American Army base is the 106th Division. When do you want to meet?"

"As soon as possible. I'm leaving here very soon."

McDonald glanced at his watch. It was 0900. They were an hour ahead in Belgium. "I can get a plane out of here later this morning. I'll meet you there about mid-afternoon. "I'll call the base and tell them to expect you."

Chapter Fifty-Seven

The local gendarme in Grote Brogel sat in a café, sipping his coffee. He should get back out on the road, but something stuck in his mind. He pulled out the bulletin from the Antwerp police department and looked it over again.

Councilman Peeters

Wanted for Treason

.... collaborating with Nazi Germany

.... leading to the arrest of allied aviators

The gendarme examined the photo more closely than he had the first time, thinking, trying to recall if he'd seen this person before. Finally, it dawned on him. He *had* seen him before, more than once, as a matter of fact, right here in Grote Brogel.

He remembered seeing Peeters in town several times during the last two years of the occupation, though he never knew his name until now. He never stayed very long and always seemed to be in the company of an older man named Gaston, who had a farm just outside of town.

The gendarme also recalled that a few other people in town had mentioned it to him on those occasions, wondering who he was and what he and Gaston might be up to.

But he'd never paid much attention to comments like that. During the occupation, a lot of people were suspicious about things, cooking up stories about their neighbors collaborating with the Germans.

But there was also that girl who lived with Gaston, who would disappear for weeks at a time. Where she would go and what she was doing was always a mystery. He remembered asking Gaston about it one time, but the old farmer just said she was visiting relatives.

And now Peeters is wanted for treason and collaborating with the Nazis? What did that say about Gaston... and the girl? Were they involved as well? Perhaps the police in Antwerp hadn't made that connection yet, but what else would explain Peeters' visits here, all the rumors, the girl's frequent disappearances?

The gendarme finished his coffee, slipped the bulletin back into his jacket pocket, and pushed away from the table. He left the café, got in his auto, and drove slowly through the village, wondering what to do. Should he contact the police in Antwerp and tell them what he knew? But what did he really know, other than the fact that Peeters had been in town several times? Wasn't the rest of it just a lot of gossip and supposition?

On the other hand, if there really *was* a connection, and if Gaston and the girl had been working with Peeters and collaborating with the Germans, it would mean a big boost for his career if he was the one who discovered it and turned them in.

The gendarme drove out of town and, a few minutes later, approached the gravel drive leading to Gaston's farm. He slowed the car. There were lights on inside the house, so he knew someone was home. But who? It could be just the old farmer himself. Then again, Peeters may be there as well. If he's running from the Antwerp police, this would be a logical place for him to hide.

He passed the house and continued driving slowly, thinking about the situation. He needed to question Gaston about Peeters; that was his job. But if Peeters was there, it could be dangerous. He stopped the car, thought about it again, then turned the car around and drove to the station.

Back in his office, the gendarme picked up the telephone and called his deputy.

"I want you to round up two of your friends and meet me at the station in an hour." He listened to the expected question from the deputy, then cut him off. "It's about that bulletin from Antwerp, that guy named Peeters who's wanted for treason. I think I know where he is, and we're going to arrest him."

Chapter Fifty-Eight

Claire stood near the door of the abandoned warehouse and watched as Lukas and Gaston helped Peeters down from the loft. She took one of his arms, Lukas took the other, and they led him slowly through the orchard to the barn and into Gaston's truck. She knew from the grimace on Bart's face that all the movement was painful for him, but it was necessary. There had been too much activity here, and someone may have noticed. He would be in less danger at the safehouse with Jo.

Claire stepped up on the truck's running board and gave Peeters a hug. He looked her in the eye and said, "I agree with Gaston. Going to St. Vith today is a bad idea."

"It's the only way. Something very wrong is going on, you know that. Besides, your friend McDonald says there hasn't been any enemy activity in the area in months."

"Promise me you will be careful. If there's any sign of—"

"I'll be fine. I won't be alone. Lukas will be there and so will McDonald." Then she smiled and squeezed his hand. "So will the American Army."

She stepped down from the truck and left the barn. Lukas' old Citroen was parked on the gravel driveway, and he was already sitting behind the wheel. Gaston opened the passenger door for her. "We'll wait for about a quarter of an hour after you leave so we don't attract attention," he said. "There's always someone watching; you know how it is."

Claire nodded and gripped the old man's hand. "I know you'll keep him safe. And thank Jo for me again." Then she got in the car, closed the door, and nodded at Lukas. "Let's go."

Chapter Fifty-Nine

Stalag Luft POW Camp

Jack gritted his teeth and slowly rubbed his hands up and down the sides of his legs, trying to stop shivering. It was five o'clock in the morning and snowing as he stood with the other ninety-six attempted escapees under harsh floodlights in the camp's central parade ground.

Twenty-four hours earlier, the last of the escape attempts were crushed when all but three of the group Jack had led to the railway platform were returned to the camp in chains. The other three had been shot while trying to run away. The other eighty men in the camp waiting for their turn in the tunnel had been rounded up hours earlier in a surprise action by the guards.

As they stood in silence, waiting for the Commandant to deliver their sentence, Jack's mind drifted back to yesterday when he was brought back into the camp in handcuffs. The other captured escapees had been huddled on the parade ground, surrounded by the guards, under strict orders of silence. Jack had wandered slowly through the group until he was alongside Barrows, who whispered in his ear, "It was Bucher."

Now, the guards suddenly shouted for the escapees to come to attention. They quickly divided the group into two parallel lines facing each other about ten meters apart, then backed out of the way. A moment later, the Commandant's voice crackled over the loudspeaker. "I have received instructions directly from Berlin," he barked. "Our *Fuhrer* has decided to be lenient. Only fifty of you will be executed. The rest will be assigned to manual labor and half rations for the duration of the war. The executions will be random and will commence immediately."

Jack swallowed hard and stared at the line of men opposite him, making eye contact with Barrows. The New Yorker nodded and flashed a quick thumbs-up.

Then the gunfire erupted.

Jack went rigid and closed his eyes, trying desperately to recall an image of Claire as the blast of gunshots reverberated through the parade ground.

The soldier standing next to him staggered, spattering blood over the side of Jack's face, then collapsed at his feet.

An instant later, the one on the other side slumped against him, almost knocking him down.

Jack tensed, waiting for the bullet.

He waited, teeth clenched, his hands balled into fists.

Then it stopped.

He stood ramrod stiff, frozen in place, waiting for more gunshots.

But it was quiet except for sporadic cries and groans from the fallen men, which slowly faded away.

Jack kept his eyes closed for what seemed like an eternity until he summoned up the courage to open them and look at the opposite line.

Through the cloud of acrid gun smoke, he spotted Barrow's body, crumpled on the blood-stained snow.

Chapter Sixty

Eifel region, near Bitburg, Germany

East of St. Vith in the Belgian Ardennes

SS-Hauptsturmfuhrer Becker sat at a table under a flimsy, hastily constructed canvas tent that served as the company commanders' headquarters and checked his watch in the light of the single kerosene lantern. It was a little before midnight, and the cold dampness seemed to penetrate straight through to his bones. He had been cold in Russia, to be sure, so cold that he was practically paralyzed. But this was a different kind of cold: damp and gray, the snow turning to sleet, the roads ankle-deep in mud, a different kind of cold, but equally miserable.

One of the other company commanders ducked his head as he stepped into the tent, water dripping from his helmet. "Christ! What shitty weather!" he moaned, glancing around for the coffee pot. "I'd rather be back in Russia."

Becker knew that none of them, under any circumstances, would want to return to Russia, but he ignored the comment.

"Coffee's all gone," Becker advised him. "Have you heard anything more? Are we getting ready to move out?"

The other commander cursed the lack of coffee and then slumped down on a folding chair next to Becker. "*Nein*, nothing definite. Everything is still a fucking secret, and the chain of command is all fouled up."

Becker nodded. The highly secret, meticulously planned offensive was getting off to a rocky start. A few days ago, the 1st Panzer Division had moved into position as the lead unit of the entire offensive, which the *Fuhrer* was convinced would win the war for Germany. Becker knew it was sheer folly and cursed his rotten luck that he was stuck here in this shit hole rather than carrying out the mission he'd planned for so many months.

He stood and leaned over the table, taking another look at the map that was spread out, examining it again in even greater detail. The first major target of the offensive was the main highway and rail junction of St. Vith.

Becker traced the route marked on the map from their location to St. Vith. It was a single, narrow road through the hilly, wooded terrain of the Belgian Ardennes, passing through a small village named Lanzerath. It snaked through tiny farm hamlets, over single-lane bridges, and made innumerable twists and turns through towns along the way, a road that was now a quagmire of snow and mud. It was a route better suited to horse carts than 70-ton Tiger tanks. Sheer madness, he thought.

Regardless of the last-minute confusion, Becker sensed that the offensive would be launched soon, probably within the next 24 hours. The fact that over two hundred thousand troops and hundreds of vehicles had managed to make their way in secret to within a few miles of the Allied lines without detection was a remarkable feat. But everything depended on surprise, and a force this size couldn't avoid discovery much longer.

It would start very soon; Becker felt certain of it. Fortunately, he'd had advance warning and had managed to get Wagner and the others out of Germany ahead of schedule. And by now Lukas would have made sure they were all at the *Viscount's* estate in Namur. And DeVos would have all the money well hidden.

So, all *he* needed to do was get there himself. It had been a major blow to his plans when that shithead Steiner 'rewarded' him by getting him back into the action. But the more he thought about it, perhaps it was possible that the distraction and chaos of this insane offensive may actually help get them through Belgium and out of Europe. It certainly made no difference to him if the offensive was successful or not as long as *he* survived and got to Namur. And fortunately, he'd had time to establish a backup plan for that as well.

Chapter Sixty-One

Stalag Luft POW Camp

Faint streams of sunlight filtered through the tiny, barred window of the cooler, and Jack stirred at the sound of a key rattling in the lock. When the door swung open, the guard motioned for him to stand and follow him. Shielding his eyes against the bright sunlight and weaving on unsteady legs, Jack followed the guard across the vast compound, aware but not acknowledging the subtle waves and muted nods of encouragement from the other inmates.

The guard led him to the Commandant's office and pointed to a chair just outside the door. Jack sat down, appreciating the simple comfort of a chair after sitting on the thin straw-filled mattress in the cooler for the past two weeks. Two inmate clerks sat at small desks across the room, their heads down, typing ponderously and shuffling papers from one stack to another. Neither looked up at him.

Jack glanced at the sign next to the door of the Commandant's office, which read, *Obersleutnant Erich von Lindemann.* Even though he'd been back in solitary confinement the last two weeks, rumors had reached him that a new Commandant had taken over after the escape attempt. He was reported to be a career Luftwaffe officer who was vehemently opposed to the execution order and no friend of the SS or the Gestapo.

A moment later, Jack was shown into the Commandant's office. The guard left the room and closed the door behind him. The Commandant took several long moments flipping through papers on his desk before he finally looked up. He took a cigarette from a silver case and offered one to Jack. "So, have you had enough time in the cooler, Lieutenant Richards?" he asked in English after he lit both cigarettes.

Jack took a long, welcome drag on the cigarette and nodded.

The Commandant held his eye for a moment, then placed his cigarette in an ashtray and tapped his finger on a file folder. "I've been reviewing your file, Lieutenant, and it is very curious indeed."

"Curious in what way?"

"It appears you have spent an inordinate amount of time this past year in solitary confinement as a result of your classification as a *besonder fall...* a 'special case' as you would say in English. Do you know the reason for this?"

Jack hesitated for a moment before responding, wondering where this was going. "No sir, I don't."

"Well, I didn't either, so I did some investigating. Apparently, none of your previous Commandants or jailers bothered to inquire about this." He removed a sheet of paper from the file and glanced at it. "You are a 'special case' because you have been accused of espionage. They think you're a spy, Lieutenant."

Jack flinched, almost dropping the cigarette. "A spy... don't—"

The Commandant held up a hand, stopping him.

Jack sat in silence as the Commandant flipped through some of the other pages in the file. "You were the pilot of a B24 Liberator shot down over Belgium in September of '43, is that correct?"

Jack hesitated again. In every interrogation he'd been subjected to since his arrest in Spain, he had never responded with anything except name, rank, and serial number.

The Commandant looked up at him. "Perhaps I should explain something to you, Lieutenant. The Americans and the British have liberated France and Belgium, and their armies are positioned all along our western border. The Russians have liberated Poland and are massed along our eastern border. The war will be over in a matter of months, and Germany will be defeated." He said this very matter-of-factly, with not a hint of anger or sorrow, as though it was as obvious as the passing of time. He paused, watching the smoke rise from his cigarette, then continued. "The execution of prisoners that took place in this camp was a war crime, and when the Allies achieve the inevitable victory, the perpetrators will be hanged. I do not intend to be one of them."

Jack remained silent and stared at the Commandant. To hear such admissions from a uniformed German officer was so incredible he was speechless.

The Commandant took another drag on the cigarette and then crushed it out. "If you are wondering why you are sitting here, Lieutenant, it's because I'm trying to help you. Based on the information in this file, I'm amazed you are still alive. I can only assume that because you have been in the custody of the Luftwaffe since your arrest in Spain, and not the Wehrmacht, or God help you, the SS, no one bothered to investigate your 'special case.' Perhaps your previous Commandants thought it sufficient to just give you extra time in the cooler."

Jack leaned over and crushed out his own cigarette. "I cannot imagine what could be in that file that would suggest I was a spy."

"Then perhaps you should answer my initial question," the Commandant said. "Were you the captain and pilot of a B24 Liberator shot down over Belgium in September of '43?"

Jack nodded. "Yes, I was."

"You were rescued by one of the escape organizations in Belgium and eventually led through France and over the Pyrenees mountains into Spain."

Jack nodded again.

"But then you were arrested, apparently betrayed by someone."

Hearing it said out loud was like a dagger thrust into Jack's heart.

The Commandant continued. "The SS and the Gestapo have collaborators in all of the occupied countries; I'm certain you knew this."

Jack nodded, recalling the terrible moment when the Guardia Civil snapped the handcuffs on him in the farmhouse.

The Commandant folded his hands on the desk and continued. "It is important that you understand just how dangerous the SS and the Gestapo are, Lieutenant. But I also want you to understand that, as officers of the Luftwaffe, my colleagues and I take no part in their treachery. We are no different than you and your fellow Allied officers. We do our duty, as do you." He paused and glanced up at the ceiling. When he continued, his eyes had a fierce intensity. "The terrorizing of non-combatants, the women, and children in the occupied countries is something that *none* of us in the Luftwaffe officer corps, or the Wehrmacht officer corps, have ever condoned. We may have to pay the price, but we *never* condoned it or participated in the crimes. That is probably why none of your Luftwaffe interrogators turned you over to the SS, as these notes indicate should have happened."

Jack sat back in the chair and stared at the Commandant, trying to comprehend what he was hearing, not knowing what to say.

They sat in silence for a few moments, the Commandant occasionally glancing down at the file. Finally, he looked Jack directly in the eye. "You will most likely survive the war, Lieutenant. However, you should know that there is someone back in Belgium who wanted to make sure you did *not* survive."

Jack stiffened and met the Commandant's eyes. "And who is that?"

"There are some notes in this file, notes made by a certain SS officer who was apparently receiving information from a collaborator in Belgium. There is a reference to the name of the collaborator, most likely a code name, but it may mean something to you."

Jack held his breath.

"The name is Lukas."

Chapter Sixty-Two

St. Vith, Belgium

St. Vith was nestled in a hilly, wooded region of the Belgian Ardennes, bordering Germany's Eifel region. It was a quiet, rural area of farms and orchards, cold and crisp on this sunny afternoon, with snow clinging to the branches of pine trees.

But Claire had to admit she felt uneasy. With Belgium liberated and Germany all but defeated, this densely forested area was considered relatively safe. But they were just a few miles from the German border, and all the signs in shop windows and street corners were in German. As they drove through the town and up to the 106th Division headquarters housed in St. Josef's Covent, she thought that security would have been a bit tighter than it seemed to be.

The young army clerk at the front desk led Claire and Lukas down a marble-floored hallway and into a small room with a single window furnished with just a rectangular metal table and six chairs. A few minutes later, the door opened, and a thin middle-aged man with neatly trimmed dark hair and wearing a three-piece suit entered the room and closed the door behind him. He stepped up to Claire, extended his hand and said with a smile and a cultured British accent, "I'm Matthew McDonald. You must be Claire. Thank you for contacting me, and I'm very sorry to hear about Councilman Peeters."

Claire shook his hand, thanked him, and introduced Lukas.

McDonald gestured toward the table. "Well then, shall we take a seat? I gather we have a lot to discuss."

McDonald opened his briefcase and set a pad of paper and a pen on the table in front of him. "Let's start at the beginning, shall we? If I understood you correctly on the telephone, this all started when you happened to discover a transfer of funds from the German company, *I.G. Farben,* to Niels DeVos's family company."

For the next fifteen minutes, Claire explained everything that had happened over the last few weeks.

McDonald listened patiently, taking several notes. When she finished, he asked, "Was Councilman Peeters able to recall exactly what he overheard while he was locked in the chapel?"

Claire took a moment, trying to recall Bart's exact words. "The policeman asked DeVos if he had heard from Becker. He heard DeVos say, 'Yes, more shipments are on the way, coming to St. Vith, same as before.' Then DeVos stopped, and Bart said he heard footsteps on the gravel drive. Apparently, DeVos and the policeman moved further away from the door because he couldn't hear well enough after that to know what was being said."

McDonald nodded and jotted down a note. "Do I understand that you were part of the escape line with Peeters?" he asked.

"Yes, Lukas and I both were operatives in the escape organization. For a time, Captain DeVos pretended to help our organization, but we've come to believe he's a traitor, a collaborator with the Nazis, and he's being paid for some type of mission."

McDonald glanced at his notes. "And you said that Peeters believed this person named Becker was a German officer?"

Lukas spoke up for the first time. "We don't really know—"

Claire interrupted him, "*I* think he's a German army officer who is giving orders to DeVos, and so did Bart. You've worked with Bart for a long time, and you met with him and DeVos that day at the Café Brig. What do you think?"

McDonald set his pen down and folded his hands on the table. "You are correct; I have worked with the councilman—'Bart' as you call him—for a long time. He was MI9's main contact in Belgium, always very thorough and reliable, though I only met him in person one other time before the meeting at the café with DeVos. Tragic day as it turned out."

McDonald sat back in his chair, folded his arms across his chest and stared up at the ceiling as though trying to decide what to say next. Several moments passed in silence. Then he reached into his briefcase, removed a file folder, and set it on the table before him.

He took a breath, glancing at each of them. "As to this person, Becker, I'm going to share some information with you that I normally wouldn't do. But I trusted Peeters and the bartender, so I will trust the two of you. I fear you may have inadvertently stumbled into something potentially very dangerous, so you have a need to know."

"This file contains information we have been compiling for some time concerning *SS-Hauptsturmfuhrer* Konrad Becker, whom I believe is the same person DeVos mentioned during that conversation Peeters overheard." McDonald folded his hands on the table and glanced again at each one of them. "Shall I proceed?"

Claire responded immediately. "Yes, by all means." She turned to Lukas, who just stared straight ahead, not making eye contact. He looked pale, and she noticed a few beads of sweat dripping down the side of his face. She wondered if he wasn't feeling well. "Lukas?"

Lukas quickly cleared his throat and said quietly, "Yes, go ahead."

"Very well," McDonald said. "Konrad Becker is connected through marriage to the Chairman of the Board of the German conglomerate, *I.G. Farben.* This company has been closely aligned with the Third Reich and is known to be complicit in the use of forced labor for the production of war materials. Among the products they produce is the poison Zyklon-B, discovered in several of the Nazi concentration camps liberated by the Russians. We've been aware of Konrad

Becker for years and started watching him more closely when he returned from Russia in 1943 and began recruiting certain individuals in Belgium who are sympathetic to the Nazi cause."

"Was one of those Nazi sympathizers Niels DeVos?" Claire asked.

McDonald took a moment to light a cigarette before answering. "Yes, I believe so. I had never met DeVos before that day at the Café Brig. But we knew that the Germans had commandeered his family's business, *Produits Agricoles Echange*, some time ago. The Jerries had taken over many businesses in the occupied countries, so there was no real reason to suspect DeVos of anything. But when I returned to London after the meeting—just before you called me, as a matter of fact—I was given a copy of this bulletin." He removed the bulletin from the file and showed it to them. It was the one DeVos had issued about Peeters being a traitor.

"Yes, we've seen it," Claire said, glancing at Lukas again, who remained silent.

"The bulletin confused me at first," McDonald said. "Why would DeVos attend a meeting with Peeters one day and issue an arrest warrant for him the next?"

Claire chimed in. "But when I told you Bart had been shot after you left the meeting, you knew something was wrong."

McDonald nodded. "Precisely. And I had some time before I could get a transport plane to Belgium, so I went back through some of our files. I discovered that

DeVos attended a meeting in Germany in 1938 as a representative of the Belgian fascist organization known as VNV. Konrad Becker was a supporter of the VNV and used it for recruiting collaborators. And it turns out that Becker was at the same meeting. I suspect the two of them struck up a relationship that resulted in a connection between DeVos' company, *Produits Agricoles,* and *I.G. Farben.*"

"Is it true that *Produits Agricole* was producing Zyklon-B for the Nazis?"

"It's true," McDonald said, taking a drag on the cigarette, "but I suspect that was just incidental, a cover; it wasn't the main reason for the connection. It was only the tip of the iceberg, so to speak. As I said, Becker is part of the *I.G. Farben* organization. And even though he is just a mid-level SS officer, his family has important connections. While he was stationed in Belgium, we have evidence that Becker set up a conduit—a 'pipeline' of sorts—for smuggling vast sums of money out of Germany in case they lost the war. Becker wasn't the only one. Other business organizations in Germany had similar conduits in other occupied countries, all very secret, of course. But Becker has his own operation in Belgium, and I now believe that DeVos is an important part of it."

"Where is all this money?" Claire asked.

McDonald shrugged. "We don't know. Some of it is in banks, but we believe a lot of it is in cash, probably Swiss Francs, hidden somewhere in Belgium. It's possible that hiding the cash was DeVos' part of the operation." He paused for a moment and tapped the thick file folder before continuing. "There is another reason for these conduits, one that is much more important than the money.

"Let me guess," Claire said. "High-level executives of *I.G. Farben* who don't want to get trapped in Germany when they lose the war."

McDonald nodded, "And executives from other German companies as well. Men who know they could be arrested and tried for war crimes."

"And where are they hiding?"

McDonald shrugged again. "Just like the money, we don't know. Perhaps they're not even here yet or may have just come very recently. We don't know."

"So, what do we do now?" Claire asked.

McDonald put the file back in his briefcase and snapped it shut. "I need to meet with my American counterpart in their G2 Intelligence unit and get his take on this. He won't be back in his office until morning. I'll have the clerk here book a couple of rooms for you at Hotel Zur Post, and we can meet again tomorrow."

Chapter Sixty-Three

Stalag Luft POW Camp

Two days after their first meeting, Jack was again summoned to the Commandant's office. The temperature had dropped overnight, and there were snow flurries in the air. Jack pulled his cap down to cover his ears and thrust his hands in the pockets of his overcoat, wondering what it was about this time.

With the arrival of the new Commandant, things had been relatively calm in the camp, despite the trauma of the executions... until early this morning. The arrival of an SS staff car had sent a flurry of new rumors circulating through the barracks. The long, black auto was parked in front of the administration building, and Jack averted his eyes as he followed the guard into the two-story, concrete block structure.

When Jack was shown into the office this time, the Commandant stood at his desk, hands clasped behind his back. Two other officers stood off to the side, both wearing the black uniforms of the SS.

The Commandant cleared his throat and spoke slowly and deliberately; his demeanor completely changed from the last time. His eyes darted around, and he spoke as though reading from a script. "Lieutenant Richards, I must inform you that, effective immediately, you are being transferred to the Hinzert

Concentration Camp at Trier, Germany. These officers will escort you there. That is all."

Jack went rigid as though he'd received an electrical shock. He tried to say something, but no words would come. The two SS officers abruptly stepped forward and motioned toward the door.

The Commandant looked away.

Jack sat in the back seat of the SS staff car and stared out the window at the somber-looking American and British airmen who were lined up along the road near the gate. Arnie Thompson stood at the head of the line holding up Ned Barrow's favorite Brooklyn Dodgers t-shirt.

As the car exited the camp, Jack looked out over the gray, snow-covered landscape of rural Germany, bewildered and terrified about what had just happened. Neither of the two SS officers in the front seat had said a word to him, but he knew that what lay ahead was not good.

He had heard about the Hinzert Concentration Camp, located near the city of Trier in southwestern Germany. All the POWs knew the stories of other camps, and Hinzert was one of the worst: a brutal forced labor camp run by the SS and the Gestapo for political dissidents, insurgents and others accused of treason or espionage. A camp from which no one survived.

Though he had no idea how or why, it was obvious that his 'special case' status had finally caught up to him; perhaps the Commandant's investigation of his case had gotten someone's attention and aroused suspicion. That would explain the sudden arrival of the SS and the Commandant's rigid demeanor, whose own future was probably now in jeopardy.

As they drove on, the two SS officers chatted and joked with each other as though Jack wasn't there. His mind wandered, and he recalled the aerial reconnaissance maps of Germany he'd studied before each of his bombing missions. He knew that Trier was located just south of Bitburg in the southwest part of the country, very near the border with Belgium, in the area of the Ardennes forest. His gut churned, and he clenched his teeth over the cruel irony that he would be so close to Claire and never see her again.

Because of Lukas!

They drove for another two hours to a railway station just outside of Berlin, teeming with hundreds of weary-looking, emaciated civilians in worn, tattered clothing. The war was finally taking its toll on the perpetrators, Jack thought smugly.

The SS officers turned him over to two burly Feldgendarmes, wearing green uniforms with chain-link medallions around their necks. The notoriously brutal German military policemen shoved their way through the sullen crowd, swinging nightsticks at anyone too slow to get out of their way.

They boarded the train and shoved Jack into an empty compartment. One of the Feldgendarmes immediately pulled out his nightstick and slammed it into Jack's stomach. When he doubled over in pain, gasping for breath, the other one kicked him squarely in the back, sending a searing jolt of pain all the way to his shoulder blades. They left him on the floor of the compartment and locked the door.

As the train chugged its way southwest through the night, Jack finally managed to crawl up on the seat and look out the window, trying to keep track of their location. They stopped at Hanover, Dusseldorf, and Cologne before arriving just after dawn at the railway junction of Stadkyll in the Eifel Region of southwest Germany. It was one of the strategic landmarks Jack remembered from the aerial maps.

The Feldgendarmes unlocked the compartment, grabbed him violently by the arms and pushed him out of the railcar. Jack stumbled and fell on the gravel rail siding, his back still aching from the earlier kick. They hoisted him to his feet and led him through the station.

To Jack's surprise, the station teemed with Wehrmacht soldiers, hundreds of them, occupying every square foot of the building and spilling over to the outside. They were all dressed in battle gear, carrying backpacks and rifles.

They exited the station, and the Feldgendarmes hustled him across a parking area, then shoved him into the back seat of a powerful German-built Horch. As they sped away from the station, Jack glanced out the window and was astonished to see a long line of tanks and armored half-tracks being unloaded from a string of flatbed rail cars.

What the hell are they doing down here?

If what the Commandant had told him about the Allies closing in on Germany was true, the build-up of German troops would almost certainly happen much further north, in the area the Allies would most likely attack. That would be in the Ruhr industrial region near Cologne and Frankfurt—the area the train had passed through hours ago—not way down here, in the middle of the Ardennes forest.

It doesn't make any sense!

Chapter Sixty-Four

Near Bitburg, Germany

After leaving the railway station, the Feldgendarme driver followed the main highway leading to Bitburg and Trier, then eventually turned onto a narrow, gravel road hard-packed with snow. It was bumpy and rutted, and the powerful, stiff auto made for a rough ride.

They continued southwest when Jack suddenly heard sounds of aircraft approaching from the north. He looked out the back window but couldn't see anything. He turned back to the front of the car and saw the two Feldgendarmes glance at each other. The driver sped up, and the car bounced hard over the ruts and potholes, the rear end sliding on the slick, snow-packed surface.

The aircraft were getting closer, the deep, reverberating noise louder, and Jack suppressed a smile when he realized these weren't just any aircraft. The very familiar, unmistakable drone of the four Pratt & Whitney supercharged engines told him these were American B-24 Liberators!

It suddenly became clear why the Feldgendarmes had turned off the main road, and a moment later, Jack heard the rolling thump of bombs dropping several miles to the south and east. The Americans—

his Americans, in *his* B24s—were pounding the hell out of Bitburg. It was all he could do to remain in his seat and not jump up and shout. But a nasty glance from the thick-necked Feldgendarme in the front passenger seat was warning enough.

The rolling thumps of the bombs continued, becoming more frequent, and the driver sped up again, driving faster on the bumpy, slick road.

Then Jack heard another sound, the same powerful drone as the other B-24s, but this one much louder and much closer, as though it was heading *toward* them. It must be off-course, Jack thought, or—

The blast came before he could register another thought, and the road in front of them exploded. A massive upheaval of dirt, snow, and rocks rained down on the powerful auto, which swerved wildly, then flipped over and bounced. Glass shattered, and metal screeched, then a jarring *Thump* as the inverted vehicle slammed to a jarring halt.

Some time passed, perhaps only seconds or a minute; it was impossible to know when Jack slowly opened his eyes and blinked. He was lying in the snow, the branches of a tree looming over him. He tried to move but couldn't. His head pounded. Blood trickled down his forehead and across his cheek.

He smelled smoke, then tried again, and finally sat up.

He looked to his left and saw the car upside down, the roof caved in, and the front end smashed against the tree trunk. Flames spurted from under the hood.

Hanging out of the front door was the blood-drenched head of one of the Feldgendarmes.

As his mind slowly cleared, Jack pressed his hand against his forehead. Blood spurted between his fingers as he slowly got to his knees.

Then he spotted the other Felgendarme staggering toward him from the other side of the car. The big man's uniform was ripped and soiled with blood, and his left arm hung limply at his side. But his right hand held a pistol, pointed at Jack.

The Feldgendarme shouted and motioned with the pistol for Jack to stand up.

The smoke thickened. The flames grew larger and hotter. Jack kept his eyes riveted on the Feldgendarme. He felt around with his right hand for a rock, a stick, anything—

The Feldgendarme shouted again, but this time, his voice croaked, and his hand trembled, the pistol wavering back and forth.

Jack's right hand gripped something cold and solid, a rock partially buried in the snow. He clawed at it with his fingers, got his hand under it and with one swift motion threw it at the Feldgendarme... an instant before the gunshot.

Jack froze for a second before he realized the shot had missed, then frantically crawled away from the car, choking on the hot, acrid fumes.

A second gunshot rang out.

Jack got to his feet and stumbled up a hill into the trees.

His head pounding, his eyes blurry, Jack braced himself against a tree and turned back. The Feldgendarme stood near the rear of the car, partially obscured by smoke. Blood streamed down his face from a huge welt on his forehead.

The burly man wiped away the blood and pointed the pistol toward the trees.

Then the vehicle exploded, and he vanished in a thunderous blast of white-hot flames.

Chapter Sixty-Five

St. Vith

Lukas could hardly breathe as he and Claire left the 106th Division headquarters building and stepped out into the cold, crisp air. He knew coming down here was a risk, but he also knew that when Claire was determined to do something, there was very little that could stop her. And it would have been worse if he'd stayed behind, not knowing what was going on. But now he felt like he was caught in a vice that was slowly closing in on him.

"Lukas, did you hear me?"

He blinked at the sound of Claire's voice and looked at her. "I'm sorry, what did you say?"

"I asked if you were feeling all right. You were very quiet in there, and you don't look good. You seem to be limping more than usual."

He took a breath of the fresh air. "I'm fine, just a bit of a headache and a cramp in my leg. It was very stuffy in that room, and… what we heard was very alarming." The Hotel Zur Post was just a few blocks away, and his mind churned at how he would handle meeting Frau Brunkhorst again. She was very discreet, but he'd been here four times in the last two weeks and—

"Do you know where we're going?" Claire asked.

"Yes... I know the hotel. I've stayed here before... just a few days ago, actually, when I was... helping my friend rebuild a tractor. It's just up ahead." It sounded incredibly weak, but it was all he could come up with. He looked straight ahead, not daring to make eye contact with Claire.

Frau Brunkhorst was indeed very discreet when Lukas and Claire entered the quaint, three-story hotel situated on Hauptstrasse in the center of St. Vith. Lukas quickly introduced Claire and said, "We've just come from a meeting at the American Army base, and I've told Claire what a wonderful café you have here. I believe the clerk at the base called ahead."

Lukas noticed a slight flicker of confusion in Frau Brunkhorst's eyes, but she recovered in an instant and smiled. "*Ja, ja*, they called. I have two nice rooms for you with a good view. You come down when you freshen up and have a nice dinner."

***

Claire sat across from Lukas at a small table in the café sipping coffee after a surprisingly decent meal of sliced ham and boiled potatoes. Unfortunately, there were several other guests dining at the café, so there was no opportunity to discuss the information they'd learned from McDonald.

Claire finished her coffee and said, "Let's take a walk outside."

Lukas nodded, finished the last of his coffee and pushed his chair back.

The night air was cold, but there was no wind, and the skies were clear and filled with stars. As they walked away from the hotel, Claire glanced up and down the street. No one else was around. She turned to Lukas, who'd been unusually quiet during dinner. "Are you feeling any better?" she asked.

He nodded. "Yes, the food helped."

"I agree with what you said earlier. What we heard from McDonald was definitely alarming. What do you think we should do now?"

Lukas shrugged. "I'm not sure. I think we need to be very careful. McDonald said this could be very dangerous."

"Well, I think they should arrest DeVos right now."

Lukas didn't respond, and they walked on in silence. Claire felt a burning anger in her gut. DeVos was a traitor, a kidnapper, and involved in some massive smuggling operation. He should be arrested and hanged. But he's also a captain in the police force, so she knew how difficult it might be for someone like McDonald to just go out and arrest him. Maybe after McDonald talked with his American counterpart, they'd have a plan. But she hated just waiting for someone else to do something!

She shook her head and decided to change the subject and clear her mind for a moment. "Frau Brunhorst seems very nice, though I detected a look of sadness in her eyes," she said to Lukas. "Does she manage this hotel alone?"

Lukas nodded. "Yes, she does. I've heard a rumor that her husband is serving time in jail for refusal to serve in the Allied army and fight the Germans."

Claire sighed, imagining how difficult that must be. She knew that St. Vith was the most important town in this tiny, German-speaking corner of Belgium. The area had historically been part of Germany until after the Great War when it was carved out and handed over to Belgium. Tensions and divided loyalties had existed ever since and had only worsened during the last few years of German occupation.

When they returned to the hotel, the café was empty, and Lukas said he was tired and went up to his room. Claire noticed Frau Brunkhorst sitting at the front desk, going through some papers. A picture of a handsome young man hung on the wall behind her. Claire stepped over to the desk, and as Frau Brunkhorst looked up, she pointed to the picture and asked, "Is that your husband?"

Frau Brunkhorst glanced at the picture and nodded. "*Ja*, that is Kurt."

"I'm sorry, it must be difficult for you," Claire said, hoping she wasn't getting too personal, but she was curious about Lukas' comment.

Frau Brunkhorst shrugged, seeming very tired. "In St Vith, some fight with the Allies, some with Germans. Kurt's family lives in Germany; he could not fight them. But would not fight against Allies." She wiped some dust from the picture. "So, I do what needs to be done and hope it all works out."

Later, as Claire sat on the single bed in the tiny hotel room, she thought about the conflict confronting Frau Brunkhorst. Her husband was of German heritage, and they were living in an area that had been part of Germany until twenty years ago when the Versailles Treaty gave it to Belgium. Could anyone really blame them for having divided loyalties in a country where even the Flemish-speaking Belgians in the north and the French-speaking Belgians in the south had difficulty getting along? It was a question she knew no one would ever be able to answer.

She lay back on the bed and stared at the rough plaster ceiling, wondering if Jack's parents and sister had been notified that he was missing in action. She didn't know them, but her heart ached when she thought about how devastated they would be. She'd been able to put it out of her mind the last couple of days, but now it all rushed back, everything, every moment she and Jack had together those few short weeks. She remembered how she'd helped him tie the laces on his boots, how they laughed about *Treasure Island,* Jim Hawkins, and Sir Lancelot, how she woke him up from his nightmare, and how he wanted her to stay and talk. That was the moment she knew she was in love with him. As crazy and improbable as it was... she knew. And most of all, she remembered the night they made love in the cabin before setting out over the mountains. If only that night could have lasted forever.

Claire sat up and wiped the tears from her eyes, picturing his face. Where was he right now? The pit that formed in her stomach told her she would probably never see him again, but she knew, in her heart, that she would never, ever give up hope.

She also knew she would never rest until Niels DeVos and whoever else was involved in all of this paid for what they had done.

Chapter Sixty-Six

Near Bitburg Germany

Jack plodded deeper into the forest, trying to put some distance between himself and the burning auto. Fortunately, the thick stand of trees had shielded him from the full force of the blast when the Feldengarme's auto exploded, but his ears still rang from the shock wave.

He slumped down next to a tall pine tree and removed the scarf he'd tied around his forehead—now sodden with blood—wrung it out and re-tied it. The bleeding had slowed to a slow oozing, but he was still dizzy, and his head hurt like hell.

He waited a bit longer, taking slow, deep breaths to clear his head, then stood up and glanced back. A thick, black cloud of oily smoke spiraled upwards above the trees, a clear signal for any German troops in the area. He took another deep breath, pushed away from the tree, and trudged deeper into the woods.

He stopped again after climbing another steep grade and tried to get his bearings. He knew they had been heading south when the bomb exploded in front of the car. And he'd been thrown out of the right side of the car, so when he scrambled up the hill into the trees, he was heading west, which was good. He was probably still in Germany, but Belgium wasn't far away.

It was snowing again, and heavy, slate-gray clouds hovered just above the tops of the trees, obliterating any notion of directions. But he could no longer see the smoke from the car or smell the burning fuel, so he knew he was putting some distance between himself and the wreckage. Shivering from the cold, he glanced around, but wherever he looked, the terrain appeared the same. So, with no better idea, he continued in the same direction, hoping for the best.

He continued trudging through the forest, pushing himself through the heavily wooded, hilly terrain. His head throbbed, and his back still ached from where he'd been kicked, not helped by being thrown from the car.

As dusk approached, it finally stopped snowing, and he found himself at the edge of a farm field. Beyond was a flickering of light and the dark outlines of a barn and a house. He stopped for a moment to catch his breath.

Were the people who lived there Germans or Belgians? He was either still in Germany or perhaps in the German-speaking part of Belgium that Claire had told him about. There was no way to know for sure. What would they do if an American soldier knocked on the door?

He was freezing cold, lost, and injured. His clothes were ripped, soaking wet and filthy. He needed help.

But he was so close... so close to being back in Belgium. Could he really take the chance?

He decided to approach the house slowly, along the edge of the clearing. Perhaps there was a barn or shed he could hide out in until—

Suddenly, a dog barked inside the house. A moment later, the front door opened, and a man emerged, holding a rifle.

Jack edged back into the trees, but the dog squirted out through the man's legs and raced across the clearing. Jack stood still, just as he had when he and Claire confronted the three dogs after they left Gaston's warehouse.

The dog charged up to him and then stopped, circling around him, alternately sniffing and barking.

The man whistled sharply, and the dog instantly retreated to the house. Then the man shouted something to Jack in German and motioned for him to come forward.

Jack hesitated. But his eyes were blurry, he felt lightheaded, and his legs were shaking. He knew he had no chance on his own. He stepped forward, keeping an eye on the rifle. As he approached the house, he said, "American... I'm an American soldier... a pilot. Can you help me?"

The man stood in the doorway for a long, tense moment before finally stepping back and beckoning for him to enter the house. When Jack stumbled at the door, the man grabbed him under the arm and helped him inside.

Chapter Sixty-Seven

It was a small, sturdily built home with thick stone walls and a hand-hewn, timbered ceiling. Kerosene sconces bathed the tiny parlor in a warm glow, and a fire crackled in the stone fireplace, a welcome relief to Jack after the numbing cold and dampness of the forest.

The man set the rifle down and called out to someone. A woman appeared from an adjacent room that Jack guessed might be the kitchen. The man and woman exchanged a few terse words in German before the woman stepped forward, took Jack's arm, and led him to the kitchen, the dog following close behind.

It was a small, square room with white-painted stucco walls, a giant wood-burning stove, and an oak table with four hand-made chairs. Something was simmering in an iron pot on the stove that filled the air with an aroma that reminded Jack of the beef stew his mother used to make. For a moment, he could almost see her standing by the stove in their home in Sturgeon Bay, telling him to be patient and that dinner would be ready soon.

The woman pulled out a chair, took his arm and helped him sit. She seemed to be in her late fifties or early sixties, with graying hair pulled back in a bun. Her manner was reserved and somewhat guarded, though Jack detected a kind of softness in her eyes. As she removed the blood-soaked scarf and examined the lacerations on his forehead, he could feel the calloused, rough fingers of someone used to hard work.

"Is not so bad," she said in thickly accented English. "Will clean it now."

She methodically went about dabbing the cuts on his forehead with a warm, wet cloth, carefully avoiding the golf ball-sized lump that had developed. Then, she produced a strip of white cloth and wound it around his head.

Her husband stuck his head into the kitchen, and the woman turned toward him. There was a brusque exchange in German, and the man disappeared.

"He brings dry clothes," she whispered to Jack. "He worried you are here, but it is okay."

The man reappeared a few minutes later carrying some clothing, which he set on a chair. Then he took a hat and coat from a hook on the wall and left the house.

When she finished wrapping Jack's head, the woman handed him the clothes and motioned for him to go into the other room. When he returned to the kitchen, the woman glanced at him and nodded. "Look better now. Sit and rest."

She stepped over to a cupboard, produced a bottle of red wine, filled a glass, and set it in front of him. Then she filled a bowl with stew and brought it to him. "You eat now," she said and turned back to the stove.

The wine was sweet, and the first few sips sent a little surge of warmth through his body that took the edge off the throbbing pain in his head. The aroma of the hot stew brought back another wave of memories of home. His eyes clouded up, wondering if he'd ever see his mother and father or his sister, Mary, again. Claire would love Mary, he thought as he brushed away a tear.

A short time later, the husband returned, along with another man. He was shorter and stockier than the husband, with a thick neck and a full, black beard. They both stood at the doorway of the tiny kitchen and stared at Jack for a moment. The woman poured a second glass of wine and set it on the table. Then she and her husband disappeared.

The bearded man pulled back a chair, sat down and took a small sip of wine, never taking his eyes off Jack. He set the glass down and said in English, "You are American?"

Jack nodded. "Yes, Lieutenant Jack Richards, Army Air Corps."

The man appeared surprised, and Jack wondered if he'd made a mistake. He still didn't know exactly where he was or anything about these people, except that they spoke German.

The man seemed to sense his unease. "Have not seen an American airman before," he said, speaking slowly and deliberately. "My name is Gunter. This is the home of Franz and Hilda."

"Is this Belgium?" Jack asked.

The man smiled and nodded. "Ja, you are in Belgium. This area has been occupied by American soldiers since last September. You are safe here; it's okay."

Jack relaxed a bit and took another sip of wine. Then he said, "I was a prisoner and being taken to a concentration camp near Trier by two Feldgendarmes when the car was bombed. The Feldgendarmes were killed in the crash and fire, but I escaped."

The man nodded and said, "American planes bombed Bitburg every day last week. We hear them come and go. War cannot last much longer."

"When I arrived by train in Stadkyll, the Germans were unloading tanks and half-tracks, many of them, maybe a hundred or more. There were also several hundred German soldiers at the station. Why would they be way down here?"

"Tanks and soldiers? In Stadkyll?" The man shook his head. "No German soldiers around here, all further north, at West Wall, near Cologne, Frankfurt."

"But I saw them early this morning. I'm a bit confused about directions. Exactly where are we?"

Gunter got up and went into the parlor. After a moment and a few comments with Franz, he returned carrying a map, which he spread out on the table. "We are here," he said, pointing to a spot near a small town named Lanzerath, several kilometers north and east of St. Vith. Very close to the German border.

Jack studied the map for a moment, locating the railroad station at Stadkyll. "It was here, at the railroad station," he said. "They were unloading tanks, and there were hundreds of German soldiers, all dressed for battle."

Gunter called out to Franz, who appeared a moment later. The two of them conversed in German, Gunter pointing to the area Jack had identified on the map. After a moment and a few more comments from Franz, Gunter glanced at Jack and then tapped his finger on the map again. "Some American soldiers are here, in Lanzerath, part of 106th Division in St. Vith," he said. "They patrol this area, come through here, good men, give us coffee and cigarettes."

"Have they said anything about German tanks or a build-up of German infantry in the area? Any warnings?"

Gunter shook his head. "As I said, no German soldiers this far south. They are in the north, behind West Wall."

"When was the last time you saw any of the American soldiers?"

Gunter shrugged. "Perhaps, two, maybe three days."

"Listen to me," Jack said, leaning forward. "The tanks I spotted today were probably moved in overnight, and they were unloading them this morning in Stadkyll. I should go to St Vith and report this. Can you help me?"

The two men conversed again in German, and this time, Franz grew more agitated, shaking his head. Finally, he left the room, and Gunter turned back to

Jack. He propped his elbows on the table and sighed. "Franz is worried you put us in danger. You know about people in this area?"

Jack shook his head. "No, not really."

"I explain," Gunter said. "There are some here who side with Allies, but many side with Germany. This area was part of Germany until the Great War. Many here still believe they should be Germans. When Americans arrived in September and drove out the Germans, many followed the Wehrmacht back across the border into Germany. But some stayed, believing Germans would return. Now, we have many empty houses, and it is hard to know who to trust; we must be careful.

"But you stayed, and so did Franz and Hilda."

He nodded, "We stayed. Where would we go? My wife died two years ago. No children. Believe Americans will win. So, we stay."

"Then I was lucky to knock on the right door?" Jack said with a thin smile.

"Yes, lucky. But if what you say about tanks is true, maybe Germans will be back soon. Then all in danger."

"Can you help me get to St. Vith?" Jack asked again.

Gunter downed the last of his wine and stood up. "Not St. Vith, too far. Come with me now, to my house, just down the road. Franz and Hilda are frightened, so better if you come with me. I have wagon, and in

morning, I take you to American soldiers in Lanzerath.
You tell them your story."

Chapter Sixty-Eight

Jack snapped awake at the first thunderous blast and sat bolt upright. A second blast, louder and closer, shook the tiny attic room, rattling the single window.

Gunter yelled from down below, "Jack! Get up! Germans coming!"

Jack jumped from the narrow cot, pulled on his trousers and boots, and scrambled down the steep, narrow stairway. He grabbed the woolen coat Gunter had given him last night and ran through the open front door.

Gunter was a few yards ahead of him, a black silhouette sprinting toward blazing orange flames that had engulfed the roof of the barn. Jack caught up to him just as he pulled open the barn door and ducked inside.

Jack followed him inside, then stopped short, suddenly paralyzed by the thick, choking smoke, the crackling flames and searing heat overhead. Visions of his burning airplane flooded back into his mind. He flinched and stumbled backward as a terrified horse reared up and kicked violently at the wooden slats of its stall, whinnying and snorting, tossing its head from side to side.

Suddenly, Gunter appeared through the smoke, leading a frantic, bellowing cow with a rope. He reached out and handed the rope to Jack, pointing at the door.

Jack took the rope and turned back toward the open door, tugging, pulling, as the massive animal balked, then slowly lurched forward, following him out of the barn. He plodded forward, leading the cow until they were in the clear, then glanced back toward the burning building.

A wave of panic washed over him as the rear section of the roof collapsed in a sickening *thump,* and a flash of flames and debris shot high in the air. Then, an instant later, Gunter emerged through the smoke, backing out of the barn, leading the bucking horse, now blindfolded with a hastily tied rag coat over its head.

An artillery shell screamed overhead, and an explosion shook the ground, leveling a house on the other side of the road.

Gunter yelled for Jack to follow him as he led the bucking horse to an orchard behind the house. Jack pulled on the rope, and the cow lumbered forward.

Gunter quickly secured the horse to an apple tree, then took the rope from Jack and led the cow to another tree. He gripped Jack's arm and pointed toward the burning, wrecked house across the road. "House empty, no people. We go in my cellar now."

Chapter Sixty-Nine

St. Vith

Claire woke abruptly as a crack of thunder shook the room. She lay still, staring into the darkness, listening for the rain. Then, a second crack, louder and closer.

She jumped from the bed and scrambled to the window.

My God, it's not thunder!

Claire quickly got dressed and burst from her room. As she ran to the stairway, she heard someone running down the hall behind her. It was Lukas. They quickly descended the stairs, ran through the lobby and out through the front door.

The quiet town of St. Vith was abruptly jarred awake. Deep, booming thuds echoed from the east as Claire and Lukas stood in front of the hotel. Across the street, window shutters banged open, and people poked their heads out. Other people emerged from doorways, and soon, a small crowd gathered near the hotel, everyone staring into the sky and talking at once.

"Is it the Germans?"

"No, it's the Americans!"

"Are they bombing us?"

"We've got to leave!"

Claire backed up against the wall of the hotel building and stood next to Lukas, wrapping her arms over her chest as the shelling continued, a crescendo of thumping bursts lighting up the eastern sky.

What the hell is happening?

An hour later, it suddenly stopped, but clouds of thick, black smoke rose above the tree-lined hills in the east, blotting out the morning sun. Rumors spread wildly up and down the street as some people scurried home to pack up their belongings. Others lingered on the corner, arguing about what to do.

American soldiers suddenly appeared. Jeeps and trucks roared into the small city, clogging the streets, all seemingly headed in different directions.

A little before noon, Claire and Lukas sat at a table in the hotel's café. They were the only patrons. Frau Brunkhorst nervously poured coffee for them and produced a small plate of cheese and bread. "The Germans are coming back," she said anxiously, "We are in trouble now."

Claire turned to Lukas after the woman disappeared into the kitchen. "Do you think this is the real thing? Could the Germans really be attacking us down here?"

Lukas shrugged. "I don't know, it sure sounds real, but I can't believe they would try this now; down here, in this weather, it doesn't make sense."

"I think we should—"

She stopped abruptly as Matthew McDonald entered the café. He stepped directly to their table and took a seat. Claire thought he looked a bit pale and tense.

"I'm glad I found you here. I would have come sooner, but things are a bit dicey at the base right now."

"What's happening? Claire asked. "Are the Germans attacking us?"

"No one knows for sure," McDonald replied. "It could be just a diversion, to draw attention away from their defenses up north. We'll know more in a few hours. If it *is* real, it's a major intelligence failure. No one expected this, and certainly not down here."

"What should we do?"

"At this moment, we have no idea how many enemy troops are in the area or where they are headed. The 106th Division has secured St. Vith for the moment, so the safest place you can be is here at the hotel. I'm still trying to track down my American colleague with G2, but all the phone lines are jammed right now. I've got to get back, but you both need to stay here. I'll send someone for you if the situation changes."

Chapter Seventy

When the shelling finally stopped, Jack looked across the cellar at Gunter. The stocky man's face was streaked with dirt, his black beard speckled with plaster dust. Neither of them said anything as they stared silently at the ceiling. The wooden support beams had creaked and groaned, the ground shook, and chunks of dirt and plaster had rained down on their heads. But the beams held.

Time passed, half an hour or an hour; it was hard for Jack to know. Then he heard sounds from outside, voices and boots tramping along the gravel road.

The voices got louder, men shouting orders... in English!

Jack motioned for Gunter to stay where he was. Then he climbed the wooden ladder, pushed open the trapdoor in the floor of the hallway, and crept to the window.

Two American soldiers stood in the road, looking at the house. When a third soldier joined them, they moved closer.

Jack stood and stepped over to the door, slowly pushing it open. He stuck his head out and shouted, "I'm American, an American soldier! It's okay! I'm American! I'm coming out!"

He pushed the door open further and stood in the doorway with both hands in the air. "I'm an American soldier! I'm unarmed!"

The three soldiers looked at each other in surprise. Then one of them stepped forward, pointed his rifle at Jack and motioned for him to step outside. "Is anyone else inside?" he asked.

"The owner of the house," Jack replied. "He helped me last night. He's Belgian, he's on our side."

"Tell him to come out here where we can see him," the soldier said.

When Gunter joined Jack outside, another group of soldiers had arrived. One of them stepped forward and looked Jack up and down. "I'm Lieutenant Dugan, 41st Reconnaissance Platoon," he said sharply. "Who the hell are you?"

Jack took a step forward, acutely aware of the civilian clothing he was wearing. "Lieutenant Jack Richards, US Army Air Corps. I was a prisoner of war in Germany but escaped near Bitburg. This man's name is Gunter, and he came to my assistance. We were going to try and contact you this morning so I could report what I'd seen over there. But I guess it's a little late for that now."

Lieutenant Dugan looked at him like he didn't understand. Then he shrugged and said, "Well, all I know is there's a whole shitload of enemy infantry and a couple hundred tanks heading this way right now. So, you better come with us."

"Where are you going," Jack asked.

"We've been ordered to fall back to Lanzerath. We can escort your friend that far, but no further."

Jack glanced at Gunter, who shook his head. "No, I stay. Must look after animals. I speak German; they leave me alone. You go, you are soldier, go with your men."

Jack doubted the part about the Germans leaving him alone, but he reached out and gripped the stocky man's hand. "Thank you. Good Luck."

Chapter Seventy-One

Lanzerath

Jack followed the reconnaissance platoon through the tiny village of Lanzerath. He counted about twenty small, brick and wood frame homes along the narrow, gravel road that led to a church in the center of the town. It was mid-morning, but the town looked deserted, shutters closed, doors shut, not even a stray dog wandering around.

They passed through the town and followed the road to the west, where it skirted a pasture before bending to the north. Lieutenant Dugan halted the platoon and pointed to a hilltop ridge on the other side of the pasture. "That's our position," he said. "We'll have a clean line of fire onto the road. Our orders are to dig in and hold that position until reinforcements arrive."

Jack looked up at the ridge, a flat area just inside the tree line of a forest. He remembered Dugan's words back at Gunter's house.

There's a whole shitload of German infantry and tanks...

The platoon numbered twenty-five men plus him and a solitary Jeep with a 50-caliber machine gun. He glanced at Dugan, a first lieutenant no older than he was when he'd flown his first mission over Germany almost two years ago. But he had to admit, the guy seemed to know what he was doing... or he was doing a hell of a job faking it.

They spent the next two hours on the ridge top, improving foxholes left behind by some previous troops in some previous battle. When they were deep enough to stand in, they covered the holes with pine logs and brush. The wind picked up, and it started to snow again.

Dugan approached Jack and handed him a Colt 45 pistol. "This is what you fly boys carried, isn't it?" he asked.

Jack nodded.

"Ever fire it?'

Jack shrugged. "Once or twice, on the range back in the states."

Dugan slapped him on the shoulder. "Stay in the back and try not to shoot any of our guys. It won't be long now."

It wasn't.

Jack swallowed hard when the first wave of German infantry emerged from Lanzerath just after noon, marching along the road in a column five men wide that extended back into the town as far as he could see. He put his hand in his coat pocket and felt the grip of the Colt 45. It suddenly seemed very inadequate.

The tiny platoon was hunkered down in their foxholes at the top of the ridge, forming a wide semi-circle over-looking the pasture and the spot where the road turned to the north. The Jeep was hidden in the trees just above the line of foxholes, and Jack kept telling himself that he'd better not raise his head when the machine gun started firing.

Dugan stuck his head out of his foxhole at the center of the group and said, just loud enough to be heard, "They've got their rifles slung over their shoulders, so they're not expecting any trouble. As soon as that first group gets to the bend in the road, we open fire."

Jack's first thought was that Dugan had lost his mind.

There's only twenty-five of us...

But he never completed the thought as the big 50-caliber machine gun cut loose with a deafening clatter that sent vibrations rippling down his spine. He reflexively ducked his head, pulled the pistol from his pocket, and gripped it with shaking hands.

A few moments later, Jack looked up from his position at the rear of the semi-circle and almost pissed his pants. Down on the road, dozens of German soldiers lay sprawled out on the blood-stained ground. But a mass of enemy troops charged across the meadow... heading right at them!

Jack watched in stunned amazement as the platoon opened fire from their elevated position, picking off the front line of enemy troops like duck pins.

But more kept coming.

A second line, then a third. Each one getting farther and farther up the hill, closer to the ridge top.

With the big 50-caliber banging away above his head, Jack clutched his pistol with both hands, hunkering down, wondering what he would do when the enemy troops climbed over the ridge top.

Then Dugan yelled, "Cease fire! Cease Fire!"

Jack looked up as the line of enemy soldiers fell back, retreating down the hill toward the road, climbing over the bodies of their fallen comrades.

Dugan shouted. "Re-load, re-load. It's not over."

Jack inched up a bit higher, looking down at the road. The orderly line of enemy troops had broken formation in a chaotic exodus to the ditches along the road.

Dugan was on the radio, pleading for reinforcements and artillery cover. Jack heard him shout, "There's hundreds of them! We're a recon platoon, we're not trained for this, we can't—" Then Dugan flinched and stared at the handset for a moment before tossing it back to the radio operator. "The son-of-a-bitch said I must be seeing things," he snapped, then stood for a moment as though to calm himself. He glanced around at the platoon, "Okay, stay alert. Help is on the way."

The next attack came an hour later. At least twice the number of enemy troops charged up the middle and along both sides of the pasture. The 50-caliber mounted on the Jeep clattered away, and the platoon fired their carbines from the foxholes as fast as they could re-load.

But this time, the German troops kept coming. They ducked behind the dead bodies for cover and tossed grenades that splattered the line of foxholes with dirt, rocks, and snow.

Jack heard someone shout and looked up just as three German soldiers crested the hill and charged the foxholes on the right side of the line. Two of them were shot down instantly, but the third tossed a grenade toward the Jeep.

The explosion knocked Jack to his knees as a searing blast of heat, and a cascade of rocks and dirt pelted him from behind.

He looked up at what was left of the Jeep, a burning, tangled mass of metal, then turned to the right as two of the Americans jumped from their foxholes, knocked a German trooper to the ground and shot him at point-blank range.

But German troopers swarmed up the hill from both sides.

Gunfire was non-stop, coming from all directions.

The Germans tossed more grenades onto the ridge top, and the Americans tossed them back. One exploded just in front of Jack's foxhole, showering him with snow and dirt. Another exploded behind the foxhole to his left.

Two enemy soldiers suddenly appeared, charging toward the foxhole. Jack stood and fired his pistol twice.

The soldiers hit the ground and disappeared.

Jack's ears rang, and his eyes watered, but he thought he hit one of them.

Then enemy mortar shells screamed in. They all fell short, killing several of their own men.

It continued for over an hour, wave after wave of German troops threatening the hilltop, then backing away, over and over again, under withering fire from the platoon's strategic advantage above them. Jack hunkered down, gripping the pistol so hard his hands cramped up. He kept looking left and right, watching for any other enemy soldiers cresting the hill.

Gradually, the onslaught slackened, and the enemy troops backed away a second time. The gunfire became sporadic and then finally stopped as the targets disappeared.

Another hour passed in the quiet with German troops milling about on the road below. It was getting dark, and it was hard to tell how many were left, but it seemed to Jack that they were still vastly outnumbered. Remarkably, the platoon hadn't suffered any casualties beyond a few minor wounds, cuts, and bruises.

Jack slumped back, leaning against the dirt sides of the foxhole. His hands shook, and he set the pistol on the ground so he wouldn't accidentally pull the trigger. One of the riflemen, his face streaked with dirt, turned around and smiled at him. "They probably didn't teach you any of this shit in flight school, did they?"

Jack shook his head. "No... not even close."

"Well, I think you got one of them. Not bad, fly-boy."

Dugan was on the radio again, this time seeming calmer than before. With a brisk, "Yes sir," he handed the handset back to the radioman. Then, he motioned for the platoon to gather around. "We've been ordered to pull back. Reports are that a squad of enemy tanks is heading to Lanzerath to open this road. So as soon as it's dark, we're hauling our asses out of here through these woods."

Chapter Seventy-Two

SS-Hauptsturmfuhrer Becker stood alongside a halftrack, wondering if they would ever get moving. The 1st Panzer Division—the elite unit hand-picked to spearhead the offensive—had lost the entire first day and stalled just a few miles from where they started because their advance infantry units were beaten back near an obscure hamlet called Lanzerath.

Darkness settled in, with bone-chilling rain slowly turning to sleet, and the mood among the division was as dismal as the weather. Five thousand troops and hundreds of tanks sat idle in the rain and fog, stalled at what was supposed to be the weakest point in the entire line of American forces.

The night passed in agonizingly slow motion until finally, just after dawn, they received word that the American troops in Lanzerath had fallen back, and the road was open. Within minutes, the lead tanks rolled forward, diesel smoke filling the air, steel treads clanking, and mud flying in all directions.

The division commander was incensed at the delay and ordered everything in their path to be destroyed: houses and barns, livestock, and stray dogs. From his half-track trailing behind the lead Jeep, Becker watched as the commander personally shot down a stocky, bearded man standing in an apple orchard tending to a cow and a horse.

It was midafternoon when the 1st Panzer Division arrived in Lanzerath, now deserted and eerily quiet. Becker sat pensively in the rear seat of the half-track as they passed through the tiny village, following the road alongside a pasture littered with the dead bodies of German soldiers. The meticulously planned offensive was a whole day behind schedule, and casualties had already started mounting.

But that was not Becker's concern... staying alive was the important thing. And staying out of the line of fire as much as possible until he found the chance to get away. If they actually made it deep into Belgium close to Namur, that would, of course, be ideal. But there was no assurance they would get that far, and if they didn't, he just had to manage a way to stay alive and get there himself.

Chapter Seventy-Three

Near Grote Brogel

Niels DeVos had a lot on his mind as he drove from Antwerp to the out-of-the-way spot he'd selected near Grote Brogel. When the local gendarme had telephoned with the news of Peeters' arrest, he'd breathed a sigh of relief. Peeters knew too much, and his escape from the Café Brig had been a disaster. How those two dumb bastards got taken down by a bartender with a club was beyond belief. But there was no time to dwell on that now.

He'd deal with Peeters, of course, as well as his cohort, Gaston, who'd also been arrested. But there was still the question of that damn girl, Claire. DeVos assumed that Peeters had told her everything he knew; she was an old family friend and probably an escape line operative, so it would make sense she knew everything. That's why he had set up the attack near the old *Vleeshuis.* Then someone happened to come by and ruined the whole Goddamn thing. And now *she* was missing.

Was Lukas involved in her disappearance? He had no evidence of that, but someone had to have helped her get away. And she and Lukas were living together. DeVos had called Lukas' home and his shop twice since Claire disappeared and no one answered. Lukas *had* to be involved.

There wasn't much he could do about that right now. Becker trusted Lukas, so he knew he had to be careful. But he had to know where the girl went. And Peeters was the one who knew.

DeVos turned on to a narrow dirt road and followed it around a bend to the spot where it ended in front of an abandoned barn hidden in a grove of trees. One of the men he usually hired for side jobs like this stood outside the barn, leaning on an old, battered truck, smoking a cigarette. He was a thick-necked brute who could be relied on to do almost anything as long as he was paid.

DeVos got out of the car and approached the barn. "Are they inside?" he asked.

The brute nodded with a grunt and ground out the cigarette with the heel of his boot.

DeVos stepped into the barn and saw Peeters sitting on the concrete floor, his hands cuffed behind him, his legs shackled. He glanced over to the opposite corner of the damp, foul-smelling building where Gaston lay unconscious on the filthy floor, blood streaming from the back of his head. The brute followed him in and pushed the door closed, slapping an iron bar into his hand a few times.

DeVos stood over Peeters and looked down at him. "You know how this will end," he said calmly, "but it could be done quickly and painlessly. Just tell me where to find your friend, Claire."

Peeters shrugged as a bead of sweat trickled down his face. "I have no idea. I've been in jail for the last several days, if you recall."

DeVos turned away and glanced at the brute, casually flicking his head toward Peeters.

The big man immediately lunged forward and swung the iron bar, clobbering Peeters on his right kneecap. Peeters howled, rolled on his side, and curled into a fetal position. The brute smacked him along the spine, snapping Peeters' head back so hard DeVos thought his neck might break.

DeVos quickly stepped in and pulled the brute back. He leaned down close to Peeters and said, "Tell me where the girl is, and this will stop now."

Peeters slowly turned his head, looking up at him. His eyes were closed, and he wheezed heavily. "I... said... I don't know—" He suddenly broke into a heaving fit of coughing and curled up again.

The brute stepped up, twirling the iron bar. "I'll give him a few whacks in the shoulder," he grunted. "That'll shake it out of him."

DeVos glanced at him and nodded. Obviously, the bastard was good at this sort of thing.

When the brute whacked him on his bandaged left shoulder, Peeters shrieked in agony, writhing and shaking from head to toe.

DeVos stepped forward and once again motioned for the burly man to back off. He knelt down and whispered in Peeters' ear. "I'll give you one more chance to tell me where the girl is, or it will be the end for your friend, Gaston."

The brute dragged the still unconscious Gaston across the floor until he was lying next to Peeters.

DeVos drew his service revolver and pointed it at Gaston's head. He leaned closer to Peeters and whispered again. "Last chance, where is she?"

For a long moment, Peeters didn't move, his body quivering. Then, very slowly, grunting and breathing heavily, he pressed his right hand on the floor and, inch by inch, pushed himself up so that his head was even with DeVos.'

Then he spit in his face.

DeVos flinched, and his head jerked back. Then he stood slowly and wiped his face with the back of his hand. He glanced down at Peeters, then cocked the pistol and shot Gaston in the back of the head.

Peeters collapsed onto his side and curled back into the fetal position.

DeVos turned to the brute. "Finish him off, then get rid of both bodies."

Chapter Seventy-Four

Antwerp, Belgium

DeVos spent most of the next day in his office at police headquarters on the telephone and listening to the radio, shocked at what he heard about a surprise German offensive in the Ardennes. Becker hadn't said a word about this. Did he know? Was he involved?

Everything depended on Becker arriving in Namur.

And now there's another battle underway?

The reports were all sketchy, and he had no idea how extensive the fighting was, but it would certainly create chaos.

He knew how resourceful Becker was and what a meticulous planner he was. Perhaps he knew this was going to happen and planned accordingly. Perhaps he thought the chaos of an offensive would provide cover for getting out of Europe with all the money. DeVos knew the original transfer of funds from *I.G. Farben* was just the beginning, a token to earn his loyalty, even though Becker had threatened his family after taking over the business.

The real plan was to get out of Europe before Germany collapsed, with enough money to live in style in South America or the Caribbean. Whatever else might be part of Becker's plan, DeVos didn't know and didn't care. He only hoped that if he remained loyal and carried out his part of the mission, what was left of his family would be safe... and he'd be rich.

He'd been receiving shipments of money—wooden crates filled with bags of Swiss Francs—for months at the rendezvous point in St. Vith. He knew where the money was hidden, and Becker knew how to get out of Europe. Nothing else really mattered.

But what were his options if Becker got killed or injured in the fighting and never made it to Namur? If the Allies put down this offensive, the Germans would be driven back across the border, and the search for traitors and collaborators would intensify to feverish proportions. And that meant he was vulnerable. He'd committed treason and murder, and if it became known he was finished, even his position as a police captain wouldn't protect him. Peeters and his friend, Gaston, were out of the way, but there were still loose ends. And the biggest loose end was that damn girl, Claire, who knew everything. Somehow, he had to deal with her.

He needed air and decided to take a walk. He put on his hat and coat, left the station, and stepped into the cold, crisp air of the late afternoon, still deep in thought, wondering what had happened to Claire and where she could have gone.

She was obviously trying to find Peeters, and he was certain Lukas was helping her. He knew they hadn't gone to the police or gendarmes, or he would have heard about it. She was obviously very determined and resourceful, but...

DeVos stopped walking as he suddenly had a thought.

McDonald, the MI9 agent.

Did Claire know about him?

He started walking again, slowly, thinking it through. It was certainly possible she did. After what happened to Peeters at the Café Brig, he could have told her to go to McDonald for help. The more he thought about it, the more he began to worry. He had to get to Claire before McDonald or anyone else could protect her.

DeVos walked on in silence, past the cathedral and across the Grote Markt. It was getting dark, and the streetlamps cast shadows along the narrow streets when the idea suddenly hit him.

Put out another bulletin!

Of course, that was it. He could issue a second bulletin announcing that Peeters has been apprehended, but he had an accomplice who is still at large... an accomplice by the name of Mariette Janssens, AKA 'Claire.'

Chapter Seventy-Five

After holding off the German offensive for four days, the beleaguered forces of the 106th Division finally received the order to withdraw from St. Vith. Enemy artillery fire had intensified every night that Claire and Lukas had been confined to the hotel, and at times, Claire was certain the shells would burst right through the roof. Getting a full night's sleep had been impossible, and she passed most of the long nights sitting on the narrow cot, thinking about Jack, wondering if he was in a POW camp in Germany, wondering if he was injured, wondering, worrying...

Just after sunrise on the fifth day, a young lieutenant came to the hotel to escort Claire and Lukas back to the base. Claire buttoned up her coat against the cold as she sat with Lukas in his ancient Citroen outside the 106th Division HQ, watching the semi-organized commotion. The HQ command center had been dismantled, radios were disconnected, file cabinets emptied, maps taken down, and everything hauled outside to waiting trucks. Overnight, the temperature had dropped to below freezing, but at least the snow and sleet had ended, and the skies were clear.

Someone knocked on the passenger side window. It was McDonald. His three-piece suit was now replaced with a brown leather jacket and a black beret. "The road heading west to the Salm River is already jammed, and nothing's moving," he said. "So, just sit tight until I return with a Jeep. You can follow me. The good news is that the roads are frozen, so we won't get stuck in the mud. And now that the skies have cleared up, we might finally get some air cover."

Chapter Seventy-Six

Fourteen hours after leaving St Vith, Claire and Lukas, along with several hundred exhausted infantrymen of the 106th Division, descended on the town of Salm-Chateau on the west bank of the Salm River. Most of the houses and shops were deserted as people had packed up and fled further west to get out of the line of fire. The Americans controlled the area for the moment, but that could change at any time.

The soldiers found their way into empty houses, barns, and shops, bunking down wherever they could, knowing they'd be given only a day or two to rest up before being tossed back into the fight. There was a small hotel on the main street, and the rooms were quickly claimed by officers, but McDonald managed to secure a small room for Claire on the third floor. Numb with cold from the long ride, Claire pulled off her shoes, crawled under the covers of the bed and was asleep within minutes.

Early the next morning, she awoke slowly and grudgingly to a persistent knocking sound. When she finally realized that someone was at the door, she pulled back the covers and reluctantly crawled out of bed, hopping quickly over the cold floor in her stocking feet. She opened the door to see Lukas standing in the narrow hallway with a napkin-covered plate in his hand and a triumphant smile on his face.

"It's bacon," he said, as though he'd just discovered a cache of diamonds.

Claire took the plate and removed the napkin, revealing the delicious aroma of freshly cooked bacon. There were three thick pieces and a slice of brown bread. "How is this possible?" she asked, quickly snatching up one of the pieces and taking a bite.

"A local farmer showed up at the hotel this morning lugging a basketful, and the officers fired up the stove in the kitchen. I was lucky enough to grab some for you before they devoured all of it."

"It's morning already?" Claire asked, glancing at the still, dark window.

Lukas nodded. "It's only 6:30; it won't be light for a while yet."

Claire held out the plate, but he shook his head. "No, I've already had some. That's for you. Enjoy it, but don't take too long. McDonald wants a word with you."

"What about?"

"I don't know; he just said he needed to see you."

Fifteen minutes later, Claire descended the stairs into the hotel's small parlor. It was crowded with officers, laughing and joking, obviously enjoying the surprise breakfast treat and savoring a few hours away from the battle. A good-natured cheer went up for the girl in their ranks, along with a few high fives, as Claire pushed her way through the crowd to the front door where McDonald was waiting.

The freezing morning air hit her with a jolt as she stepped outside, but McDonald quickly took her arm and steered her toward an idling car parked in front of the hotel. "I've got the heater on," he said, "it's not the best, but it's better than standing out in the bloody cold."

Claire buttoned her coat as they jogged to the car.

"Did you sleep ok?" he asked when they had climbed in and closed the doors.

"Like a rock," Claire replied, "I can't remember when I've been that tired before." She motioned toward the hotel. "The officers seem to be in a good mood."

McDonald nodded. "We got word last night that the Jerries' spearhead unit, The 1st Panzer Division, has been spotted near La Gleize. The air corps will be hitting them at first light."

"That sounds like good news."

"It is, but this thing is far from over," McDonald replied. "The telephone lines are all jammed, but late yesterday, I finally contacted my counterpart in G2 Intelligence, Colonel Worthington. He's up in Liege, working like hell trying to figure out what's happening. But he's agreed to meet with me in Liege tomorrow so I can brief him on what we know so far about DeVos and the smuggling operation."

"Will he be able to help us get DeVos?" Claire asked.

"That's what I need to find out. I can't do this on my own. DeVos is an officer in the police department, after all. But the Americans have the most influence in

Belgium right now, so I'll need their help. Worthington's aware of what we've been investigating, but he needs to know about DeVos."

"I certainly hope he can help. I'm sure DeVos is hunting for Bart now right now. Bart knows too much; he knows about St. Vith; he knows about the money transfer from *I.G. Farben,* the document I found…" Her voice trailed off as she thought about the day she discovered the document, the day that started everything.

"Do you have that document?" McDonald asked.

Claire shook her head. "No, I gave it to Bart."

"Listen, Claire, this has now become very complicated… and very dangerous for you, and probably Lukas as well."

"So, what do we do?"

"You both stay right here. I've spoken to the 106th commander, and he'll post a guard in the hotel. I'll be back as soon as I can. If they need to move out before I return, they'll take you with them. That's the safest thing for you now. I'll know where to find you."

Chapter Seventy-Seven

Near La Gleize, Belgium

The instant Becker spotted the American Thunderbolts roaring in at tree top level, he grabbed the canvas bag at his feet and jumped from the half-track. He rolled on the ground and buried his head in his hands as the planes opened fire.

The hammering machine-guns and thundering rockets ripped through the tank convoy. The ground heaved as if an earthquake had erupted, sending mountains of snow, rocks and shrapnel soaring in all directions. Becker felt searing waves of heat wash over his back as tank after tank exploded, and the terrified crewman of the 1st Panzer Division scrambled to escape the burning infernos.

Becker crawled forward, away from the road, desperately clawing through the snow-covered, rocky ground. Suddenly, a shock wave from a deafening blast smashed him flat into the snow as chunks of debris the size of car doors crashed to the ground.

His ears rang, and his eyes burned from the smoke as he started to crawl again, making his way slowly, inch by inch, into the field along the road. Choking and coughing from the thick, acrid smoke, barely able to see, he kept crawling further into the field, ignoring the screams and shouts from his wounded and dying comrades.

Finally, he hunkered down in a hollow and scooped up handfuls of snow, wiping his burning, half-closed eyes. Then he slumped down as low as he could and covered his head with his arms as the horrific sounds of blast after blast echoed across the frozen terrain.

It was Russia all over again, and Becker's mind reeled with the memories. The snow and bone-chilling cold, the fire and smoke, the screams, the blood... and the never-ending, paralyzing sound of machine-gun fire and rocket blasts. Gripped with fear on those ghastly days on the Russian steppes, his only instinct had been exactly the same as it was now. Get away!

Suddenly, it was over. The American planes disappeared into the morning sky, leaving behind a long line of wrecked, burning tanks and hundreds of dead, wounded, badly burned and maimed German soldiers. Becker used the cover of the thick, oily smoke to emerge from his hiding place. Turning away from the crackling glow of the fires, away from the screaming and moaning of the tank crewmen, he hoisted the canvas pack on his back and set off in the opposite direction.

Chapter Seventy-Eight

Liege

McDonald sat at a glossy, wooden table in a conference room in Liege across from Colonel Sam Worthington of US Army G2. It was a windowless room on the ground floor of a former bank building. McDonald had worked with Worthington on numerous occasions, and he always had a calm, congenial manner. But today, he seemed tense and on edge. The surprise German offensive had been an intelligence failure of epic proportions, especially for the Americans, and it was obviously taking its toll.

"Thank you for agreeing to meet with me this morning, Colonel," McDonald said, "I'm sure you've got a lot more important things on your mind at the moment."

Worthington shrugged. "Yeah, all hell's breaking loose right now. You know what it's like when the top brass gets surprised by the enemy. But tell me what you've got. I know this is also pretty damn important."

McDonald explained what had happened to Peeters after their meeting with DeVos and what he'd learned from Claire about the smuggling operation through St. Vith.

When McDonald finished, Worthington said, "I've read all your intel reports about this German SS officer, Konrad Becker. Is he still involved with this?"

McDonald nodded. "I'm certain that Becker is orchestrating the entire operation, smuggling not only money but high-level people out of Germany."

Worthington opened a file folder and removed a single sheet of paper. "After we talked on the telephone, I called an inspector at the Liege police department. We're on pretty good terms, and I wanted to find out if he knew Captain DeVos. He doesn't know him personally, but he sent this over."

McDonald took the paper and flinched when he saw Claire's photo at the top of a police bulletin. As he read the bulletin, a pit formed in his stomach.

Alert to Belgian police officers and gendarmes:

The Antwerp Police Department has issued an arrest warrant for a fugitive believed to be an enemy collaborator and spy for the Third Reich. The fugitive being sought is a young woman by the name of Mariette Janssens, also known as 'Claire,' who is an accomplice of Bart Peeters, a known enemy collaborator who was recently apprehended in Grote Brogel. The exact whereabouts of this woman are unknown, but anyone with information about this person should report it to Captain DeVos at the Antwerp Police Department."

McDonald dropped the bulletin on the table and looked at Worthington. "Good God, DeVos is more desperate than I thought to invent a story like this. But the part about Bart Peeters being apprehended is very disturbing. He's been a friend and a great asset all through the war. Do you know if it's true?"

"No, I don't. But I did ask the inspector that same question, and he has no reason to doubt it."

"Does he know where they took Peeters?"

"Worthington shook his head. "No, he doesn't, and neither does the gendarme in Grote Brogel."

"I've half a mind to go to Antwerp and confront the son-of-a-bitch myself."

"He'd stonewall you," Worthington said. "And neither of us has any direct authority over local police departments."

"Yes, you're right, of course. For now, it's probably best if DeVos doesn't know we suspect him of anything. But I've got to find out about Peeters. He's the one with first-hand knowledge about this operation. And I need to find out who else is involved."

"Any thoughts about that?' Worthington asked. "In something this big, there have to be others involved."

"I agree, but we only know about DeVos and Becker, of course."

"So, I assume the part about the young woman, Claire, being a collaborator is all a fabrication. Correct?"

"Yes, a bloody lie, every bit of it. This chap, DeVos, is the collaborator."

Worthington propped his elbows on the table and let out a long breath. "I don't have to tell you that this young lady is in extreme danger right now. Every police station and gendarmerie in Belgium will post this on their boards. Where is she right now?"

"She's with the 106th Division. Their commanding officer assigned one of his men to watch over her until I get back."

"Well, I think the 106th is about to give up Salm Chateau and head west. Things are likely to get very dangerous. I'll get word to them to have Claire taken to the field HQ at Haute Bodeux. All the brass are there, and she'll be safe until you can get there."

"Much appreciated. One more favor to ask. Can you set up a meeting for me tomorrow with the inspector in Liege? I'd like to talk with him about DeVos."

"Sure, no problem. I'd go with you, but I'm swamped. You should go talk to that gendarme in Grote-Brogel as well. But if DeVos is anything like you've described, he's probably bribed or threatened him into silence."

Chapter Seventy-Nine

The next day, Claire woke up just after dawn, shivering under the thin blankets. She glanced at the solitary, frost-covered window and closed her eyes again. She had not felt this isolated and alone since the day she returned to Antwerp from Brussels and learned that her parents had been arrested by the Gestapo.

Ever since that day, the only thing that gave her hope was her belief that the war would not last forever, that the Allied armies would prevail, and the Nazi menace would be defeated. That belief and her friendships with Bart, Gaston, Lukas, and the other patriots who helped her and protected her had kept her going in the dangerous, clandestine world of the escape line.

And then... there was Jack.

She thought about the last morning they spent together, standing on a rock over-looking Spain, holding hands, the warmth of their lovemaking still radiating in her soul. She remembered every single detail of his face, his dark brown eyes, the damp mist that clung to his hair. At times, it was almost too much to—

She was abruptly roused from her thoughts by the sound of vehicles in the street and men shouting. Then someone knocked at her door. She pulled on her shoes, slipped on her sweater, and opened the door to find Corporal Dennison, the young soldier assigned to guard her, standing in the hallway. "We're bugging out, Miss," he said in his ever-polite tone, with an accent she had learned was from the American south.

"Bugging out?" It was a term she didn't know.

"We're leaving, retreating," the corporal explained patiently, "and establishing a new line of defense further west. We got word that the Germans were heading in that direction toward Dinant. We've got to go now."

"Is Mr. McDonald here?" Claire asked.

"No, Miss. But I have strict instructions to stay with you and make sure you're safe."

Outside the hotel, the street was mobbed with hundreds of infantrymen forming up and heading out of town. Jeeps and trucks moved slowly through the narrow, crowded streets intermixed with foot soldiers, all heading west, leaving Salm Chateau to the enemy.

Corporal Dennison led the way to a Jeep that was parked in front of the hotel and held the door open for her.

"What about Lukas?" Claire asked.

"I saw him about an hour ago getting into his car. He said to tell you that he had to get back to Antwerp. Better climb in now; we'd best be going."

Later that afternoon, Claire sat in the back seat of the Jeep with a blanket wrapped around her shoulders, her back aching, and her mind numb after hours creeping along narrow roads choked with American Jeeps, trucks, and tanks along with hundreds of exhausted-looking infantrymen. She was still annoyed that Lukas left so abruptly without saying anything to her. She couldn't imagine what was so important that he had to get back to Antwerp, but perhaps something had—

Corporal Dennison abruptly leaned over the front seat and tapped her knee. "We'll be leaving the convoy now, Miss, at that crossroads up ahead." He pointed to a narrow lane marked with a wooden sign in the shape of an arrow and faded letters spelling out *Haute Bodeux, 3km.*

"Why are we going there?" she asked.

"There's a field HQ in a chalet down this way," he replied, "Mr. McDonald will meet you there later."

As they entered Haute Bodeux, Claire glanced around in amazement at the tiny village of a half-dozen sandstone farmhouses clustered around the grounds of a grand, three-story chalet. It was a majestic structure, complete with peaked tile roofs, stained glass windows and turrets, surrounded by at least fifty acres of snow-covered lawn. She wondered who had lived here and what happened to them.

The driver pulled up and stopped in front of a massive stone archway guarded by three US Army MPs. One of the MPs approached the Jeep. He was a master sergeant whose name tag said, 'O'Reily.' He glared at the driver and Corporal Dennison suspiciously. "You lost, son?" he asked with more than a bit of condescension in his tone.

"No sir," Dennison replied, "I have orders to meet Matthew McDonald, British MI9 here."

"McDonald? No one here by that name. Let me see your orders."

"Uh, they're not written orders, sir. We received a message by radio from the 106th Division Commander to meet Mr. McDonald at the chalet in Haute Bodeux later today.

Claire shifted uneasily in her seat when the master sergeant turned his attention to her. "Who's this?" he demanded.

"She's a civilian assistant assigned to McDonald, sir. That's the reason we're here. I believe Colonel Worthington of G2 called here to set it up."

O'Reily glared at Dennison as though he were an impertinent pest. Then he turned to one of the other MPs. "Go inside and find out if they have any orders to expect a Brit named McDonald." Then he turned back to Dennison. "You have any idea who's staying in this place? All the top brass, that's who. If your story doesn't check out, your ass is grass."

The other MP returned a few minutes later and whispered something to the master sergeant, who nodded and turned to Dennison, glancing briefly at his uniform shirt, which bore his name above the left pocket. "So, you're name's Dennison?"

"Yes, sir."

"Let me see your tags."

Seemingly unruffled, Dennison removed the dog tags from around his neck and handed them to O'Reily.

The master sergeant studied them for a moment, then tossed them back. "What's your name, Miss?" he said to Claire. When she confirmed her name, he looked momentarily disappointed, then quickly reverted to his condescending manner. "You are cleared to proceed. Apparently, this McDonald guy has been delayed and will arrive here later. Christ, MI9, G2, they're all a bunch of spooks. No wonder this thing is so fucked up." He paused, still glaring at Claire and Dennison. Then he jerked his thumb toward the chalet. "The corporal will escort you to the chalet and show you where you can wait for him. Do *not* under any circumstances go anywhere else in the chalet until McDonald arrives. Is that clear?"

"Crystal clear, sir," Dennison replied.

O'Reily's eyes briefly narrowed as though he might make a move toward Dennison. Then he turned and walked away.

"Asshole," Dennison quietly whispered as they drove through the archway.

Claire glanced at Dennison. "Crystal clear?" she asked as they drove slowly up the long gravel drive, following the corporal who walked ahead of them. "Were you *trying* to piss him off?"

Dennison shrugged. "He was already pissed off, and he *is* an asshole."

Chapter Eighty

Lukas rolled down the driver's side window and took a deep breath of the cold air. He'd left Salm-Chateau early to get ahead of the convoy, but the narrow road was still clogged with military vehicles, and their ponderous pace was causing him to doze off at the wheel. He needed fresh air. The breeze drifting in through the open window was cold but mixed with dust, grit, and diesel fumes; it was anything but fresh.

He blinked a few times to clear away the cobwebs and stared ahead at the seemingly endless line of American troops and military vehicles, thinking about Claire. He was conflicted about leaving her behind but knew he had no choice. He was due to meet Becker in Namur and had to be prepared.

He was exhausted after the rushed ordeal of transporting twelve of Becker's associates to the *Viscount's* estate. But at least that part was behind him. Now, the mission was approaching the final stage. If all went according to the plan, he would soon lead the *SS-Hauptsturmfuhrer* and the others out of Belgium and on their way to their eventual destinations.

Then, his task would be completed. And, after that, perhaps there would be a chance to build a future with Claire. He certainly hoped there would be, but the double life he'd been leading was weighing on him more and more as time went on. He felt certain he'd been successful in concealing it from Claire, but how much longer could he keep it up?

He regretted leaving her without so much as a word, but he knew Claire too well. She'd want to know why he was leaving where he was going, and it was impossible to lie to her. Claire was clearly in danger; there was no question of that, even if she didn't fully realize it herself. She knew too much, and with people like DeVos, that was extremely perilous. But at least he'd left her in the custody of the American Army. Considering the circumstances, she was probably as safe as anyone could be.

Lukas sighed and rolled the window up a bit. There was a time in his life when he was certain there was a future with Claire. He knew she was fond of him, even referring to him as 'the brother she never had.' But he had always hoped for more, always thought that, perhaps, someday...

Then Jack came along.

He knew how she felt about Jack; he had sensed it immediately the day they arrived at his safehouse. He could see it in her eyes when they looked at each other. It was frustrating and unfair. They had only known each other a few weeks... and he had known Claire her entire life.

Lukas took a last deep breath of the cold, foul air and rolled the window up the rest of the way with the reassuring thought that it no longer mattered. Jack was gone, and *he* was still here. And Claire was safe, in the hands of the US Army... beyond the reach of Niels DeVos.

Chapter Eighty-One

Becker was exhausted. He was also wet, cold and aching from the long trek through the hilly, rocky terrain. He had pushed himself hard for the first hour after leaving his hiding place in the hollow, trying to put as much distance as possible between himself and the battered convoy. But it was tough going as he trekked across snow-covered fields, crossing icy streams, avoiding roads as much as possible, and his progress had slowed considerably the last couple of hours.

All afternoon, he'd pressed on as the clap of artillery fire in the distance grew louder, American airplanes crisscrossed the skies, and plumes of black smoke rose above the trees. The battle was raging, and now he had to make sure to avoid it.

The sun was going down as Becker slogged up another hill and stopped to catch his breath. Then he spotted it, a barn, on the other side of a field, less than a hundred meters away. He dropped to his knees and took a moment to scan the area.

Beyond the barn was a small stone house. There was no sign of activity, no neighbors he could see in any direction. There had to be a road, of course, probably on the other side of the house, out of sight from his vantage point.

Off to his left was a small outcropping of rocks and two trees. He glanced at the setting sun, then stepped over the outcropping and settled down with his back to one of the trees.

Becker woke with a start. It was completely dark, and he was shivering.

Christ, I must have dozed off.

He slowly got to his feet, moving his head back and forth and shaking his arms. Then he stamped his feet on the ground, picked up the canvas pack and set off toward the barn. He moved slowly across the open field, pistol in hand, listening for any sound of dogs. The night sky was black and overcast save for wisps of light snow that blew about in the breeze.

When he reached the back of the barn, he waited for a few minutes, listening. Hearing nothing, he stepped to the corner, keeping his back pressed against the rough brick wall. He inched his way to the front of the barn and peered around the corner; his eyes focused on the farmhouse. The house was dark and quiet, so he inched along the front side of the barn until he reached a large wooden door that slid on rails mounted above. He nudged it carefully. It moved with only a slightly audible squeak. He pushed it again, gently, just enough so that he could squeeze through.

He slowly pulled the door closed, then turned around and flicked on his flashlight. The barn smelled of hay and cow dung, and as he passed the light around, he noticed an old tractor, a plow and several cows resting in stalls at the rear of the barn. They ignored him.

He stepped over to an open area under a hay loft and checked his watch. It was a little past nine. Most likely, whoever lived in the house—if they hadn't already abandoned it—would be going to bed soon. He had plenty of time to get ready.

He opened the canvas sack and removed a US army field uniform, a colt 45 pistol and a garrison cap with a captain's insignia. He didn't bother to smooth out the wrinkles because he'd made sure the uniform was supplied complete with dirt and blood stains as might be expected of a soldier in battle. The fact that the 1st Panzer Division had been stopped was a set-back, but not entirely unexpected. Becker had thought from the beginning that the offensive through the Ardennes was doomed to fail, and he had come prepared. *He* was not about to fail.

Chapter Eighty-Two

When DeVos returned to the police station late the next day, the clerk at the front desk said he had a telephone message and handed him a small slip of paper.

DeVos took the slip of paper and read the message.

Urgent that you contact MP Master Sergeant O'Reily at Chalet Haute Bedoux regarding the fugitive sought named Mariette Janssens.

DeVos stared at the message and read it a second time, scarcely able to believe his luck.

Was it possible that the US Army had tracked down the girl?

Had the plan really worked?

The message included a telephone number, and he went to his office to make the call. This may be just the break he'd been hoping for. That bitch had caused enough trouble, and he would take great pleasure in doing away with her.

"O'Reily, here," the voice on the other end of the line snapped crisply.

"This is Captain DeVos from the Antwerp Police Department. I understand you have some information about a fugitive we are searching for."

"Yeah, that's right," O'Reily said. "I had to make a trip over to MP Headquarters in Spa earlier today, and I spotted your bulletin on their board. This person you're looking for, Mariette Janssens, AKA 'Claire,' is here at the chalet in Haute Bedoux. She was brought in the day before yesterday under very strange circumstances. The bulletin said to contact you."

DeVos paused before responding and took a deep breath. "Are you sure it's the same person?"

"Yeah, I'm sure. I was at the gate when some snot-nosed corporal drove her in. She gave me her name, and this is her in the photo. It's the same person, no doubt about it."

"Was anyone else traveling with her?"

"No, just the corporal that drove her in."

"In that case, Sergeant, I will leave first thing in the morning and drive down to pick her up. This person is a spy and a traitor."

There was silence on the other end as though the sergeant was thinking it over.

DeVos waited.

When O'Reily spoke again, there was a note of uncertainty in his voice. "Apparently, some British Intel officer arranged for her to come here. He's not on the base at the moment, and I don't know when to expect him." There was another long pause. "But if she's what you say she is—"

"You can be assured of that," DeVos cut in. "She's a traitor, and she's responsible for the torture and deaths of several American aviators. We have been searching for her for several weeks."

"Well, if that's the case, come on down here and get her."

Chapter Eighty-Three

Becker exited the barn at three o'clock in the morning wearing the US Army uniform that identified him as Captain Rickert, G2 Intelligence and crept slowly to the farmhouse. He stepped up on the wooden porch at the back of the house, paused and listened. It was quiet, no movement from inside, no dogs barking, nothing.

He tried the door. It was open. He slipped inside and removed his shoes, then flicked on his flashlight and moved slowly through the dark kitchen. He spotted a telephone on the wall, a stroke of luck. He passed through to the parlor until he located the staircase.

Upstairs, Becker discovered two small bedrooms, both with open doors. One was empty, but from the other, he heard the sounds of someone snoring. He kept the flashlight pointed at the floor and snuck into the second bedroom, where he found a man and woman sound asleep. Slowly, silently, he stepped up to the bed and pointed his pistol at the man's head.

Just as he pulled the trigger, Becker saw the woman move. When the blast of the gunshot reverberated through the tiny room, the woman sat bolt upright, staring at him with wide, uncomprehending eyes, spatters of blood running down her face. She turned toward her husband and shrieked, a loud, wild howling that caused Becker to flinch. He stumbled backward and almost dropped the flashlight.

The woman shrieked again—

Then he shot her.

Becker stood motionless for a moment, staring at the couple he'd just murdered. They appeared elderly, gray-haired and thin. He quickly holstered his pistol and backed out of the room, closing the door behind him.

Back downstairs in the kitchen, he rummaged through the cabinets and found a dusty, unmarked bottle of calvados, probably something the old man distilled himself. He poured some into a glass and knocked it back. Then he poured another and sat in the dark, sipping it slowly.

He sat quietly in the dark kitchen for over an hour, thinking and planning his next move. Finally, he stood and picked up the telephone.

***

Niels DeVos woke up instantly when the telephone rang.

"Becker," came the sharp response on the other end of the line.

It took a moment for the fog of sleep to clear away. "Yes... of course, what—"

Becker cut him off. "I will be in Namur tomorrow."

DeVos rubbed his eyes, glancing at the clock. "Namur? Tomorrow?"

"Go there today, to the hotel where you made reservations."

DeVos was alert now, thinking as fast as he could. He had to tell Becker about the girl. He should also—

"Did you hear me?" Becker said sharply.

"Yes, of course. The *Grand Hotel de Flandre*. But... something has come up just yesterday, something you should know about."

A pause. Then Becker said sharply, "What is it?"

DeVos closed his eyes for a second, took a deep breath and said, "There is someone else who may know about our plans, a young woman who was an associate of Peeters, and—"

Becker cut in. "Peeters? You've taken care of him, I hope!"

"Yes, of course, he and his friend, Gaston. But there is this girl, a young woman named Claire, who probably knows everything Peeters did. She worked for him at the Department of the Interior; she's the one who discovered the funds transfer from *I.G. Farben*. I put out an arrest warrant for her and just received a call from an American MP who is holding her in custody in Haute Bedoux."

"How long have you known about her?" Becker asked, his voice like ice.

"Just a few weeks, we tried to pick her up once before, but—"

Becker cut him off again. "Forget it; we can discuss that another time. Just go and get her before she gets away again."

"Yes, of course, I'm going there this morning. But there is another ah... complication. Claire is a close friend of Lukas'. I believe she was working with him in the escape line, and lately, she has been living with him."

Becker was silent for what seemed like a long time. Finally, he said, "Is Lukas with her now?'

"No, apparently, she was alone when she arrived in Haute Bedoux, except for an army corporal who drove her to the base."

Another pause while DeVos wiped the sweat from his brow.

Then Becker continued. "Bring her to Namur. I will meet you at midnight on the other side of the Jambes Bridge at the base of the Citadel. Then we'll find out what the hell is going on."

***

The sun was rising when Becker stepped outside the farmhouse and took a walk around the property. The house was surrounded by snow-covered fields on three sides and fronted a narrow dirt road. He walked out to the road and looked in all directions, not spotting any other homes or farms. It was perfect.

He went back into the house and fried some eggs and bacon he'd found in an ice box. Then he stood near a window in the parlor where he could watch the road, listening to the sound of artillery fire in the distance. He wondered if it was the Americans finishing off the 1st Panzer Division.

An hour passed, and he was just about to light a cigarette when he spotted vehicles approaching about a half mile down the road. He stepped out onto the porch and raised his binoculars, relieved to see they were Americans. There were two Jeeps and a canvas-backed truck. Becker stepped out to the road and waved them down.

A lieutenant jumped out of the lead Jeep and saluted when he spotted Becker's uniform. "Lieutenant Anderson, 3rd Battalion, 82nd Division," he announced.

Becker smiled and returned the salute. "Captain Rickert, G2 Intelligence. Can you give me a lift?"

"We're headed to La Gleize, where some hot-shot Panzer group is trapped," the lieutenant said. "You're welcome to ride there with us."

Becker surmised which 'hot-shot Panzer group' the lieutenant was referring to and emphatically shook his head. "No, it's extremely important that I get to Antwerp without delay. I'm an enemy interrogator with G2 and was on my way to a meeting at G2 headquarters last night when our Jeep got lost and hit a mine. I'm the only one that survived."

The lieutenant looked uncertain about what to do, but Becker didn't give him a chance to reply. "Are you in command of this unit?" he demanded.

"Uh, yes, sir, I am now. Captain Johnson was shot by a sniper yesterday afternoon."

It was a stroke of good luck, and Becker knew exactly what to do. "I'm sorry to hear that, lieutenant. But I'm afraid I will have to pull rank on you and take one of your Jeeps. You may follow your orders and continue with the others to La Gleize."

The lieutenant blinked, and for a moment, Becker thought the young man would object. Instead, the lieutenant glanced at the sergeant who was driving the Jeep, a husky man at least ten years older. The sergeant just shrugged and climbed out of the Jeep.

"Have you got a map?" Becker asked.

"Yes sir, there's one under the driver's seat," the sergeant replied.

Becker climbed into the Jeep and waited until the Americans drove off, then opened the map and figured out the best route to Namur.

Chapter Eighty-Four

Jack trudged along with the 41st Reconnaissance Platoon as they headed west, following a single-lane dirt road that meandered past farm fields, through hilly forests, and over rickety bridges. He could hear artillery and small arms fire from behind them, but they hadn't encountered any other troops—friendly or enemy—since pulling out of Lanzerath.

In the middle of the afternoon, Dugan ordered a halt at a crossroad. Nearby was a small cluster of houses and barns. Standing alongside Dugan, Jack looked around at the tiny hamlet. There were no signs of life in any of the houses, and save for a few cows feeding on hay near the barns; the tiny settlement looked deserted.

"The people are still here," Dugan said, motioning toward the small, sturdy-looking stone structures, "most likely peeking out the windows wondering if we're Germans or Americans."

"Which are they hoping for?" Jack asked.

Dugan shrugged. "Hard to know, isn't it? My guess is they really don't care as long as we just leave them alone."

Then Jack heard the sound of vehicles approaching from the south. He glanced at Dugan, who had already pulled out his binoculars and peered down the road.

"They're Americans," Dugan said. "Three men in a Jeep and two Sherman tanks." Dugan stepped out into the middle of the road as the vehicles approached the crossroads and motioned for Jack and the others to follow, holding their weapons high over their heads. "Americans!" Dugan shouted. "We are Americans!"

The Jeep skidded to a stop, and one of the three soldiers stood up, staring at them. Then he sat back down and motioned to the driver, who accelerated up to the crossroad.

An officer climbed out of the Jeep and stepped up to Dugan. "Major Wells, 106th Infantry."

Dugan saluted, "1st Lieutenant Dugan, 41st Recon Platoon. We've come from Lanzerath."

"You were at Lanzerath? We heard about that. Sounded like a hell of a fight."

Dugan nodded. "We held out as long as we could, sir, before we received orders to fall back."

"Well, you delayed the enemy attack by at least a couple of days, Lieutenant, a heroic effort." He paused for a moment, then glanced at Jack, obviously noticing his lack of uniform. "Who are you?"

Jack spoke up and explained his situation.

The major stared at him for a moment, then nodded and said to Dugan, "Well, Lieutenant, you're a Captain now. We finally had to abandon St. Vith, and what was left of the 106th is a few miles behind us. Take these two tanks and you and your men keep heading west.

I'm on an advance scouting mission so contact me by radio if you encounter enemy troops."

Chapter Eighty-Five

Claire was getting restless, wondering what was going on. She hadn't heard from either Corporal Dennison or McDonald since her arrival at the chalet, and it was beginning to concern her. It was mid-afternoon, and she was re-reading a copy of *Treasure Island* she'd found in the chalet's library, thinking about Jack and how they'd laughed about the Jim Hawkins character.

There was a knock on the door.

She opened it to find Corporal Dennison standing in the hallway. "Hello, Corporal. How are you today?" she asked.

Dennison didn't smile, as he almost always did. Instead, he just nodded politely and said, "If you'll come with me, Miss, and bring your coat. You are being transferred."

"Transferred? To where?" It was a surprise, for sure, but not altogether unusual given that she'd had to move every few days to stay clear of the fighting.

"I don't know, Miss. I was just ordered by Master Sergeant O'Reily to come and get you. They've got a car waiting."

"Has Mr. McDonald returned from Liege?" she asked.

"No, he hasn't."

Maybe they're taking her to Liege to meet with him, Claire thought. But that optimistic thought vanished in an instant when she and Dennison arrived at the front entrance. Master Sergeant O'Reily abruptly gripped her arm and led her to a car waiting in the driveway.

A stocky, bald man with gold-rimmed glasses, wearing a police officer's uniform, stood by the car. "This is Captain DeVos of the Antwerp Police Department," O'Reily said crisply. "He is taking you into custody."

Claire instinctively tried to jerk away, but O'Reily's grip was vicelike. "What the hell is going on?" Claire demanded. "I am here under the specific orders of Matthew McDonald with British MI9."

"Yeah, but he's not here, lady and Captain DeVos has a warrant for your arrest."

"No! This is a mistake!"

DeVos stepped forward, holding a pair of handcuffs.

"Wait, no, this is crazy; someone has made a terrible mistake!" Claire shouted, trying again to break away.

But DeVos grabbed her other arm, spun her around and snapped on the cuffs behind her back. Then he and O'Reily pushed her into the back seat of the car.

Claire glanced back and made eye contact with Corporal Dennison, silently mouthing the words, *Get McDonald!*

Chapter Eighty-Six

Claire studied the bald man as he started the engine and drove away from the chalet. She had wondered what Niels DeVos looked like, and now she knew. "So, Mister DeVos, where are you taking me?" she asked, making no attempt to hide her contempt.

He turned abruptly and glared at her. "It's *Captain* DeVos, and if I were you, lady, I'd keep my damn mouth shut."

"I saw your phony bulletin calling *me* a traitor. *You're* the traitor, and everyone will know as soon as—"

DeVos stopped the car abruptly, swung his right arm across the back of the seat and caught Claire squarely on the side of her jaw. Her head snapped back so hard she thought her neck would break, and a lightning bolt of pain shot through to the back of her head.

Her ears rang so loudly that she barely heard him say, "And that's just the beginning of what I will do to you if you utter one more goddamn word." He turned away, put the car back in gear and started driving down the road.

A moment later, when Claire yelled, "Go to hell!" he flinched but did not turn around again.

It was over an hour before the pain in Claire's head subsided, and she was able to work her jaw back and forth. Her teeth were all intact, and her jaw wasn't broken, but the welt on the side of her face had swollen up and was extremely tender to the touch.

She hadn't expected the sudden eruption of DeVos' temper, and she certainly didn't like getting smacked in the face. But she had discovered a potentially valuable bit of information. He probably intended to kill her; that seemed certain. But if he was so thin-skinned that a few smart-assed remarks could cause that kind of reaction, she had to be very careful and not let him go over the top.

They were driving west, weaving through massive groups of American army troops clogging most of the roads. Every town they passed through was crawling with American infantrymen, Jeeps, and trucks. It was hard for her to resist screaming for help, but she knew that no one would hear her above the cacophony of engine noise, men shouting and clanking tank treads. And, even if she did manage to get someone's attention, DeVos was a police officer, and she was a fugitive under arrest.

She assumed DeVos was eventually going to rendezvous with the SS officer, Becker, who was directing the smuggling operation. But would he get rid of her before that? Or did Becker know about her, and was DeVos bringing her to him? She wasn't sure which was worse.

As time passed, the concentration of American soldiers began to thin out. But, from the east, Claire could still hear the steady, rolling thump of artillery fire, much like a gathering thunderstorm. She had kept track of the towns they passed, and it seemed that DeVos was continuing west toward Dinant. But she remembered what Corporal Dennison said about the Germans heading in the same direction. DeVos would need to turn north before too long to avoid the worst of the fighting.

She looked through the windshield and noticed a bank of dark clouds that had moved in from the west, blocking out the setting sun. The wind had picked up, and it looked like it might begin to snow again.

Chapter Eighty-Seven

Matthew McDonald returned to the US Army G2 base in Liege after a frustrating day with the inspector of the Liege police department and the gendarme in Grote Brogel. He stood in the doorway of Colonel Worthington's office, waiting for the beleaguered Intel officer to get off the phone.

"Christ, the situation's changing every hour out there," Worthington said as he hung up the phone and motioned for McDonald to come in. He ran a hand through his gray hair and took a deep breath. "So, how did you make out?"

"The inspector was quite cordial but said he wasn't in a position to do anything about DeVos. He would have to take it up with his chief, and they would have to go to the chief in Antwerp—"

Worthington held up a hand. "Yeah, I get it. Same type of bureaucratic run around as the military. How did it go with the gendarme in Grote Brogel?"

"Worse, complete stonewall, claims DeVos and a couple of other policemen waltzed into the gendarmerie and took Peeters and someone else away."

"Did he—"

Worthington was interrupted by a clerk who stepped into the doorway and spoke to McDonald. "I'm sorry to interrupt, but you have a phone call. It's from a Corporal Dennison in Haute Bedoux. He said it's urgent."

McDonald's thoughts immediately turned to Claire. He glanced at Worthington, who gestured to the clerk. "Transfer the call in here."

McDonald picked up the phone with some trepidation. He listened silently, growing sick to his stomach, as Corporal Dennison related what had happened. He set the phone down and stared at Worthington. "Claire was taken into custody an hour ago in Haute Bedoux by Captain DeVos of the Antwerp police department."

"What? How the hell did that happen?"

"Some MP sergeant named O'Reily apparently saw the bulletin DeVos issued and contacted him. But that doesn't matter now… we've got to find her and nail that son-of-a-bitch."

"I doubt DeVos is taking her back to Antwerp," Worthington said, "not with that phony arrest warrant he cooked up."

"I agree," McDonald said. "But DeVos probably needs to meet up with Becker somewhere, perhaps wherever he's hidden all the money. So, is he taking her with him so Becker can deal with her?"

"Or now that this offensive has thrown everything into chaos, maybe DeVos will try to get out of the country and head to Switzerland. You said he transferred a lot of money there." Worthington stepped over to a large map on the wall, filled with scribbles of arrows and circles from an intel briefing earlier. "So, DeVos and Claire left the chalet in Haute Bedoux a little over an hour ago. He would have to go south through Luxembourg and France to get to Switzerland. But if he knows anything at all about the current battle situation, he won't drive straight south, or he'd run into one hell of a shit storm. He would have to drive west, all the way around Dinant, to stay out of the line of fire."

"But what will he do with Claire?" McDonald stared at Worthington as the question hung in the air... a question they both knew the answer to. He paced around the small office, remembering how he had told Claire she would be safe when he left her. He turned back to Worthington. "My orders from London are specific. They want Becker and the Nazis from *I.G. Farben* and DeVos will lead us to Becker. But if we act fast and get lucky, maybe we can save her. She's a bloody hero; she risked her life rescuing Allied airmen and risked her life coming down to St. Vith to meet me."

"No question about that," Worthington said. "So, let's think this through. We have two possibilities. DeVos is either heading to some unknown location in Belgium to meet Becker; or he's on his way to Switzerland by way of Dinant."

"We don't have much time," McDonald said. "If he makes it to the French border, our chances of finding him will be nil. The country is in disarray, the government is a mess, and no one is going to care too much about a civilian fugitive from Belgium.”

He stared at the map for a moment, then said, “I’m going to Dinant.”

Worthington nodded. “I’ll call the police chief in Dinant and ask him to put every one of his officers and the local gendarmes on the lookout. We know what kind of car DeVos is driving, and there aren’t that many private autos on the road. When you get to Dinant, check in with the CO of the 4th Armored Division. I’ll let him know to expect you. I’ve got to stay here and monitor the progress of the offensive.”

“While you’re at it, call that dumbass MP sergeant O’Reily and let him know how badly he screwed up!” As McDonald was pulling on his coat, the same clerk stepped into the room and handed a note to him. When he read it, he looked up at Worthington, slowly shaking his head. “This is a message from that gendarme in Grote Brogel. He just learned that Bart Peeters and his friend, Gaston, were both shot and killed as they attempted to escape.”

Chapter Eighty-Eight

Darkness came quickly as the snow moved in, huge flakes cascading down harder every minute, forcing DeVos to slow down as the roads turned slippery. Claire closed her eyes and visualized a map of Belgium, once again recalling what she'd heard from Corporal Dennison about the present battle situation. The Germans were heading west toward Dinant. The Americans would certainly mount a counterattack to stop them, Claire thought. But where would it take place? Would it be near Dinant, just where DeVos appeared to be heading?

She wondered how much of all this DeVos understood and where he was really going. Was he going to meet Becker, and where would that be? If it was in Antwerp, Namur or Brussels, he would have to start heading north. Or had he abandoned that mission and was now planning to get out of the country and go to Switzerland?

She visualized the map again. If DeVos was trying to flee the country and go to Switzerland, he needed to get west of Dinant before heading south toward France to avoid the fighting. But that would take time. If he got impatient and turned south *before* they got to Dinant, they could get caught up in the middle of a major battle.

An hour later, the wind had increased, and it was snowing harder. The road ahead was almost a whiteout, save for the faint beam of the car's headlights, which barely penetrated the blowing snow. Claire glanced at DeVos, who was concentrating hard, both hands gripping the steering wheel, his shoulders hunched forward as the auto slipped and slid on the snowy, icy road. Claire shifted in her seat, trying to relieve the ache in her shoulders and wrists from the damn handcuffs. With her arms pinned behind her back, it was impossible to find a comfortable position.

As she turned to the left, she glanced out the window and noticed a flash of light off in the distance. It was hard to see what it was through the falling snow, but she kept watching, squinting through the fog on the glass. She saw another flash, a yellowish, white burst, this one much larger. She continued to watch as the light intensified, then slowly faded into a steady flickering, like a fire. Perhaps something exploded and was burning. But where? They had traveled quite far west, so perhaps it was somewhere just east of Dinant.

She turned her head and looked back at DeVos. Had he noticed it? It didn't seem like it because he was staring straight ahead at the slippery, snow-covered road. She turned back and looked out the window again. It was dark except for the faint glow of the fire, partially obscured by the falling snow.

Something is out there.

Chapter Eighty-Nine

Along with the blowing wind and snow, the temperature had dropped, and Claire was shivering, her teeth chattering. The auto had a heater but didn't do much good in the back seat. She hadn't said anything in a while, so she decided to take a chance. "Hey, could you turn up the heat? It's freezing back here."

She obviously surprised him because he flinched, causing the car to swerve on the icy road. "Goddamn it, quit complaining," he snarled. "Don't make me reach back there and whack you again."

"Yeah, that's what you're good at, whacking women."

Suddenly, DeVos slammed on the brakes, and the car swerved wildly. Then, apparently realizing his error, he stepped back on the gas pedal and turned the wheel into the spin. The rear of the car swerved again, then spun a full ninety degrees before coming to a halt.

"You Goddamn bitch!" he screamed. He spun around amazingly fast for a big man and swung his fist at Claire's head. But this time, she anticipated it and ducked down below the back of the front seat. He half-climbed over the seat and beat her on the back with both of his fists, swearing and shrieking like a madman.

It hurt like hell, but he wasn't inflicting the damage that he'd have caused if he had hit her in the face again. She hunkered down further, and a few seconds later, he stopped.

She heard him turn back toward the front of the car, breathing heavily and muttering "fucking bitch," under his breath. He ground the gearshift, stepped on the gas, and the car started moving forward again.

Claire waited a few minutes, then slowly got back up on the seat. She sat in silence, rotating her head and squeezing her shoulders back and forth. She knew she'd probably have some bruises, but she wasn't really injured.

She glanced out the window to her left and, through the snowfall, was still able to make out the faint flickers of light from the fire. She stared at it for a moment... thinking, *Something is different.*

She kept watching as the fire slowly faded away... then it hit her. Instead of coming from the left and the *rear* of the car as before, the light was now coming from the left but the *front* of the car.

We're traveling in a different direction.

Instead of heading west, they were now heading south. She thought about how it could have happened. They must have been at a crossroads at the instant DeVos slammed on the brakes. Maybe that's why he did it. He could have suddenly gotten confused. The car had spun ninety degrees, and, in his rage, he hadn't noticed. Then, after turning around and pummeling her, he just put the car back in gear and started driving again.

Under these conditions, there was no frame of reference save for the position of the fire, which had now died out. DeVos obviously hadn't realized he was now heading south and probably wouldn't for quite some time. Claire sat back in the seat as best she could and thought about it. Most likely, they were still east of Dinant and now heading south, possibly right into the line of fire between the Germans and whatever American battle group was out there and caused that explosion.

Suddenly terrified at the thought of being handcuffed in the back of a car in the middle of a battle zone, Claire took a deep breath to calm herself and closed her eyes, exhaling slowly.

He's going to kill me anyway.

This may be my only chance.

A few minutes later, the car slowed down. Claire spotted something just ahead on the left side of the road. DeVos slowed even more as they approached it, and Claire leaned toward the window, peering through the snow. It looked like a building. The car finally stopped.

It was a two-story house set back several meters off the road. A farmhouse, she assumed, and there was probably a barn and some other outbuildings beyond it, but it was impossible to see that far. The house was dark. Most likely, they were all asleep, or perhaps the house was abandoned. That wouldn't be unusual with all the fighting going on.

She glanced at DeVos, who had rolled down the window and was staring at the house. A moment later, he rolled the window back up and got out of the car. He slogged through the snow to the rear. Claire heard the trunk open and then slam shut again. Then DeVos pulled open the rear door of the car and snapped, "Get out. We're going into this house." He held a pistol in one hand and a flashlight and a coil of rope in the other.

As Claire stepped out into the snow, DeVos pointed the pistol at her head. "If you so much as squirm," he snarled, "I will blow your fucking brains out."

The house was unlocked, and DeVos shoved her through the doorway ahead of him. Claire glanced around at the dark, cold interior. The house seemed vacant, apparently abandoned.

Behind her, DeVos shouted to see if anyone was home, then kicked the door closed, keeping a tight grip on the handcuffs that bound her wrists. She thought about what she might do to break free but decided to bide her time. At least she was finally out of the car and standing on her feet. That was an improvement.

DeVos snapped on the flashlight and slowly moved the beam of light around the room, calling out again, apparently wanting to make sure they were alone. It was a small, open room with two rocking chairs near a stone fireplace and a wooden staircase at one end.

At the other end stood a table and four wooden chairs, with a doorway beyond that, Claire guessed, led to a kitchen.

DeVos showed the light back to the staircase and then, jerking on the handcuffs pulled her over to it. There was a thick wooden post at the base of the stairs that extended up to the wooden ceiling. DeVos put a hand on Claire's shoulder and shoved her into a sitting position. He looped the rope around the post, through the handcuffs and tied it off, jerking it short enough that Claire's back was pressed against the post.

Sitting on the hard, wooden floor with her back and neck aching in pain, Claire wanted nothing more than to lash out at him and curse him for the sick bastard he was. But she kept silent. She needed to think.

She watched as DeVos rummaged about, shining the flashlight around the small house. Finally, he found a kerosene lamp and some matches. He lit the lamp, set it on the table and sat down on one of the wooden chairs. Then he pointed the gun at her. "You know this won't end well for you," he sneered, "but it won't happen right away, and certainly not quickly... not after all the goddamn trouble you've caused." He had a smirk on his face as he set the gun on the table and lit a cigarette, obviously enjoying himself before the kill.

Claire leaned her head back against the post and closed her eyes. Is this how it's going to end, she thought? Dying at the hand of the same son-of-a-bitch that betrayed Jack?

Chapter Ninety

The first thunderous blast jarred Claire so hard it felt like her right shoulder had been ripped from the socket. The second blast, louder and closer, shook the entire house to the point she thought the roof would collapse.

DeVos scrambled to his feet and looked out the window. "What the fuck was that?" he shouted.

"There's a war going on, you dumb bastard, and we're right in the middle of it!"

DeVos spun around, a look of confusion in his eyes. "But we're nowhere near... we're too far—"

He never finished the thought as another massive explosion blew away the outside wall of the house. The shock wave slammed Claire's head and neck backward against the wooden post, pelting her with a spray of dirt, snow, and wood splinters.

A moment later, she opened her eyes and stared dumbfounded at the wreckage on the other side of the room. Remarkably, the table was still standing, and the lantern was still lit, but wind and snow whipped into the room through a massive, jagged hole the size of a horse cart. She glanced down at the floor and spotted DeVos' body under a pile of rubble.

Artillery shells screeched overhead as Claire squirmed violently, twisting her body, trying desperately to get her fingers on the rope. But it was no use. She looked at DeVos again, and her heart sank when she saw his feet move.

Damn it! He's not dead!

She squirmed again and jerked on the rope, praying in vain that she might break it. But all she did was send jolts of pain through her back and neck, forcing her to stop. She glanced at DeVos, and a wave of panic swept over her. His arms were moving now, his right hand reaching out, pushing away rubble.

The bastard will get out of here and leave me to die!

He'll get away!

Then, another jarring concussion rocked the building. Plaster rained down on Claire's head, and the ceiling above her sagged, creaking and groaning.

Wooden boards cracked and snapped.

Claire instinctively closed her eyes and ducked as an entire section of the ceiling suddenly crashed to the floor, taking half the staircase and the thick wooden post with it.

A moment later, she glanced up at a gaping hole in the roof, staring at falling snow against the blackness of the sky above. It took a moment to sink in. Then she realized what had just happened.

The post had split in two and was lying on the floor!

She got to her knees and slid along the floor, pulling her cuffed hands and the rope along the length of the fallen post.

She glanced at DeVos. He was still lying on the floor, half covered in rubble, but now moving both arms and hunching his back.

She crawled faster, ignoring the sharp pains in her knees as she slid over chunks of plaster and broken boards littering the floor. She jerked her arms violently along the length of the post, the broken, jagged end of it now less than a meter away.

DeVos muttered something and tried to lift his head just as Claire managed to jerk the rope all the way to the end of the post.

She staggered to her feet, her hands still clasped behind her back, the rope now right at the broken edge of the post. She jerked the rope upward, but the post didn't move.

Goddamn it!

She jerked again, harder this time, and yet again, until finally, the post lifted just an inch.

Then another inch.

Then, one more... and she yanked the rope from beneath it.

Dragging the rope behind her back, she stumbled across the floor toward DeVos, kicking debris out of the way.

Another explosion rocked the building, knocking her off her feet, and she fell hard onto the floor. The table collapsed, and the kerosene lantern fell to the floor in a burst of flames.

Claire scrambled to her feet and staggered over to DeVos.

Just as she got to him, he turned over, raised his head, and tried to sit up. Without thinking twice, Claire kicked him violently in the side of the head.

Flames swept across the floor as Claire sat down with her back to DeVos, struggling to find the pockets of his trousers.

The key to the handcuffs!

They must be in his pockets!

DeVos moved! And grunted!

She felt his hand on her back, pushing her away.

She got to her feet and kicked him again.

But this time, he grabbed her ankle, trying to pull her down.

She jerked free and jammed her boot into his face.

She stared down at his face in the flickering firelight. His nose was smashed, and blood gushed over his chin. There was a massive welt on the side of his bald head. His eyes were glassy and dim, but she heard him mumble, "Fucking bitch... I'll—"

Claire didn't hesitate. She raised her right foot over his head and screamed as loud as she could, *"This is for Jack, you son-of-a-bitch!"* Then, with every ounce of effort she could muster, she jammed the heel of her boot into his forehead.

The fire spread rapidly. Gagging from the smoke, Claire grabbed DeVos' limp arm and dragged his body away from the flames. She sat down again, frantically digging into his trouser pockets.

She found it! A ring of keys.

She got to her feet and, without looking back, staggered out of the house.

She stumbled through the snow and slumped down behind the car. Clutching the ring of keys in trembling hands, she located the one for the handcuffs and then fumbled around behind her back, trying to unlock the damn things. Shivering from the cold, her arms and wrists going numb, she prayed she wouldn't drop the keys in the snow.

At last, she got it. The lock clicked open, and she shook the blasted things off her wrists.

It was only then she realized the shelling had stopped.

A wave of heat washed over her as blazing flames completely engulfed the house, illuminating the dark night sky. Claire struggled to her feet and leaned against the car for support. She spotted the silhouettes of dozens of tanks in the fields beyond the road, many of them shattered or burning.

Christ, we stumbled right into the middle of it!

It was impossible for her to tell which tanks were German and which were American, but those from the west were advancing while those from the east were retreating.

She continued to lean against the auto, watching the advancing tanks. A moment later, one of them turned and headed directly toward the burning house. It stopped about fifty meters away, and two crewmen jumped out and jogged toward the house.

Every bone in her body ached, her arms and wrists were bleeding and numb, and her head throbbed so badly that she thought it would split. Even if she had the energy to try, she knew she would never be able to get away. So, she just closed her eyes and waited, hoping they were Americans.

Chapter Ninety-One

Jack sat in the lead Jeep next to Captain Dugan as the 41st Recon Platoon pressed on for another hour, following a narrow, snow-covered road. The immediate area was quiet, though the ever-growing sound of shelling in the south and east was proof the battle was raging on several fronts just a few miles in either direction.

They crested a hill and, up ahead, perhaps a half mile down the road, Jack spotted a lone farmhouse and a barn, surrounded by fields on three sides. Dugan raised his hand, signaling the platoon to a halt. He tapped the shoulder of the radio man in the front seat and said, "Get four men up here to go with us down to that farm. The rest of the platoon and both tanks stay here and keep a lookout."

Following the four infantrymen, the Jeep proceeded slowly down the road toward the farmhouse. When they stopped in front of it, the four men spread out and circled the house while the driver and radioman got out and stood in front of the Jeep, aiming their submachine guns at the house.

Dugan nudged Jack and pointed to the tire tracks in the snow-covered road just ahead of them. "A couple of vehicles have come through here not long ago, but nothing big. Probably just a couple of Jeeps, maybe ours."

A moment later, the front door of the house opened, and one of the infantrymen appeared. "It's all clear, Captain!" he yelled. "But you'd better come in here and have a look. It's bad!"

Jack followed Captain Dugan into the house and up the stairs into a bedroom. He took a step back at the sight of the blood-covered bodies lying in the bed.

The two infantrymen, both young and nervous, were waiting for them in the small parlor when Dugan and Jack came back down the stairs. "What should we do with them, sir?" one of the men asked.

Dugan removed his helmet and ran a hand through his hair. "This doesn't look like a military action to me. The house isn't damaged, hasn't been ransacked, and there are only a couple of tire tracks outside. I'd say these poor people were murdered, probably by a civilian, maybe an intruder." He glanced back at the staircase and then put his helmet back on. "Let's go outside and look at the map. I think there's a town up ahead. If there's a gendarme, we'll report this. Looks like a civilian crime to me."

It turned out there was a small village two miles down the road with a French name Jack couldn't pronounce. The small convoy approached the village slowly until they arrived at a crossroad just outside the town and halted.

413

It was a tiny settlement with a single road fronted on both sides by a half dozen simple brick structures. A few farmhouses and barns dotted the hillsides beyond the town, but there appeared to be no sign of enemy activity.

"Looks pretty quiet right now," Dugan said as he handed the binoculars to the driver. "But it won't be that way very long." He tapped the radioman on the shoulder. "Send that French-speaking guy up here. He can go with us, but the rest are to stay here and keep a lookout."

It turned out there *was* a local gendarme who apparently doubled as the area blacksmith. A faded wooden sign that read, *Gendamarie,* hung above the open doors of a dusty blacksmith shop.

A portly, middle-aged man, wearing a black apron and beret stood in the open door of the shop, obviously surprised and nervous to see an American Jeep roll into his little village. He held a double-barreled shotgun in his hands.

After a tense moment of shouting back and forth, the blacksmith/gendarme finally lowered his shotgun and motioned for them to enter the shop. He dusted off a table and motioned toward an equally dusty chair, but Dugan indicated he would stand.

The shop was small and cramped, and Jack stood outside the door while Dugan and the interpreter tried to explain what they had found at the farmhouse. While he was standing there, looking around, something caught Jack's eye. It was a bulletin tacked to the inside of one of the wooden doors. The bulletin was written in three languages, including English, but what jumped out at him was the black-and-white photo at the top.

A photo of Claire!

He ripped the bulletin off the door and stared at the heading in English.

Notice to all police officers and gendarmes...

He kept reading, incredulous, stunned to the core by what it said.

Arrest warrant... fugitive and enemy collaborator...

Mariette Janssens, also known as Claire... accomplice of Bart Peeters

Report to Captain DeVos, Antwerp police department

Jack rubbed his eyes, certain he was hallucinating, then read the entire bulletin again, slowly and carefully, his hand trembling as he did.

Mariette Janssens, Christ, that's her real name!

And Bart Peeters!

He stood in silence for a moment, riveted to the spot. Then, he abruptly pushed past Dugan and the interpreter and held up the bulletin in front of the gendarme. "Ask him when he got this," Jack snapped, glancing at the interpreter.

"What the hell are you talking about?" the interpreter shot back.

"This! This bulletin! Ask him when he got this!"

Jack felt a hand on his shoulder and turned around. Dugan was looking at him like he'd just gone crazy. "Jack, what the hell are you doing?"

Jack took a breath to settle down and tried to keep his hands from shaking. He handed the bulletin to Dugan. "When I was shot down over Belgium last year, I was rescued by a young woman named Claire."

Dugan nodded and glanced down at the bulletin.

"That's her, Mariette Janssens, also known as Claire! That's her photo. She's the one who rescued me. That's the reason I came back here when I escaped from the Germans, to find her!"

Dugan finished reading and then looked up at Jack. "And now there's a warrant out for her arrest?"

Jack shook his head. "It's a lie. I know her! I know this man, Bart Peeters; they're patriots, Resistance fighters; they helped me escape!"

Dugan stared at him with an uncertain look. "But you haven't seen her in over a year, maybe—"

Jack interrupted him and then caught himself. "Excuse me, I'm sorry, sir. But the one thing I learned while they were helping me get out of Belgium is that there are spies and traitors everywhere, even in the government and the police departments. This arrest warrant is a lie! The Nazis are trying to get her!"

Dugan stared at him for another moment, then handed the bulletin to the interpreter. "Ask him when he got this; how long ago?"

The interpreter exchanged a few words in French with the gendarme, then turned back to Dugan. "He just received it yesterday. Someone called a provincial guard, or messenger, something like that, rode up on a motorcycle and gave it to him."

Jack stared at the interpreter, feeling like he was floating in a bad dream.

Yesterday? Christ, what were the chances?

Jack reached over and took the bulletin. "Ask him if I can take this," he started to say, but the gendarme apparently knew what he meant and made a gesture that he should keep it.

Captain Dugan confirmed through the interpreter that the gendarme would look into the murder at the farmhouse, then motioned that they should leave. He was silent as they left the village and drove back to join the rest of the platoon at the crossroads. Jack sat in the back seat next to him, re-reading the bulletin over and over.

When they arrived, the radioman walked up to the Jeep and said to Dugan, "We just received a radio message from the 106th, sir. We are to proceed immediately to La Gleize and rendezvous with the 82nd. They've apparently surrounded the enemy's lead panzer unit."

Dugan nodded, "Okay, let's move out." He glanced at Jack and pointed to the bulletin. "This will have to wait, but we'll discuss it later. In the meantime, keep it to yourself."

Chapter Ninety-Two

Dinant

Claire walked slowly down the crowded hospital corridor, glancing at the wounded soldiers slumped over in chairs, lying on gurneys, or simply leaning against the drab gray walls smoking cigarettes. She reached the end of the corridor and pushed open the swinging door, wincing at the pain in her wrists. She glanced around at the equally crowded waiting area and managed a smile when she spotted Matthew McDonald.

With a look of surprise on his face, McDonald pushed through the crowd and gently put a hand on her shoulder, leading her to a chair in the far corner of the room. "I didn't expect to see you up and around," he said, pulling out the chair.

Claire shook her head. "I'm fine, just very sore. I'd rather just get out of here."

McDonald draped his coat over her shoulders as they stepped out into the cold and walked to his car.

"It was DeVos," Claire said as she got into the passenger seat.

McDonald nodded. "I know. Do you want to talk about it?"

She thought about it for a moment, then shook her head. "Not right now.

What about Bart, has he been released from—?"

As the color slowly drained from McDonald's face, Claire knew it was bad news. "What happened? Is he...?"

McDonald slowly shook his head. "Bart and Gaston were both shot and... killed... as they tried to escape," he said.

Claire stared at him as though she hadn't heard correctly, then suddenly felt like she would throw up. She clasped her hand over her mouth and swallowed hard, then slowly turned away and slumped against the passenger door as everything closed in around her.

Some time passed, and Claire suddenly felt chilled and opened her eyes. McDonald sat in the driver's seat, patiently looking over at her. "I'm sorry," she said. "I just don't know what to do."

"What would Bart have wanted?" he asked quietly.

Bart, dear Bart.

Her friend, her mentor... her rock.

Now... gone!

She sat up straight and wiped her eyes. "He'd want me to finish this."

McDonald nodded. "Then let's finish it." He put the auto in gear and pulled away.

Claire's head began to throb, and she pressed her fingers to her temples. She closed her eyes as images flashed through her mind: Bart in the loft on Gaston's farm struggling to tell the story, Gaston putting his craggy hand on her shoulder the night she and Lukas arrived, Jack standing on the rock overlooking the river... gone... all gone. Then she shuddered at an image of DeVos, sprawled on the floor, blood streaming down his face, just before she—

McDonald glanced at her as though he had read her mind. "DeVos is gone, Claire. He died in the fire. He can't hurt you or—"

"He didn't die in the fire! I killed him! I smashed his head in with the heel of my boot. Then I left him there to burn in hell!"

McDonald pulled over and stopped the car in front of the 4th Armored Division HQ. He turned to her with wide eyes. "My God, Claire, I..."

His voice tailed off, and they were both quiet for a while.

Then Claire said, "I think I know where DeVos was going."

"Was he trying to get out of the country to Switzerland?"

Claire shook her head and reached into the pocket of her trousers, removing the key ring she'd taken from DeVos. "These are the keys DeVos was carrying. I needed them to get out of the handcuffs. Look at this key." She held up an ancient brass key, discolored with age but still intact.

McDonald looked closely at it, pointing to a small square emblem on the bow of the key where it attached to the ring. "What is that?" he asked.

"It's the coat of arms of the city of Namur," Claire replied. "I think that's where he was headed."

"Go on. I'm listening," McDonald said.

"After we left Haute-Bodeux DeVos kept heading west. I also thought he might be trying to get out of the country because if he was going to meet Becker anywhere near Antwerp, he would have turned north right away. When I found this key in his pocket, it all made sense. He was heading west toward Namur."

McDonald looked her in the eye for a moment, then said, "I'll be right back. I've got to get ahold of Worthington and ask him to meet us there."

Just before he closed the door, Claire held up her hand, stopping him. "Ask him to find out if there is a locksmith in Namur."

Chapter Ninety-Three

Namur

Becker was pleased with how well his masquerade as a US Army officer had held up on the drive to Namur. The country was crawling with American and British soldiers, and he'd been forced to stop several times because of the congestion caused by the massive troop movements. His fluency in English had served him well, but it was his choice in selecting his specific American uniform and insignia that really made the difference. No one seemed remotely interested in what a lone G2 Intelligence officer was up to or where he was going.

As he crossed the Jambes Bridge over the Meuse River in the center of Namur, Becker saluted sharply to the American soldiers sitting on tanks guarding both sides of the bridge. He guessed it would be the same in every other city along the river, clear evidence that the German offensive was doomed to end in failure.

As he drove off the bridge, Becker glanced up at the Citadel of Namur, the sprawling, thirteenth-century fortress that overlooked the city, where he would meet DeVos and the girl at midnight. Then he'd find out if DeVos' paranoia about Lukas was warranted or not.

He hoped it wasn't... he hated the thought that he could have misjudged Lukas.

A few minutes later, he arrived at the *Grand Hotel de Flandre,* where the concierge at the front desk seemed relieved that 'Captain Rickert' was finally checking in.

"Bon Jour, Monsieur, we have been holding your rooms but with some difficulty. Every hotel in the city is full, as you can imagine."

Becker smiled. "Thank you. I appreciate it."

"Oui, bien sûr." The concierge glanced down at the large book on his desk. "I see that you also reserved a room for *Monsieur* DeVos. Will he check in soon as well?"

"Yes, I'm sure he'll be along very shortly," Becker replied as he took the room key, picked up his pack and walked through the crowded lobby, nodding to a group of American soldiers standing near the bar.

***

It was well after dark when Claire and McDonald arrived in Namur after a long, tedious drive, slogging their way through the mass of American troops and armament, all heading in the opposite direction.

Claire stared out the window at the wreckage of much of Namur's central square, illuminated by the faint glow of streetlamps in the gloom of dusk descending on the city. The wreckage from the original German invasion four years ago still littered many of the narrow, twisting streets in this historic, picturesque city that she remembered visiting with her parents before the war… before they disappeared. How much longer will this go on, she wondered for perhaps the thousandth time, and who else would she lose before it's finally over? Her thoughts turned to Jack, wondering where he was at this moment, if she would ever see him again if he was safe.

The car slowed to a stop in front of a stately, four-story building across from the central railway station. A brass plaque next to the entrance read *Grand Hotel de Flandre.*

"The city is crawling with American troops," McDonald said, "but the clerk back at 4th Armored HQ thought he could pull some strings and get some rooms at this hotel. Let's go find out if he was successful."

The concierge took his time flipping pages in the book and scratching notes while McDonald impatiently drummed his fingers on the counter.

"*Oui,* our General manager did receive a call," the man said with a weary tone. "As you can imagine, we are nearly full… but I shall do what I can."

Claire spoke up, smiling and speaking French, which seemed to help, and assured the man they would be most appreciative of his help. A few minutes later, he produced two room keys. "The name of the third member of your party is Worthington, is that right?" the concierge asked.

"Yes," McDonald answered. "Colonel Worthington, US Army G2. He will arrive a bit later."

"Ah, G2, the Intelligence group. I hadn't heard that term before until a few hours ago when another officer of G2 checked in."

"Really, that's interesting," McDonald said. "I know most of the G2 officers in Belgium. What's his name?"

"He checked in right here. Let me see. Ah, here it is... a Captain Rickert."

McDonald thought about it for a moment, then shrugged. "No, that name's not familiar. But Worthington might know him. We'll wait for our friend in the bar."

Chapter Ninety-Four

The hotel bar was packed with American and British officers taking advantage of their last night in Namur before heading south to the Ardennes. There was also a contingent of young, local women looking for a free drink and companionship.

Claire leaned close to McDonald so she could be heard over the clamor. "Good luck finding a table. I'm going up to my room to call Lukas. I'll be right back." When she returned, she was surprised to see McDonald sitting at a table in the corner with a bottle of red wine and three glasses.

"I had to buy drinks for a few of my fellow Brits, but they gave up their table," McDonald said as he poured two glasses of wine. "Did you have any luck?"

She shook her head. "No answer."

"It's a mess out there, Claire. It could take him some time to get back to Antwerp. But at least he's heading away from the fighting."

Claire smiled without answering and took a sip of wine. After hearing about Bart and Gaston, she wasn't sure she could handle it if anything happened to Lukas.

"Have I told you how much you remind me of my daughter?" McDonald asked as he picked up his wine glass.

Claire blinked at the surprise question. "No, you haven't. What's her name?"

McDonald took a sip of wine. "Her name is Jenny, she's twenty-one, a senior at Cambridge. She's a lot like you, very smart, opinionated, speaks her mind freely, cares a lot about other people."

"Well, I'm not so sure how smart I am all the time, but thank you. You must be very proud of her. I've been to Cambridge several times; it's lovely."

"Really? What brought you there?"

"I studied in London for two years and—" She stopped abruptly, looking past him at a young American aviator who had just entered the bar. Her hand trembled, and she quickly set the glass down before it spilled.

McDonald had obviously followed her gaze. "Do you know him?" he asked.

She stared at the aviator another moment, then turned back. "No... for a moment, I thought it was... no, never mind."

McDonald sat quietly, watching her.

Claire took a deep breath. "His name is Jack, Jack Richards. I helped him escape in September last year. That aviator looked a bit like him, but... that's not possible because... I know he's..."

As her voice trailed off, McDonald folded his hands on the table and waited.

She took another breath. "We only knew each other for a few weeks. I know how it must sound, but there was something between us, a connection... no, it was more than that... a lot more. I knew we both felt it, but there was nothing we could do. He had to go... and then he was... betrayed."

She glanced up at the ceiling and then looked back at him, wiping away a tear. "When he was recovering at Gaston's farm, I gave him a book to read, *Treasure Island,* one of several I have in English, and we used to laugh about this character, Jim Hawkins, and how he sort of came of age, and then I would say to Jack that I should have picked a different book because he seemed more like Sir Lancelot than Jim Hawkins, and we would..." Her voice faltered, and she looked down at the table, wiping away another tear as it all suddenly flooded back. "I'm sorry, I must sound like some love-sick schoolgirl."

"He was betrayed?" McDonald asked,

Claire nodded slowly. "I got a letter from the air corps... he never returned. I was with him all the way to the Bidasoa River, the crossing into Spain... but he never made it back to England." She closed her eyes and clenched her hands until it hurt. Then she glared at McDonald. "It was DeVos! He did it; he betrayed Jack. I *know* he did!"

McDonald started to say something but stopped and waved his hand at a tall, dark-haired American officer who had just stepped into the bar.

When McDonald introduced Claire to Colonel Worthington, he extended his hand and said, "I'm pleased to meet you, and I'm very sorry about what happened at Haute Bedoux."

McDonald poured a glass of wine for Worthington and said to Claire. "Perhaps you can explain to the Colonel why we're here in Namur. I didn't want to go into it on the telephone."

Claire took another sip of wine to help collect her thoughts and nodded. "Shortly after DeVos abducted me, he proceeded to drive west for the next several hours in the direction of Dinant. Certainly not the direction he would take if he were heading anywhere near Antwerp. Then, after he... died... I found this key in his pocket." She placed the key on the table and pointed to the small rectangle on the bow inscribed with a lion behind a diagonal band. "The colors have faded over time, but that is the coat of arms of the city of Namur. I believe that DeVos was coming here to meet Becker."

"Do you think DeVos told Becker about you, and Becker instructed him to bring you here?" McDonald asked, glancing around, not that anyone could hear them over the shouts, laughter, and clink of glassware in the crowded room.

Claire nodded. "DeVos never said that, but yes, I think that's possible. Do you have any idea where Becker is right now?"

McDonald shook his head. "No, I don't. We know he was back in Germany before this offensive started. And I suspect it has fouled up his plans. But this chap is very well-connected and very resourceful. I think we can assume he had backup plans."

"But if Becker intends to meet DeVos, he'll eventually realize that he isn't coming. What does he do then?" Claire asked.

"There have to be others," Worthington said. "This thing is big enough that Becker and DeVos couldn't be in it alone."

"Do you have any ideas?" McDonald asked, looking at Claire.

"I've been thinking about it constantly," she replied, "but Bart told me that when DeVos came to him in January of '43 and wanted to help the organization, it was decided he would work mostly alone, reporting only to him. DeVos did help Lukas find some new safehouses, but as far as I know, that was it."

"Lukas?" Worthington asked. "Who is that?"

"My closest friend. I've known him all my life. He was an operative in the escape line with Bart and me."

"Lukas was with Claire when they came to St. Vith," McDonald added. "He's been helping her with this whole thing."

Claire nodded. "You must remember that our organization had been infiltrated, and dozens of our operatives had been arrested and executed. Knowing who to trust was the biggest problem we had. Bart said he had known DeVos since before the war and trusted him." She paused for a moment and slowly shook her head. "It was the worst mistake he ever made."

The three of them sat in silence for a while then McDonald abruptly turned to Worthington and said, "By the way, apparently one of your G2 colleagues is staying here at the hotel."

Worthington looked surprised. "Really, what's his name?"

"According to the *concierge*, it's Rickert, Captain Rickert."

Worthington was quiet for a moment, then shook his head. "Never heard of him. He must be new."

Chapter Ninety-Five

Gerhard Wagner always thought the *Viscount's* estate was one of the most magnificent he'd ever seen. Set on fifty acres in the hills overlooking the Meuse River, three kilometers south of Namur, the five-story Renaissance structure consisted of more than forty rooms, including eighteen bedrooms, three dining halls and an elegant, gilded-wall parlor half the size of a soccer field. The main residence was surrounded by terraced French gardens with a crystal-clear stream flowing gracefully down to the river below.

It was early in the morning, crisp and cold, as Wagner wandered slowly along the cobblestone walkways through the maze of gardens, as he'd done every morning since he arrived. He found a bit of solace in the peaceful tranquility of the gardens, a quiet respite that settled his nerves, allowing him to prepare for what lay ahead.

Wagner always knew it could happen. Ever since the defeat of the Wehrmacht at Stalingrad, it had been a possibility that Germany would lose the war. And now it was a reality. Escape or get caught up in defeat and the retributions that the victors would extract. No other decision was possible, not with what was at stake.

Wagner sighed, suddenly shivering from the cold, and headed back inside.

A fire was crackling in the giant stone fireplace as Wagner entered the massive, two-story parlor. The morning light streamed through stained glass windows, illuminating the priceless Renaissance paintings that hung on the walls. He nodded to Koch, Braun, and Fuchs, all of whom stood near the fire sipping coffee.

"Guten Morgen, meine Herren," Wagner crisply said as he proceeded to the buffet and poured a cup of coffee. The three men had been his closest and most trusted colleagues at *I.G. Farben,* members of the inner circle who had carried out his every order without question. They had supervised the slave labor camps and the production facilities that supplied the German war effort with synthetic fuel, rubber, and chemicals... like Zyklon-B. They would also play an important role in what lay ahead.

Others were here as well, executives from other German companies, who would be joining them shortly, coming down from their rooms for coffee. But his three colleagues from *I.G. Farben* were always up early, as he was. He could tell they were nervous, eager to be on their way, as far away from Europe and the vengeance of the Allies as they could get.

"Is there any news?" Koch asked when Wagner joined the group near the fireplace.

Wagner nodded. *"Ja,* I met with the *Viscount* last night. He informed me that the Americans have secured all the bridges over the Meuse River, in Liege and Huy, as well as here in Namur."

"So that's it then?" Koch asked, his face turning pale, "The offensive has been stopped?"

"It would appear so," Wagner said calmly. "The *Viscount* reported that there is still considerable fighting going on to the east and south, with thousands of casualties on both sides. But the element of surprise was lost, and there is no longer a chance for victory."

Braun set his empty coffee cup on a low table and asked, "Where does the *Viscount* get his information?"

Wagner waved a hand dismissively. "That does not concern us. His family has been in Belgium for centuries; he is very well connected."

"Can he be trusted?"

Wagner sipped his coffee, glancing at Braun as he did, purposely letting his subordinate wait a few moments before responding to the impertinent question. Finally, Wagner set his cup down and took a step closer to Braun. "Of course, I trust the *Viscount.* Our families have been closely related since the thirteenth century. He is a man of integrity whose loyalty to the Reich is beyond question... certainly beyond *your* question."

Braun took a step back, his eyes dropping to the floor. Then Koch spoke up, changing the subject. "Pardon me, Herr Wagner, but has this offensive affected our plans for departure?"

Wagner waved a hand, cutting him off as well. "Becker planned for that possibility. We are to wait here until it is time to depart the country."

"And the changes in our travel plans?"

"Everything is arranged," Wagner said curtly. "Lukas has taken care of it."

Chapter Ninety-Six

La Gleize

During the two hours it took the 41st platoon to travel to La Gleize, Jack sat in the back seat of Dugan's Jeep, overwhelmed with the incredible bulletin he'd found at the blacksmith shop.

Claire is alive!

I know her real name!

I could find her!

He kept glancing at the bulletin, at her picture, scarcely able to believe it was real and that he might find her again.

But this was an *arrest* warrant! It didn't make any sense. Arrested for being an enemy collaborator? He knew that wasn't possible; it had to be some terrible mistake, some colossal bureaucratic blunder. As he stared at the bulletin, his mind went back to the question that had been troubling him, nagging at him ever since that first meeting with the Commandant of the POW camp. The question of *Lukas.*

If Lukas could betray *him,* could he betray *Claire?*

He shook the thought out of his mind. Lukas cared about Claire, had always loved her, and wanted to *marry* her someday. Lukas would never hurt Claire.

But someone wanted to.

And what could he do about it? Even though he now knew her real name, he had no idea where she was. It had been over a year since Belgium was liberated. Would she still be in Grote Brogel? Or had she gone back to Antwerp?

And why would a police captain in Antwerp want to arrest her?

Who could he contact? The bulletin mentioned Bart Peeters, but he had no way to contact him, no telephone number, and no idea where he lived. He had only a vague recollection of where Lukas lived, not that he would think of contacting him.

In fact, the only real contact he had was this police captain in Antwerp named DeVos, but would he dare to call him?

He was suddenly jolted from his thoughts when the Jeep stopped, and Captain Dugan climbed out. Jack joined him, along with a couple of riflemen. They were situated on the top of a hill overlooking a now quiet battlefield in the valley below. Dozens of burned-out German tanks still smoldered with black, oily smoke drifting up the hillside. Wrecked half-tracks and Jeeps littered the blackened field, and several hundred dejected-looking German prisoners, who'd been disarmed and herded into a farm field, were being guarded by 82ⁿᵈ Airborne troopers.

"Looks like this is pretty much all over," Dugan said. "Let's head into the center of town."

The town of La Gleize was just coming back to life when the platoon drove in. Most of the villagers had taken refuge in a crypt under the church and were now emerging into the sunlight, wary and cautious, though seemingly happy to see American soldiers.

Directly across the road from the church was the town hall, and Dugan told the driver to pull up there. "Let's go see if anyone's in there. Maybe they have a telephone."

The *Bourgmestre* of La Gleize charged out of his office when Jack, Dugan, and the interpreter entered the building, shaking their hands, speaking rapidly and excitedly in French. The interpreter tried to keep up, but Dugan finally waved him off. "Don't worry, I get it. He's happy he still has a town. Hopefully, it'll stay that way." Then he had the interpreter ask for permission to use the telephone and nodded at Jack.

With no other alternative, Jack made the decision to call the Antwerp police station and ask for Captain DeVos. It took them a moment to find someone who spoke English, but the woman turned out to be very helpful, answering Jack's questions.

"I'm sorry, but Captain DeVos is not in at this time."

"Yes, I am familiar with bulletin... you are the second American soldier to call about it."

"The first? Let me... ah yes... MP Sergeant O'Reily at Chateau Haute Bedoux."

Jack almost dropped the phone.

An American MP Sergeant knows about Claire?

What the hell is going on?

When he recovered from the shock, he thanked the woman and then called the number she had given him.

A gruff voice came on the line. "O'Reily here."

"Sergeant O'Reily, my name is Lieutenant Jack Richards with the Army Air Corps. I got your number from the Antwerp police department. I'm calling about a woman named Mariette Janssens, also known as Claire."

There was silence on the other end. Finally, O'Reily spoke up. "Are you working with McDonald?"

"McDonald? Who is that?"

"Some fuckin' British Intelligence spook who is hell-bent on finding this girl."

"Well, sergeant, I'm hell-bent on finding her as well. Now, how do I get ahold of McDonald?"

"Last I knew, he went up to the G2 Intelligence base in Liege. I'll give you the phone number."

When Jack hung up the phone and returned to the outer office, Dugan was talking with a major from the 82nd Airborne. After a moment, he excused himself and stepped over to Jack. "Any luck?" he asked.

Jack nodded. "More than I expected." When he related what he'd just learned, Dugan took his arm and led him to a far corner of the room. "Okay, here's the situation. While you've been on the phone, we received orders to head back south and hook up with the rest of the 106th. The Germans have taken St. Vith and Bastogne."

"Ok, I understand."

"No, Jack, you're not going with us."

"What do you mean? What else would—"

Dugan stopped him, "Listen to me, Jack. You've seen enough of this Goddamn war, more than most. You flew over a dozen combat missions, got shot down, lost your crew, got betrayed by some low-life Nazi collaborator and spent the last year as a POW. After escaping, you almost got yourself killed at Lanzerath, for Christ's sake. I just explained all this to Major Broward with the 82nd. You are ordered to stay right here in La Gleize. He's already set it up with the *Bourgmestre*. There's a small hotel here, and they'll take care of you for a few days. You have his permission to contact this MI9 agent, McDonald and see if he can help you."

"Captain Dugan, that's very kind, but I can't just—"

Dugan interrupted again. "Yes, you can, Jack, because I'm your commanding officer, and the major is mine. And he just gave you an order. Besides, you're a Goddamn flyboy who can't shoot straight... and you're not in uniform. Now, go find that young lady."

As he started to leave, Dugan stopped and looked back at Jack. "Oh, one more thing. If you manage to live through all this, make your way to the 1st Army HQ in Brussels, General Hodges's office. Tell them to contact Major Broward with the 82nd Airborne, so they don't court-martial you for desertion."

Chapter Ninety-Seven

Namur

The locksmith met Claire at his shop first thing the next morning. He was a prim, white-haired man who appeared to be in his late sixties. In a strange contrast to his dusty, cluttered shop, he wore a tweed jacket and bow tie. He had a neatly trimmed goatee, which he gently stroked as he examined the key at a small table in the rear of the shop. Claire sat across from him on a rickety, wooden chair.

"Très intèressant," the locksmith said in French. "Where did you find this, if I may ask, in a museum or antique shop, perhaps?"

"Non, not in a museum or shop; I found it among the remains of a... 'friend' that passed away."

"Ah, je vois. So, how can I help you?"

"We know that is the coat of arms of Namur," Claire said, "but perhaps you may have some idea where this key came from, what type of building, anything like that?'

The locksmith nodded and examined the ancient brass key again. He held it up close to Claire and pointed to the coat of arms embossed on the bow of the key. "You are correct; it is the coat of arms of the city. But it is an old version, dating back well before the turn of the century. And look at this." He pointed to the bit of the key. "This is a very old design as well, perhaps mid-nineteenth century. But it is quite complex for that period, designed for a very secure lock. I have seen specimens like this before, but not for a long time."

"Do you have any idea what type of lock... in what type of building... anything that might—?"

The old man suddenly opened a drawer and removed a magnifying glass. He held the glass close to the shaft of the key, slowly nodding his head. After a moment, he smiled, nodding his head. "*Oui, oui, bien sûr, le Citadel.*" He motioned for Claire to look at the key through the magnifying glass while pointing to some faint scratches on the shaft of the key. "Do you see that?" he asked.

Claire blinked and then squinted to try and make out the scratches. "It looks like a date," she said, "17—?"

"1792," the locksmith said with a ring of triumph in his voice. "This key opens a lock in the Citadel."

Claire looked at him with confusion. "I don't understand."

The locksmith held up both hands. "*Pardonne-moi,* I will explain. In 1792, France invaded Belgium at the beginning of the Great European War. They attacked Namur and captured the Citadel. If I recall from my reading of history, the soldiers of the garrison of Namur were imprisoned there for a time. Somewhere in the tunnels below the fort, there are cells and gates.

I have not seen them in many years; no one goes down there now. But this key could be for the lock on one of those gates."

It suddenly became clear. DeVos was hiding money in the abandoned tunnels beneath the Citadel. But, like the locksmith, Claire also remembered some of the history of the Citadel. There were more than seven kilometers of tunnels.

Chapter Ninety-Eight

Later that same morning, Lukas sat at a table in the back room of a café in the *Quartier du Vieux* in the center of Namur. The café's proprietor was a friend, a trusted confidant who would make certain they had privacy when *SS-Hauptsturmfuhrer* Konrad Becker arrived.

Lukas took a sip of coffee, his nerves on edge in anticipation of seeing Becker again after these past few months. They were getting close to the end, he thought with relief, and he felt confident he'd carried out his part of the mission. He hoped Becker would be pleased, but with Becker, you could never be certain.

Lukas heard footsteps on the café's wooden floor and looked up as Becker appeared, striding purposely across the room, followed by the proprietor carrying a tray of fresh coffee, croissants, and a plate of cheese.

Dressed in a black turtle-neck sweater, black leather jacket and dark wool trousers, Becker stood by the table while the proprietor silently set down the tray, poured coffee and departed, closing the door behind him. "Have you heard from DeVos?" Becker abruptly said as he sat down.

Lukas was surprised by the question. "No, I haven't heard from him for some time, but I didn't expect to. As you know, I wasn't involved in—"

Becker cut him off. "Yes, yes, I know. But I was supposed to meet him last night." He stared at Lukas for a moment as though he had more to say, then reached over and took a croissant, broke it in half and took a bite.

"What about the offensive?" Lukas asked, "Is there still a chance—?"

Becker cut him off again, this time with a wave of his hand. "No, there is no chance of success. There never was. It was just another desperate move by our illustrious *Fuhrer,* who refused to accept the fact that Germany was finished. But *our* mission is unchanged; everything will proceed as planned, though now with more urgency." He took a sip of coffee and then asked, "Have you been to the chalet? Have you seen Wagner and the others?"

"Yes, of course. They are waiting for you."

Becker nodded slowly then his expression abruptly darkened, "Tell me about Claire."

Lukas blinked. A cold shiver ran down the back of his neck, but he knew he couldn't divert his eyes. "Claire? She's a long-time friend of mine; we grew up together. Why do you ask?"

"Are you aware that DeVos put out a warrant for her arrest?"

"What!?" Lukas snapped. Then sat back hard in his chair and stared at Becker.

Was this a lie, a ruse on Becker's part to rattle him?

No, Becker wouldn't waste time on that.

Lukas swallowed hard, struggling to regain his composure. "No, I didn't know that. But... I can't say I'm surprised."

"And why is that."

Lukas paused for a moment, breathing slowly to settle down. "DeVos has known about Claire for some time. She works with Bart Peeters at the Interior Department. I'm pretty sure he knows Claire and I have been living together, and I think he has always suspected she was part of the escape organization."

"Was she?"

Lukas shook his head. "No, never! I wouldn't allow it. I've always looked after her, ever since we were kids, and I would never allow her to be in that kind of danger. If DeVos put out a warrant for her arrest, he probably did it to make me look bad."

"Why would he do that?"

Lukas paused again, this time more for effect, though he knew he was treading on thin ice. "I will be honest with you. I don't trust DeVos. I don't exactly know why, but I don't, and I don't think he trusts me either."

Becker stared at him silently for a moment, the long, hard stare with those ice-blue eyes Lukas remembered from previous meetings. "Why was Claire at a US Army base in Haute Bedoux?"

Now Lukas could feel cold sweat dripping down his back, but he forced himself to ignore it. "Haute Bedoux? I don't even know where that is. The last time

I saw Claire was over a week ago when I drove her to the home of her friend, Gaston, in Grote Brogle. I have no idea why she would be at an American army base. She's been sharing my apartment with me since the liberation because she works in Antwerp, and it's been impossible for her to find anything else. We're friends, that's all, not lovers. And we don't keep track of where either of us goes or what we do."

"You don't know about the money?" Becker finally asked.

Lukas shook his head. "No, nothing about any money." He knew it wasn't completely true since Claire had told him about the money transferred from *I.G. Farben* to DeVos' company. But he suspected there was more to it than that.

Becker was quiet for another moment while he sipped his coffee. Then he set the cup down and leaned forward. "The associates of mine whom you have been transporting from St. Vith to the *Viscount's* estate are only half of the mission. The other half is money, a lot of money smuggled out of Germany. DeVos has been secretly transporting that money and hiding it here in Namur."

"And now he's missing? Perhaps with the collapse of the offensive, he got spooked and is making a run for it, heading for Switzerland. I said I don't trust him."

Becker smiled and shook his head. "That's not possible. DeVos has more to lose than just his life. I made sure of that. He knows he could never escape from us. I'm sure you... and your friend, Claire... know that as well."

Lukas saw the expression on Becker's face and decided he didn't want to know anymore. "Do you know where DeVos was hiding the money?" he asked.

"Not precisely," Becker said. "Somewhere in the tunnels under the Citadel. But I've been in Germany since the Allies liberated Belgium, and I don't know the precise location."

It was an obvious flaw in the plan, but it was Becker's plan, and Lukas knew better than to pursue it. Becker was a close confidant and friend of the *Viscount,* and he had connections high up in the German Reich. And despite his loyalty to him, Lukas knew Becker had always been, and still was, a very dangerous man.

"What about the escape routes out of this godforsaken country?" Becker asked, changing the subject with a decided edge in his voice. "That part of the plan is *your* responsibility. Is it all arranged?"

Lukas nodded, thinking of the countless hours he had spent arranging—then re-arranging—the meticulous details of smuggling a dozen men out of Belgium and on to various secret locations in South America, Australia, Canada and even the United States. "Yes, it is all arranged."

Becker motioned toward the plate of croissants and cheese. "Very good. Then have something to eat. If DeVos doesn't show up, *you* will have to find a way to get the money."

Chapter Ninety-Nine

The stately, black Mercedes-Benz was parked behind the Cathedral of Saint Aubain, near the center of Namur, on a quiet street of bombed-out buildings near the *Quartier du Vieux.* Becker stood hidden in an alcove of the Cathedral and waited while a police car drove past. Then he stepped quickly to the Mercedes, opened the back door, and slid in. The chauffeur immediately put the auto in gear and drove away, heading for the *Viscount's* estate.

"Has DeVos arrived yet?" the *Viscount* immediately asked when Becker got in the car.

Becker shook his head. "No, not yet." He could feel the *Viscount* staring at him, knowing what the blue-blooded nobleman was thinking and hating the fact that he was under scrutiny. But, in fact, he *was* concerned. DeVos may have faults, but he'd never been late before.

"Is that a problem?" the *Viscount* persisted. "You expected him by now, did you not?"

"Yes, of course. But, regardless, he is not critical to the mission, doesn't know anything of importance that—"

"But what about the money?" the *Viscount* snapped, cutting him off. "I thought DeVos was the one who—"

Becker held up a hand, interrupting him in return. The *Viscount* was a powerful aristocrat, well-connected within the Third Reich, and a close friend of Wagner's. But, aside from providing a secure location for their rendezvous, he didn't add anything to the final mission. In fact, Becker had already decided he was expendable. "Don't worry about the money," Becker said curtly. "I've already handled that. Lukas will get the money."

The *Viscount* exhaled slowly. "Well, if you've entrusted it to Lukas, then it's in good hands."

"Are the others prepared to go?" Becker asked.

The *Viscount* nodded, "They are all here, awaiting your instructions."

Chapter One Hundred

When Claire finished with the locksmith, she walked back to the hotel. As planned, McDonald and Worthington were waiting for her in the lobby. As soon as McDonald spotted her, he and Worthington headed for the door and motioned for her to follow.

They turned a corner and stepped into an alcove on the side of the hotel building, where they were out of the wind. McDonald glanced at Worthington, then said quietly, "I was walking past the concierge's desk this morning when he waved me over and asked if I had connected with this other G2 officer, Captain Rickert."

"Really? Why would he care about that?" Claire asked. "I'm surprised he even remembered, given all the crowds and activity in the hotel."

McDonald nodded, "Precisely what *I* thought. I told him I hadn't met Rickert and asked if there was anything I should know. He just shrugged and said that he'd seen Rickert earlier this morning wearing civilian clothing—a black sweater and black leather jacket. The concierge said they only exchanged a few words, but Rickert mentioned he had a few days' leave, then dropped off his key and walked away rather abruptly. Well, then I was curious, so I asked the concierge if Rickert had met or was expecting anyone else. It turns out he *is* expecting someone else, a certain *Monsieur* DeVos."

Claire flinched and took a step back. "My God... *DeVos*?"

"Exactly right," McDonald said. "And now I know why neither of us ever heard of a G2 officer named Rickert. Because he's—"

"Becker!" Claire cut in. "It *has* to be Becker."

Worthington nodded. "He is obviously impersonating an American G2 officer; that's how he made it here through all the checkpoints."

"But why a G2 officer? That's a hell of a coincidence."

Worthington nodded. "Perhaps. But it's also damn smart on his part. If he tried to impersonate a standard line officer, he'd have a unit insignia on his sleeve, which could be a risk if he was challenged at a checkpoint not knowing anything about the whereabouts of that unit. But a G2 officer could be anywhere."

Claire felt the tingling in her spine again, this time all the way up to the back of her head. "So, Becker is here, in Namur... waiting for DeVos."

"Who we know will never show up," McDonald said, looking at her with raised eyebrows.

"But Becker doesn't know that," Claire replied, suddenly feeling very unsettled, as though someone was sneaking up behind her.

The three of them all looked at each other in silence for a moment before McDonald continued. "Okay, so Becker is smuggling money and people out of Germany. And now he shows up here in Namur expecting to meet DeVos—"

"Who was carrying this," Claire said quickly, holding up the ancient key. "The locksmith thinks it might belong to an old lock somewhere in the tunnels under the Citadel."

"That could be where the money is hidden," McDonald said, "But what about the people? Where are *they*?"

The group lapsed into silence again as they walked back to the hotel. Suddenly, Claire thought about Lukas and said, "I tried to call Lukas again early this morning but still got no answer. I'm really getting worried."

"The roads are a mess, but I'm sure he'll turn up soon," Worthington said.

She glanced at him, knowing he meant well. "Thanks, but I'll feel a lot better when I actually see him. Besides, we could use his help. He knows this area quite well."

Chapter One Hundred and One

When they returned to the hotel, McDonald stopped at the concierge's desk to check for messages. Claire had decided to take a walk, and McDonald said he'd meet Worthington in the bar for coffee. He did, indeed, have a message. It was from Colonel Worthington's clerk in Liege.

"There was a telephone call for you earlier today, and it was a bit odd," the clerk said. "It was from an American who said he was in the Air Corps. He was inquiring about that missing woman, Claire."

McDonald thought it was a lot more than odd; it sounded suspicious and dangerous. Considering the type of traitors and collaborators they'd been dealing with, this could be another one, perhaps someone DeVos hired, trying to track down Claire. "Did he give his name?" McDonald asked.

"Yes, he said his name was Jack Richards."

Jack Richards?

Now, McDonald was really alarmed. The real Jack Richards was either dead or rotting away in some POW camp in Germany, and now, whoever this guy is, he's using Jack's name to get to Claire.

"Mr. McDonald, are you still—"

"Yes, yes, I'm still here, just thinking. Did this person say where he was?"

"Yes. He called twice. The first time from the town hall in La Gleize. Then, about an hour later, he called back and said he was staying at the hotel. He asked if you would call him there."

McDonald hung up the telephone and found Worthington in the bar. When he told him about the phone message, Worthington shot a hard look at him. "What? Who was it?"

"He said his name was Jack Richards."

"Who is Jack Richards?"

"The American aviator Claire was escorting, the one who was betrayed and captured. As far as we know, he's a POW in Germany... or worse."

"So, what the hell is going on?"

"Damned if I know," McDonald said. "But we need to find out who this son-of-a-bitch is and what he's after, especially if he could lead us to Becker. He told your clerk he was staying at the hotel in La Gleize.

Worthington nodded and pushed his chair from the table. "Okay, I'll send a couple of men over there to arrest this guy and take him to Liege. Then I'll drive back there in the morning and find out who he is and what he's up to."

Chapter One Hundred and Two

As she left the hotel, Claire's mind was a jumble of emotions, and she needed to be alone for a while to think things through. Two weeks ago, it seemed like the long nightmare of the war had ended; Belgium was liberated, and she had made it through. Bart, Gaston, and Lukas had made it through. Jack had made it back to Britain, and there was hope that one day they would be together again.

Then, without warning, her life turned completely upside down—indeed, it almost ended. Bart and Gaston are dead. And Jack is missing, at best, a prisoner of war.

The nightmare had returned... in the form of Niels DeVos! She shivered as another image of DeVos flashed through her mind, lying in the pool of blood on the floor of the burning house.

She shook the gruesome thought out of her head and started walking. A few blocks from the hotel, she stopped abruptly and stared at a slender man on the other side of the street, walking with a slight limp. She recognized him... but how could it be?

Lukas?

It took her a moment to find her voice. Then she shouted, "Lukas!"

He stopped and turned toward her. When their eyes met, he took a step back and then immediately crossed the street, sidestepping a group of soldiers. "Claire? My God, it's really you!"

She stared at him for a moment, checking once again to make sure she wasn't seeing things, then threw her arms around him. "Yes, it's me... I can't believe it. What are you doing here?" Her memory flashed back to that moment when Lukas suddenly appeared at the tunnel in Antwerp and rescued her from an attacker.

Like a guardian angel.

"I should ask you the same thing," Lukas said. "But let's get in out of the cold where we can talk.

Lukas led the way to another café he knew about, several blocks away from the one where he'd just met Becker. It was nearly deserted in the late morning save for a group of American soldiers at a large table near the front window.

They took a seat at a table in the rear, and Lukas ordered coffee. It was then that he noticed the bruises on Claire's face.

"What happened to you?" he asked quietly. "I thought McDonald was taking care of you."

She reached over and touched his hand. "Yes, he was. I was driven to a chalet in Haute-Bedoux, a headquarters for American officers. But he had to go to Liege, and while he was away... DeVos showed up."

"DeVos? Christ almighty, how?"

"He had put out an arrest warrant for me. I think an MP sergeant at Haute Bedoux saw it and called him. And they let him take me."

Lukas stiffened at the thought of DeVos laying a hand on Claire, a lump rising in his throat. Fortunately, their coffee arrived, and it gave him a moment to recover. When the waiter departed, he asked quietly, "Did DeVos do that to you?"

She nodded, then touched his hand again and squeezed it. "I'm fine. It's over... at least that part is."

"My God, Claire, what happened? Was he captured, did the Americans—?"

"He's dead, Lukas." Claire was silent for a moment, staring at her coffee cup. Then she looked up at him. "I killed him."

Lukas sat back slowly, staring at her, swallowing hard.

She killed DeVos?

Before he could respond, Claire picked up her coffee cup, but her hand trembled, and she quickly set it back down. When she looked up at him again, there were tears in her eyes. She brushed them away and took a deep breath before continuing. "There's something else I need to tell you. Bart... and Gaston... they're both..." She slumped back in her chair, tears streaming down her face.

Lukas reached across the table, but she waved his hand away. "Give me a minute, I'll be... just a minute."

She wiped her eyes with a napkin and then looked back at him. "Bart and Gaston were both shot; they're... dead!"

Lukas put his hand over his mouth. He looked down at the table, taking short breaths, desperately trying not to throw up.

Bart and Gaston... dead?

Claire was abducted and forced to kill DeVos?

How did this happen?

I never meant for it to go this far; I never—

"It was DeVos," Claire snapped, jolting him back to the moment. "I'm certain of it. He had them arrested and then had them shot! He *murdered* them, Lukas. He murdered *Gaston... and Bart!*"

Lukas stared at the ceiling, rubbing his temples, his mind racing. He knew what DeVos was like. But he had made sure Claire was safe. At least he thought he did, that's why he drove her to St. Vith, that's why he left her with McDonald and the American Army! "Claire, I am so sorry... I thought you were safe. Tell me what happened!"

Claire shook her head. "I'll tell you, but not now, some other time." She paused for a moment, then asked, "What about you? You left early, and I've been worried ever since. Why are you here in Namur? And why the hell did you leave without saying anything to me!?"

The shock of seeing her again and what she'd just told him was so complete that it took Lukas a moment to think of a response. "I had to... get back to my shop. I had a lot of work piling up, and... you were safe. I was up before dawn, and Corporal Dennison told me the whole unit was bugging out, so I wanted to get ahead of them." It was a lie and not a very good one, but it was the best he could come up with. He could sense her skepticism, could see it in her penetrating eyes. He continued quickly, making things up as he went along. "This is as far as I got. I thought I'd be ahead of the convoy, but it didn't matter. It was slow going, every road was jammed with American troops, and my car kept over- heating. I finally had to stop here at a repair garage I know about. The owner is a friend, someone I've done business with. Fortunately, he was able to repair the radiator. And why are *you* here?" he asked to change the subject.

She looked him in the eye for a long moment, then slowly shook her head. "It's a long story, but I'm not here alone. McDonald is here, along with an American G2 colonel named Worthington. They're at the hotel; I just went out for a walk." She paused for another moment, and he was afraid she was going to question his story. But instead, she leaned over the table and motioned for him to do the same. "We're certain that Becker is here," she whispered.

Lukas felt his face flush like he had just been caught stealing. "Becker? You mean—?"

"Yes, of course, the German SS officer, Konrad Becker. McDonald has known about him for years. He's involved in something very treacherous."

"And... what is that?" Lukas asked cautiously, knowing he was treading on very shaky ground.

"He's been smuggling money out of Germany for years, hiding it here in Belgium, in Namur, we believe. But more importantly, Becker has been smuggling certain *people* out of Germany, high-ranking businessmen, from places like *I.G. Farben*, war criminals who are trying to escape. We believe they are hiding somewhere, perhaps right here in Namur or someplace close by."

Lukas squirmed in his chair and quickly took a sip of coffee to hide it, giving himself a moment to think, knowing he had to choose his words very carefully. "That's incredible information," he said at last, "but how did you connect with McDonald and this colonel... I don't understand."

"I know it's hard to believe, and I really will tell you the whole story, but, quite honestly, I'm not up to it right now. McDonald found me in Dinant and brought me here. He and Worthington had put all the pieces together. Except that they didn't know where DeVos and Becker were going to meet."

"And how did they find out it was here?"

"Because of this." Claire reached into her pocket, withdrew an old key, and handed it to him. "DeVos had it on his key ring. He was obviously coming here to meet Becker. You can see Namur's coat of arms right here." She pointed to the emblem on the bow of the key."

Lukas could feel sweat dripping down his back, and he struggled to stay calm, but it was becoming more difficult by the second. The fact that Claire had the key and that she and the others had figured out Becker was here in Namur could ruin the entire operation. But more importantly, it put *her* in grave danger. "Do you know what this key unlocks?" he managed to ask. He reasoned, of course, that it unlocked a cell somewhere in the tunnels under the Citadel, but not which one. That secret apparently died with DeVos.

"We showed it to a locksmith here in town," she replied, with the eagerness of someone about to solve a puzzle, "and he thinks it may be a gate or a cell somewhere in the tunnels under the Citadel. That may be where Becker and DeVos hid the money."

She reached over and squeezed his hand again. "Lukas, I can't tell you how relieved I am that you're safe. I'm still annoyed that you left without saying anything to me, but I'm so glad you're here. You can be a big help to us. You've got to come back to the hotel with me and meet the others. McDonald will be amazed."

Chapter One Hundred and Three

That evening Lukas stood near the fireplace in the parlor of the Viscount's estate, sipping a twelve-year-old whiskey, carefully watching the others in the room. The servants had disappeared after serving drinks, and the Viscount was circulating among his guests.

Lukas had settled down a bit after what was, for him, a very stressful meeting with Claire, McDonald, and the American, Colonel Worthington. He was satisfied they didn't suspect anything, but he knew he was trapped in a lie that couldn't last.

For the moment, however, he had to set that aside as best he could and blend in with the very same war criminals that Claire and her friends were hunting down. Though he had transported each of these men from St. Vith, Lukas had not been formally introduced to them. But the Viscount discreetly pointed them out as they arrived in the massive parlor. Besides the Viscount's close friend, Gerhard Wagner, and the other executives from *I.G. Farben*, there was Dr. Kaspar, chairman of a steel company, Herr Kardos, leader of a truck manufacturer, and Dr. Sinderen, an aircraft manufacturer. Several others represented mining companies and manufacturers of munitions, tanks, and railroad locomotives.

Conspicuously absent for the moment was SS-Hauptsturmfuhrer Konrad Becker, though Lukas was certain he would soon make a grand entrance. Meanwhile, the Viscount played the part of the genial host, making sure his guests had ample drink and were enjoying the array of sumptuous hors d'oeuvres.

A few minutes later, the Viscount broke away from a group he'd been talking with and joined Lukas near the fireplace. "Becker will be arriving soon," he said quietly, "but I understand DeVos is still missing. Do you suppose something has happened to him?"

Lukas took a quick sip of the whiskey, giving himself a second before answering, hoping he could keep up with all the lies he'd been telling. "It's certainly possible with all the fighting going on. I wouldn't have expected him to miss this."

The Viscount turned his head slightly, glancing at the crackling fire and speaking so as not to be overheard. "In reality, it is of no consequence. DeVos never played an important part in the mission beyond transporting and hiding the money… not anything like the part you have played." He paused for a moment, then looked Lukas directly in the eye. "I'm very proud of you, Lukas. I hope you know that. And whatever happens from this point forward, you will continue to play an important role."

"Thank you, sir. You know I will always be grateful for—"

The Viscount gently laid a hand on Lukas' shoulder, stopping him with a smile. "Yes, of course, but it's no longer just about gratitude. You are part of us now, and that will never change."

Then, the Viscount stepped back to the center of the grand room and spoke up loudly enough to stop the conversations. "Gentlemen, please, let us welcome our special guest, SS-Hauptsturmfuhrer Konrad Becker."

Becker strode briskly into the parlor, an imposing figure dressed in the crisp, black uniform of the SS, complete with twin lightning bolts on the collar and a red & white swastika armband. He stood in the center of the room, silently making eye contact with each man. Then he abruptly stiffened, clicked his heels together, raised his right arm and barked, "Heil Hitler!"

Lukas raised his right arm and glanced around the room, watching as the others, including the Viscount, did the same. It was then that he realized that Becker had not arrived alone. Quietly and almost unnoticed, two other men had slipped into the room. They wore dark suits and stood along the back wall of the parlor with their hands clasped behind them. Neither Becker nor the Viscount made any effort to acknowledge them. It was as if they were meant to be invisible, though their mere presence was all the introduction anyone in the room needed.

The Viscount quickly snapped his fingers, beckoning a waiter who stepped into the room carrying a silver tray with a single glass of whiskey. Becker picked up the glass and nodded at the assembled group. "Welcome, gentlemen. Let us raise a toast to our host for the evening, my good friend and loyal supporter of the Reich, Viscount Maurice de Berg.

The evening proceeded in a congenial manner, the aperitifs followed by an elaborate meal of lobster bisque, quail, and roast venison. When the table had been cleared and the cigars and port passed out, Becker rose from his seat at the head of the table, thanking the Viscount once again for his hospitality. Lukas took a sip of the sweet wine, wondering what was coming next.

Becker took a moment, glancing around at each of the men, then proceeded in a calm, measured tone. "Gentlemen, while there have been some military setbacks, let me assure you that the German Reich will survive. It will live on, beginning right here, right now, in this magnificent estate and in other similar locations in France, Italy, and beyond. There are others like you, specifically chosen to carry on the mission of the Third Reich outside of Germany."

Lukas glanced around at the others, all of whom had their eyes riveted on Becker, their expressions grave and serious. Becker continued as calmly as though he were giving a weather report. "It is now apparent that this war cannot be won. Regardless of how much longer the fighting continues, the ultimate outcome is no longer in doubt. But the mission of the Reich will carry on, it will be re-invented in other places, one day to return to Germany, stronger than ever. That is where all of you come in. That is why you are here."

A low murmuring wafted around the table as Germany's great and powerful industrialists shifted uneasily in their seats, taking quick sips of port, waiting to learn their fates.

Becker stood ramrod straight, hands clasped behind his back, as he continued. "The Reich will live on, but for now, we must go underground and operate in secrecy. Plans have been made to finance the establishment of post-war industrial enterprises in foreign countries. Each of you will be tasked with carrying on the enterprises you control and continuing your individual research and development projects.

"You will create secret technical offices, bureaus and laboratories in Canada, Australia, Brazil, and even in America, where you will continue the final development of our new weapon, a weapon unlike anyone could have previously imagined. Your task— our task, working together as one—is to bring this weapon into reality. Then, one day, when our task is complete, and the Reich is once again strong enough to re-establish control over Germany and the rest of the world, you will all be handsomely rewarded."

With that, Becker sat down and took a sip of port.

Lukas was dumbfounded. He hadn't known what to expect from this meeting except perhaps details of when the assembled German industrialists were going to embark on their journeys to avoid the prisons and gallows of the allied victors. But what he had just heard was something so completely astonishing, something so audacious he could barely comprehend its implications. As he looked around the room at the faces of the other men, he could tell he was not alone. Even the Viscount looked surprised. In fact, the only other one besides Becker who appeared completely unfazed was Gerhard Wagner.

The silence that had settled over the group was finally broken when Dr. Sinderen spoke up. He cleared his throat and folded his hands on the table. "About this new weapon Herr Hauptsturmfuhrer, are you certain it is something that our adversaries do not possess, not the Russians or the Americans?"

"They do not yet possess this technology," Becker said. "However, they know that it exists, and they are desperate to get their hands on it. That is why you are all here. We must act quickly and in total and complete secrecy. Right now, our courageous armed forces are continuing to fight the war, knowing in their hearts it is unwinnable. Our leaders know that as well. But it is imperative that they keep our enemies at bay; it is imperative that they keep them occupied with fighting the war, giving us the time and opportunity to get you out of here and re-established beyond the borders of Europe while we still can."

Dr. Kaspar spoke up next. "On instructions from the party, our firm has been secretly sending millions of Reichsmarks out of the country. You are aware of this, I know. Is this how the funds are to be used, to develop this new weapon and start another war?"

Once again, the room became deathly quiet. Lukas held his breath, waiting for an eruption from Becker at the impertinent question. Becker, however, appeared quite calm as he took a long, slow sip of port and slowly set the glass down. He folded his hands on the table, his gaze fixed on Kaspar. "Nein, Dr. Kaspar, we do not intend to start another war. That will not be necessary. When all of you have done your job, and this weapon is functional, the mere fact that we possess it will be enough of a deterrent for our adversaries to give us what we want. We shall regain our rightful position in the world without firing another shot."

Becker paused for a moment, his eyes fixed on Kaspar, his expression hardening. "You are correct about the money, however. That is exactly how it is to be used. And not only the measly funds you and your greedy colleagues have so reluctantly paid—and is safely hidden away here in Belgium—but all of it, every mark and pfennig in your treasury."

Becker then stood abruptly and swept his hand in an arc across the table. "And that goes for every one of you and your companies. There will be no holding back. The future of The Reich, indeed your future, depends on it." Then he drained his glass and set it down hard on the table. I suggest you all get a good night's sleep. You will receive travel instructions within the next forty-eight hours. Auf wiedersehen!

Chapter One Hundred and Four

Late that evening, after the others, including Becker and the strangers in the dark suits, had retired to their quarters in other wings of the vast mansion, Lukas sat near the crackling fire in the parlor, thinking about Claire. He hated himself for all the lies he'd told her, and for the hole of deceit he had fallen into, which was getting deeper every day.

The *Viscount* joined him and handed him a snifter of cognac. "You were a bit quiet after dinner," he said, "is anything troubling you?"

Lukas took a sip of cognac, shaking off his thoughts about Claire. "Just thinking about all that has to be done in the next 48 hours."

The *Viscount* nodded, "Yes, after all this time, it does seem quite abrupt. But with the surprise German offensive, things have changed. Does it concern you?"

"No, the arrangements have all been made, the passports are secure, and travel schedules and reservations have been in place for some time. I will need to contact a few people with revised dates, but it can be done."

"What about the money? Now that DeVos has disappeared, Becker tells me that he has left that up to you as well."

Lukas was still trying to absorb the incredible fact that Claire had killed DeVos, and his skin crawled whenever he thought about it. He took another sip of cognac before responding. "I will start investigating that in the morning." A task made a bit easier now that Claire has the key, he thought to himself. At least he knew where to start. They just had to find the cell down in the tunnels.

The *Viscount* nodded, "I'm sure you will take care of that as efficiently as you do everything else.

"Were you surprised at what Becker presented tonight?" Lukas asked, changing the subject.

The *Viscount* was silent for a moment. Then he slowly nodded. "Yes, I was *very* surprised. Wagner has never said anything about the development of a new weapon. And he certainly never mentioned any plans to continue this work in secret and abroad."

"Is that even possible," Lukas asked.

"Quite frankly, I doubt it. And it causes a great deal of concern." He paused for a moment, glancing down at the glass in his hand before continuing. "There are those within the Third Reich who will never abandon the dream of German supremacy and will try to keep it alive even after their defeat in this war. My dear friend, Gerhard Wagner, is one of those, as is his protégé and son-in-law, Konrad Becker, of course. But it probably won't succeed. It will only be a matter of time before more powerful countries like America and Russia develop this same weapon. As for most of the others in that room tonight—you and I included—it would have been sufficient just to escape what's left of Europe while we still can."

Lukas stared at the *Viscount,* surprised at what he'd just said.

You and I included... Escape Europe while we still can?

A heavy cloud suddenly enveloped him. There was so much he hadn't known, could not even have imagined, that he felt like a fly caught up in a spider web. "I had never imagined that I could not remain in Belgium, I don't want to leave... I can't leave."

The *Viscount* shrugged. "Neither do I," he said matter-of-factly. "I love Belgium; I love my life here. But Becker would never allow us to stay behind, not with what we know." He paused, looking at Lukas with a smile. "Don't worry. We will have to leave for a time. But I will make certain the two of us return when the war is over. I've already planned it."

Lukas stared into the fireplace, thinking about that. He realized that he'd begun to question his loyalty to Becker. Or, more precisely, Becker's loyalty to *him.* Becker's questions about Claire had unnerved him. He'd always known Becker was dangerous, but the fact that he knew about Claire was frightening. Lukas had at one time admired Becker, obeyed him, and had been loyal to him. But it was the *Viscount* he trusted! If they *did* have to leave, he took some solace in what the *Viscount* had just said about returning to Europe after the war ended.

"Who were the two men in the dark suits?" Lukas asked.

The *Viscount* shrugged again. "I have no idea. Becker obviously brought in some extra security. Just another surprise from an unpredictable person." He leaned back in the plush leather chair and sighed. "I had hoped it would turn out differently. Despite my friendship with Wagner, I certainly do not share his passion for continuing the German Reich." Then he drained the last of the cognac, set the glass down and looked Lukas in the eye. "We need to be careful, you and I, and get through the next two days. The war will be over soon, and we will return. But now, I shall retire. I suggest you do the same. We have a lot ahead of us."

Chapter One Hundred and Five

The next morning, when Claire entered the hotel dining room, she spotted McDonald sitting at a table set for two. "Isn't Colonel Worthington joining us for breakfast?" she asked.

"He had to tend to some business back in Liege," McDonald said, pouring a cup of coffee for her. After the waiter took their order, McDonald said, "We know that Becker is here in Namur or somewhere nearby. And I'm betting that wherever he is, so are the bloody war criminals he's smuggled into the country. We know he left the hotel yesterday dressed in civilian clothes, and I spoke with the concierge just now, and Becker has not checked out of his room. His key is still at the desk."

"Is he still waiting for DeVos to show up?"

"Perhaps," McDonald said, "but my gut instinct is that Becker's not coming back to the hotel. I'll get the key and search his room. Doubt if I'll find anything useful, but you never know. After that, I'll check in with the police here in Namur and find out if they've seen or heard of any foreigners in town during the last few weeks. I met the chief at an intel meeting in Brussels a couple of months ago. I think I can trust him."

"But several thousand Allied troops have been passing through here the last several days," Claire said, "It would be quite easy for a few foreign civilians to get lost in the crowd, wouldn't it?"

McDonald nodded. "Yes, it's a long shot, but we don't have a lot of options at this point. Are you meeting Lukas this morning?"

Claire held up the ancient key. "Yes, he'll be here in about an hour. Then we're going to search the tunnels for the money." She saw the dubious look on McDonald's face and smiled. "Don't worry, I'll be fine. Lukas said he's familiar with the tunnels and has some ideas about where to look."

Chapter One Hundred and Six

McDonald was getting impatient as he sat in the chief's office in the Namur central police station. The chief was a calm, serious sort who remembered McDonald from the intel briefing. He patiently listened as McDonald related the events of the past few weeks and the search for an SS officer named Becker. The chief jotted notes from time to time, mentioning how hectic the city had been recently with hundreds of American and British troops coming and going. And the more they talked, the more it seemed to McDonald like a waste of time.

He was about to give up when the chief abruptly held up his hand as though he'd suddenly thought of something. "I just recalled something one of my officers told me late yesterday afternoon. It may not mean anything, but it was a bit strange."

"What was it?" McDonald asked."

The chief continued. "The officer said that he spotted *Viscount* de Berg's automobile in town yesterday morning."

"Who is that?" McDonald asked.

"The de Berg family is one of Belgium's oldest nobilities," the chief said, "descended from the House of Berg in Germany back in the 13th or 14th century. The *Viscount,* I believe, is the last surviving member of the family in Belgium, an extremely wealthy man, an international art collector with connections all over Europe and beyond. The family estate is just a few miles out of town, overlooking the river."

"Why would it seem strange that his car was in town?" McDonald asked.

"The *Viscount* is a very private man, quite reclusive, actually," the chief explained. "His chauffeur and one or more of his servants will occasionally drive into town for supplies, but the auto was apparently sighted in a rather unlikely location."

"And your officer recognized the car?" McDonald asked.

The chief nodded. "It's hard to miss, a long, black Mercedes-Benz, the only one I'm aware of in the area."

McDonald was about to ask how this could be relevant when the chief continued. "I believe the car was there to meet someone," he said. "Let me see if the officer is here in the station. Perhaps he can provide more detail."

It took a few minutes to locate the officer, a middle-aged man with a slight paunch. He appeared a bit nervous when introduced to a British Intelligence officer but relaxed a bit when the chief told him what he wanted to know.

"I recognized the auto right away," the officer said, "seen it once or twice before, in the city center or market area, that big Mercedes, all of us know whose it is. But yesterday, it was parked on the street behind Saint Aubain's Cathedral, which seemed odd since there's nothing on that street except a few bombed-out buildings. After I drove past, I glanced in the rear-view mirror and saw a man walk up to the car, open the rear door, and get in. Then they drove away."

"Do you know who this man was?" McDonald asked.

The officer shook his head. "I have no idea. He seemed like he was in a hurry, though."

"What was he wearing?" McDonald asked.

"I just caught a quick look, but a short jacket, I think... and he had blond hair, I remember, because he wasn't wearing a hat."

McDonald recalled what the concierge had told him about Becker wearing a black leather jacket. He turned to the chief. "You said the de Berg family was descended from the House of Berg... in Germany?"

The chief nodded. "Yes, that's right, but what does that...?" He stopped in mid-sentence and motioned to the officer, dismissing him. After the officer left and closed the door, he continued. "I understand what you may be thinking, but, as I said, the de Berg family has been in Belgium for generations. The *Viscount's* father was a decorated officer in the Belgian army during the Great War, an associate of King Albert. I cannot imagine that he could—"

McDonald held up a hand, interrupting him. "I realize this may be a very sensitive matter. But I want to visit the *Viscount...* this morning. And I would appreciate your assistance."

The chief was silent for a moment, staring down at his desk, obviously uncomfortable at the prospect of offending a nobleman of such high stature. Finally, he looked up at McDonald and said, "I could call and make an appointment, but I'm not sure what good it will do. A hundred men could be hidden on that estate, and you would never know it."

McDonald stood up. "All the more reason for a visit. And no need to call ahead; it will be best if we just show up unannounced.

Chapter One Hundred and Seven

Liege

Jack paced back and forth in the small jail cell, furious with himself for being so stupid. What did he expect would happen when he called a G2 army intelligence base out of the blue, that they would run out and greet him with open arms? Claire was being sought as a fugitive, and every policeman and gendarme in Belgium was on the lookout for her. On the other hand, what options did he have? He had no idea where to start looking for her, no idea if she was even still alive... a thought that made him sick to his stomach.

Jack stopped pacing as a key rattled in the cell door. A guard pulled the door open and motioned for him to step out. "Colonel Worthington wants to see you."

He was led to an austere conference room and stood across the table from a serious-looking, middle-aged army officer. The man looked up at him and pointed to a chair. "I'm Colonel Worthington, US Army G2." he said crisply, "who are you?"

Jack blinked at the abrupt comment, then cleared his throat and replied, "My name is Jack Richards, 1st

Lieutenant, US Army Air Corps. As I said to the lady on—"

Worthington interrupted him. "Why aren't you in uniform, Lieutenant?"

In uniform? What the hell?

"I've been a prisoner of war in Germany for the last year. They took our uniforms. I managed to escape about—"

The colonel interrupted again, "Did you get those clothes from the Germans?"

Jack reflexively glanced down at the woolen coat Gunter had given him that first night, just before the offensive started. It was filthy now and ripped in several places, but he was still wearing it because it had been cold in the jail cell. "No, I got this from a farmer in Lanzerath. As I was saying, I managed to escape during an air raid near Bitburg and made it over the border to Lanzerath. Then I met up with—"

"What were you doing in La Gleize?"

Jack sat back in his chair and took a breath, recalling the same interrogation technique he'd been subjected to in the German POW camps. Keep interrupting; keep them off balance. After a moment, he continued, "In Lanzerath, I met up with the 106th Infantry, and if you would contact Major—"

"I thought you said you were in the Air Corps?"

"I was, 20th Combat Wing out of Hardwick. I flew—"

Worthington abruptly pointed a finger at Jack's face. "What is your *real* name? I know you're not Jack Richards; that's impossible. Now, who the hell are you, and what do you want with Mariette Janssens?"

It went on like this for over an hour, Jack fighting hard to control his emotions and temper. Through countless interruptions, he managed to tell almost the entire story: being shot down near Grote Brogel, his rescue by Claire and Gaston, the trek through France and over the mountains, his capture in Spain and imprisonment in Germany.

Then Colonel Worthington abruptly changed tack and asked, "Why did you call asking for Mr. McDonald? Where did you get his name?"

Frustrated and exhausted, Jack pulled out the folded, somewhat crumpled bulletin and slapped it on the table. "I first called Captain DeVos with the Antwerp police, as it said right here." He went on with the story about how he got McDonald's name, then leaned across the table and glared at the colonel. "Mariette Janssens is the person who saved my life! I've told you a dozen times, my name is *Jack Richards, and I'm an American air corps officer, and I need to find Claire! Goddamn it!*" He paused for a moment, then continued, slowly and deliberately, "Unless you've already found her. Have you found Claire, Colonel?"

"How do you know Niels DeVos?" Worthington shot back.

Jack slumped in his chair, disheartened. It was at least the third time he'd been asked that same damn question. "I don't know Niels DeVos! I never knew that name until I saw it in the bulletin. I've told you that three times. The only people I ever met besides the Basque guide who led us over the mountains were Claire, Gaston, Bart, and Lukas." He thought for a moment about telling Worthington that Lukas was a traitor, the one who betrayed him, but dismissed it. It was obvious that the man hadn't believed anything he'd told him, and that would only make it worse.

The colonel stared at him in silence, then stood up. "That will be all for now. The guard will show you back to your cell."

Jack stood as well. "You haven't answered my question. Have you found Claire?"

Worthington took a step closer to Jack, looking him in the eye. "Why do you want to know?"

"Because I need to find her, she saved my life and... because I'm in *love* with her, damn it! If anything's happened to her... I don't know what I'd..."

"The guard will show you back to your cell," Worthington repeated and turned away.

Jack stared at Worthington's back, suddenly overwhelmed with frustration and despair, terrified that he might never see her again.

It can't end like this!

Not when I've come this close!

"Wait!" Jack shouted. "Wait! Just one last thing... Please!"

Worthington stopped and turned back slowly. "What is it?"

Jack hesitated, knowing it would sound ridiculous, but it was his last chance. "If you *have* found her, tell her I'm Sir Lancelot, not Jim Hawkins."

Chapter One Hundred and Eight

It had been several years since Lukas had last been to the Citadel of Namur. Situated high in the hills overlooking the confluence of the Sabre and Meuse Rivers, the Citadel had stood since Roman times, protecting the city's inhabitants from ancient invaders. Its immense stone walls, arched bridges and circular turrets had served as impenetrable barriers against attackers until the 17th century when invading armies came equipped with horse-drawn cannons. It was then that construction began on a network of underground tunnels and galleries to protect the defenders of the Citadel and their supplies of food and armaments.

As Lukas drove his old Citroen up the narrow, winding road with Claire sitting next to him, he was decidedly on edge. The revelations during last night's meeting at the *Viscount's* estate had troubled him. The Third Reich continuing abroad, the development of a mysterious new weapon, and German supremacy rising once again like a phoenix from the ashes all seemed preposterous. But, more troubling than all of that was the prospect of leaving Claire behind since she was the only person in the world he really cared about.

Regardless of everything he'd been involved in, the thought of leaving Belgium with Becker, the *Viscount,* and the others had never entered his mind. But he now realized that what the *Viscount* said was true. Becker would never leave them behind. He felt a bit better knowing that the *Viscount* had planned for this and that they could return after the war... but it still troubled him.

He took a breath and glanced out the window to clear his mind. The massive stone structure loomed above them, blocking out the sun as though it was floating in the sky. The Citadel had been abandoned since before the turn of the century, the labyrinth of underground tunnels all but forgotten.

They came to a stop where the road finally gave way to a footpath, and Claire turned to him. "Do you have any idea where to begin?" she asked.

He shrugged. "Not exactly. But I came hiking up here a few years ago. I know this pathway winds around the base of the towers and the main fort. I recall seeing several arched doorways that could be entrances to the tunnels."

"I've heard there are several kilometers of tunnels," Claire said, sounding practical, as always.

Lukas had given that some thought. "That's right, but if DeVos was hauling sacks of money up here, I doubt he would venture too deeply into the bowels of this place before he found a hiding spot."

"The locksmith said there are cells and gates somewhere down there where soldiers of the garrison were imprisoned back in 1792."

Lukas nodded. "And I'll bet that key you have unlocks one of those gates." He opened the trunk of the car and produced two torches, a hammer, and a crowbar. "Shall we take a look?"

The tunnel was damp and deathly quiet, the cobblestone walls arching into a domed ceiling just a few feet over Lukas' head. Underfoot, the earthen floor was uneven and rocky, descending gradually downward. With the flickering light of their torches barely penetrating the blackness, Lukas proceeded slowly with Claire close behind. The tunnel eventually curved to the right and led to an ancient stone stairway descending still lower. At the bottom, the tunnel split in two directions.

"Which way?" Claire asked.

"I don't know. Let's go to the left. If we run into another stairway, we'll double back. I doubt DeVos would've wanted to carry bags of money up and down too many stairways." He had no idea if they were on the right track, and he also had no idea what he would do if they found the money. He had planned on doing this alone and completing the mission before Claire could discover his secrets.

They did run into another stairway and doubled back, following the tunnel the other way until it eventually led to an open galley with two tunnels going off in different directions. They followed one to a locked wooden door, but the key didn't fit. The second tunnel led to another stairway, steeper than the first, descending deep into the darkness.

It took another hour before they finally succeeded. After backtracking all the way outside, they climbed further up the winding path along the side of the fort and found another entrance. This led to a series of three tunnels, and on the second try, they found it. An open galley about three meters on a side with a high, domed ceiling. On one end of the galley, they found a partially rotted wooden door hanging precariously on rusty hinges. Through the doorway was another, smaller galley and at the far end, a wrought iron gate secured with an ancient lock.

Claire withdrew the key from her pocket, hesitated for a moment, then handed it to him. "Here, you try it."

Lukas inserted it in the lock, turned it, and the lock clicked open.

"My, God, I can't believe it," Claire whispered, as though afraid to be overheard.

Lukas pushed the gate open, his heart pounding. If the money was there, he would have to find a way to get it out. But how would he deal with Claire? They stepped into a short, narrow tunnel that turned to the right, opening onto a small, dead-end room no larger than an ancient crypt. Stacked along the back wall were a dozen wooden crates.

Lukas handed his torch to Claire and pried the lid off one of the crates. Inside were three canvas sacks, each filled with bundles of Swiss Franc notes.

As they stood in stunned silence, staring at the incredible stash of money, Lukas's mind was churning, wondering what to do now. He'd been considering his options for the last several hours, none of them ideal. He had a fleeting thought that perhaps he should just tell Claire the truth, tell McDonald and Worthington where they could find Becker and the Nazi war criminals. But he knew that was foolish and could never end well.

Claire broke the silence when she glanced at him, eyes wide, shaking her head. "My God, it's all true, they were really doing it—Becker and DeVos—it's all real. We've got to get back and report this to McDonald."

Lukas blinked, trying to clear his mind.

Think! Think!

"I'll take you back to the hotel and drop you off," he said as another plan formed in his mind. "We'll need help with this... a truck. The repair garage, where I got my car fixed. The owner is a friend, someone I can trust... and he has a truck."

Claire looked at him, a skeptical frown on her face. "What? Wait a minute. Who is this? I don't think that's such a good idea... I need to report this to McDonald."

"Yes, of course you do. That's why I'll take you back to the hotel right away. Is he there now?"

"I don't know. He was going to talk with the Namur police chief. But I'm sure he'll be coming back or leaving a message for me."

Lukas thought hard, working out the plan in his head. He needed some time, a few hours at least. But it was never easy to convince Claire to do something she didn't want to do. "Ok, how about this," he said, glancing at his watch, which he held up to the torchlight. "I'll drop you off at the hotel; then I'll get my friend and the truck and meet you and McDonald and anyone else he wants to include back here at the base of the footpath at four o'clock. That should give us enough time to get everyone together." The lies were spilling out so fast now he was terrified he'd never remember them all.

She continued to stare at him with an uncertain look, obviously uncomfortable not being in control of the plan, which was typical of her. Finally, she nodded slowly. "Well, I don't have a better idea, so let's get going."

Chapter One Hundred and Nine

When the chief stopped the car just outside the five-meter-high wrought iron gates, McDonald stared in amazement at the incredible sight. Beyond the gate, a smooth, gravel road lined with giant oak trees stretched for at least a half kilometer toward an immense palace just barely visible in the distance.

A moment later, a uniformed guard emerged from a small brick structure next to the gate and approached the car. The chief rolled down the window and spoke in French, explaining that they wished to see the *Viscount.* The guard looked at him curiously and then stepped back to the brick structure.

McDonald tapped his fingers on the dashboard until the guard re-emerged, pulled the gate open and motioned for them to drive through. When they arrived at the circular turn-around in front of the main entrance of the mansion, another uniformed guard greeted them and led them up the steps and through a massive set of double doors. They stepped into the marble entry hall, complete with a hanging chandelier and a large cut glass vase of flowers situated on a marble pillar, where a butler in full livery was waiting for them.

The chief introduced himself then, with a glance at McDonald, switched to English and said, "We are here to see the *Viscount.*"

The butler nodded and replied, also in English. "Do you have an appointment?"

"No, we don't. But it is quite important that we speak with him. Is he in?"

The butler nodded again. "I will see if he is available."

When the butler returned, he led them down a hallway to a sitting room lined with bookshelves and six leather chairs near a fieldstone fireplace. "The *Viscount* will be with you shortly," he said before leaving the room and closing the door behind him.

They waited more than ten minutes before the *Viscount* finally appeared. He was a tall, thin man with light gray hair, dressed casually in black trousers and a pale blue cashmere sweater. He stepped up to the chief and held out his hand, speaking in perfect English. "Ah, the chief of our very excellent police department. Good morning, sir; it has been a while since we last met."

He shook the chief's hand and then turned to McDonald. "Welcome, sir. I am *Viscount* de Berg. How may I be of service to you, gentlemen?"

McDonald introduced himself, then glanced at the chief and nodded.

"We understand your automobile was in the city yesterday," the chief said. "One of our officers happened to mention it."

The *Viscount* gave him a curious look, then replied casually, "Yes, as a matter of fact, it was. I sent my chauffeur to meet someone."

"And who was that, sir? If you don't mind my asking."

The *Viscount* looked at him for a moment, then abruptly motioned toward the chairs. "Forgive me, gentlemen, please have a seat. May I offer you some coffee, tea, perhaps?"

McDonald shook his head as they took a seat. "No, thank you. We won't take much of your time."

The *Viscount* sat next to the chief. "So, you asked whom I sent my car to meet in the city. A curious question, which makes me wonder why you would want to know." He paused for a moment, and when neither the chief nor McDonald responded, he smiled thinly and said, "Very well, if you really want to know, it was an old friend, a former employee of mine, to be exact. I hadn't seen him in quite some time, and... it seemed he'd fallen on some hard times and needed a bit of help. My chauffeur picked him up near the cathedral and brought him here. It turned out he was on his way to London, where he had family but was short of funds. He had always been a decent sort of man, a hard worker, loyal. So, of course, I was glad to help. I gave him some money, we had a bite to eat, and my driver took him to the railway station. That was it."

He glanced first at the chief, then McDonald. "So, can you explain why this is of interest to the police and the Intelligence service of Great Britain?"

McDonald spoke up. "Are you familiar with a man by the name of Konrad Becker, sir?" He watched the *Viscount* closely for any type of reaction and thought he saw a slight twitch.

"Konrad Becker? No, I don't recall knowing anyone by that name. Why do you ask?"

"He is someone we've been searching for, and according to the officer who noticed your car, your friend looks a bit like Becker."

"Well, my friend is rather ordinary looking," the *Viscount* said with a shrug. So, I imagine that could—"

"Have you had any other visitors recently?" McDonald asked.

A look of annoyance flashed in the *Viscount's* eyes, obviously not in the habit of being interrupted. "No, I have not, certainly not since all this fighting erupted. Now, unless there is anything else."

McDonald stood and held his hand out to the *Viscount*. "Thank you for seeing us, sir. Sorry to have barged in on you."

"No trouble at all," the *Viscount* replied as he stood as well, shook McDonald's hand, and motioned toward the door. "I'm always happy to be of assistance to our British friends. I just hope this awful business in the

Ardennes will end soon. Do you think you and the Americans have it under control?"

"Not completely," McDonald said, "but we've contained it. I doubt you'll have any trouble here in Namur."

The butler led them to the front door, and when they stepped outside, McDonald noticed two men dressed in dark suits standing next to one of the uniformed guards at the far end of the terrace. As they walked back to their car, McDonald also noticed another driveway that split off from the circular turn-around and curved around the corner toward the back of the mansion. "Is there another exit from this property?" he asked.

The chief shook his head. "No. I believe that's a service drive to the back of the main house. The only way in and out of the property is through the main gate."

When they were back in the car, McDonald looked up at the mansion's colossal, five-story façade. Then he glanced at the chief. "Who do you think those two men in dark suits were?"

"Employees of the *Viscount,* I suspect." The chief said. Then his brow furled, a look of concern in his eyes. "You don't believe what the *Viscount* said?"

"No, not for a bloody minute."

Chapter One Hundred and Ten

When McDonald returned to the hotel, Claire was waiting for him in the lobby. "How did you make out?" McDonald asked, glancing around to make sure no one else was nearby.

"We found it," Claire whispered, with obvious excitement in her voice. "Several large wooden crates filled with Swiss Francs."

"Where's Lukas?" McDonald asked.

As she explained the plan to him, he glanced at his watch. It was a little past noon. He thought about posting guards in the tunnel to catch anyone who showed up but knew the police chief would never authorize it with the town still full of soldiers. He was considering other options when he heard the concierge's voice behind him. "Excuse me, Mr. McDonald, but Colonel Worthington called from Liege about a half hour ago. He asked if you could call him as soon as possible. Shall I get him on the telephone?"

"I interrogated the guy pretending to be Jack Richards, "Worthington said when he got on the phone.

"And what do you think?"

"Well, he's an American, that's for sure. Either that, or he's perfected the accent, which is certainly possible. I questioned him for over an hour. He claims to be a bomber pilot shot down over Grote Brogel and that Claire and Gaston rescued him. Then he claims he was a POW in Germany for a year, escaped and somehow managed to get back across the border to Belgium just when the offensive broke out. He seems to know all the right names: Claire, of course, Gaston, Bart, Lukas."

"Well, so did DeVos and probably Becker as well," McDonald said. "That may be how he got the right names. What are the chances the real Jack Richards could escape from a German POW camp and wind up back here, looking for Claire right after she'd been abducted?"

"Slim to none."

"Right. More likely, he's part of some group of collaborators DeVos recruited, and he's trying to find Claire because she knows too much."

"I suppose we could bring him to Namur under guard and see if she can identify him."

McDonald thought about that for a moment. "Sounds like a waste of time to me. We need to focus on tracking down these bloody war criminals."

"Yes, I agree. However, he did say something that was a bit strange. He said that if we found Claire, tell her that he's 'Sir Lancelot and not Jim Hawkins.'"

McDonald was confused for a moment before it hit him. "Did you say, 'Sir Lancelot?'" he asked, suddenly recalling his conversation with Claire in the bar.

"Yes, but I have no idea what—"

McDonald cut him off. "Hold on for a second." He called out to Claire, waving her over.

She looked at him curiously and then quickly crossed the lobby to the front desk. The concierge had discreetly stepped away, leaving them alone.

"Listen to me," McDonald said to her. "This may sound strange, but do you remember telling me about you and Jack Richards discussing the book *Treasure Island* and something about Sir Lancelot and Jim Hawkins?"

Claire flinched, "Sir Lancelot? Yes... I did... But... why—"

He held the phone out so Worthington could hear, "Were you alone with him when that happened?" he asked her. "Could anyone else have overheard you?"

Claire held up both hands, "Wait a minute... what's going on? Who's on the phone?"

"It's Colonel Worthington. Please, Claire, just answer the question."

She stared at him for a long moment, her eyes tearing up. "We talked about it more than once; it was just something... between us... but we were always alone. What's going on... why are—"

"It's Jack, Claire. Worthington has found him. He's at the police station in Liege, and he's fine—"

McDonald had to drop the phone as Claire stumbled backward, and he reached out to help her.

Chapter One Hundred and Eleven

The wait was excruciating. It had been more than three hours since Colonel Worthington had called, and Claire was beside herself. She cried at the thought that Jack was alive, and she cried at the thought of what he must have endured this past year. She paced around like a nervous cat, taking deep breaths to calm down. Then the tears came again.

Is he injured?

Does he blame me for what happened?

Will he forgive me?

When he finally stepped into the hotel lobby, Claire stood frozen in place, staring at him; her mind suddenly went blank. He looked older and tired. His shoulders sagged a bit.

Then he smiled... and held out both hands.

She rushed to him, tears flowing down her face.

He wrapped his arms around her, and for an instant, she was back in the safehouse in Saint-Jeanne-de-Luz; she was in his arms; none of the rest ever happened.

But it did happen... it all happened.

Yet he's alive. He's here.

She slowly took a step back, looking into his eyes.

"I've missed you so much," he whispered as a tear trickled down the side of his face.

She reached up and brushed it away. "I never gave up hope, Jack. I thought about you every day."

They were both silent for a long moment, staring into each other's eyes. He looked older, but he was the same... the same person she'd fallen in love with. And he still loved her... she could tell; she could see it in his eyes; she could feel it. "How did you find me?" she finally asked.

He kissed her gently, then motioned to a settee in the far corner of the lobby.

"I am *so* sorry, Jack," she said as soon as they sat down. "I don't know what happened... I thought everything was; I thought you were..." She stopped abruptly, her throat catching, the words gone.

"It's over now, I'm here," he said. "I never stopped thinking about you either, Claire. Not once. I was afraid that you might also have been betrayed. That you were being hurt, and there was nothing I could do. But I knew that somehow, I would find a way to get back here."

"How *did* you get back here? Where were you? Did they... God, I sound like an idiot; I don't even know what to ask... I just missed you so much!"

"We'll talk about it," he said quietly, "We'll have time; I'm not leaving you again, not ever." He paused for a moment before continuing. "But there is something I need to tell you now."

"Yes, of course... what is it?"

He hesitated for a moment, then took her hand. "I was in a POW camp in Germany. The Germans thought I was a spy."

"A spy? That's crazy! Where would they have gotten that idea?"

"The Commandant was a Luftwaffe officer. Air Corps people look out for each other, even enemies. He wasn't inclined to turn me over to the SS even though the notes in my file accused me of espionage. But he did tell me that there was a Nazi collaborator in Belgium who accused me."

At first, Claire thought she hadn't heard correctly.

A Nazi collaborator... in Belgium... who accused him?

DeVos?

How could he have known about Jack?

"Did he say who—?"

Jack reached over with his other hand, cradling hers in both of his. "There were a lot of notes in my file full of information obtained from this collaborator in Belgium. They said his name was... Lukas."

Claire recoiled and jumped to her feet as though she'd been bitten by a wasp. "What? Did you say, *Lukas?*" She shook her head. "No! Not *our* Lukas! That's not possible!"

"Claire, listen, I couldn't believe it either, and I've thought about it every day since that moment. But it was all in my file."

She backed away, shaking her head. "A German officer told you that? And you *believed* him?"

Jack stood and stepped closer. "Claire, they knew *everything.* They knew I was a B24 pilot, shot down near Grote Brogel. They knew I'd been rescued by an escape line, that I stayed in Lukas' attic, and was escorted over the mountains to Spain, where I was immediately arrested by the *Guardia Civil.*" He paused for a moment, a painful look in his eyes. "If it wasn't true, how would they know his name?"

Claire suddenly felt very cold and wrapped her arms around her chest. Jack reached out, but she stepped back. "It's not possible, it's... *insane!* I've known Lukas since we were children. He *helped* me, Jack. When I found out you hadn't returned to England, I was devastated, and Lukas was the one who helped me. Bart was missing... and... for God's sake, it was *Lukas* who helped me get to St. Vith where I met McDonald."

"Where is he now?"

"He's here, in Namur. I was with him this morning when we searched the tunnels for the money." She stopped and took a breath, realizing Jack had no idea what she was talking about. Then she reached over and took his hand. "Listen, we are going to meet Lukas at four o'clock, and I'm sure he can clear this up.

There's been a terrible mistake. *DeVos* is the one who betrayed you."

Jack cocked his head, a confused look in his eyes. "DeVos... money... Claire I don't know what—"

She put her hand up to his lips, stopping him. "I'll explain all of that. And when we meet Lukas, I'm sure he can clear this up. But right now, you're here, you're back. That's all that matters."

Chapter One Hundred and Twelve

Claire stood next to Jack outside the Citadel and glanced at her watch another time. It was twenty-past-four, and there was no sign of Lukas. She'd been surprised when they drove up in McDonald's car at four o'clock, and she didn't see a truck, though she was certain Lukas would show up any moment. But now, as the minutes ticked past, doubt crept into her mind. Doubt about Lukas, something she could never have imagined, something that couldn't be happening.

Damn it, Lukas, where are you?

Another ten minutes passed, and she kept watching the road, hoping to see a truck coming up the hill, but slowly realizing he wasn't coming. Finally, she glanced at Jack, then at McDonald, Worthington and the three policemen who stood a few meters away. "Okay, let's go inside."

The policemen lit several lanterns as Claire led the group up the hill, around the massive fortress and through the second arched doorway leading to the tunnels. Jack followed right behind her as she carried a lantern, leading the group through a twisting, narrow labyrinth of dark stone tunnels, some so low they had to duck their heads.

They eventually arrived at the domed-ceiling galley, with a rotting wooden door hanging on rusty hinges. "That's the way," Claire said, glancing back at Jack and the others, all of whom had remained silent. They entered the smaller, lower tunnel she remembered and stopped. The flickering light of the lantern illuminated the ancient wrought iron gate... closed and locked.

"Is this it?" Jack asked.

Claire nodded, a sudden flicker of hope rising in her heart at the locked gate.

He hasn't been here!

He's been delayed!

"Yes, this is it," she said and held the lantern close to the gate, illuminating the short, narrow tunnel. "Beyond this gate, the tunnel makes a right turn into a small dead-end room. That's where the crates are stored, but you can't see them from here. The gate is still locked, and Lukas has the key. So, we'll have to wait for him."

The group was silent for a moment until one of the police officers, a tall, broad-shouldered young man, squeezed past Jack and Claire and stepped closer to the rusting gate. "This thing is so old, I'll bet a couple of us could just pull it down," he said.

"Do it," McDonald snapped.

It didn't take long. Another of the younger officers joined in, and the two of them grabbed the gate at the top. When they jerked it forward, the rusty gate sagged and fell with a thud as the hinges broke away from the rotted wooden frame.

Claire immediately brushed past the policemen, stepped over the gate and into the dead-end room.

It was empty.

She stared at the dirt floor, footprints, and scuff marks, visible in the light of the lantern, left behind when the crates were dragged out.

She closed her eyes, shaking her head, her heart breaking. She suddenly felt cold and started to tremble. Then, a hand on her shoulder.

She turned and looked at Jack, his eyes filled with compassion.

"Goddamn it!" she hissed. "How could he *do* this?"

The sun had set when the group gathered near McDonald's car at the base of the Citadel. No one said anything for a few moments as Claire stood silently, staring up at the imposing stone structure towering above them, still trying to come to grips with Lukas' deceit.

I've known him all my life... and he's a traitor!

He betrayed Jack... and now this!

Finally, McDonald spoke up. "Well, let's review what we know for sure," he said, then rapidly summarized the events of the past two weeks. "Since the money is gone, and Lukas had the key, it's safe to assume he's involved in this. But the money is secondary. The important thing is to get Becker and these Nazi war criminals before they get out of the country. And I'm pretty sure we know where they are."

"You can't mean the *Viscount's* estate." the police chief said with a note of alarm.

McDonald nodded. "Yes, I certainly do. It's perfect, tucked away on the top of the hills, completely secluded, guards at the gates. For Christ's sake, you said it yourself, the damn place is big enough to hide a *hundred* people!"

"Yes, but wait just a minute," the chief replied, holding a hand in the air. "We don't know for sure that Lukas and Becker are connected. Maybe Lukas isn't a collaborator or a traitor at all." He glanced at Claire with a shrug, "Maybe he's just a thief and went after the money."

The group fell silent again as the sky darkened and a cold breeze picked up. Claire felt everyone's eyes on her and shook her head. "No, Lukas is not a thief... he's a *traitor.* He betrayed Jack and accused him of espionage, and he's been..." She paused and glanced up at the dark sky. "He's been lying to me all along, and I should have..."

As her voice trailed off, Colonel Worthington turned to Jack. "Why didn't you tell me that Lukas had betrayed you when I was interviewing you in Liege?"

"You didn't believe a word I said about anything," Jack retorted sharply. "I thought that would only make things worse. Dealing with Lukas wasn't the most important thing to me at that moment. I wanted to find Claire."

"Okay, we're wasting time here," McDonald said. "Lukas is in this up to his neck. And I'm betting that Becker now knows we're on to him. So, we're going back to see the *Viscount.* Only this time, it's not a friendly visit." He turned to the chief again. "We'll need your men to help us search the house."

The chief took a step back, staring at McDonald like he was a madman. "Are you out of your mind… search the *Viscount's* home, his estate? I can't authorize that; it's not possible, it's not—"

McDonald cut him off. "If you can't, who can? We're wasting time!"

"I don't know," the chief sputtered, "the mayor, a judge… I don't know, but I cannot be a party to it… I'd be crucified." With that, he turned abruptly and stalked back to his car, followed by the two officers.

McDonald turned to Worthington. "What do you think?"

Worthington shrugged. "Well, technically, Belgium is under the control of the allied armies, so I guess we have as much authority as anyone."

"Can you recruit some of our troops to help?" Jack asked.

"I've already done that," Worthington said. "I got through to 1st Army HQ in Brussels before we left the hotel. They're up to their asses in this fight right now, but they understand the importance of catching these guys. They promised to dispatch a reserve platoon out of Antwerp and send them down here. But they probably won't get here before midnight."

They were all silent for a moment, and Claire glanced at the three men standing around her in the dark... a US Army colonel, a British intelligence agent, and Jack, a battle-hardened air corps pilot who had managed to escape from a Nazi prison camp. "Okay, then it's just us," she said. "What's the plan?"

Chapter One Hundred and Thirteen

Lukas once again stood near the fireplace in the parlor of the *Viscount's* mansion. This time, however, he watched Konrad Becker pace slowly back and forth, glancing at his watch. The *SS-Hauptsturmfuhrer* now wore the uniform of a US Army Captain, all part of his plan for getting out of the country. The *Viscount* stood calmly on the other side of the fireplace, smoking a cigarette, wearing the traveling clothes of a country gentleman.

Lukas took a deep breath and tried to relax, but ever since he'd unexpectedly reunited with Claire, it was impossible. He knew it was almost over; the months of planning and secrecy, the smuggling, the lies... the long road of deception he'd been traveling was close to the end.

But being with Claire had suddenly complicated everything. He had lied to her again, and this time, it was a lie from which he doubted he could recover. He'd been trapped the moment he learned that Claire knew about the money and had DeVos' key. There was no other choice than to deceive her, stall for time and grab the money. He was in far too deep to do anything else.

Becker had made that clear in the café the other morning... and Becker knew about Claire!

And yet, a part of him still believed he was doing the right thing for the cause, for the better world his friends, the *Viscount* and Becker, had assured him was coming. They had rescued him from the destitute, impoverished situation he'd been in when he returned to Belgium. It had been his one chance to make something of himself, to show Claire they could have a life together... if she never learned his secret.

But then everything went wrong. The news about Bart and Gaston disturbed him deeply. They were friends, people who had trusted him, people he had tried to protect, even while he was secretly sabotaging the escape line. Then, he almost lost *Claire,* the one person in the world who meant the most to him. Perhaps he'd been naïve to think he could protect them all, but somehow, just believing he could seem to justify what he was doing.

Now, he was eager to go. Even if it meant he would have to leave Belgium for a time. Then, when he and the *Viscount* returned, he would try to reconcile with Claire. Perhaps he could explain to her that he'd been forced to take the money, and maybe he could explain—

He was jolted out of his thoughts when Becker abruptly stopped pacing and turned toward him. "We have to leave in a few minutes. Do you have all of the travel documents?"

Lukas nodded. "Yes, right here in this pouch."

"Let me see them," Becker demanded.

Lukas hesitated for just a second, then handed over the pouch.

Becker opened it, thumbed through a few of the documents, and then shoved the pouch into his briefcase. As if on cue, the two men Lukas had seen at the reception the other night entered the room. They both wore American army uniforms.

One of them spoke to Becker in English, "The crates are loaded, and all the guests are in the vehicles. We are ready to leave."

Becker nodded and glanced at the *Viscount,* who tossed his cigarette into the fireplace and started to button his coat.

Before he fastened the first button, one of Becker's men drew a pistol from his holster and shot him squarely in the forehead.

Lukas went rigid, staring in horror as the *Viscount* slumped to the floor. For an instant, his mind went blank, not comprehending... then he whirled toward Becker, shouting, his voice cracking. "What... what the hell... have you done? The *Viscount!* Your friend... *my* friend! My God... why... why did you do this?"

Becker stepped forward. "Watch yourself, Lukas," his voice was menacing, his ice-blue eyes glaring at him. "Be very careful if you want to survive this."

"No! This is crazy! He was our friend... our—"

"Shut up!" Becker snapped, stepping closer, pointing his finger at him. "I know all about you,

Lukas. I know how you tried to protect those traitors, Bart and Gaston. I know you're protecting another traitor, aren't you... your *girlfriend,* Claire. Did you think I wouldn't find out?"

Lukas took a step back, his heart pounding. He glanced down at the *Viscount's* dead body, suddenly terrified for Claire. He looked back at Becker. "No, you're wrong about Claire! She was never involved, not ever; I told you that!"

"You lied to me, Lukas—"

"No! I never lied. I was loyal to you..." his voice faltered as he glanced again at the *Viscount's* body lying in a growing pool of blood. He turned back to Becker. "I was *loyal...* you son-of-a-bitch!"

Becker stared at him for a long, silent moment, then shook his head. "I'm sorry, Lukas."

Lukas glanced quickly at the man holding the pistol, then whirled around and bolted for the door at the far side of the room, limping as fast as he could.

Then everything went dark.

Chapter One Hundred and Fourteen

Claire sat in the front passenger seat as McDonald stopped the car half a kilometer down the road from the entrance to the *Viscount's* estate and pulled over in a flat, grassy area beneath a clump of trees. Jack and Worthington were in the back seat, and the four of them got out of the car.

McDonald opened the trunk and retrieved a battery-operated two-way radio.

Worthington grabbed a second radio and an M1 carbine. McDonald then retrieved a Colt 45 pistol and handed it to Jack. "Guess you fly-boys know how to use this," he said.

Jack nodded, checked the safety, and shoved the pistol into his jacket pocket.

"Okay, let's go over the plan," McDonald said. "This road is the only way in or out of the estate." He glanced at Worthington.

"Platoon Alpha 6 is on their way down from Antwerp," Worthington said, "about two hours out."

"So, this is a reconnaissance mission," McDonald said. "We need to know if Becker and these Nazi bastards are still here." He turned to Claire. "Do you know how to drive?"

"Yes, of course," she replied tersely, slightly annoyed that he had to ask.

"Good, then you'll drive the car slowly up to the gate. A woman driving up to the gate alone may be just unusual enough to keep the guard a bit off balance." He looked at Jack and Worthington. "The three of us will follow along on foot, keeping the car between us and the line of sight from the guard house. Jack, I want you to be in a position to overpower the guard as soon as he approaches the car. The last time we were here, there was only one guard, so hopefully, that hasn't changed, but it may have, so everyone stays alert.

Claire kept her eyes on the guardhouse as she drove up to the huge wrought iron gate, watching for any sign of the guard. She stopped the car a few meters short of the gate and rolled down the window.

No one emerged from the small brick building.

A moment later, she spotted Jack in the sideview mirror as he emerged from around the rear of the auto. Holding the pistol down at his side, he slowly approached the guardhouse. He stopped just outside the door and looked in. Then he turned around and walked quickly back to the car, shoving his handgun back into his jacket pocket. "We're too late, he's dead."

Claire flinched, "Dead?"

"Shot right through the head."

"Okay, let's get up to the house," McDonald snapped as he quickly opened the car door and slid into the front passenger seat. "Claire, drive slowly up to the mansion. You two follow on foot, one on either side of the driveway. Stay back twenty or thirty yards, but keep the car in sight. If you see anything, shoot first and ask later."

Jack and Worthington opened the gate. Claire put the car in gear and started up the long gravel drive. There were no other guards in sight as they approached the massive five-story palace, but there were lights in many of the ground-floor windows and a few on the first and second floors. "It's strange," she said, "looks like they're still here. Or else they left in a hurry."

"I'm guessing the latter," McDonald said. "As soon as Lukas told Becker about us being in town, I'll bet their plans changed."

Claire stopped the car at the top of the circular turn-around, and they both got out. She glanced back, just barely able to see Jack and McDonald walking slowly in the darkness on either side of the driveway. She turned and followed McDonald up the steps.

McDonald pulled a pistol from a holster under his jacket and tried the door.

It was unlocked, and he slowly pushed it open.

They stepped inside a marble entry hall, Claire glancing around at the chandelier hanging from the ceiling, the cut glass vase of flowers on a marble stand in the center of the entryway, not hearing a sound.

She followed behind McDonald as he proceeded slowly, gun drawn, through the entryway, down a wide hallway leading past a richly paneled room on their left that looked like a library or sitting room, and finally into an enormous, two-story parlor with a massive fireplace at the far end.

***

Jack moved slowly along the edge of the long gravel driveway, turning his head from side to side, watching for any sign of movement. Worthington was on the other side doing the same thing. He glanced up ahead at the immense mansion silhouetted against the dark sky, lights shining from many of the windows.

McDonald and Claire had disappeared inside a few minutes ago, and he was just beginning to wonder why they hadn't radioed back when a shrieking scream echoed through the still night air.

"Claire!" Jack yelled and sprinted toward the house.

He ran up the stairs and barged through the open door into a marble entry hall, almost knocking over a large vase of flowers. He ran down the hallway and stopped dead at the entrance to a massive two-story room.

In the center of the room, Claire knelt over a body lying on the blood-stained floor next to a broken coffee table.

She looked up at him, her hands covered in blood. "It's Lukas! He's been shot!"

Jack knelt beside her and placed his hand on Lukas' neck, feeling for a pulse. "He's still alive, there's a pulse, but it's weak." He rolled Lukas onto his back, and Claire elevated his feet with a pillow.

McDonald was already on the phone, yelling at the police chief to send an ambulance.

Jack pointed across the room to the body of an older man lying in a pool of blood on the floor in front of the fireplace, a dime-sized hole in the center of his forehead. "The *Viscount?*" he asked quietly.

McDonald hung up the phone and nodded. "The ambulance is on the way, and yes, that's the *Viscount.*"

Claire leaned in closer to Lukas and whispered, "Hang on, Lukas. Help is on the way. Stay with us."

Jack glanced at Claire, who had tears in her eyes. Then he looked down at Lukas, suddenly feeling very conflicted. For over a year, he had hated Lukas for betraying him and had often thought of what he would do to him if he survived the war and saw him again. Now Lukas was lying in a pool of his own blood, also betrayed by those he thought he could trust... and, at that moment, all Jack could feel for him was pity.

Sirens echoed through the open door of the mansion, and moments later, the police chief, followed by three medics wearing white coats and carrying a stretcher, charged through the front door, down the hallway and into the parlor.

Chapter One Hundred and Fifteen

As the red taillights of the ambulance disappeared down the long gravel drive, Jack stood with Claire in the open doorway. He waited for a moment, then closed the massive door and took her hand as they walked in silence through the long hallway back to the parlor.

The police chief stood near the fireplace, staring down at the *Viscount's* body, slowly shaking his head. "I'll get the coroner over here to take care of this," he mumbled to no one in particular, "but there's going to be a lot of questions."

Ignoring him, Worthington pulled a map out of his jacket pocket and spread it out on the floor, motioning for Jack, Claire, and McDonald to join him. "Based on the fact that Lukas is still alive, I'm guessing they couldn't have left more than an hour ago."

McDonald nodded. "My guess is they're heading for Antwerp to board a ship out of Europe,"

Worthington grabbed one of the radios and barked into it, "Platoon Alpha 6, this is Worthington, over."

Jack heard a crackling response a few seconds later.

"What's your position?" Worthington asked. After listening to the response, he replied, "Okay, change of plan. Do *not* come to the destination you were given. I repeat, do *not* come to Namur. Separate into three groups and set up checkpoints on the main roads heading north out of Namur toward Antwerp."

Jack watched as Worthington looked over the map again, tracing lines with his fingers. Then he rattled off the names of three towns and the corresponding roads, all of them heading in the general direction of Antwerp. "Set up checkpoints and stop every truck and automobile. You are looking for a German SS officer who will be wearing an American army uniform and will identify himself as Captain Rickert with G2, got that?"

Another crackling response, then Worthington repeated, "Yes, that's what I said. He's masquerading as an American army officer, a G2 officer named Rickert. But he's really a fuckin' SS officer and a killer, so don't take any chances. He will likely be traveling with as many as a dozen other men, all German civilians, Nazis, trying to escape. Take them all into custody. We want them alive, but if the SS guy or anyone else resists, you can take them out. Get back to me when you're in position." He stood up, running a hand through his thinning hair. "The platoon is between Namur and Antwerp, so if that's where these Nazi bastards are going, we might get lucky."

"What's this about a Captain Rickert?" Jack asked.

McDonald replied. "Right, you weren't here for that part. Becker was masquerading as an American army officer named Rickert... a bloody G2 officer of all things. He checked into the same hotel in Namur a few hours before we did, and the concierge asked me if I knew him. Damn lucky thing, or we'd never have known."

"So, that's his plan to get past army checkpoints on his way out of the country? What about all the Germans that are with him?"

McDonald shrugged. "They probably have American, British, or Canadian passports. I'm guessing Lukas and the *Viscount* probably arranged all that, and then Becker decided he didn't need them anymore." He glanced at Claire. "I'm sorry."

She nodded. "It's okay, thank you." Then she turned to Jack and squeezed his hand. Her dark eyes were still as sharp and penetrating as they had been back at the Citadel. "I just hope they can save him... because I want to know *why!*"

Chapter One Hundred and Sixteen

Konrad Becker sat in the passenger seat of the truck, still annoyed at the hasty departure they were forced to make after all his meticulous planning. It was that idiot DeVos that caused the mess, he thought, still wondering what had happened to him. He actually felt bad about Lukas, but that was the price for disloyalty. Now, he had to set that aside and focus on getting out of Belgium.

They had left the *Viscount's* estate less than an hour ago, and Becker knew that as soon as that girl, Claire, and the G2 officer, McDonald, discovered the money was missing, they would start hunting him down. They would undoubtedly focus on Antwerp as the most likely escape route and alert all the authorities at the ports and railway stations. The offensive was still creating enough chaos that it was possible they might slip through, though not very likely. And Becker was not inclined to take any chances. As usual, he had a backup plan.

Their small convoy consisted of two vehicles: the truck Becker was riding in with the crates of Swiss francs and a small bus the *Viscount* had secretly purchased over a year ago with all the German executives and his father-in-law. His two English-speaking thugs served as the drivers.

Becker glanced at his driver as they approached a crossroads at a small settlement consisting of three or four single-story buildings, all of which looked abandoned. "Pull up next to that building on the right," he said. When the truck stopped, Becker jumped out and walked briskly to the bus, which had pulled up behind them. He leaned into the open door of the bus and said to the driver. "One of the crates has come loose, and we have to secure it. You go on ahead and we will meet at the designated spot in Antwerp."

Becker watched as the bus continued north toward Antwerp. Then he walked back to the truck and pulled a small canvas bag out of the back. He walked to the vacant building and slipped inside. A few moments later, he emerged from the building wearing the uniform of a British lieutenant colonel.

When he got back in the truck, Becker nodded at the driver, who headed southwest toward France. By nightfall the next day, they would be in Switzerland. A second canvas bag in the back of the truck contained a navy blue, three-piece suit and the identification card of a prominent Swiss banker. Becker had always enjoyed Zurich.

Chapter One Hundred and Seventeen

Three days later, Claire stood at the foot of Lukas' bed in a second-floor room of the Namur hospital. It was a double room, but one of the beds had been removed. Lukas lay in the remaining bed, his head propped up with a pillow, his eyes closed, his face pale, a thick bandage wrapped around his chest, and an IV line taped to his left wrist. His right wrist was handcuffed to the railing on the bed. A thin ray of light from the late afternoon sun filtered through the single window.

She stood at the base of the bed and watched him for a while, trying to keep her emotions in check. During the past few days, she'd gone over everything she could think of, time and time again, searching for clues she must have missed. But every time, she came away more frustrated than ever at the fact that she never suspected anything, never imagined he could do such a thing.

Finally, as though he sensed her presence, Lukas' eyes opened. He looked at her for a moment, then slowly turned away.

She stepped around to the side of the bed. "I need you to look at me, Lukas."

He opened his eyes again.

"Jack is here," she said. "He made it back. He arrived in Namur while you were taking the money from the tunnel. He was with me when we found you."

His eyes widened, and what little color he'd had in his face faded away completely.

"He knows it was you, Lukas. There were notes in his file; your name was in the file, accusing him of espionage."

Lukas nodded slowly, then whispered, his voice thin and hoarse. "What do you want me to say?"

"What I want... is to know *why*? Why did you do it, all of it? How could you do it?"

He was silent for a long time, staring at the ceiling. "I wanted to be someone," he said finally, still looking at the ceiling, his voice barely audible. "I wanted... to belong. There was nothing for me when I came back to Belgium. Everyone was gone... you were gone... Bart, my family... all gone." He closed his eyes as if visualizing an event or an experience. When he opened them and spoke again, his voice was firmer. "And then I found something. Something that made sense when nothing else did, a new order, a future, a purpose, maybe a better life... for *us*." Then closed his eyes again.

Claire watched him for a while, remembering how tough it had been for him growing up, a skinny kid with a limp whose father drank and could never hold a job, a family that never had enough money, a family that eventually abandoned him. She remembered how he'd always looked after her like a big brother. Was that the reason, she wondered? Could any of that be a reason, a justification for what he did? She pulled a chair close to his bed and sat down, leaning in closer. "What about the people in the escape line, Lukas, those you betrayed? What about Bart and Gaston?"

He abruptly turned his head toward her, wincing in pain as he did. "No! Not Bart or Gaston. I *never* wanted that to happen. And I never wanted anything to happen to *you*. I tried to protect you, always. That's why I went to St. Vith, that's—"

"But what about the others, the aviators, the ones you didn't even know, the ones who were risking their lives for us? How could you betray them?"

He lay back on the pillow, looking at the ceiling again. "It was... the war... I had orders... I... don't know."

Claire sat in silence, trying to make sense of it all. Finally, she said. "And what about *Jack*? You *betrayed* him! Why, Lukas? Why would you do that? He trusted you... *I* trusted you."

"Do you love him?"

Claire stared at him, scarcely able to believe what she just heard. "Is *that* it, Lukas? Did you betray Jack, accuse him of being a spy, and sentence him to death because you were *jealous*?"

He looked her in the eye. "Do you *love* him?"

"*Yes!* Of course, I love him! And I was devasted when I learned he hadn't returned to England."

"But you barely *know* him, Claire... and you've known *me* your whole life! You don't know anything about him. He's just another of the Yanks passing through, thinking they're helping us poor, downtrodden Europeans, prolonging the war, delaying the inevitable victory of—"

Claire abruptly pushed back her chair and stood, staring down at him, trembling with rage. "How *dare* you! How *dare* you try to justify what you did by blaming someone else, the person I *love*, the person I intend to spend my life with." She paused for a moment and took a deep breath. "I always thought of you as the brother I never had, the person I could always count on, the person I looked up to and—"

"But not the person you *loved*."

"No, Lukas, you're not the person I loved. You tried to *kill* that person." She started for the door, then stopped and turned back to him. "You never said you're sorry."

He looked up at her, a flash of defiance in his eyes. "Perhaps I'm not."

Claire stood silently for a moment before she responded, her anger slowly ebbing into sadness and pity. "You should know that all of those Nazi businessmen were caught before they got to Antwerp."

The defiant looked faded.

"But not Becker," she added. "He apparently abandoned them and escaped with all the money. So much for their *new order*." Claire stood for another moment before she left, looking him in the eye. "You'll have to live with that, Lukas. You'll have to live with the fact that you not only betrayed your country... you betrayed *me!*"

Epilogue

London, February 1945.

Jack sat with Claire and Matthew McDonald at a small round table in the *Cork and Crown* pub not far from the King's Cross Railway station. Jack had just arrived from Hardwick USAAF airbase in Sussex, his discharge papers in an envelope on the table. A waiter brought three glasses of stout British ale.

McDonald raised his glass. "I guess a toast is in order since they didn't court-martial you for desertion," he said with a grin.

Jack smiled at their friend, raised his glass with one hand and took Claire's hand with the other. "I should be the one toasting you... and Colonel Worthington. Your letters carried the day."

"We are eternally grateful," Claire chimed in, "you know that."

"Well, you both made it through," McDonald said, "That's what matters." He took a sip of ale and set the heavy glass on the table. "I assume you've heard we've re-taken St. Vith, though there's not much left of the city. But that was the last gasp for the Jerries. It will all be over soon."

"I hope Frau Brunkhorst survived," Claire said. "She was in a terrible spot, horribly conflicted, serving two masters. But I believed her heart was in the right place."

"Conflicted is one way to look at it," McDonald said. "Though from what we know about Konrad Becker and what he did to Lukas and the *Viscount,* I doubt she had much choice."

"Maybe she didn't. But *Lukas* had a choice," Claire snapped. "He made the wrong one."

Jack glanced at her and squeezed her hand. Lukas had been sentenced to fifteen years in prison, escaping the gallows only because Claire pleaded with the court for mercy, though she was very bitter about his deceit.

They were silent for a few moments until Claire spoke again. "I know how Lukas must have felt when he returned to Belgium in '41, alone, afraid, with no money and no place to live. He was desperate, searching for something, a lifeline. And the *Viscount* reached out, then Becker and..." Her voice trailed off.

"And he was swept into it and couldn't find a way out?" McDonald asked.

Jack slid his arm around the back of Claire's chair, resting his hand lightly on her shoulder. He knew how hard this was for her.

She stared into her glass of ale for a moment, then looked up. "Perhaps that's true. He got in so deep he couldn't get out. But he *did* have choices, some choices." She turned to Jack, staring at him with her dark, penetrating eyes. "He made the choice to betray *you.* He did that for reasons that had nothing to do with anything except jealousy. And I cannot forgive him for that. I couldn't stand to see him hanged… but I cannot forgive him."

"What about all the others involved?" Jack asked, glancing at both Claire and McDonald. "The others who collaborated with the Nazis? What about DeVos, or the 'section manager' that worked for Bart, or the one you called *Socrates?* What about the *Viscount* and whoever it was in Grote Brogel who called the gendarme and made us run in the middle of the night? Did they all have choices to make? Did they all have their own reasons? I just don't understand how they could do it. Belgium is complicated, you've told me that. Divided loyalties, shifting borders and all that. But I still don't understand."

McDonald folded his hands on the table and looked at Jack. "You're an American, Jack, and I love you bloody Yanks. I love how practical and matter-of-fact you all are. Claire is correct about how complicated Belgium is. All of Europe is complicated, and we've been fighting the same wars for centuries. There have always been divided loyalties everywhere, even in America, where some of your countrymen fought for the British in your Revolution and others who have called President Roosevelt a traitor for getting America into this war. There are those like DeVos whose motives were nothing more than pure greed. Others may have been frightened by what Claire, Bart and others in the Resistance were doing, fearing it would endanger them. And still others, like the women being hauled away in carts with swastikas painted on their foreheads, who did nothing more sinister than share a bed with a German soldier in exchange for some ration coupons. In the intelligence field, we try and understand human behavior so we can anticipate what people may do. I've been doing it for some years now, but I don't understand it either."

"So, no easy answers," Jack said. "I guess I'm not surprised.

Claire sat back in her chair and glanced up at the ceiling. "We have all suffered terrible losses in this senseless war, but the hardest thing for me was never knowing who to trust... that will take some time."

They were silent again for a moment. Then McDonald spoke up, a lighter tone in his voice. "So, what's next for the two of you? Heading to America?

Jack glanced at Claire, who smiled at him. "We *are* heading for America," he said. "But only for a visit with my family. Then back here."

"To London?" McDonald asked.

Claire nodded. "Yes. We've decided it's the perfect place for us to start a new life, a new beginning."

Author's Note

Road of Deception is a historical novel and is the third book in a trilogy of wartime stories set in Europe in World War Two. In writing Road of Deception, my aim was the same as it was in the first two books, Night of Flames and The Katyn Order, to honor the countless acts of nobility and courage performed by common people during one of humanity's darkest hours. The characters in this story are fictional, but the major events, organizations, and locations are real. Here is a brief explanation of some of the most important.

The "escape line" which plays a very prominent role in the story is fashioned after The Comet Line, a real escape organization that existed in Belgium during World War Two and was responsible for rescuing more than a thousand Allied aviators and escorting them to safety. The danger to the people involved in this clandestine organization was exactly as I illustrated in the story. As a result of treachery and betrayal, almost an equal number of Comet Line operatives—ordinary people, men and women, some just teenagers—were killed or captured by the enemy. Knowing who to trust was a constant problem.

The German "offensive" which is an underlying theme through Part Two of the book was an actual surprise attack by the German Army through the

Belgian Ardennes in December of 1944. It was the largest and deadliest single battle fought by the United States in World War Two, and the third deadliest campaign in American history. It is commonly known in history as The Battle of the Bulge.

In the book I describe a specific battle that occurred on the first day of this offensive at the small Belgian town of Lanzerath. This was also a real event. A single platoon of 25 American soldiers did indeed hold off the initial assault of an entire German Panzer division and set the surprise attack back one whole day, from which the German army never recovered. The commander of the fictional platoon in my story, Lieutenant Dugan, is fashioned after a real American soldier, twenty-year-old 1st Lieutenant Lyle Bouck, commander of the 394th I&R platoon. The only difference between my story and the real event was that Lt. Bouck and his men, several of whom were badly wounded, did not escape after the battle. They were captured by the Germans and spent the remainder of the war as POWs without realizing the impact of their accomplishment. Lt. Bouck and his men survived the war, but it wasn't until 1966 when the US Army finally acknowledged their achievement. Lt. Bouck was awarded the Silver Star and his entire platoon became the most decorated unit of their size in all of World War two.

Another major theme of the book is the smuggling of money and people out of Germany during the final stages of the war, which is also true. Numerous secret escape routes, often referred to as 'Ratlines,' were established by the Nazis, fascists, and other potential war criminals as way out of Germany before they could be captured by the Allied forces and brought to justice.

One of the characters in the book attempting to flee Germany is Gerhard Wagner, chairman of the German company, *I.G. Farben*. Gerhard Wagner is fictional but *I.G. Farben* was real. It was, at the time, the largest chemical company in the world, and utilized thousands of slave laborers from the concentration camps. The company also manufactured the deadly poison, Zyklon-B used by the Nazis to exterminate millions of Jews. Dozens of the key officers of *I.G. Farben* were captured by the Allies and sentenced to prison terms at the Nuremberg trials. *I.G. Farben* was subsequently dismantled by the Allied governments and broken up into a number of separate companies, some of which exist today.

About the Author

Douglas W. Jacobson is an engineer, business owner and World War Two enthusiast. Doug has traveled extensively throughout Europe, researching the stories of ordinary people who risked their lives in the fight for freedom. He has published two previous historical novels set in World War Two, *Night of Flames* and *The Katyn Order*. Doug lives with his wife, Janie, in Elm Grove, WI.